– R.A. MONTGOMERY PR...

CHOOSE YOUR OWN ADVENTURE®

EIGHTH GRADE WITCH

WRITTEN BY
Andrew E.C. Gaska
E.L. Thomas

BASED ON THE ORIGINAL BY
C.E. Simpson

ILLUSTRATED BY
Valerio Chiola

BACKGROUND ART BY
Leandro Casca

COLORS BY
Thiago Ribeiro

LETTERS BY
Joamette Gil

CHOOSECO

ONI PRESS

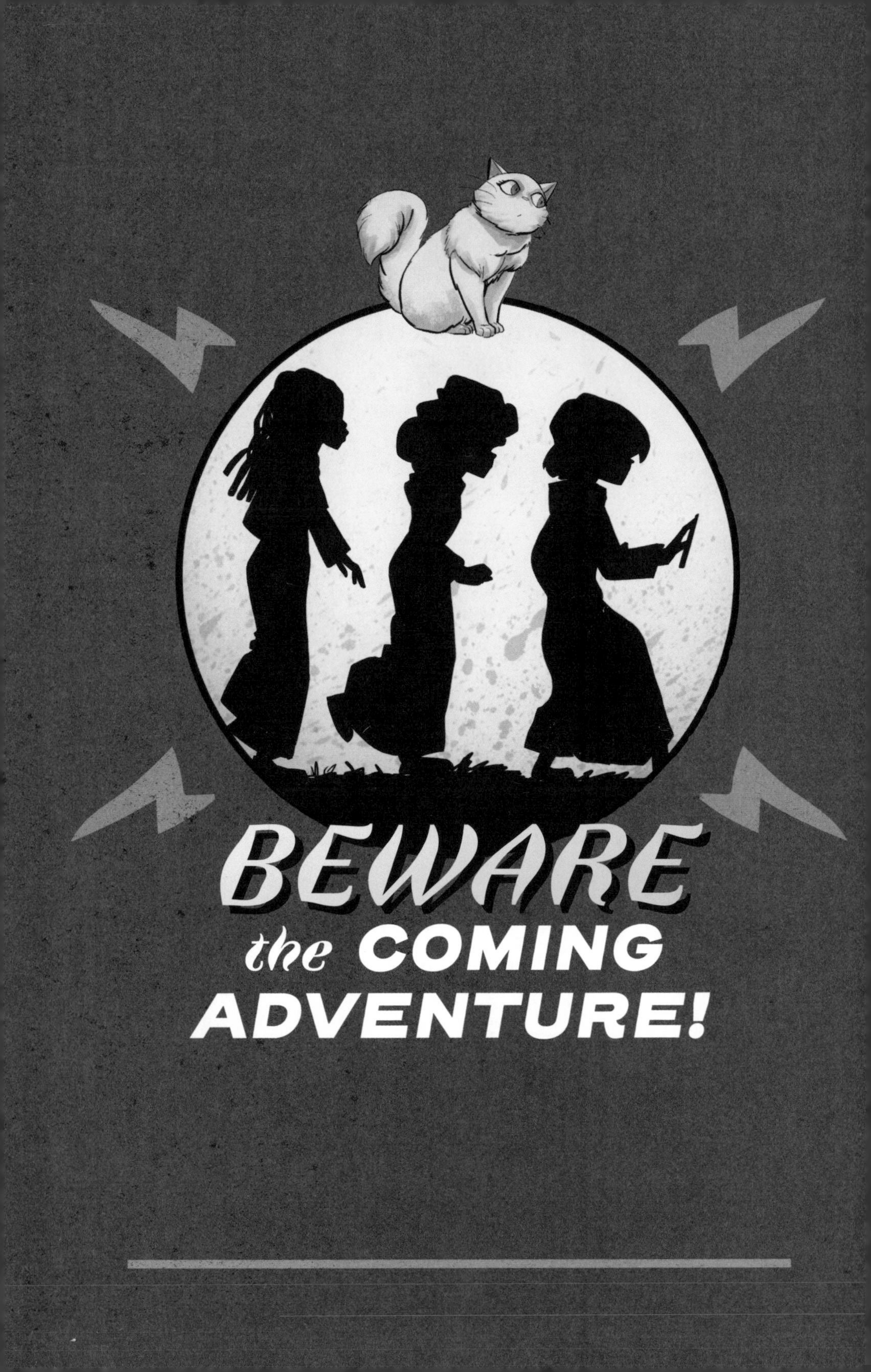

BEWARE the COMING ADVENTURE!

This book will be different from others you've encountered...

For here, **YOU**, and **YOU ALONE**, are in charge of what happens on your adventure into the witchy world located on Cherry Tree Lane...

...Where there are dangers at every corner, and choices at the turn of a page. Choices that can lead **YOU** to a thrilling magical ending, or a disastrous deadly consequence. Here, **YOU** must use all of your wits and much of your keen intelligence to find the best path forward. But, do not despair! At any time, **YOU** can go back and make another choice, alter the path of **YOUR** story, and change the result.

Your story begins with your parents, who are demonologists. Your new home may be a bit creepy, but you are happy—even if it would give other people nightmares. But, when you start your eighth grade year at a new school in Graves End, Brooklyn, chilling visions of the house's haunted past overtake, settling into a new life. Are you the victim of new kid pranks, organized by a local coven obsessed with the mythical history of your house? Or have these witches been dormant for a long time, waiting for you in particular to finally arrive?

COVER BY Valerio Chiola & Thiago Ribeiro
EDITED BY Robert Meyers & Desiree Rodriguez
DESIGNED BY Hilary Thompson

SPECIAL THANKS TO Shannon Gilligan, Melissa Bounty, and Rachel Hullett

PUBLISHED BY ONI-LION FORGE PUBLISHING GROUP, LLC.

James Lucas Jones, president & publisher
Sarah Gaydos, editor in chief
Charlie Chu, e.v.p. of creative & business devt.
Alex Segura, s.v.p of marketing & sales
Brad Rooks, director of operations
Amber O'Neill, special projects manager
Margot Wood, director of marketing & sales
Katie Sainz, marketing manager
Tara Lehmann, publicist
Holly Aitchison, consumer marketing manager
Troy Look, director of design & production
Kate Z. Stone, senior graphic designer
Carey Hall, graphic designer
Sarah Rockwell, graphic designer
Hilary Thompson, graphic designer
Angie Knowles, digital prepress lead

Vincent Kukua, digital prepress technician
Chris Cerasi, managing editor
Jasmine Amiri, senior editor
Shawna Gore, senior editor
Amanda Meadows, senior editor
Robert Meyers, senior editor, licensing
Desiree Rodriguez, editor
Grace Scheipeter, editor
Zack Soto, editor
Steve Ellis, vice president of games
Ben Eisner, game developer
Michelle Nguyen, executive assistant
Jung Lee, logistics coordinator
Kuian Kellum, warehouse assistant

Joe Nozemack, publisher emeritus

onipress.com | lionforge.com
facebook.com/onipress | facebook.com/lionforge
twitter.com/onipress | twitter.com/lionforge
instagram.com/onipress | instagram.com/lionforge

CYOA.COM
twitter.com/chooseadventure
instagram.com/cyoapub
facebook.com/ChooseYourOwnAdventure

First Edition: August 2021
ISBN 978-1-62010-941-0
eISBN 978-1-62010-954-0

1 2 3 4 5 6 7 8 9 10

Library of Congress Control Number 2020947314

Printed in Canada.

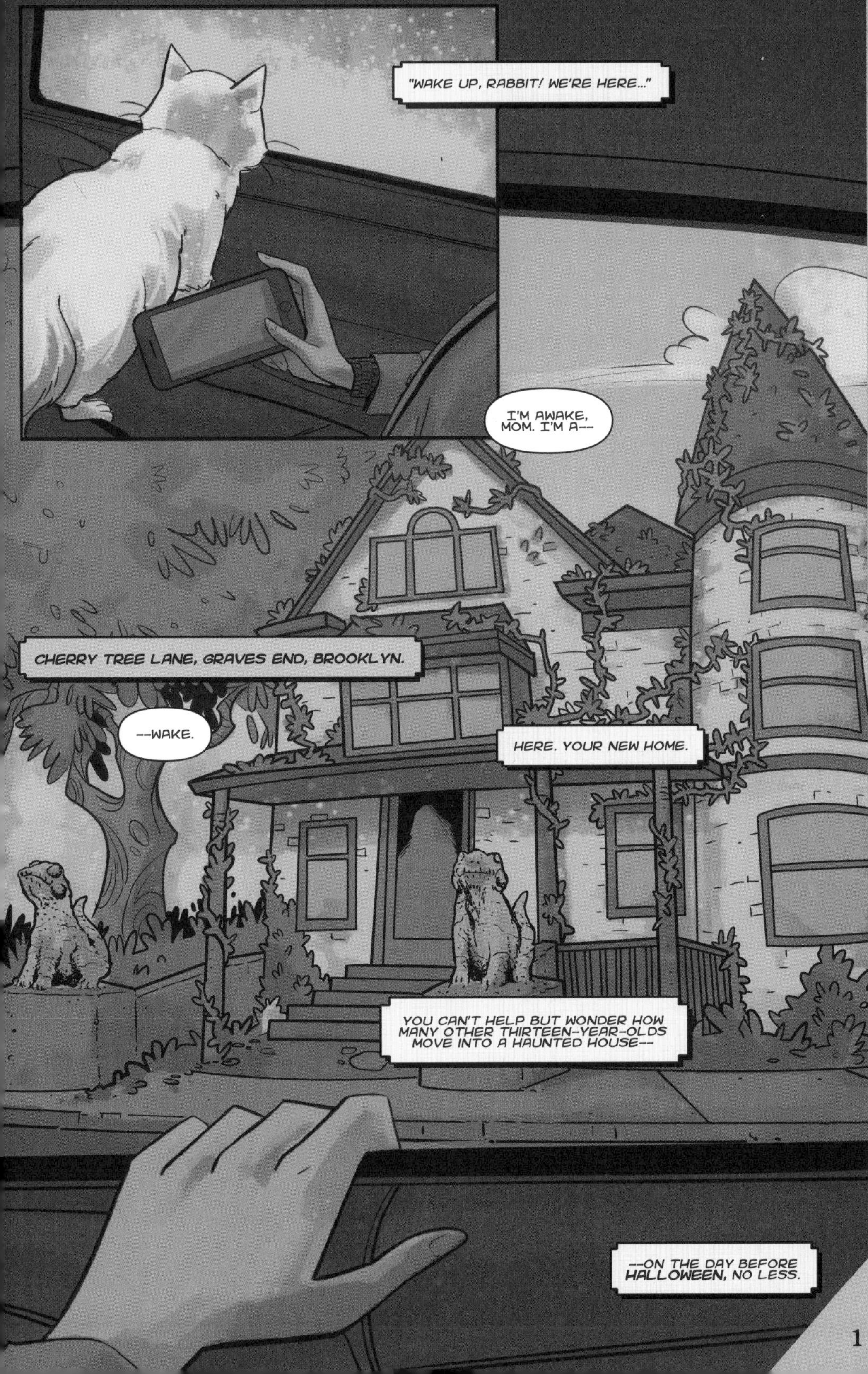
"WAKE UP, RABBIT! WE'RE HERE..."
I'M AWAKE, MOM. I'M A--
CHERRY TREE LANE, GRAVES END, BROOKLYN.
--WAKE.
HERE. YOUR NEW HOME.
YOU CAN'T HELP BUT WONDER HOW MANY OTHER THIRTEEN-YEAR-OLDS MOVE INTO A HAUNTED HOUSE--
--ON THE DAY BEFORE HALLOWEEN, NO LESS.

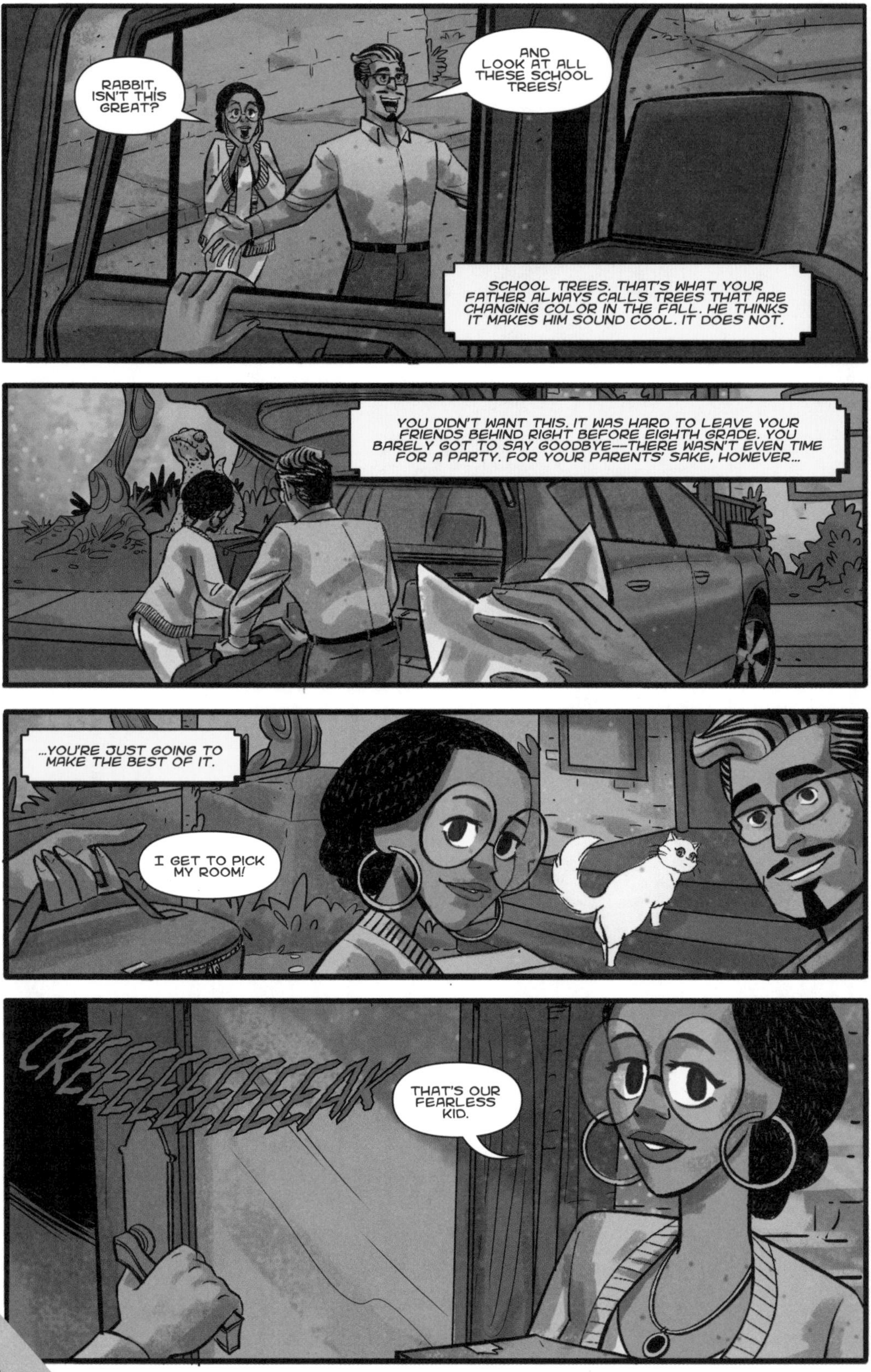

RABBIT, ISN'T THIS GREAT?
AND LOOK AT ALL THESE SCHOOL TREES!
SCHOOL TREES. THAT'S WHAT YOUR FATHER ALWAYS CALLS TREES THAT ARE CHANGING COLOR IN THE FALL. HE THINKS IT MAKES HIM SOUND COOL. IT DOES NOT.
YOU DIDN'T WANT THIS. IT WAS HARD TO LEAVE YOUR FRIENDS BEHIND RIGHT BEFORE EIGHTH GRADE. YOU BARELY GOT TO SAY GOODBYE--THERE WASN'T EVEN TIME FOR A PARTY. FOR YOUR PARENTS' SAKE, HOWEVER...
...YOU'RE JUST GOING TO MAKE THE BEST OF IT.
I GET TO PICK MY ROOM!
CREEEEEEEEEEEAK
THAT'S OUR FEARLESS KID.

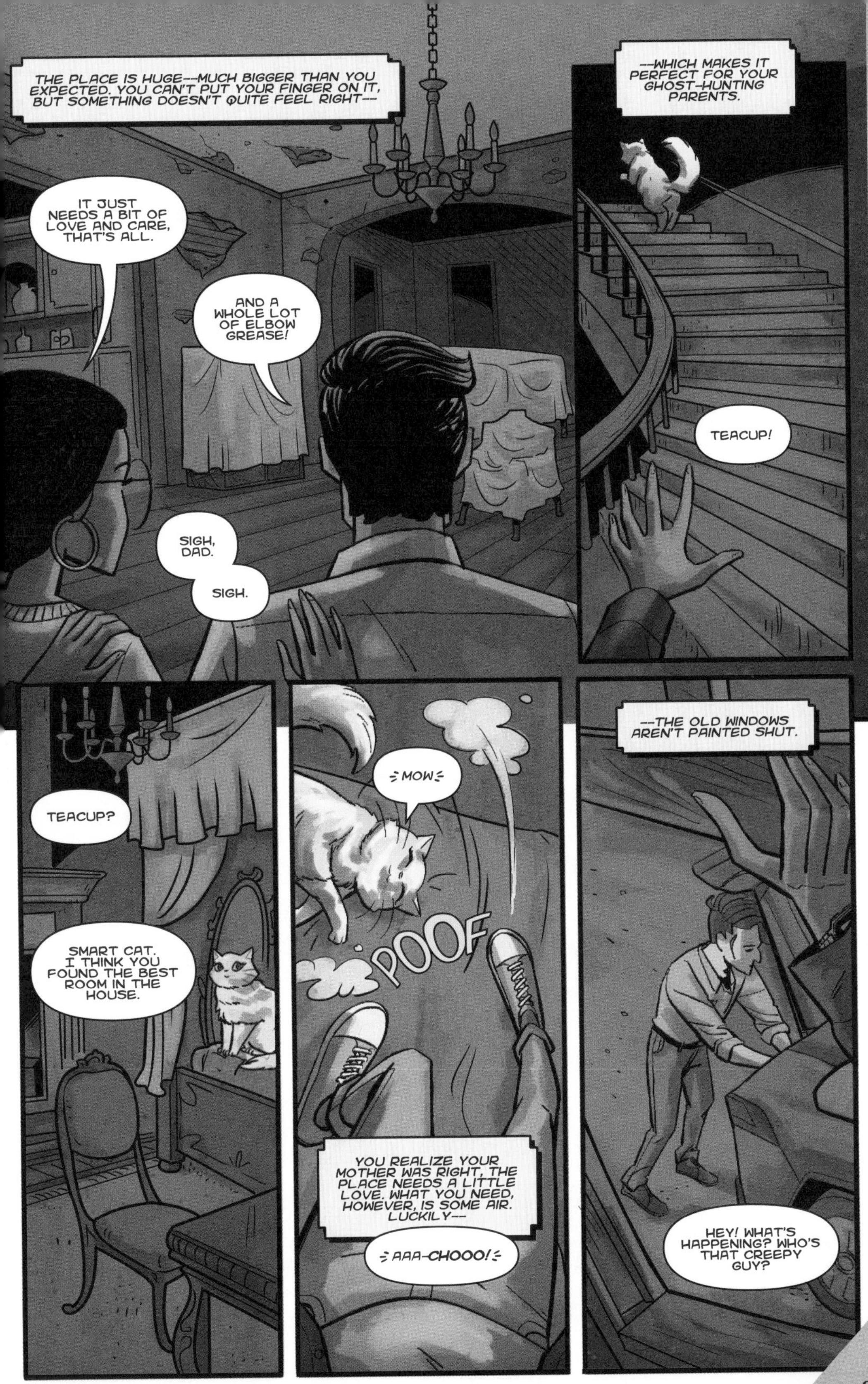
THE PLACE IS HUGE--MUCH BIGGER THAN YOU EXPECTED. YOU CAN'T PUT YOUR FINGER ON IT, BUT SOMETHING DOESN'T QUITE FEEL RIGHT--
IT JUST NEEDS A BIT OF LOVE AND CARE, THAT'S ALL.
AND A WHOLE LOT OF ELBOW GREASE!
SIGH, DAD.
SIGH.
--WHICH MAKES IT PERFECT FOR YOUR GHOST-HUNTING PARENTS.
TEACUP!
TEACUP?
SMART CAT. I THINK YOU FOUND THE BEST ROOM IN THE HOUSE.
MOW
POOF
YOU REALIZE YOUR MOTHER WAS RIGHT, THE PLACE NEEDS A LITTLE LOVE. WHAT YOU NEED, HOWEVER, IS SOME AIR. LUCKILY--
AAA-CHOOO!
--THE OLD WINDOWS AREN'T PAINTED SHUT.
HEY! WHAT'S HAPPENING? WHO'S THAT CREEPY GUY?

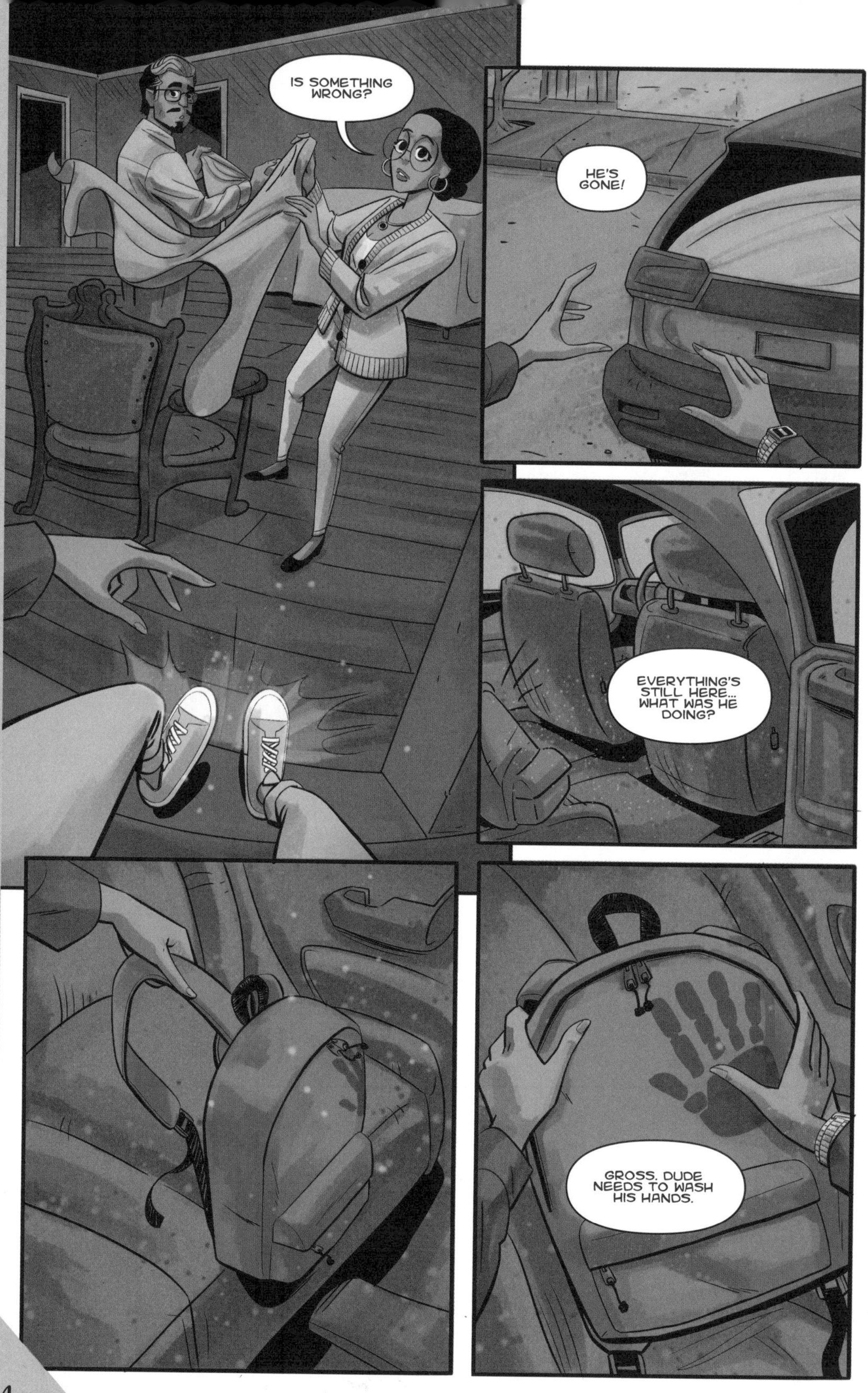
IS SOMETHING WRONG?
HE'S GONE!
EVERYTHING'S STILL HERE... WHAT WAS HE DOING?
GROSS. DUDE NEEDS TO WASH HIS HANDS.

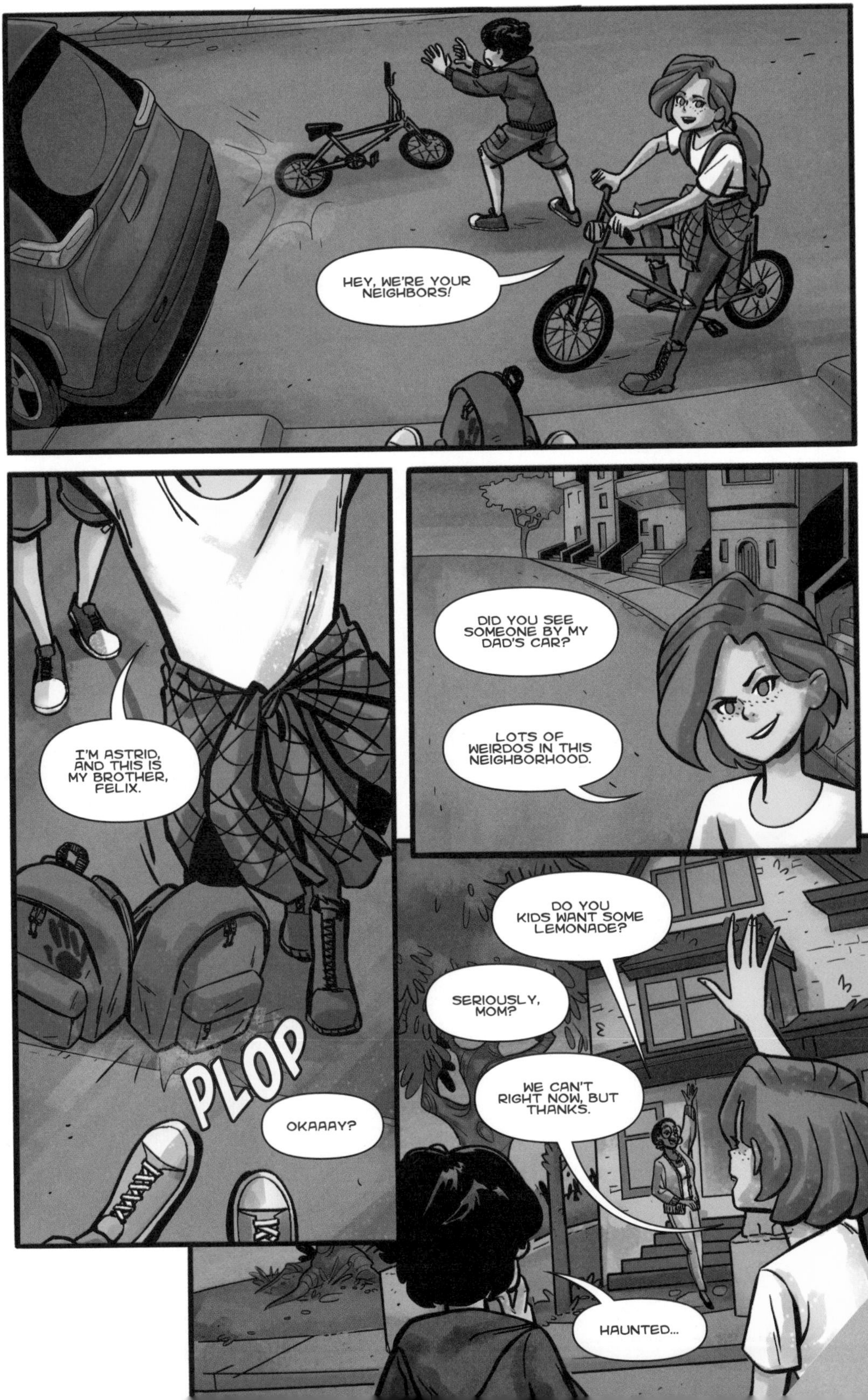
HEY, WE'RE YOUR NEIGHBORS!
I'M ASTRID, AND THIS IS MY BROTHER, FELIX.
PLOP
OKAAAY?
DID YOU SEE SOMEONE BY MY DAD'S CAR?
LOTS OF WEIRDOS IN THIS NEIGHBORHOOD.
DO YOU KIDS WANT SOME LEMONADE?
SERIOUSLY, MOM?
WE CAN'T RIGHT NOW, BUT THANKS.
HAUNTED...

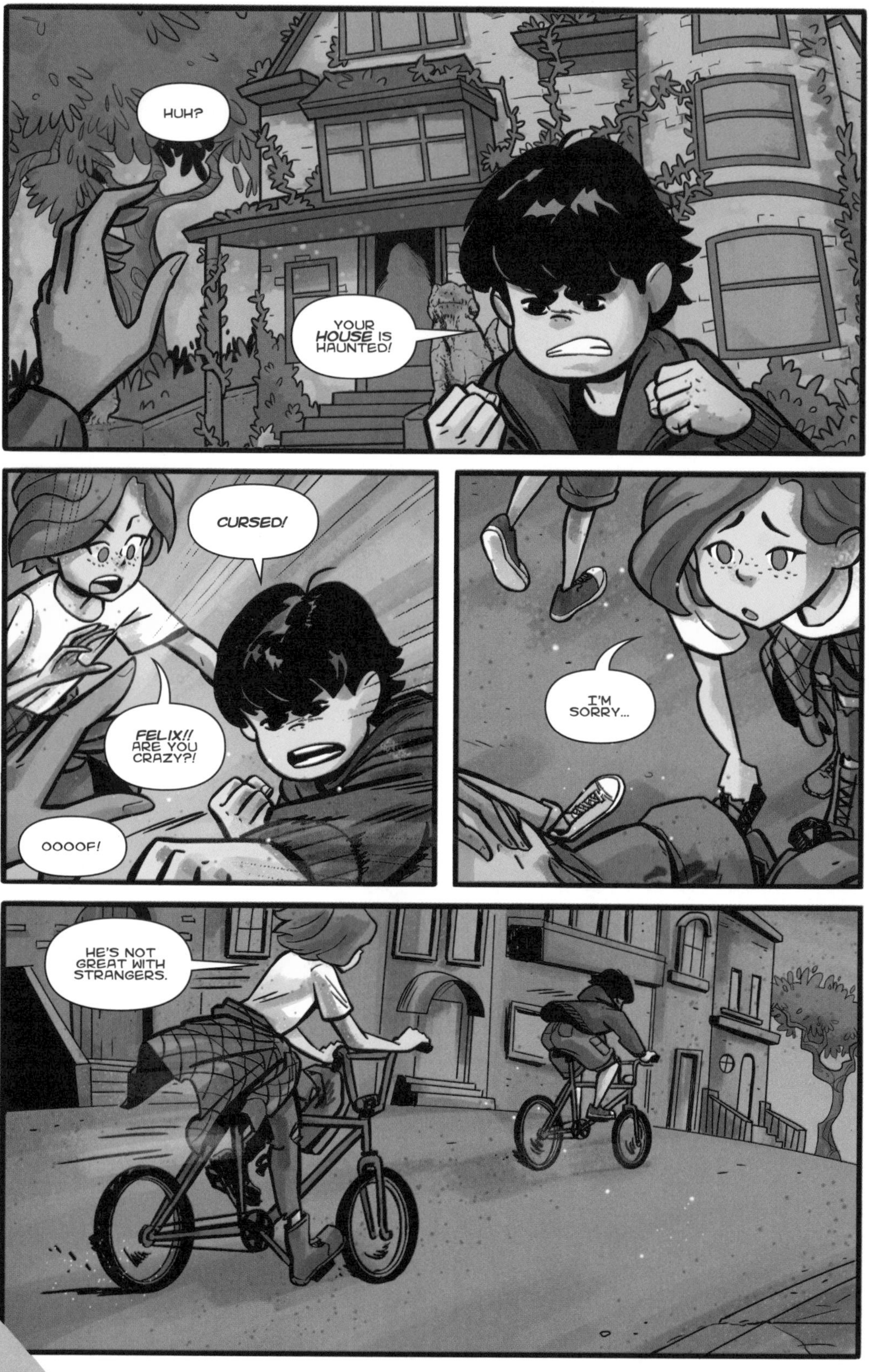
HUH?
YOUR HOUSE IS HAUNTED!
CURSED!
FELIX!! ARE YOU CRAZY?!
OOOOF!
I'M SORRY...
HE'S NOT GREAT WITH STRANGERS.

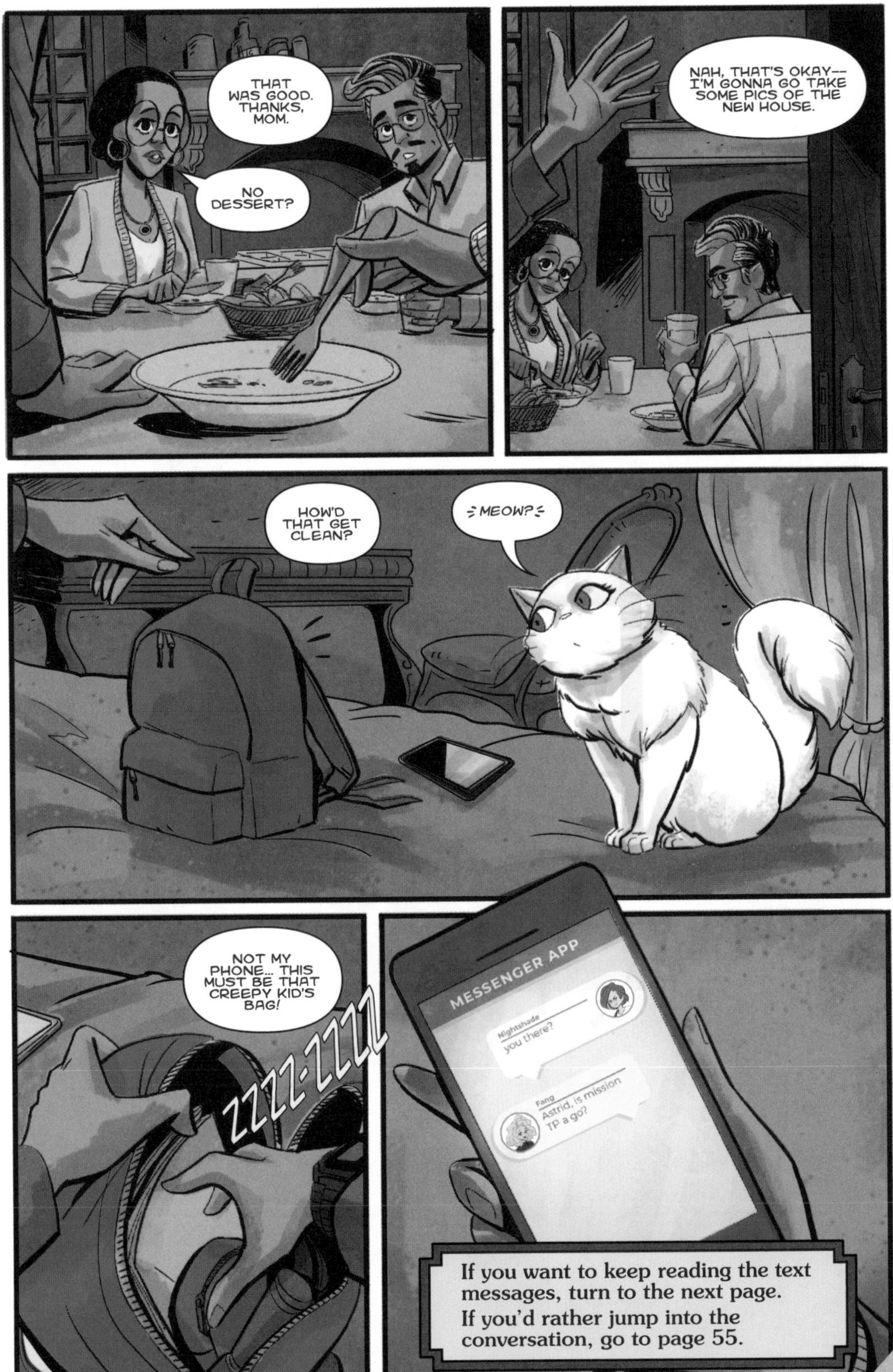
THAT WAS GOOD. THANKS, MOM.
NO DESSERT?
NAH, THAT'S OKAY-- I'M GONNA GO TAKE SOME PICS OF THE NEW HOUSE.
HOW'D THAT GET CLEAN?
MEOW?
NOT MY PHONE... THIS MUST BE THAT CREEPY KID'S BAG!
ZZZZ-ZZZZ
MESSENGER APP
MESSENGER APP
Nightshade
you there?
Fang
Astrid, is mission TP a go?

If you want to keep reading the text messages, turn to the next page.
If you'd rather jump into the conversation, go to page 55.

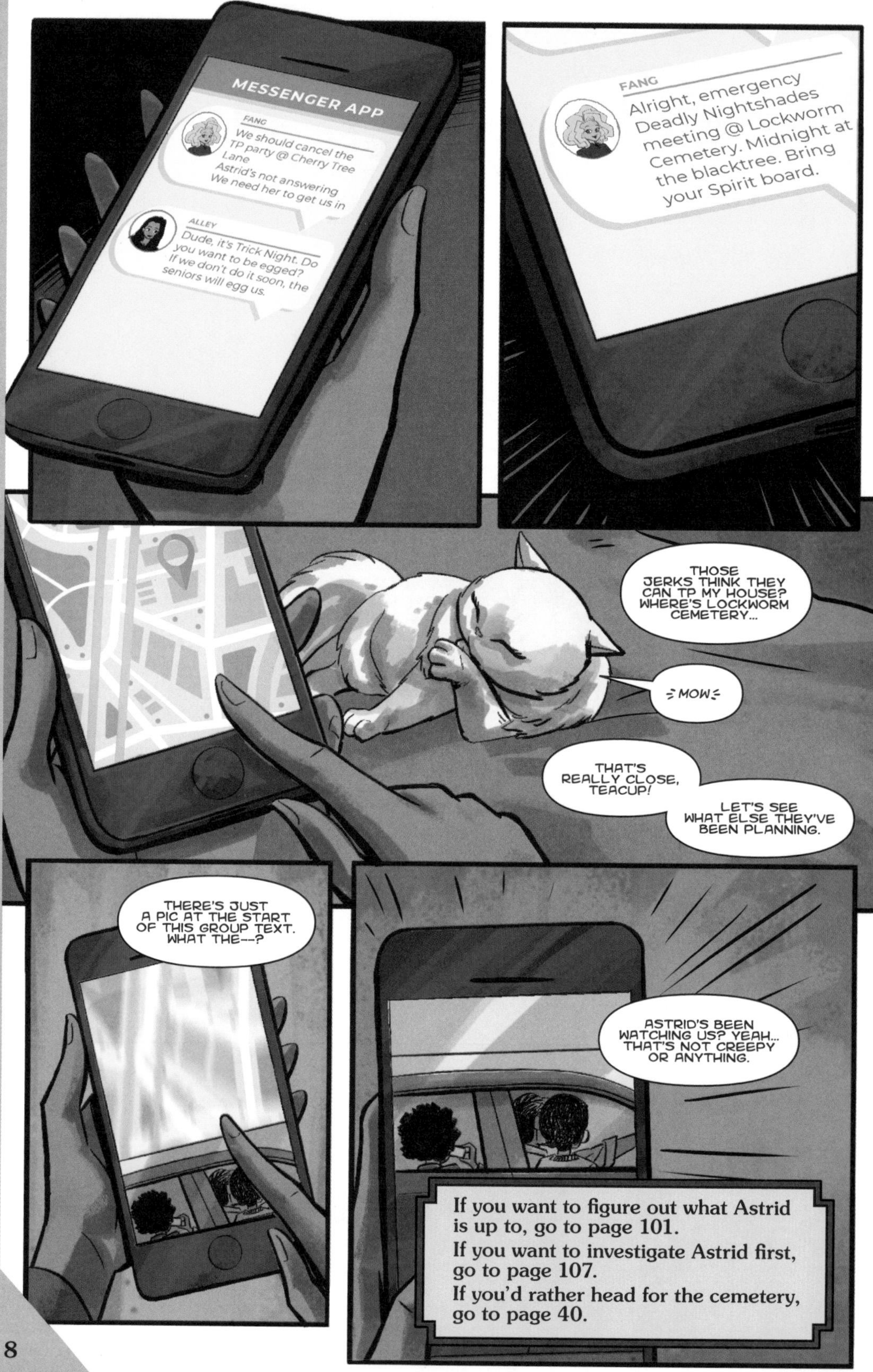
MESSENGER APP
FANG
We should cancel the TP party @ Cherry Tree Lane
Astrid's not answering
We need her to get us in
ALLEY
Dude, it's Trick Night. Do you want to be egged? If we don't do it soon, the seniors will egg us.
FANG
Alright, emergency Deadly Nightshades meeting @ Lockworm Cemetery. Midnight at the blacktree. Bring your Spirit board.
THOSE JERKS THINK THEY CAN TP MY HOUSE? WHERE'S LOCKWORM CEMETERY...
MOW
THAT'S REALLY CLOSE, TEACUP!
LET'S SEE WHAT ELSE THEY'VE BEEN PLANNING.
THERE'S JUST A PIC AT THE START OF THIS GROUP TEXT. WHAT THE--?
ASTRID'S BEEN WATCHING US? YEAH... THAT'S NOT CREEPY OR ANYTHING.

If you want to figure out what Astrid is up to, go to page 101.
If you want to investigate Astrid first, go to page 107.
If you'd rather head for the cemetery, go to page 40.

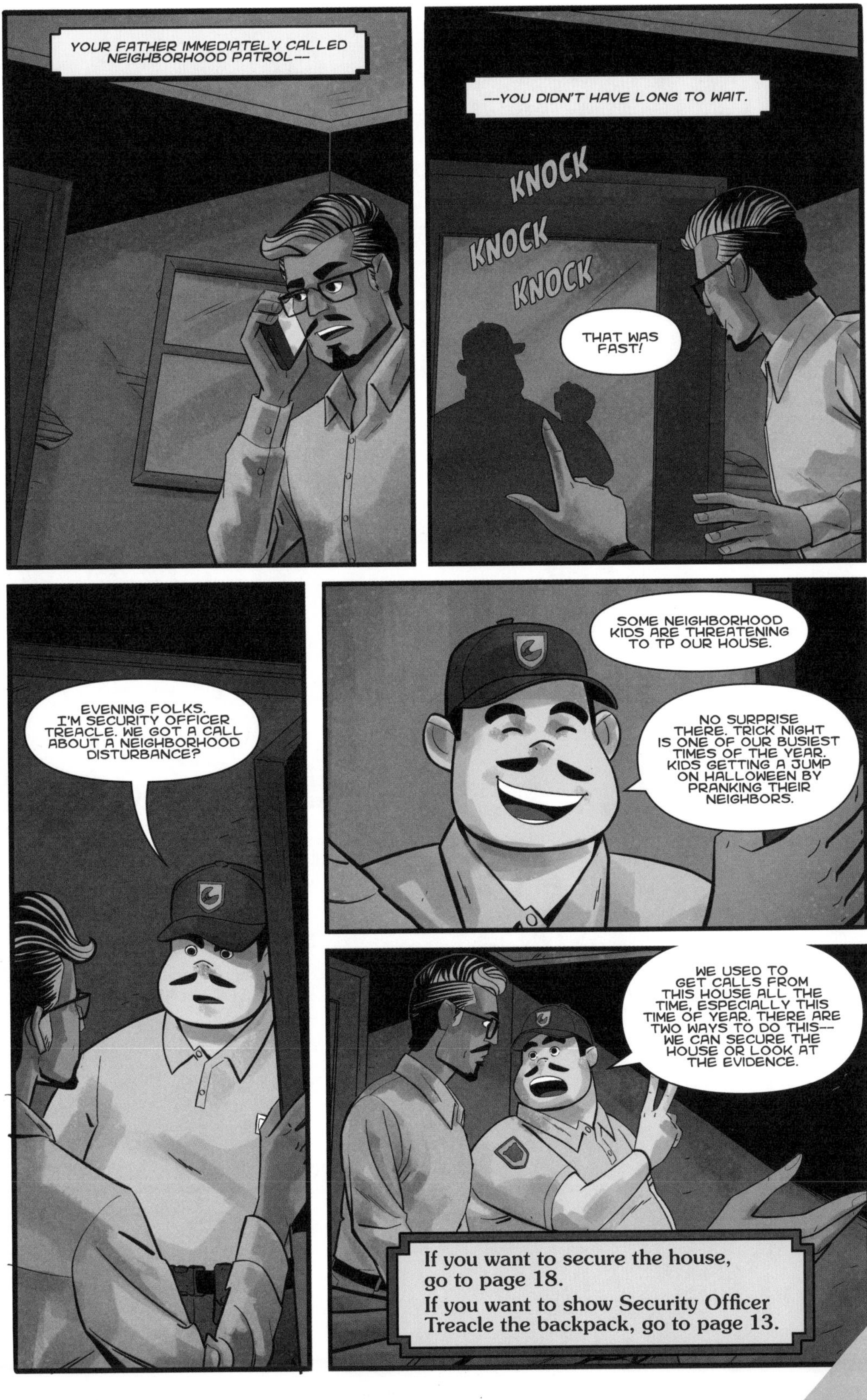
YOUR FATHER IMMEDIATELY CALLED NEIGHBORHOOD PATROL--
--YOU DIDN'T HAVE LONG TO WAIT.
KNOCK
KNOCK
KNOCK
THAT WAS FAST!
EVENING FOLKS. I'M SECURITY OFFICER TREACLE. WE GOT A CALL ABOUT A NEIGHBORHOOD DISTURBANCE?
SOME NEIGHBORHOOD KIDS ARE THREATENING TO TP OUR HOUSE.
NO SURPRISE THERE. TRICK NIGHT IS ONE OF OUR BUSIEST TIMES OF THE YEAR. KIDS GETTING A JUMP ON HALLOWEEN BY PRANKING THEIR NEIGHBORS.
WE USED TO GET CALLS FROM THIS HOUSE ALL THE TIME, ESPECIALLY THIS TIME OF YEAR. THERE ARE TWO WAYS TO DO THIS-- WE CAN SECURE THE HOUSE OR LOOK AT THE EVIDENCE.

If you want to secure the house, go to page 18.
If you want to show Security Officer Treacle the backpack, go to page 13.

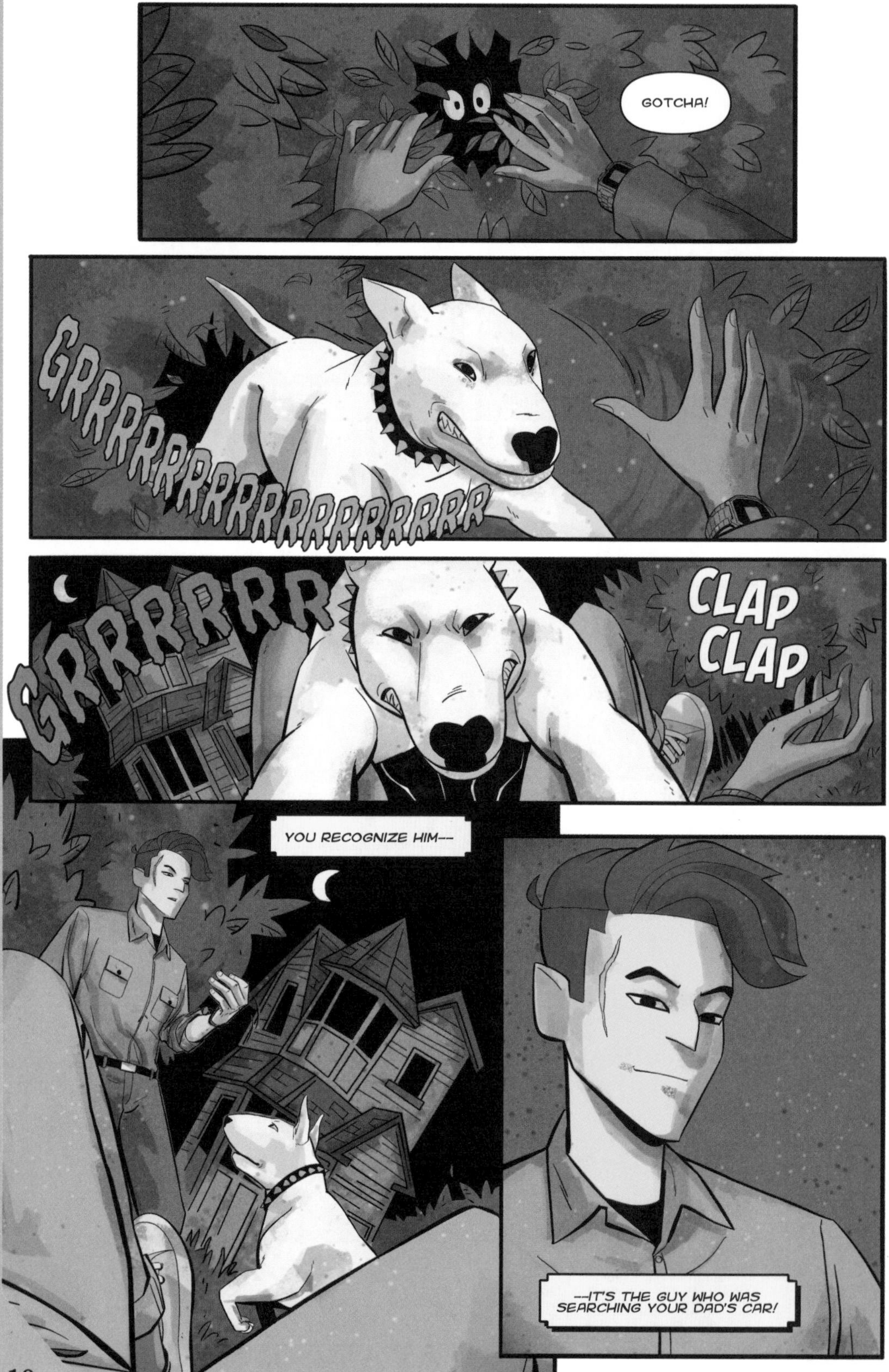
GOTCHA!
GRRRRRRRRRRRRRRRRRRR
GRRRRRRR
CLAP
CLAP
YOU RECOGNIZE HIM--
--IT'S THE GUY WHO WAS SEARCHING YOUR DAD'S CAR!

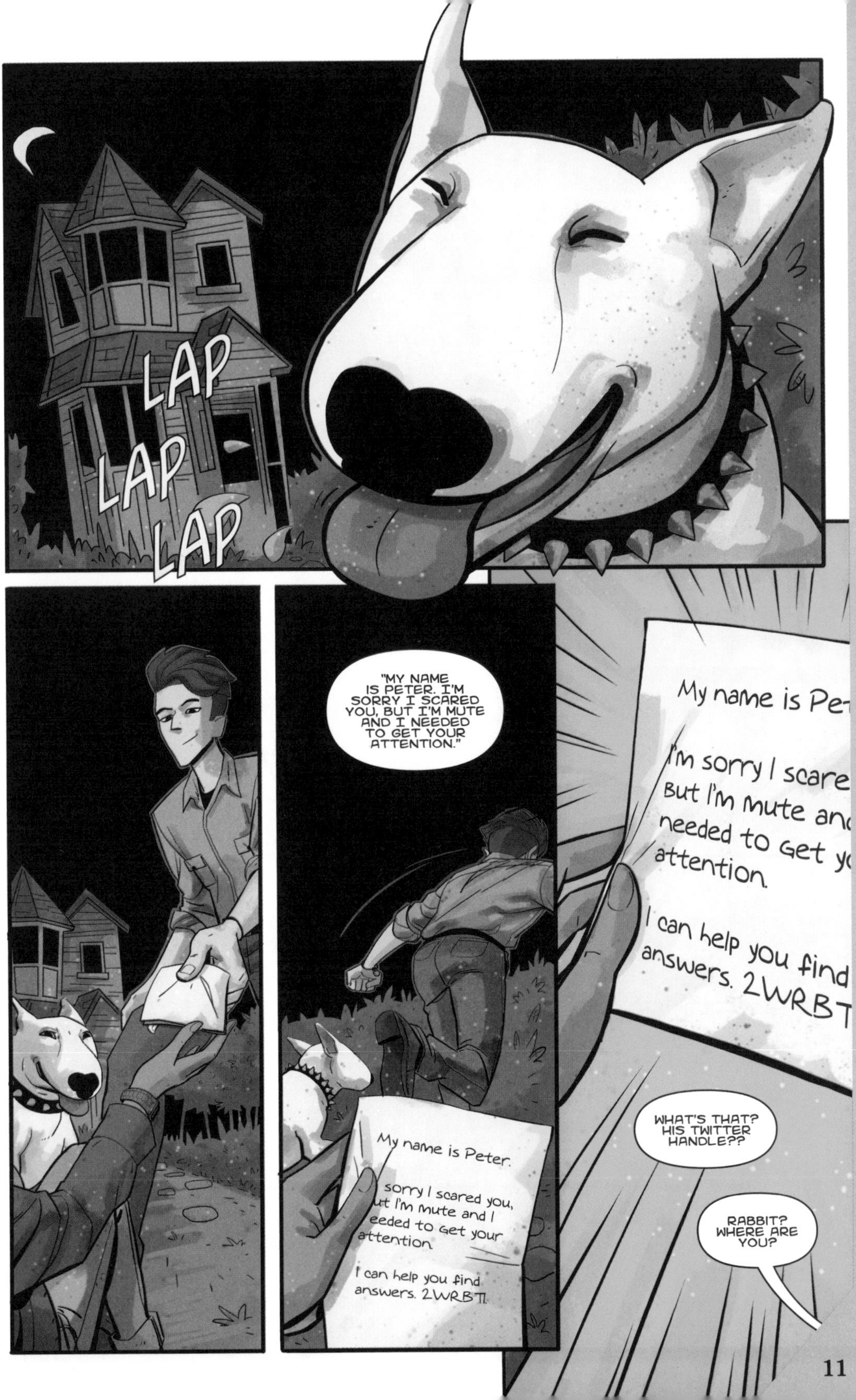

LAP
LAP
LAP
"MY NAME IS PETER. I'M SORRY I SCARED YOU, BUT I'M MUTE AND I NEEDED TO GET YOUR ATTENTION."
My name is Peter.
sorry I scared you, ut I'm mute and I eeded to get your attention.
I can help you find answers. 2WRBTI.
My name is Pe
I'm sorry I scare
But I'm mute an
needed to get y
attention.
I can help you find
answers. 2WRBT
WHAT'S THAT? HIS TWITTER HANDLE??
RABBIT? WHERE ARE YOU?

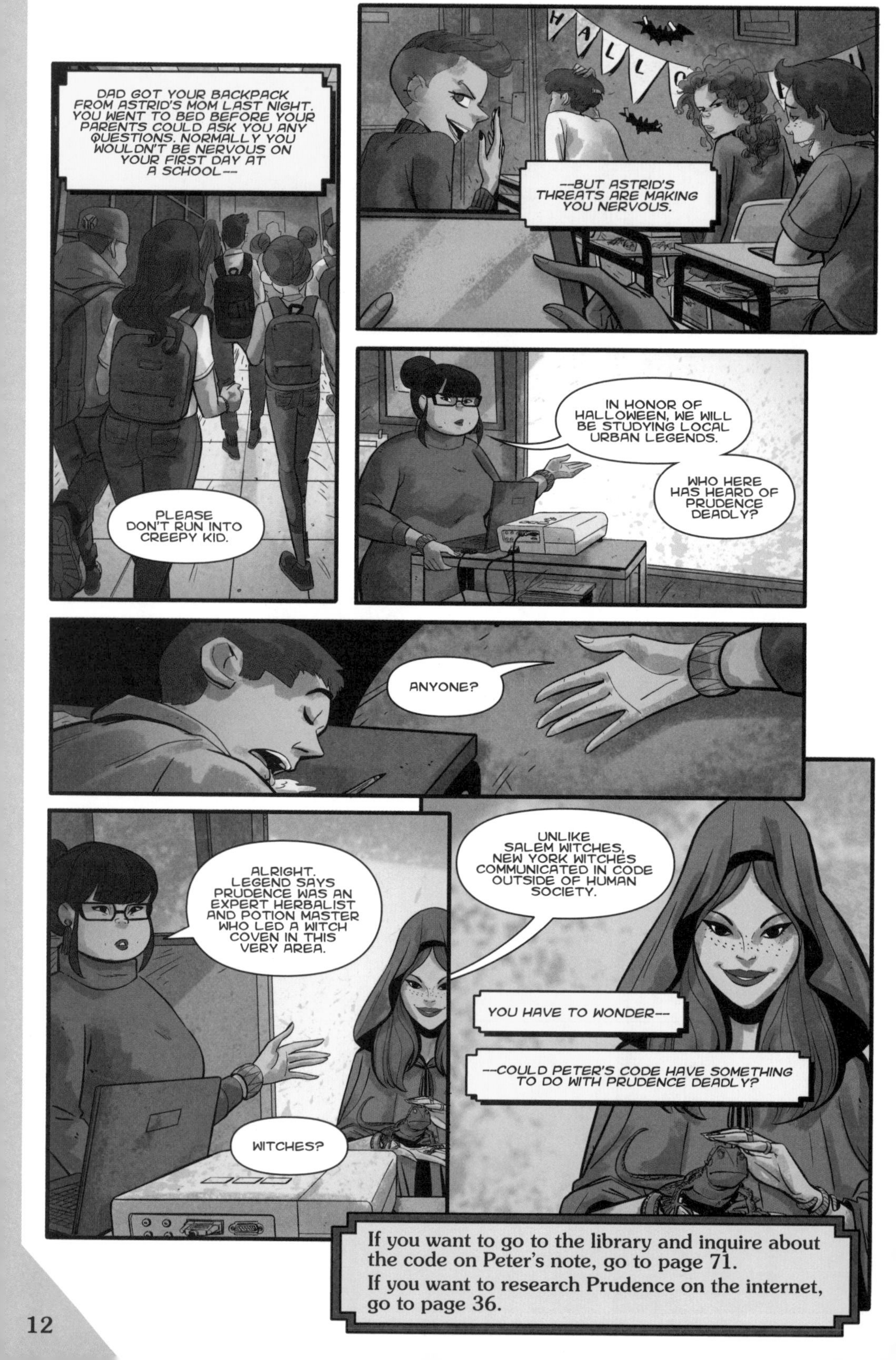
DAD GOT YOUR BACKPACK FROM ASTRID'S MOM LAST NIGHT. YOU WENT TO BED BEFORE YOUR PARENTS COULD ASK YOU ANY QUESTIONS. NORMALLY YOU WOULDN'T BE NERVOUS ON YOUR FIRST DAY AT A SCHOOL--
PLEASE DON'T RUN INTO CREEPY KID.
--BUT ASTRID'S THREATS ARE MAKING YOU NERVOUS.
IN HONOR OF HALLOWEEN, WE WILL BE STUDYING LOCAL URBAN LEGENDS.
WHO HERE HAS HEARD OF PRUDENCE DEADLY?
ANYONE?
ALRIGHT. LEGEND SAYS PRUDENCE WAS AN EXPERT HERBALIST AND POTION MASTER WHO LED A WITCH COVEN IN THIS VERY AREA.
WITCHES?
UNLIKE SALEM WITCHES, NEW YORK WITCHES COMMUNICATED IN CODE OUTSIDE OF HUMAN SOCIETY.
YOU HAVE TO WONDER--
--COULD PETER'S CODE HAVE SOMETHING TO DO WITH PRUDENCE DEADLY?

If you want to go to the library and inquire about the code on Peter's note, go to page 71.
If you want to research Prudence on the internet, go to page 36.

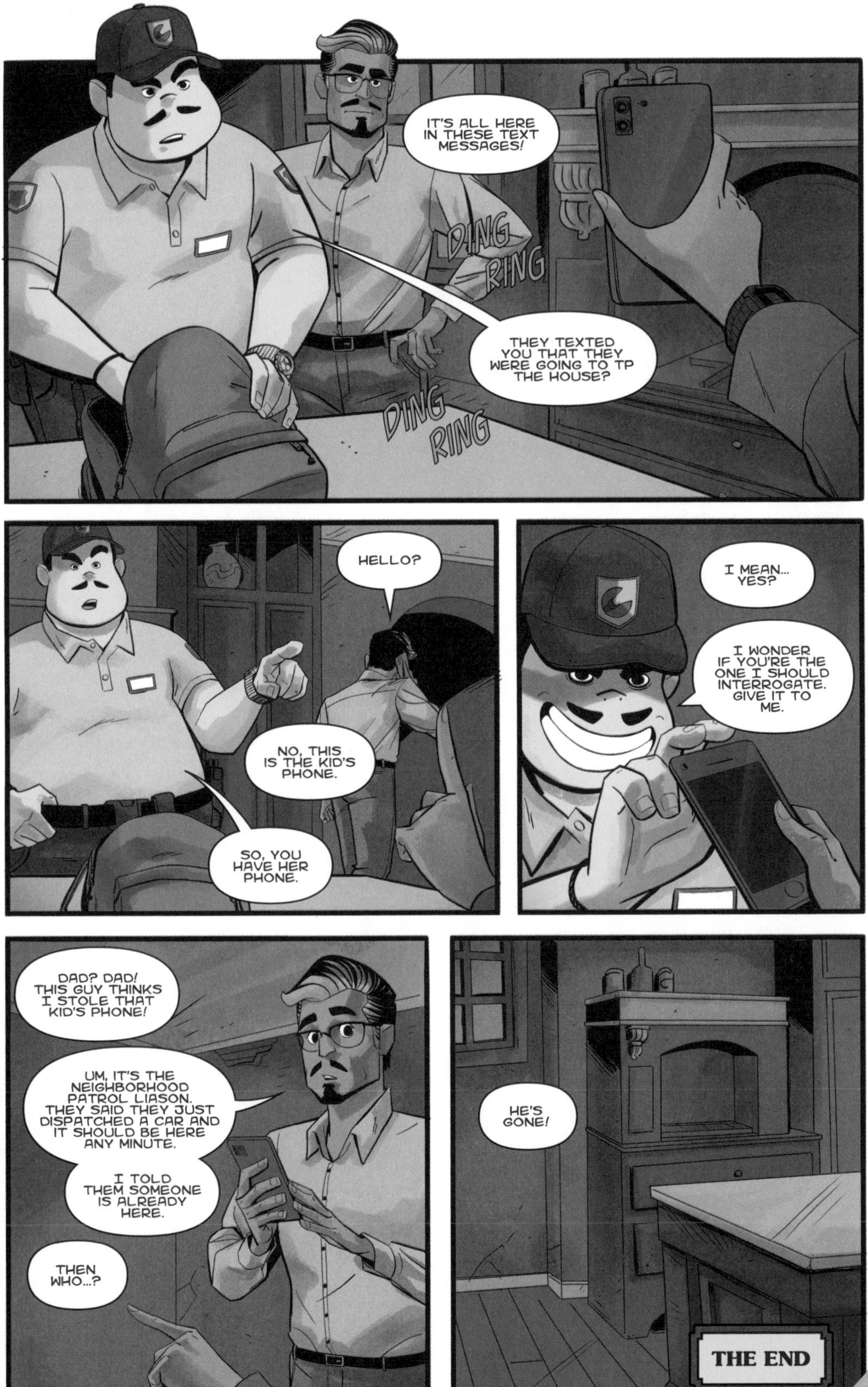
IT'S ALL HERE IN THESE TEXT MESSAGES!
DING RING
THEY TEXTED YOU THAT THEY WERE GOING TO TP THE HOUSE?
DING RING
HELLO?
NO, THIS IS THE KID'S PHONE.
SO, YOU HAVE HER PHONE.
I MEAN... YES?
I WONDER IF YOU'RE THE ONE I SHOULD INTERROGATE. GIVE IT TO ME.
DAD? DAD! THIS GUY THINKS I STOLE THAT KID'S PHONE!
UM, IT'S THE NEIGHBORHOOD PATROL LIASON. THEY SAID THEY JUST DISPATCHED A CAR AND IT SHOULD BE HERE ANY MINUTE.
I TOLD THEM SOMEONE IS ALREADY HERE.
THEN WHO...?
HE'S GONE!
THE END

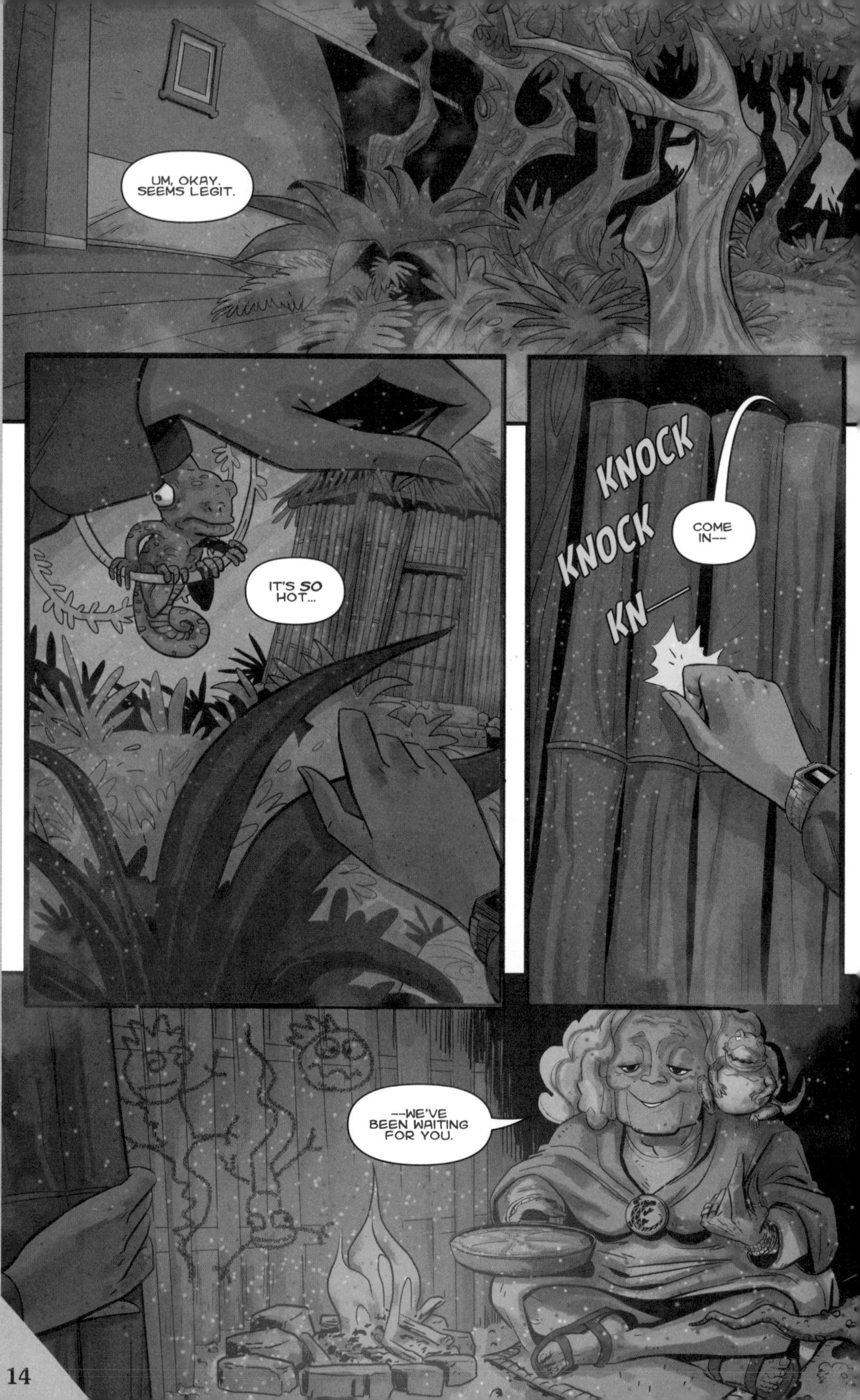
UM, OKAY. SEEMS LEGIT.
IT'S SO HOT...
KNOCK
KNOCK
KN—
COME IN--
--WE'VE BEEN WAITING FOR YOU.

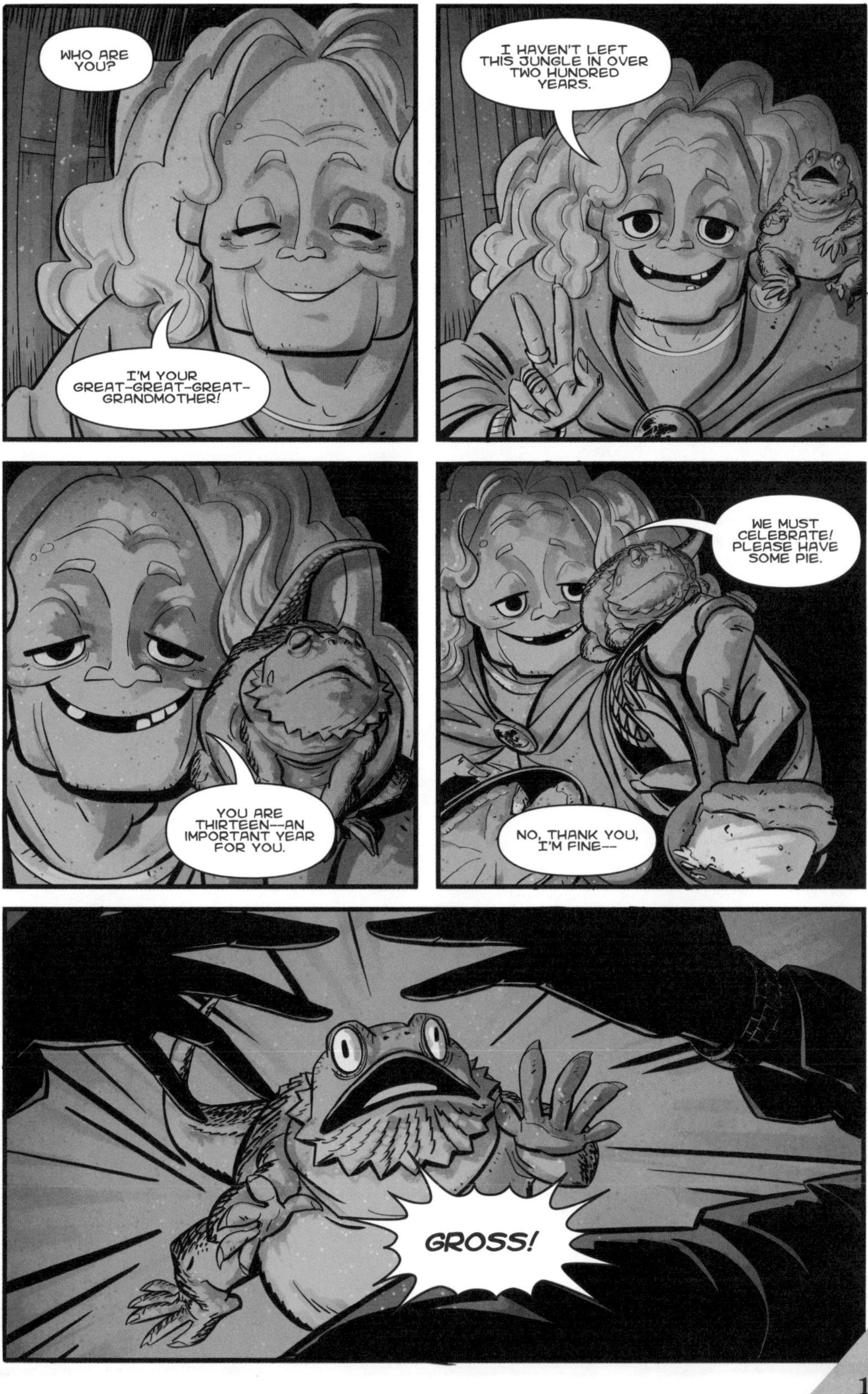
WHO ARE YOU?
I'M YOUR GREAT-GREAT-GREAT-GRANDMOTHER!
I HAVEN'T LEFT THIS JUNGLE IN OVER TWO HUNDRED YEARS.
YOU ARE THIRTEEN--AN IMPORTANT YEAR FOR YOU.
WE MUST CELEBRATE! PLEASE HAVE SOME PIE.
NO, THANK YOU, I'M FINE--
GROSS!

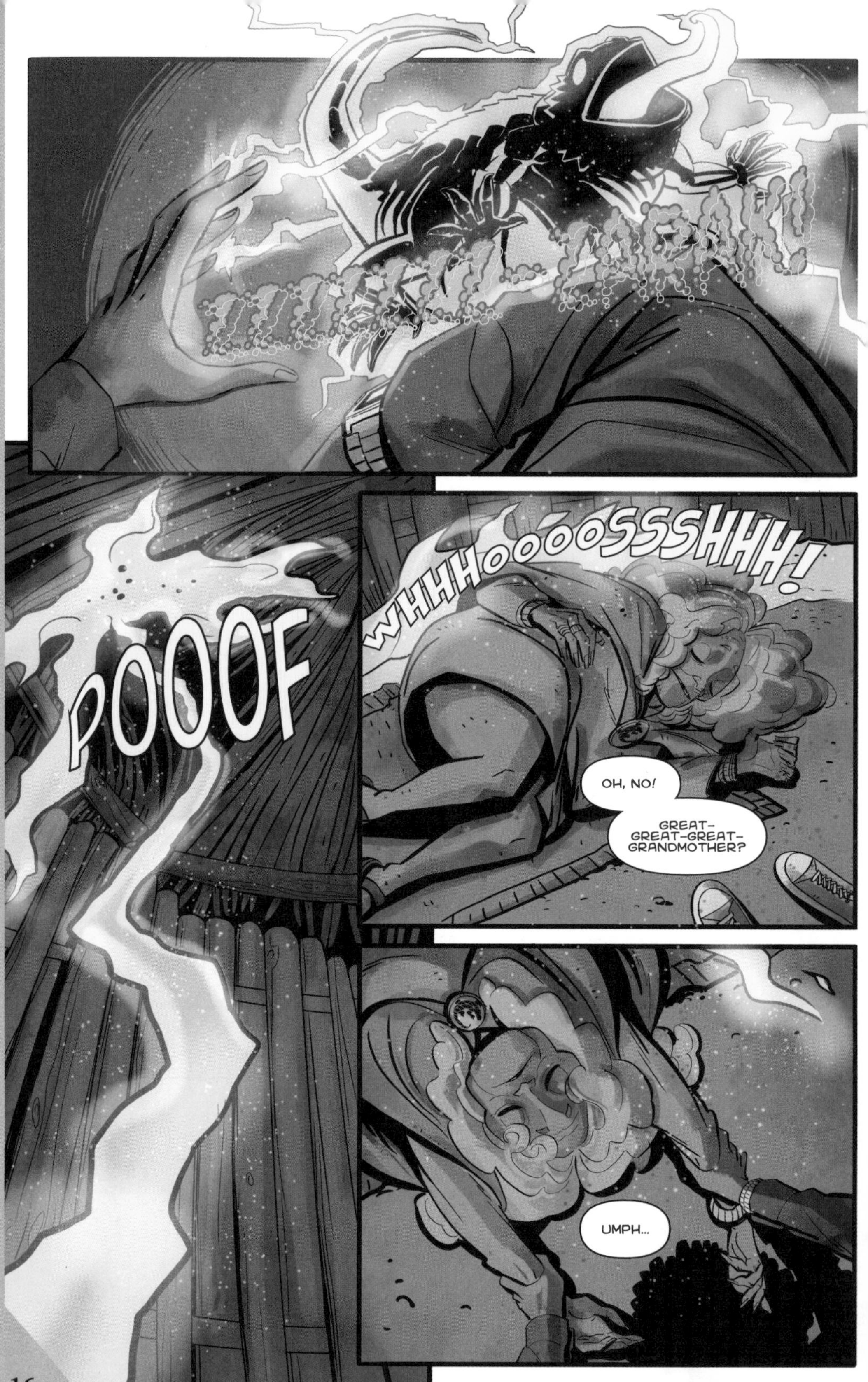
POOOF
WHHHOOOOOSSSSHHHH!
OH, NO!
GREAT-GREAT-GREAT-GRANDMOTHER?
UMPH...

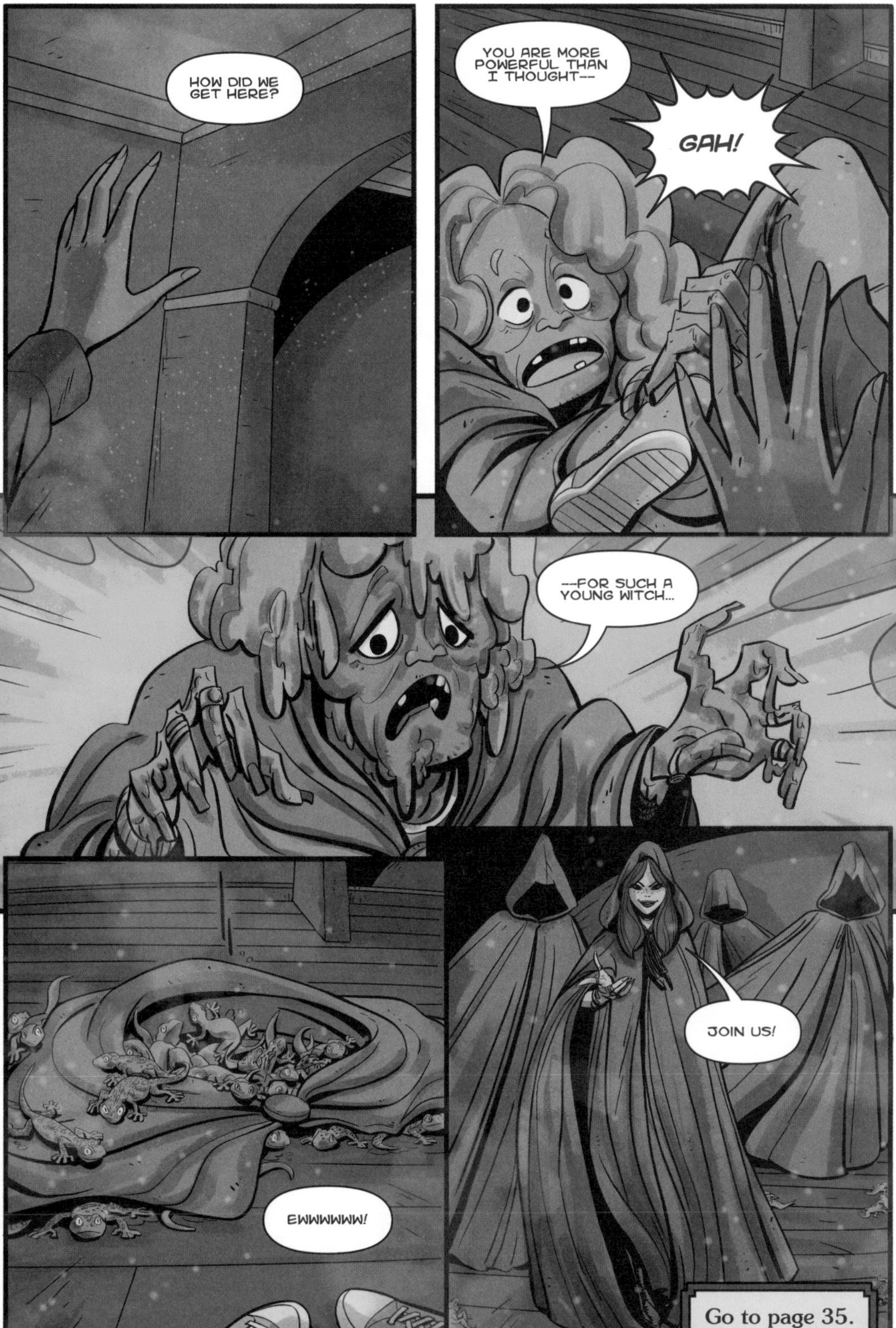
HOW DID WE GET HERE?
YOU ARE MORE POWERFUL THAN I THOUGHT--
GAH!
--FOR SUCH A YOUNG WITCH...
EWWWWWW!
JOIN US!
Go to page 35.

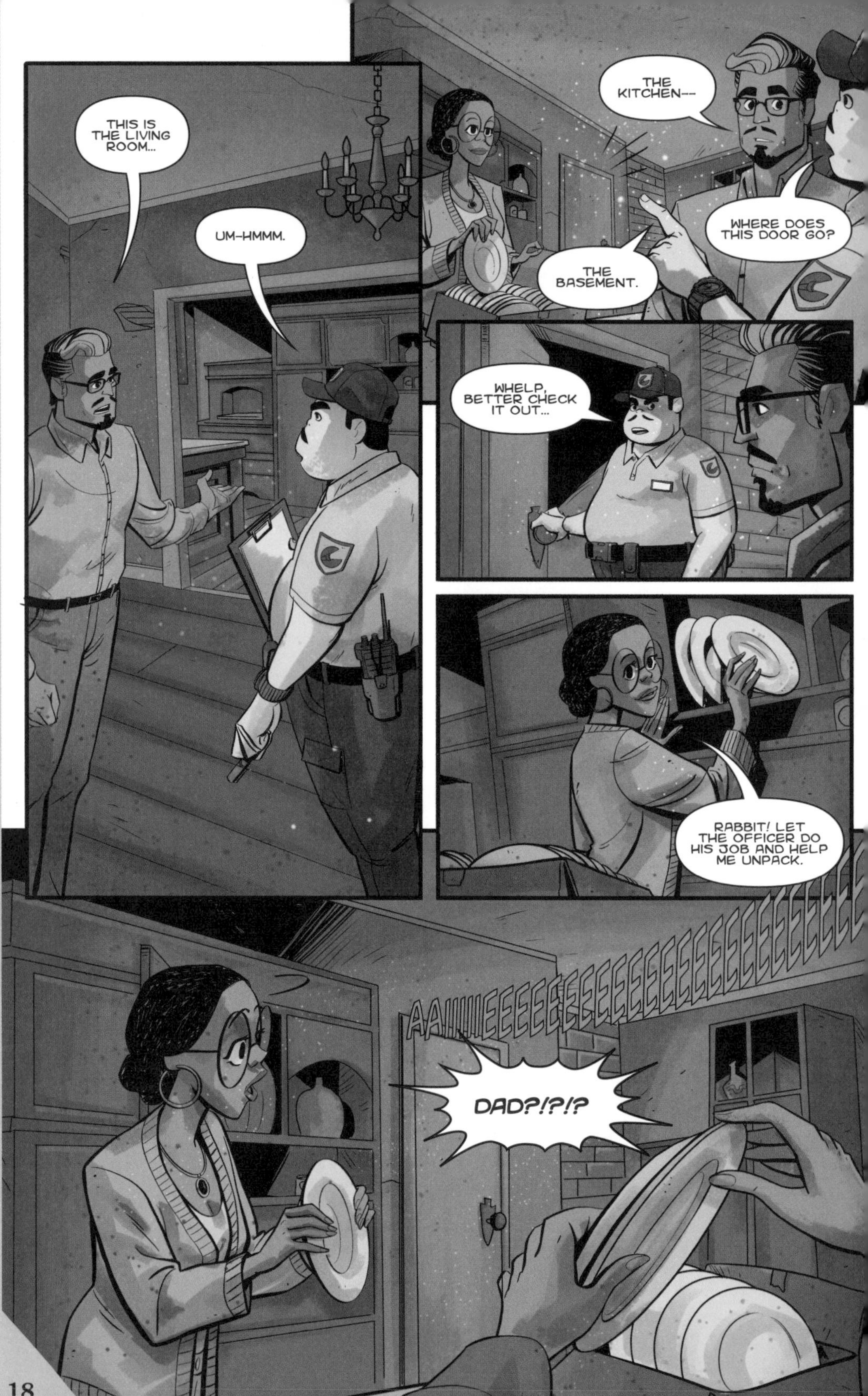
THIS IS THE LIVING ROOM...
UM-HMMM.
THE KITCHEN--
WHERE DOES THIS DOOR GO?
THE BASEMENT.
WHELP, BETTER CHECK IT OUT...
RABBIT! LET THE OFFICER DO HIS JOB AND HELP ME UNPACK.
AAIIIIIEEEEEEEEEEEEEEEEEEEEEEEEEEEEEEEEE
DAD?!?!?

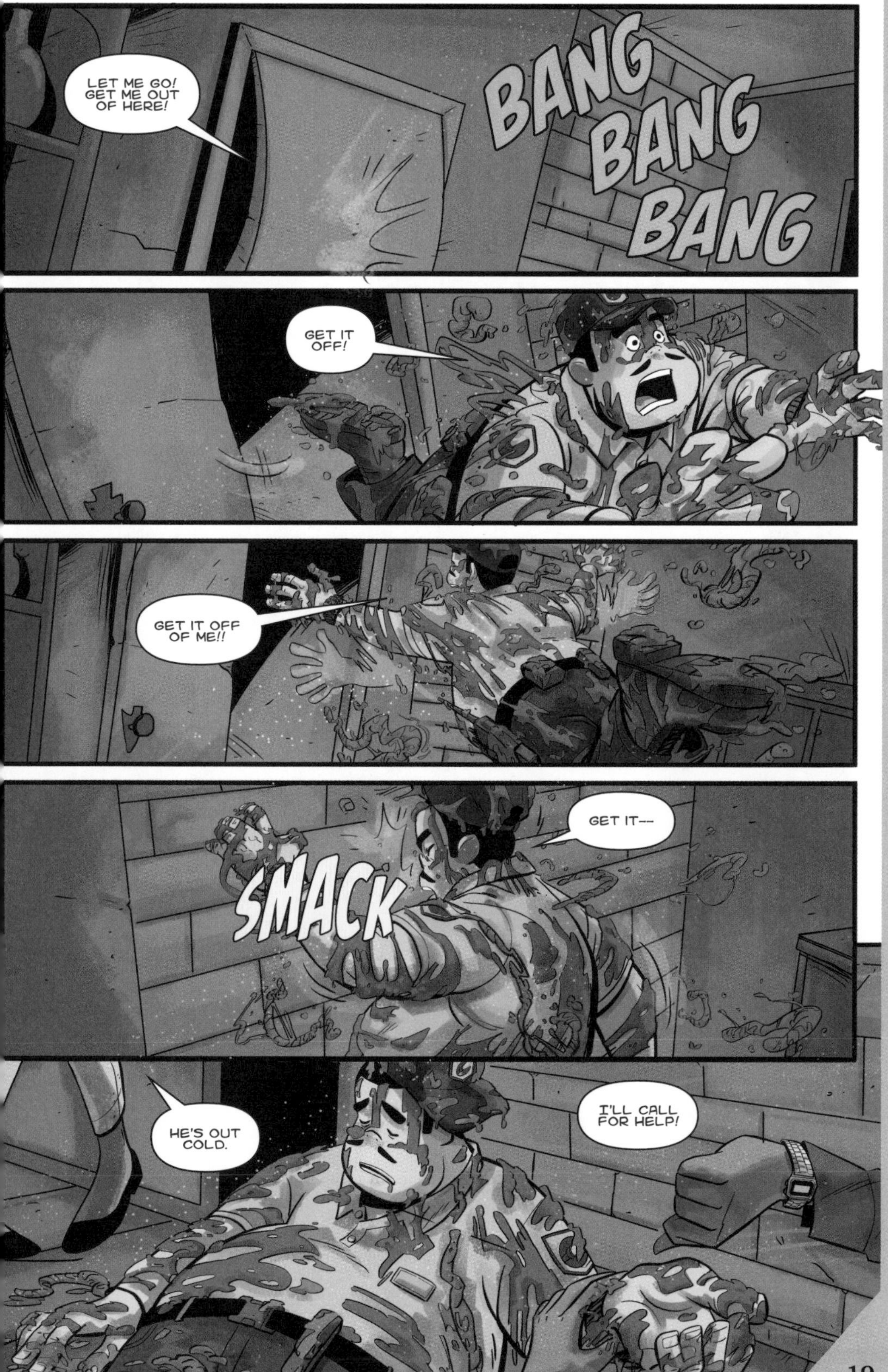
LET ME GO! GET ME OUT OF HERE!
BANG BANG BANG
GET IT OFF!
GET IT OFF OF ME!!
GET IT--
SMACK
HE'S OUT COLD.
I'LL CALL FOR HELP!

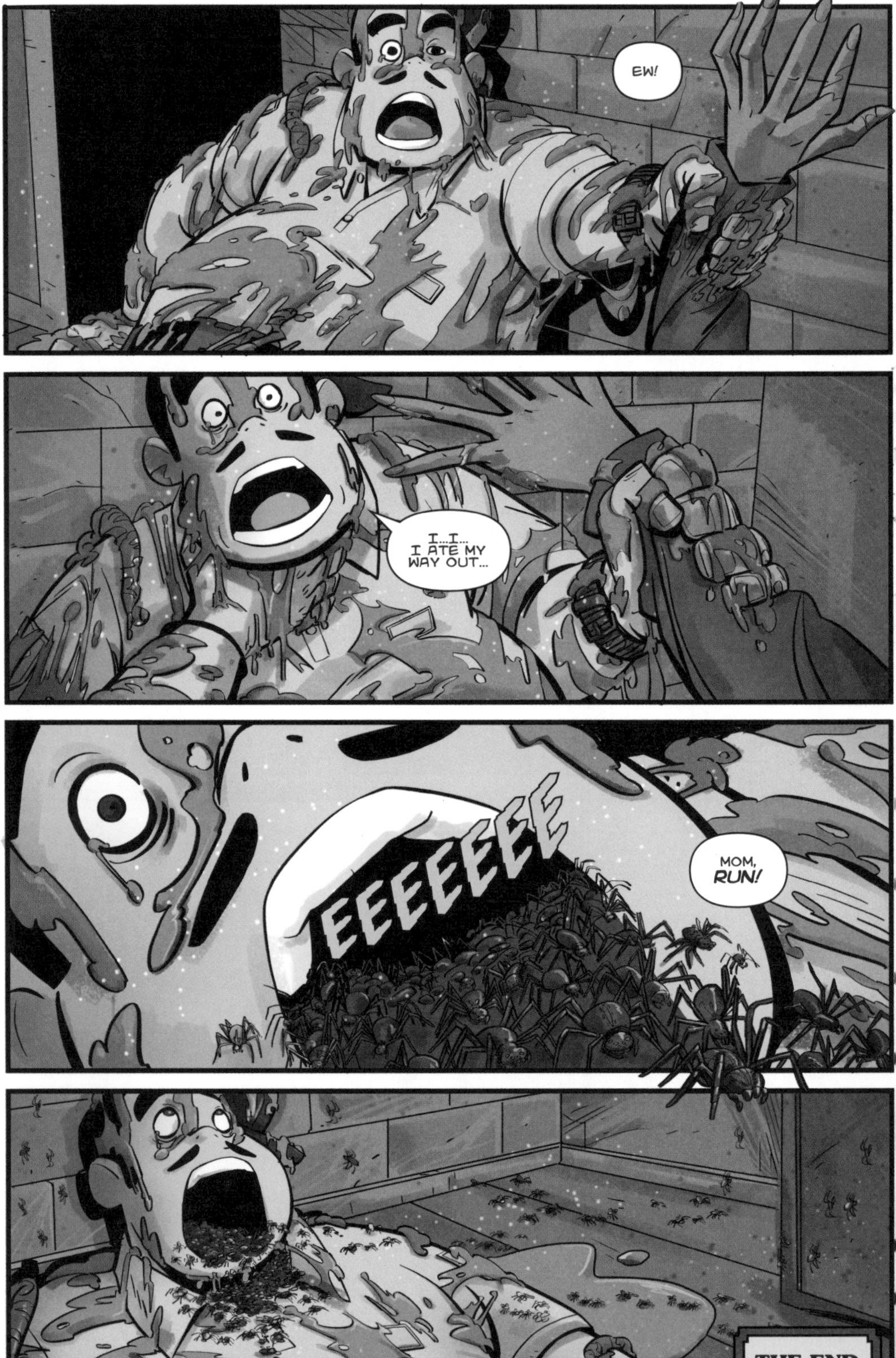
EW!
I...I...
I ATE MY
WAY OUT...
EEEEEEE
MOM,
RUN!
EEEEEEEEEEEEEEEEEEEEEEEEEEEEEEEEEEEEEEEE
THE END

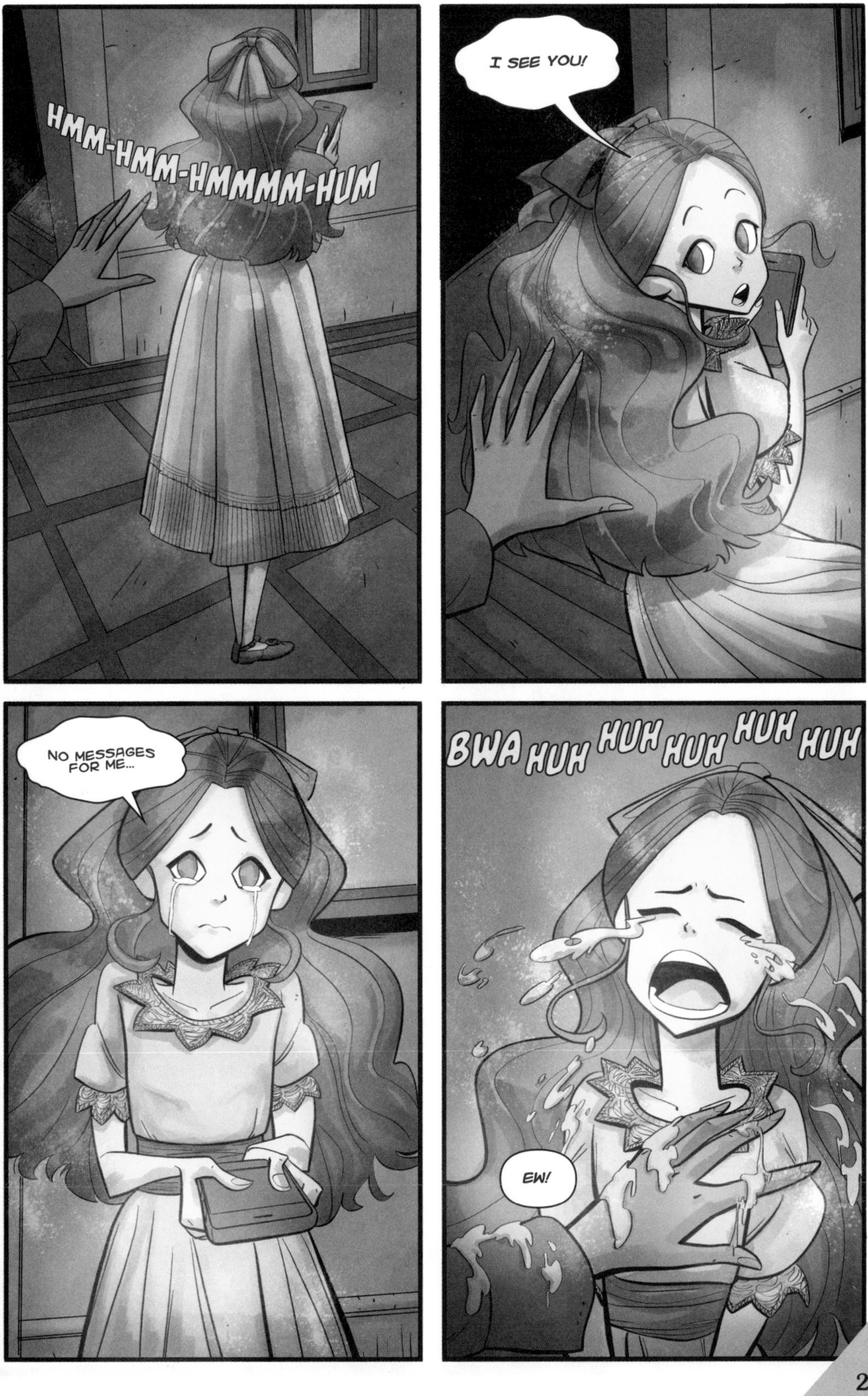
HMM-HMM-HMMMM-HUM
I SEE YOU!
NO MESSAGES FOR ME...
BWA HUH HUH HUH HUH HUH
EW!

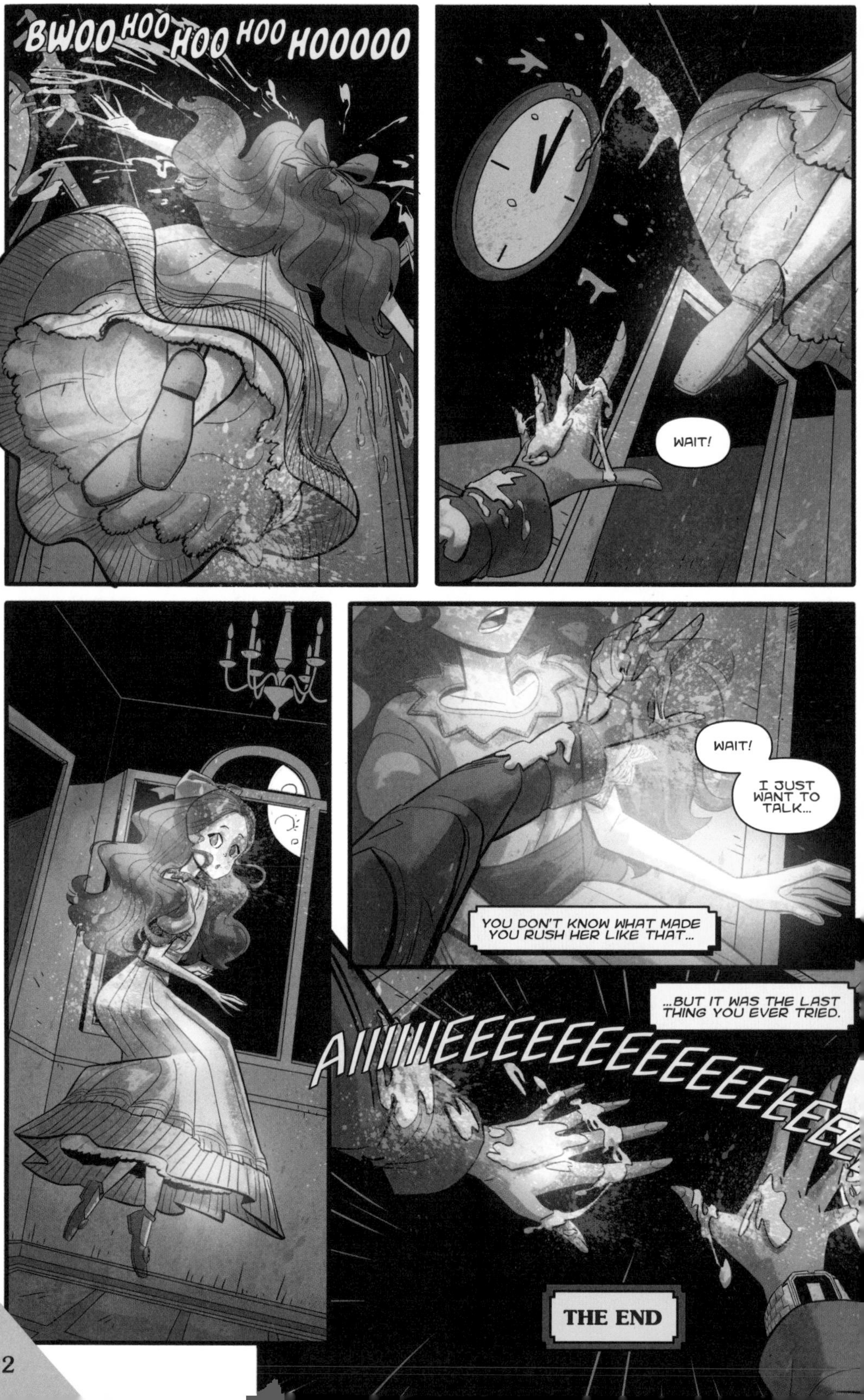
BWOO HOO HOO HOO HOOOOO
WAIT!
WAIT!
I JUST WANT TO TALK...
YOU DON'T KNOW WHAT MADE YOU RUSH HER LIKE THAT...
...BUT IT WAS THE LAST THING YOU EVER TRIED.
AIIIIIEEEEEEEEEEEEEEEEE
THE END

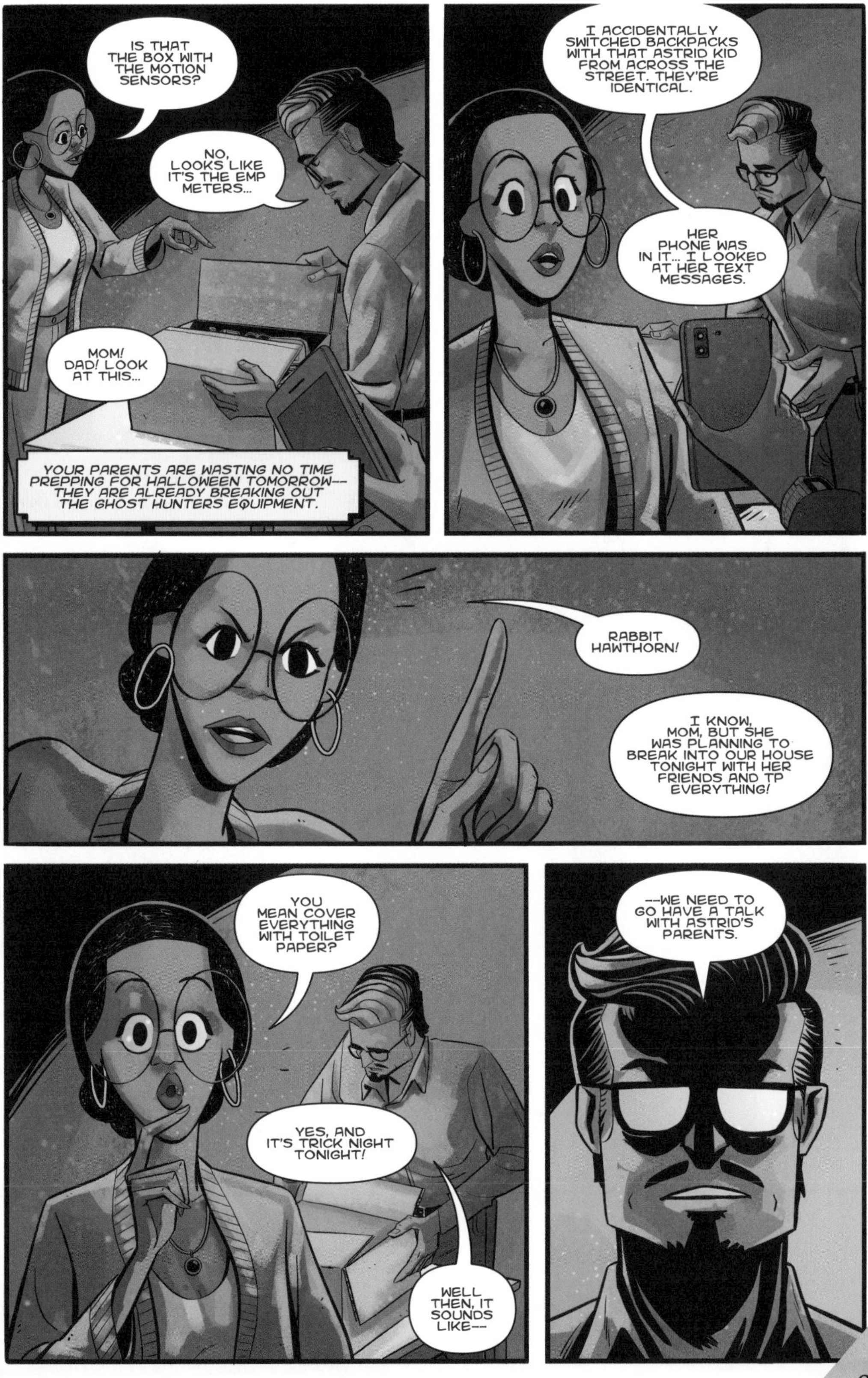
IS THAT THE BOX WITH THE MOTION SENSORS?
NO, LOOKS LIKE IT'S THE EMP METERS...
MOM! DAD! LOOK AT THIS...
YOUR PARENTS ARE WASTING NO TIME PREPPING FOR HALLOWEEN TOMORROW-- THEY ARE ALREADY BREAKING OUT THE GHOST HUNTERS EQUIPMENT.
I ACCIDENTALLY SWITCHED BACKPACKS WITH THAT ASTRID KID FROM ACROSS THE STREET. THEY'RE IDENTICAL.
HER PHONE WAS IN IT... I LOOKED AT HER TEXT MESSAGES.
RABBIT HAWTHORN!
I KNOW, MOM, BUT SHE WAS PLANNING TO BREAK INTO OUR HOUSE TONIGHT WITH HER FRIENDS AND TP EVERYTHING!
YOU MEAN COVER EVERYTHING WITH TOILET PAPER?
YES, AND IT'S TRICK NIGHT TONIGHT!
WELL THEN, IT SOUNDS LIKE--
--WE NEED TO GO HAVE A TALK WITH ASTRID'S PARENTS.

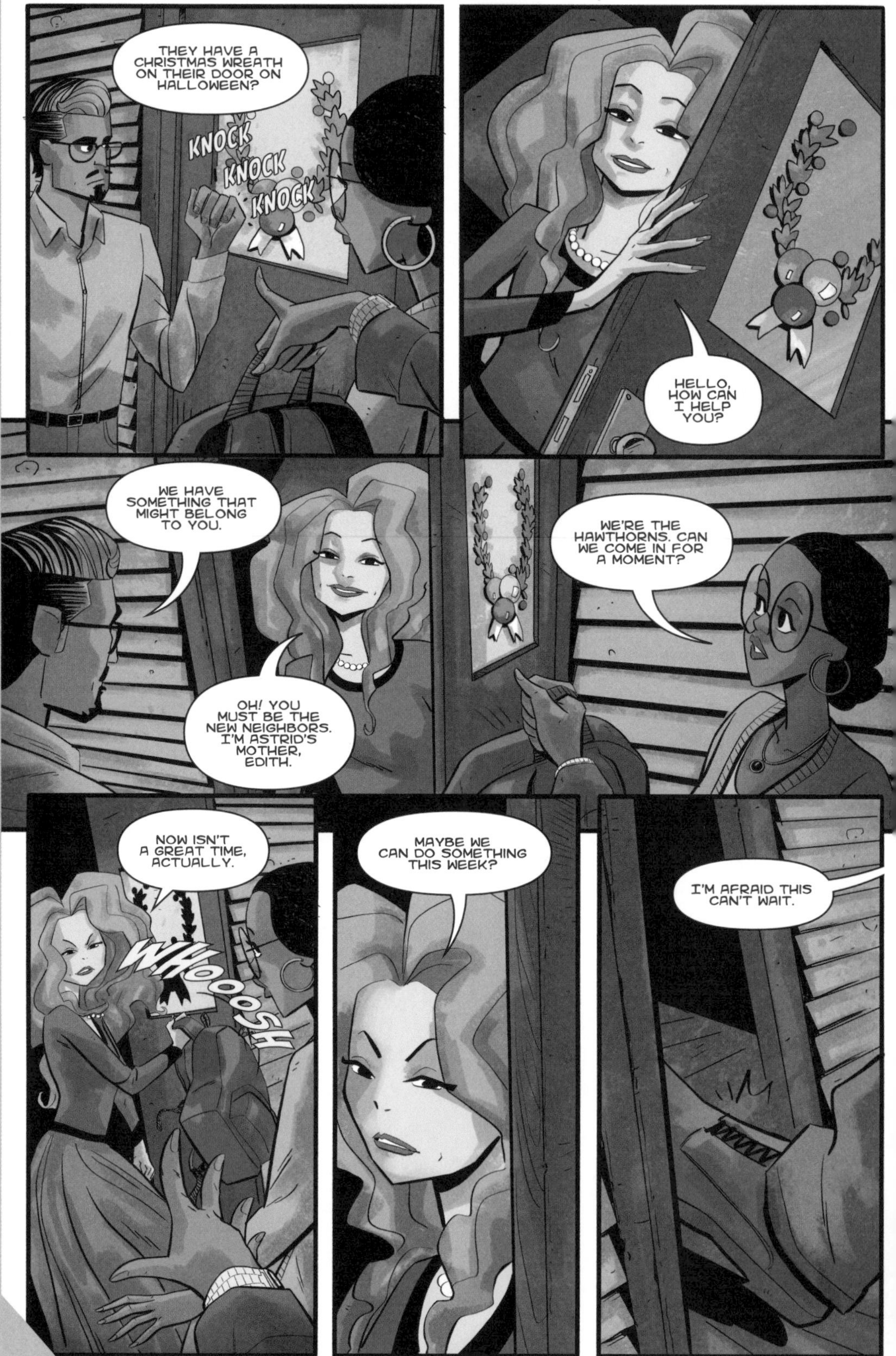

THEY HAVE A CHRISTMAS WREATH ON THEIR DOOR ON HALLOWEEN?
KNOCK
KNOCK
KNOCK
HELLO, HOW CAN I HELP YOU?
WE HAVE SOMETHING THAT MIGHT BELONG TO YOU.
OH! YOU MUST BE THE NEW NEIGHBORS. I'M ASTRID'S MOTHER, EDITH.
WE'RE THE HAWTHORNS. CAN WE COME IN FOR A MOMENT?
NOW ISN'T A GREAT TIME, ACTUALLY.
WHOOOOSH
MAYBE WE CAN DO SOMETHING THIS WEEK?
I'M AFRAID THIS CAN'T WAIT.

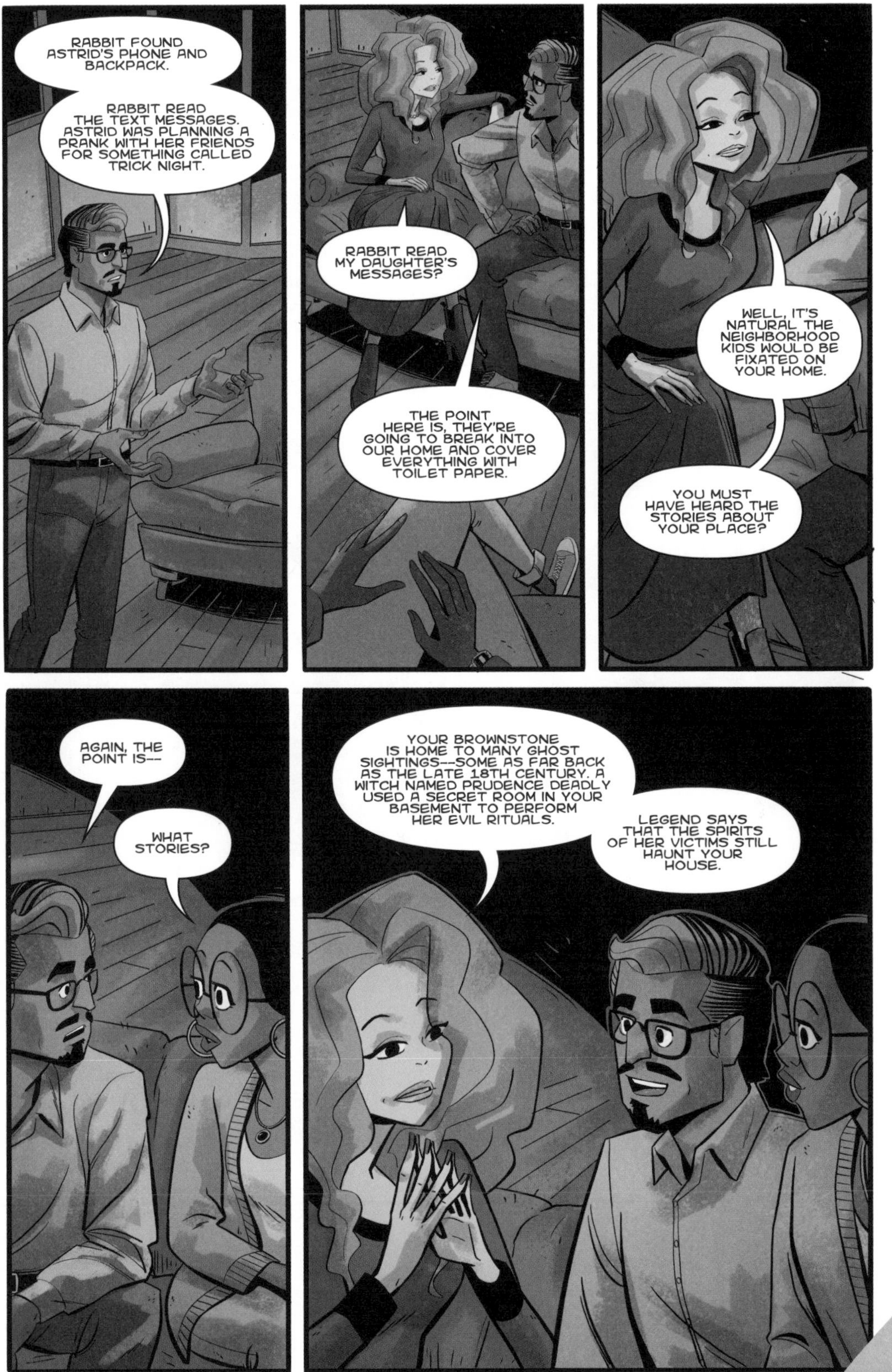
RABBIT FOUND ASTRID'S PHONE AND BACKPACK.
RABBIT READ THE TEXT MESSAGES. ASTRID WAS PLANNING A PRANK WITH HER FRIENDS FOR SOMETHING CALLED TRICK NIGHT.
RABBIT READ MY DAUGHTER'S MESSAGES?
THE POINT HERE IS, THEY'RE GOING TO BREAK INTO OUR HOME AND COVER EVERYTHING WITH TOILET PAPER.
WELL, IT'S NATURAL THE NEIGHBORHOOD KIDS WOULD BE FIXATED ON YOUR HOME.
YOU MUST HAVE HEARD THE STORIES ABOUT YOUR PLACE?
AGAIN, THE POINT IS--
WHAT STORIES?
YOUR BROWNSTONE IS HOME TO MANY GHOST SIGHTINGS--SOME AS FAR BACK AS THE LATE 18TH CENTURY. A WITCH NAMED PRUDENCE DEADLY USED A SECRET ROOM IN YOUR BASEMENT TO PERFORM HER EVIL RITUALS.
LEGEND SAYS THAT THE SPIRITS OF HER VICTIMS STILL HAUNT YOUR HOUSE.

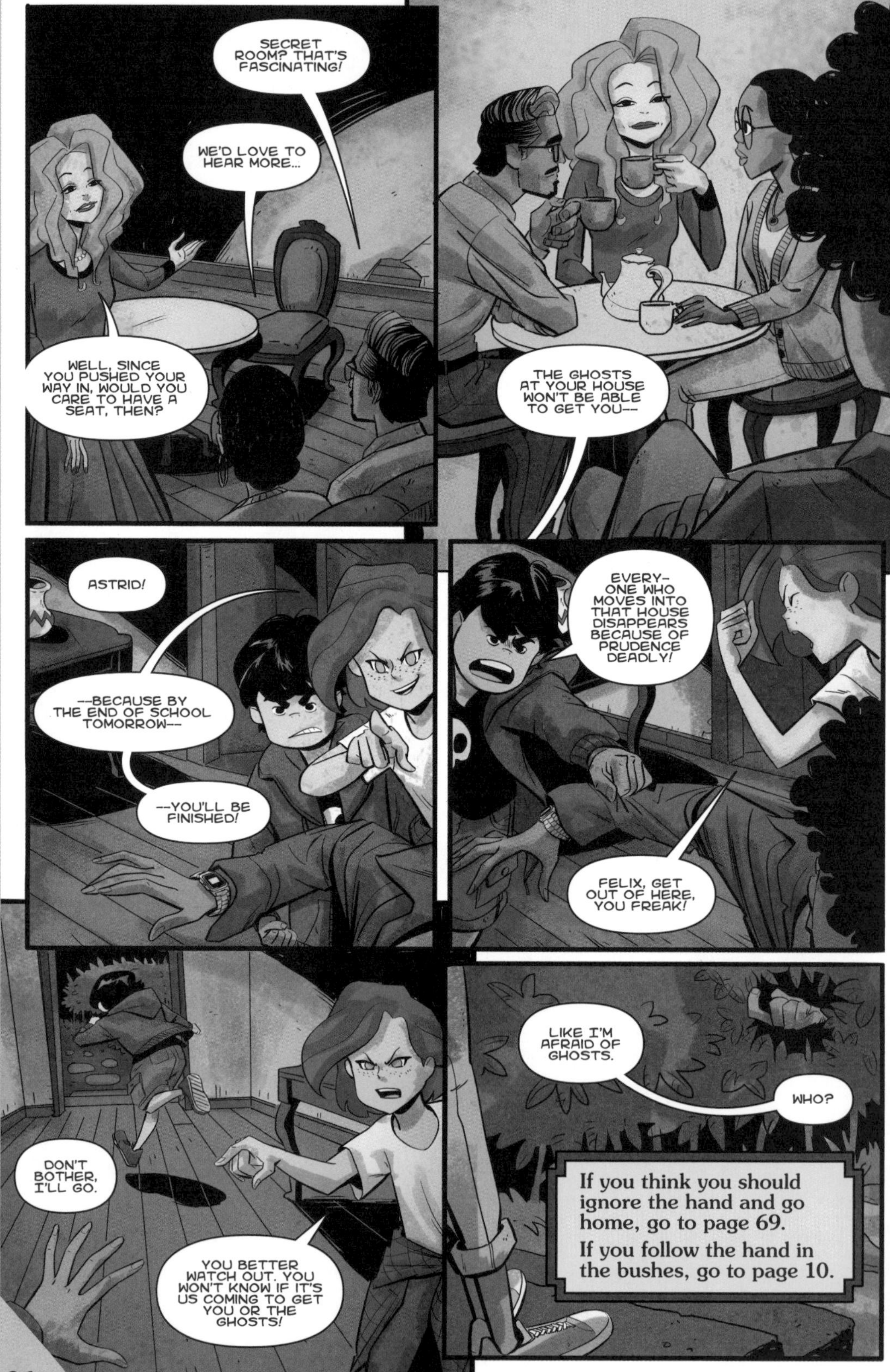
SECRET ROOM? THAT'S FASCINATING!
WE'D LOVE TO HEAR MORE...
WELL, SINCE YOU PUSHED YOUR WAY IN, WOULD YOU CARE TO HAVE A SEAT, THEN?
THE GHOSTS AT YOUR HOUSE WON'T BE ABLE TO GET YOU--
ASTRID!
--BECAUSE BY THE END OF SCHOOL TOMORROW--
--YOU'LL BE FINISHED!
EVERY-ONE WHO MOVES INTO THAT HOUSE DISAPPEARS BECAUSE OF PRUDENCE DEADLY!
FELIX, GET OUT OF HERE, YOU FREAK!
DON'T BOTHER, I'LL GO.
YOU BETTER WATCH OUT. YOU WON'T KNOW IF IT'S US COMING TO GET YOU OR THE GHOSTS!
LIKE I'M AFRAID OF GHOSTS.
WHO?

If you think you should ignore the hand and go home, go to page 69.

If you follow the hand in the bushes, go to page 10.

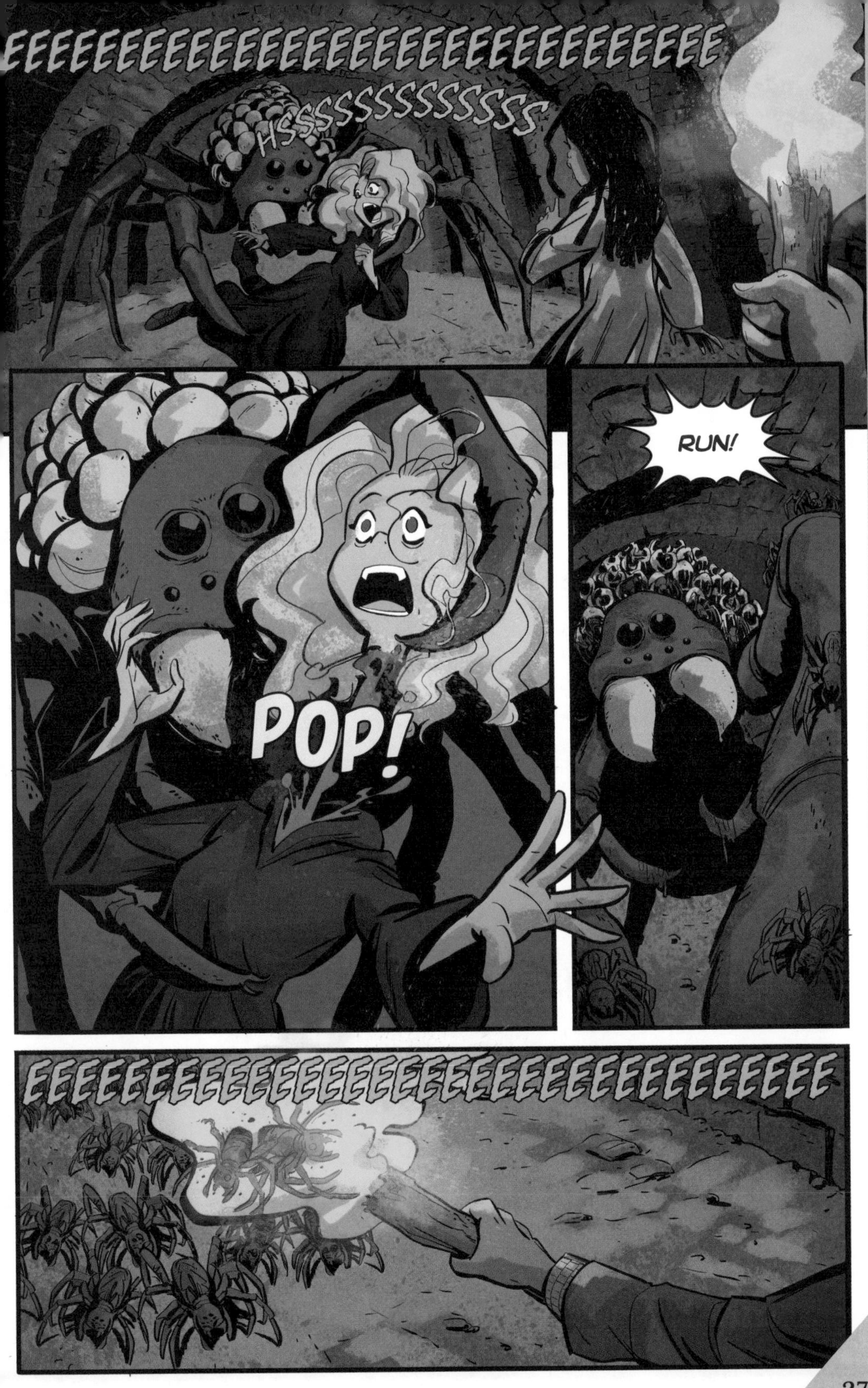
EEEEEEEEEEEEEEEEEEEEEEEEEEEEEEE
HSSSSSSSSSSSSSS
POP!
RUN!
EEEEEEEEEEEEEEEEEEEEEEEEEEEEEEEEEEEE

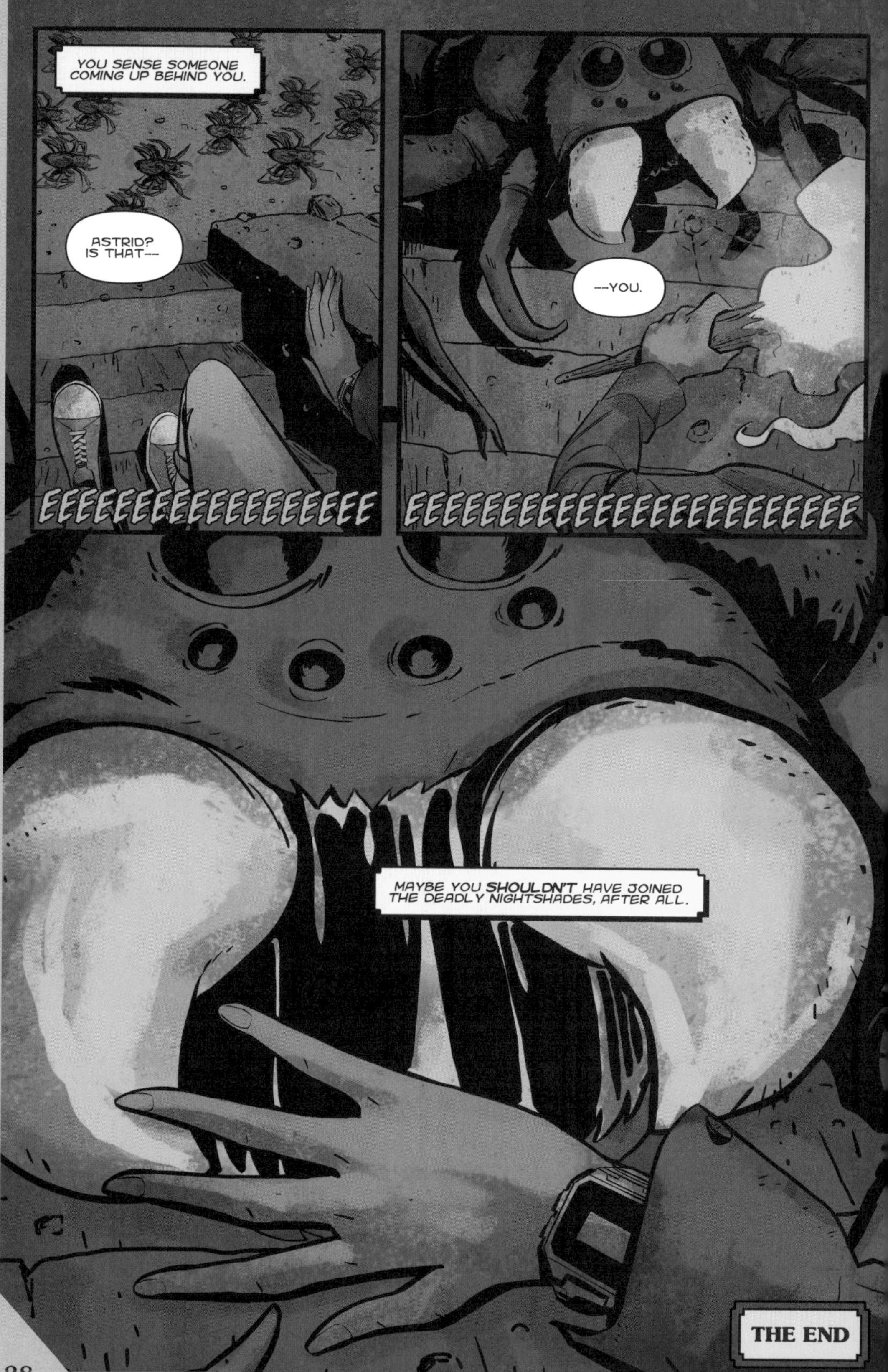

YOU SENSE SOMEONE COMING UP BEHIND YOU.
ASTRID? IS THAT--
EEEEEEEEEEEEEEEEEEEE
--YOU.
EEEEEEEEEEEEEEEEEEEEEEEEEEEE
MAYBE YOU **SHOULDN'T** HAVE JOINED THE DEADLY NIGHTSHADES, AFTER ALL.
THE END

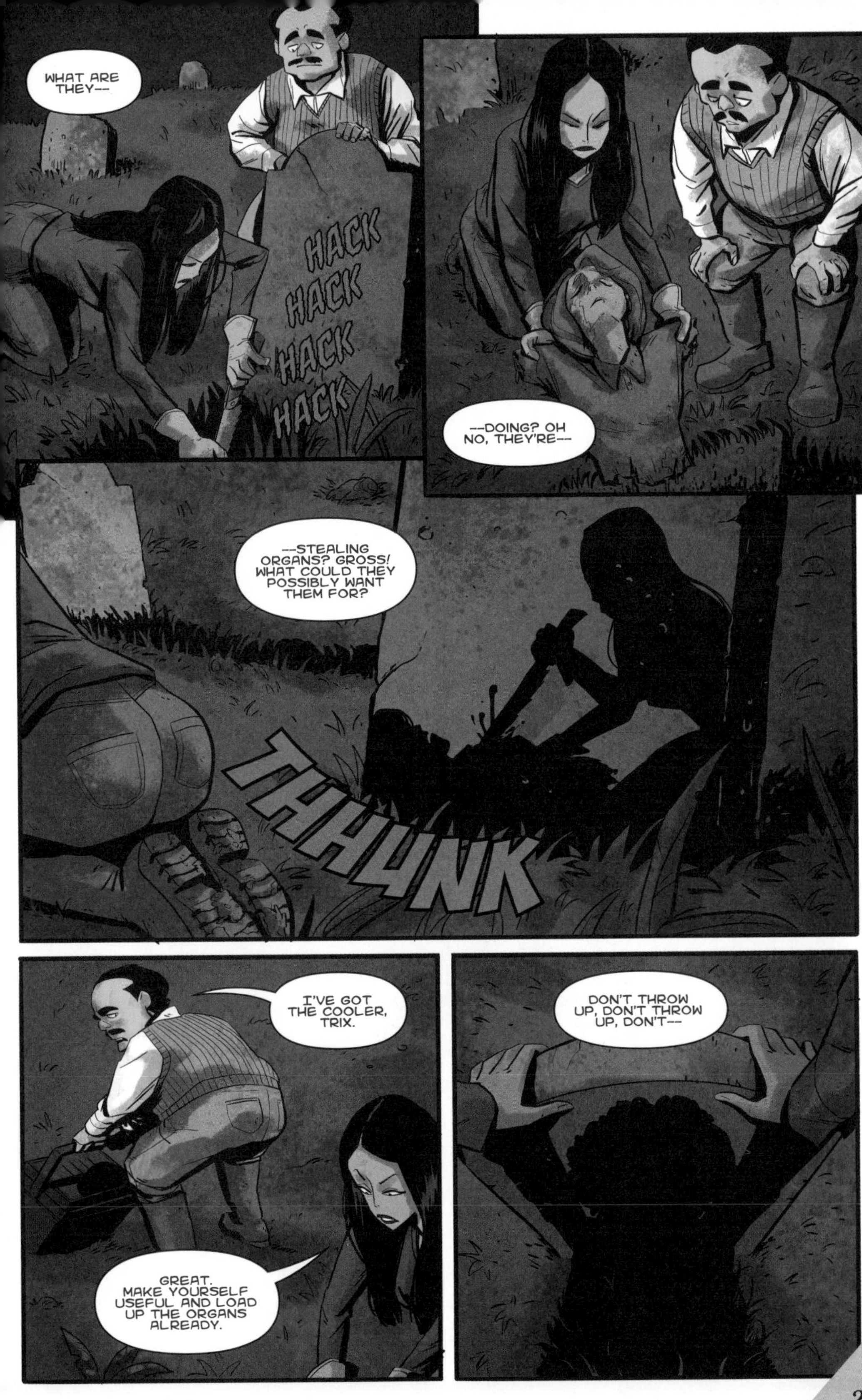
WHAT ARE THEY--
HACK HACK HACK HACK
--DOING? OH NO, THEY'RE--
--STEALING ORGANS? GROSS! WHAT COULD THEY POSSIBLY WANT THEM FOR?
THHUNK
I'VE GOT THE COOLER, TRIX.
GREAT. MAKE YOURSELF USEFUL AND LOAD UP THE ORGANS ALREADY.
DON'T THROW UP, DON'T THROW UP, DON'T--

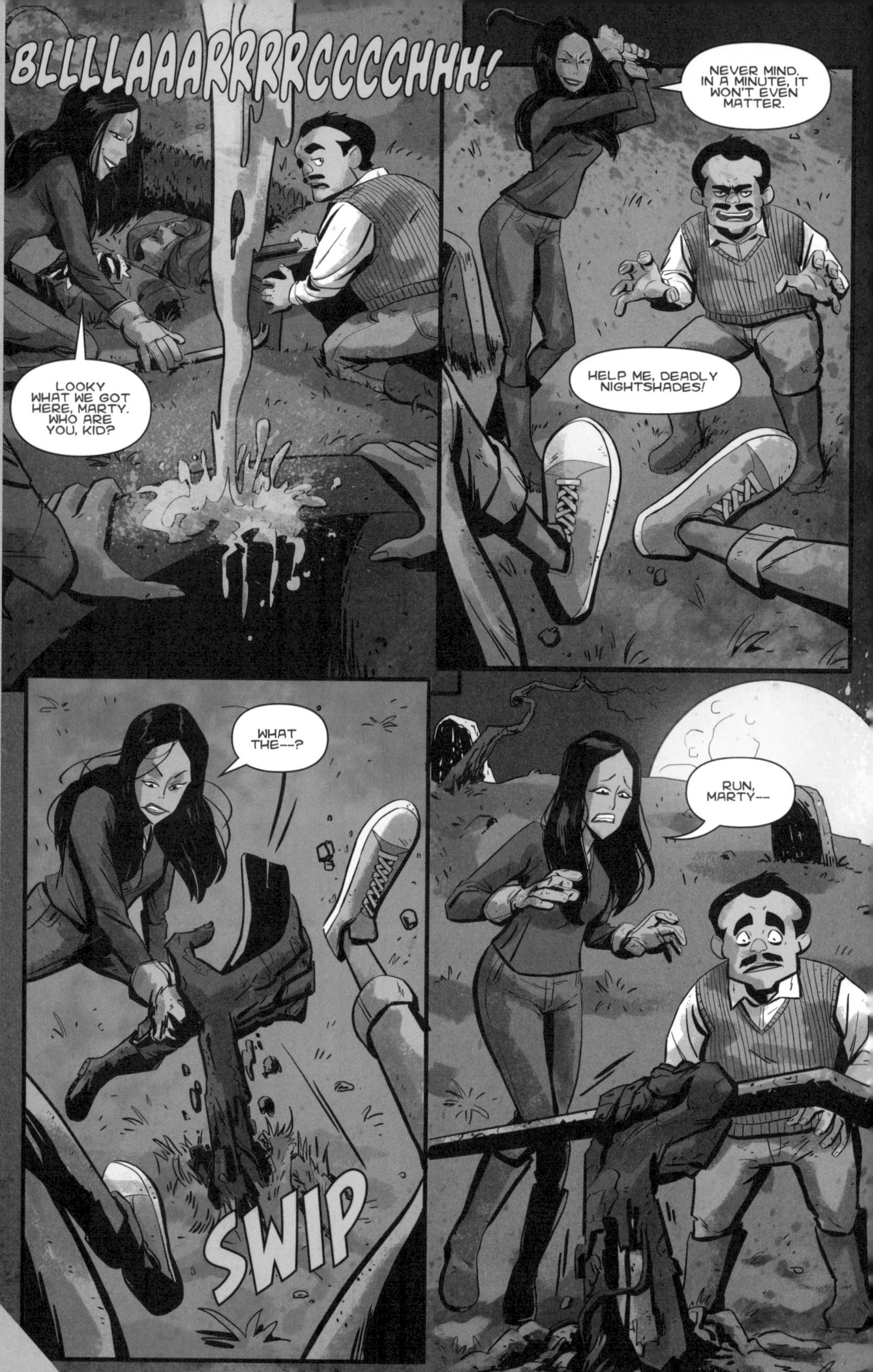
BLLLAAARRRRCCCCHHH!
LOOKY WHAT WE GOT HERE, MARTY. WHO ARE YOU, KID?
NEVER MIND. IN A MINUTE, IT WON'T EVEN MATTER.
HELP ME, DEADLY NIGHTSHADES!
WHAT THE--?
SWIP
RUN, MARTY--

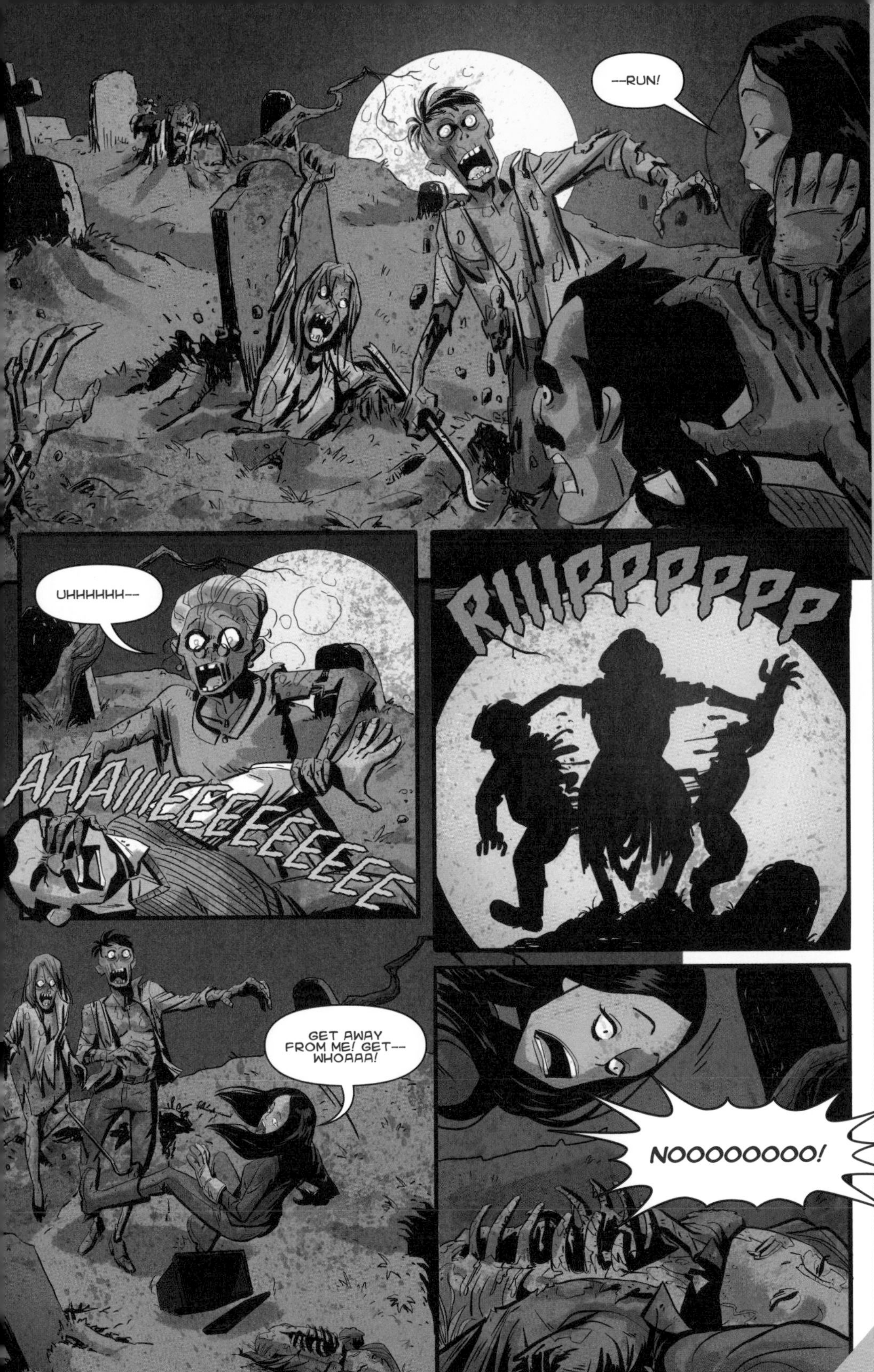
--RUN!
UHHHHHH--
AAAIIIEEEEEEEEEEEEE
RIIIPPPPPPP
GET AWAY FROM ME! GET-- WHOAAA!
NOOOOOOOO!

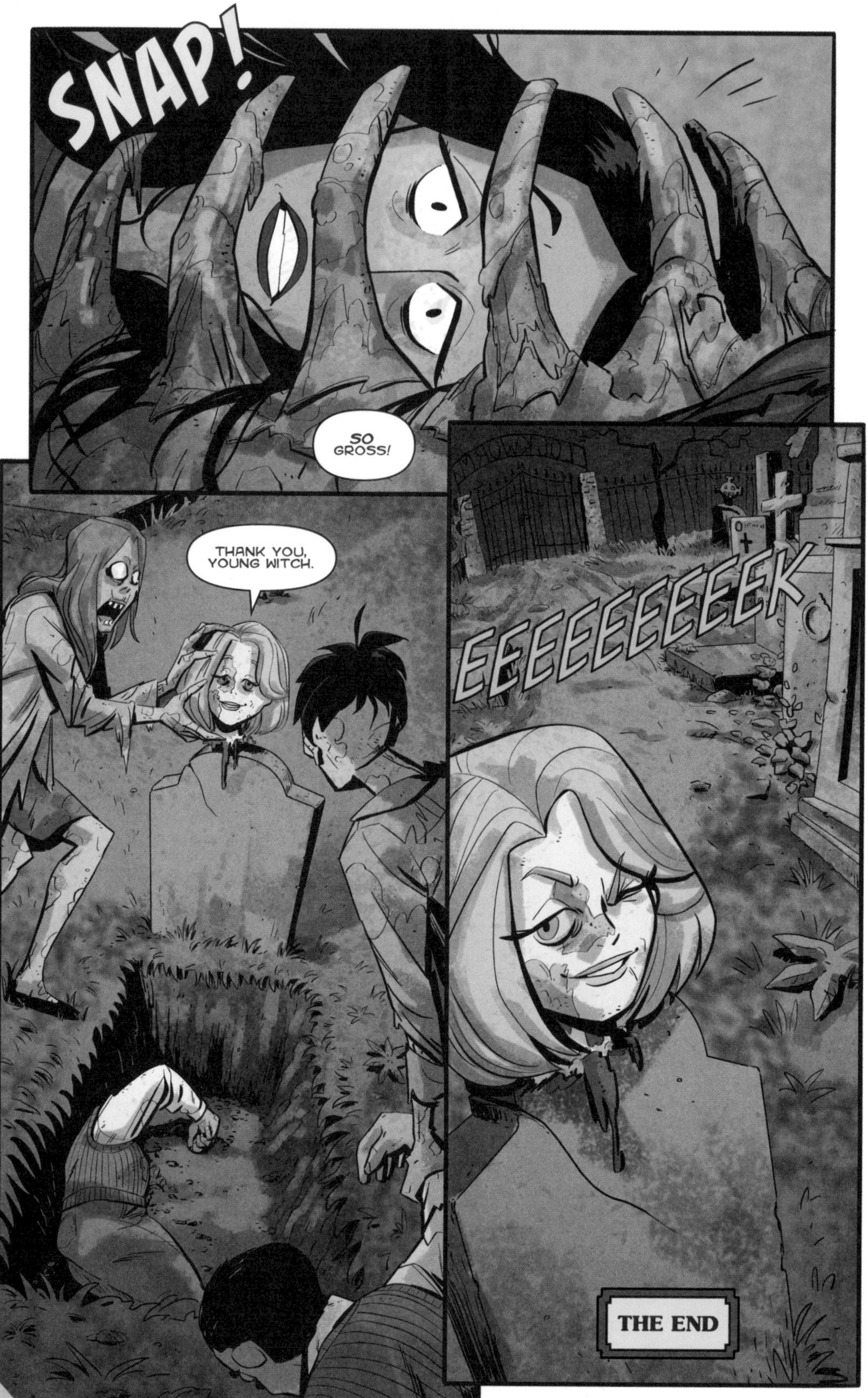
SNAP!
SO GROSS!
THANK YOU, YOUNG WITCH.
EEEEEEEEEEK
THE END

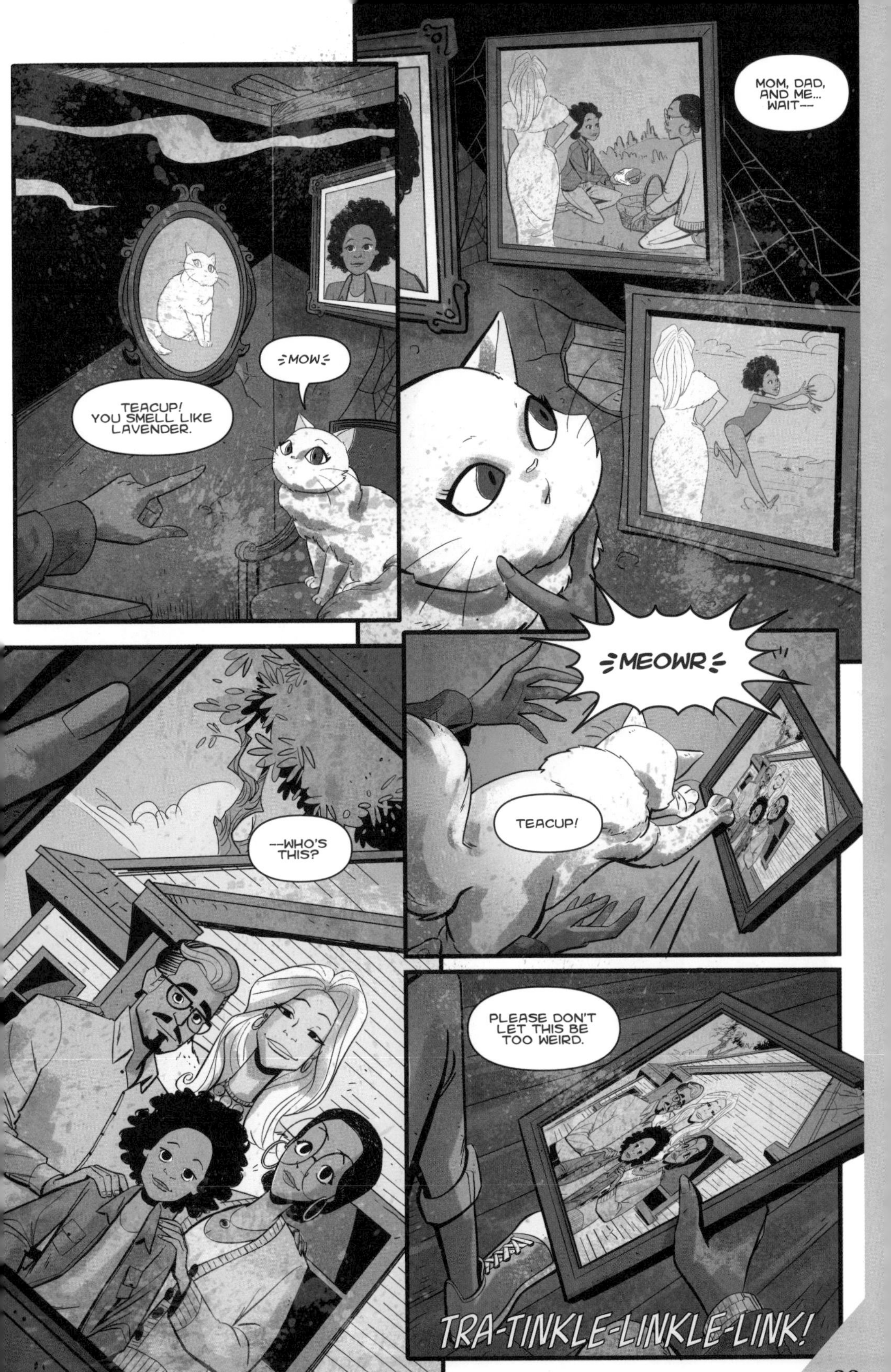
TEACUP! YOU SMELL LIKE LAVENDER.
MOW
MOM, DAD, AND ME... WAIT--
--WHO'S THIS?
MEOWR
TEACUP!
PLEASE DON'T LET THIS BE TOO WEIRD.
TRA-TINKLE-LINKLE-LINK!

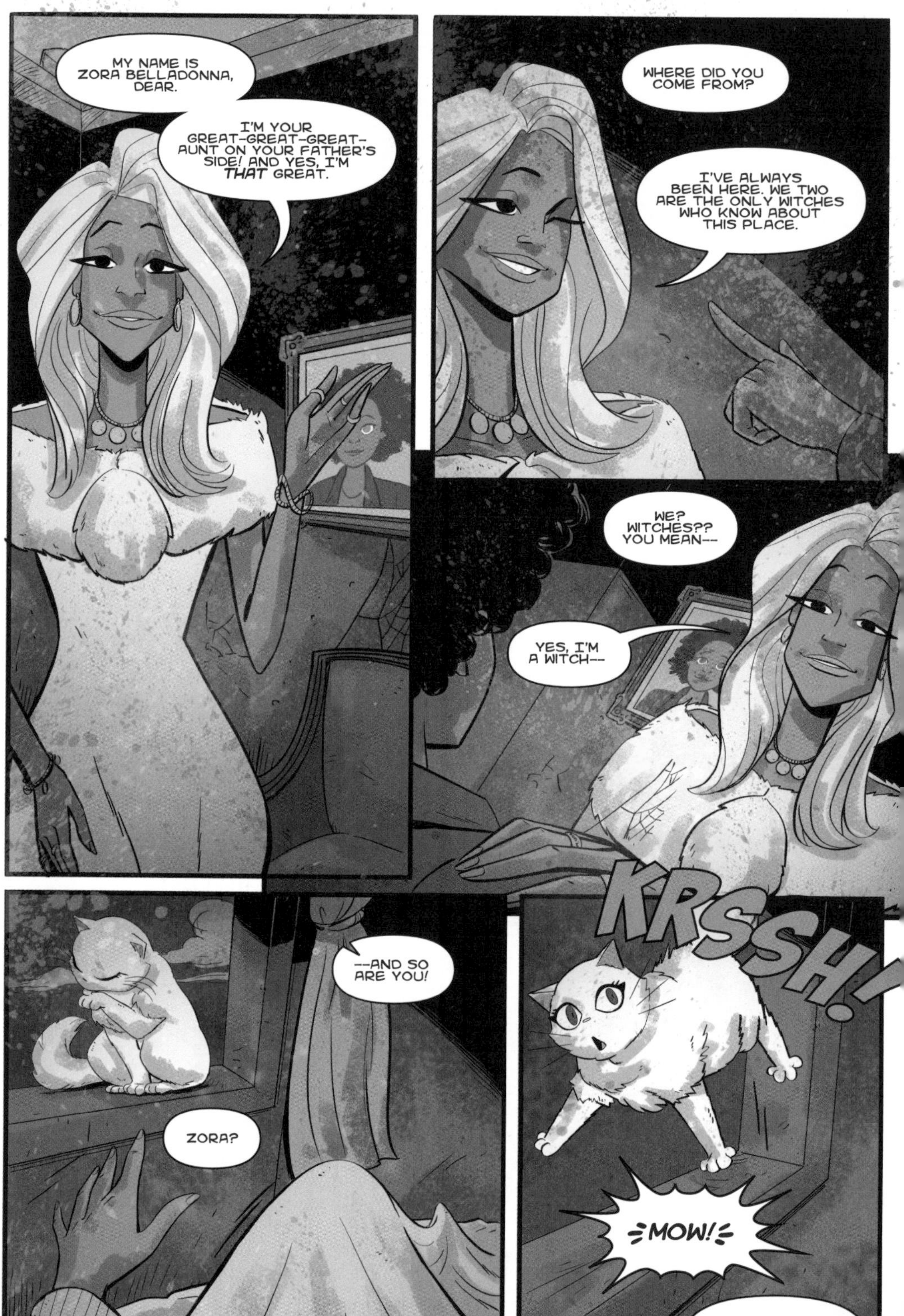
MY NAME IS ZORA BELLADONNA, DEAR.
I'M YOUR GREAT-GREAT-GREAT-AUNT ON YOUR FATHER'S SIDE! AND YES, I'M *THAT* GREAT.
WHERE DID YOU COME FROM?
I'VE ALWAYS BEEN HERE. WE TWO ARE THE ONLY WITCHES WHO KNOW ABOUT THIS PLACE.
WE? WITCHES?? YOU MEAN--
YES, I'M A WITCH--
--AND SO ARE YOU!
ZORA?
KRSSH!
MOW!
THAT CAME FROM THE LIVING ROOM! COME ON, TEACUP!

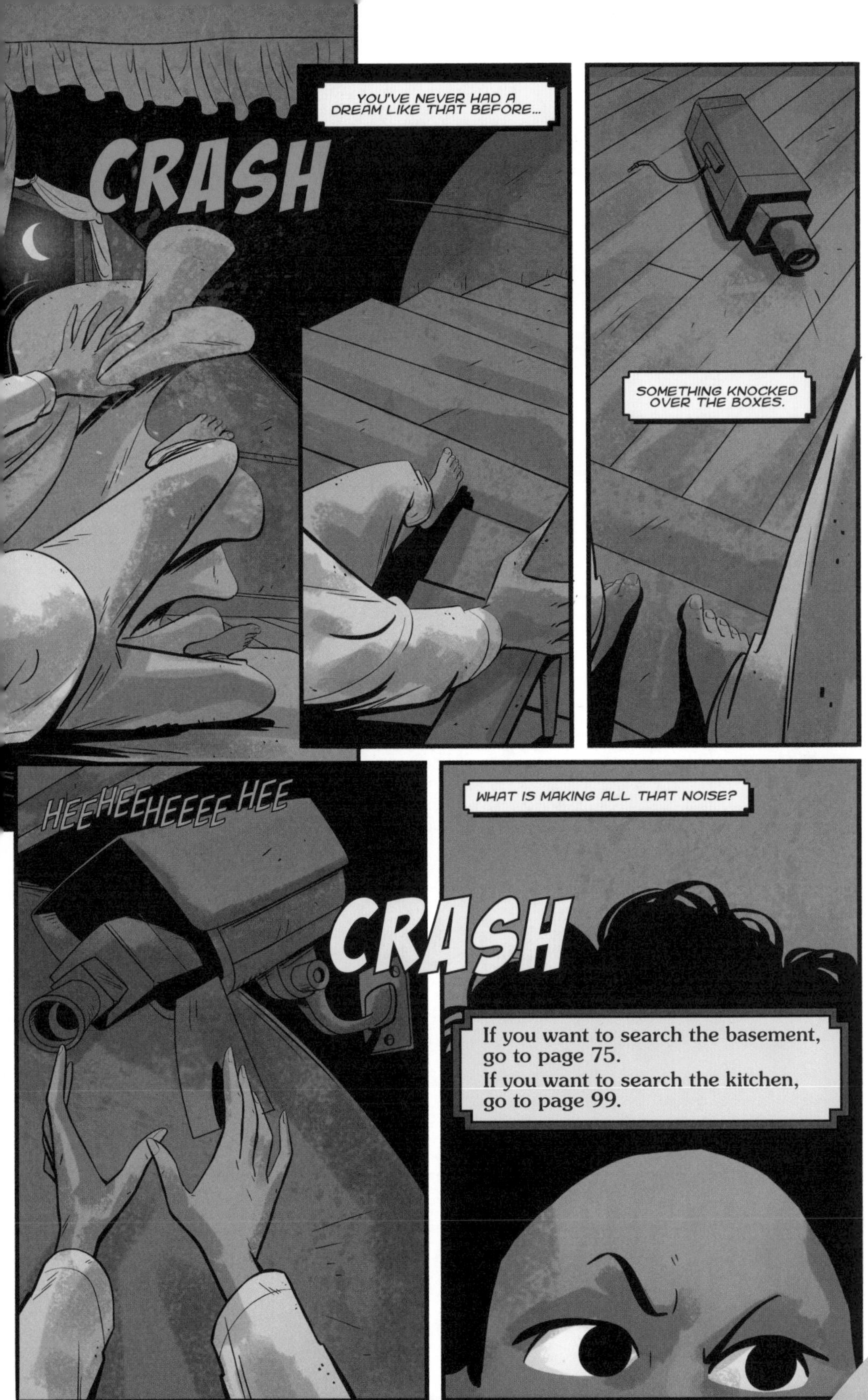
CRASH
YOU'VE NEVER HAD A DREAM LIKE THAT BEFORE...
SOMETHING KNOCKED OVER THE BOXES.
HEEHEEHEEEEE HEE
CRASH
WHAT IS MAKING ALL THAT NOISE?
If you want to search the basement, go to page 75.
If you want to search the kitchen, go to page 99.

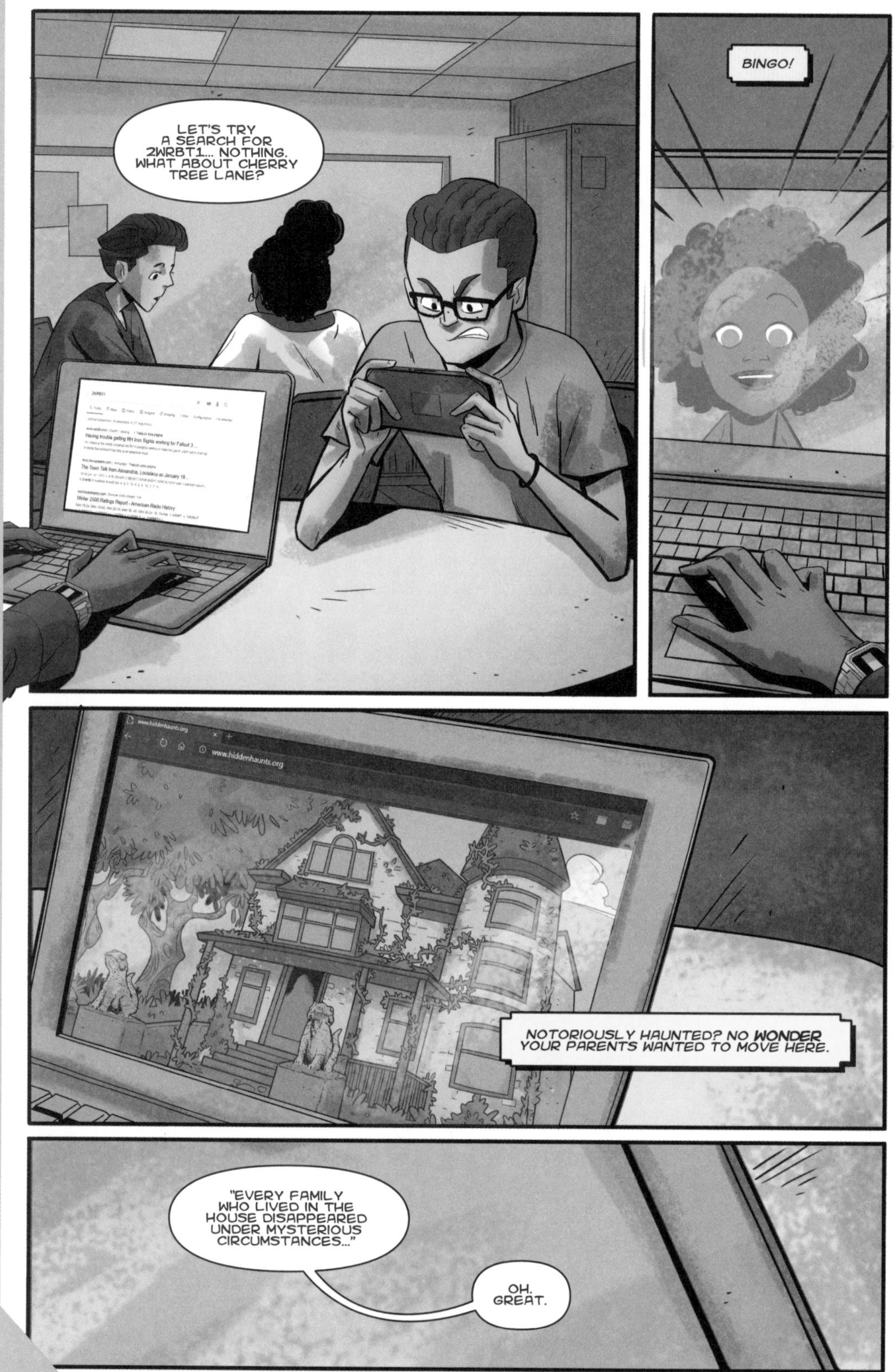
LET'S TRY A SEARCH FOR 2WRBT1... NOTHING. WHAT ABOUT CHERRY TREE LANE?
BINGO!
www.hiddenhaunts.org
NOTORIOUSLY HAUNTED? NO **WONDER** YOUR PARENTS WANTED TO MOVE HERE.
"EVERY FAMILY WHO LIVED IN THE HOUSE DISAPPEARED UNDER MYSTERIOUS CIRCUMSTANCES..."
OH. GREAT.

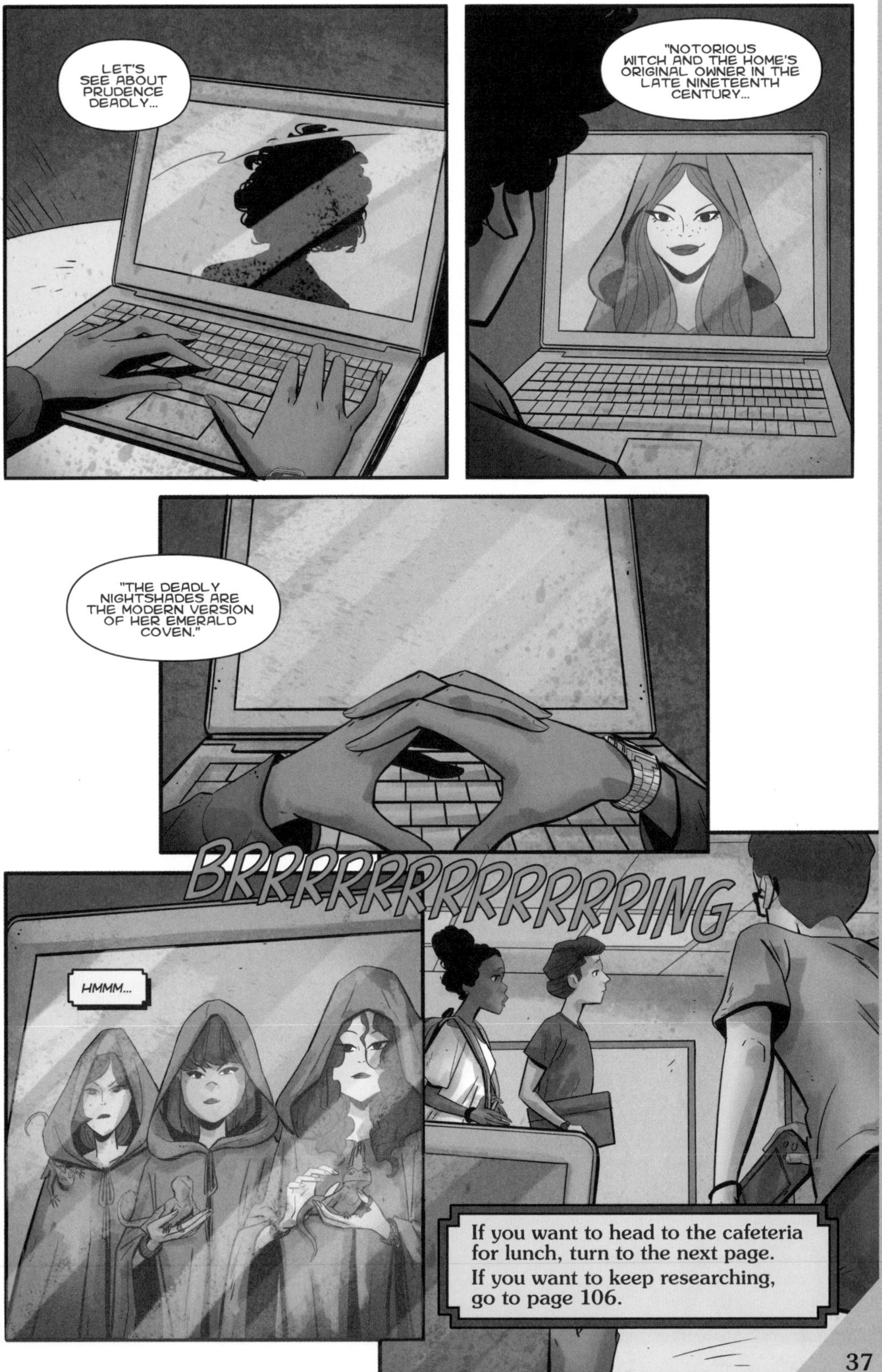
LET'S SEE ABOUT PRUDENCE DEADLY...
"NOTORIOUS WITCH AND THE HOME'S ORIGINAL OWNER IN THE LATE NINETEENTH CENTURY...
"THE DEADLY NIGHTSHADES ARE THE MODERN VERSION OF HER EMERALD COVEN."
BRRRRRRRRRRRRRRRING
HMMM...
If you want to head to the cafeteria for lunch, turn to the next page.
If you want to keep researching, go to page 106.

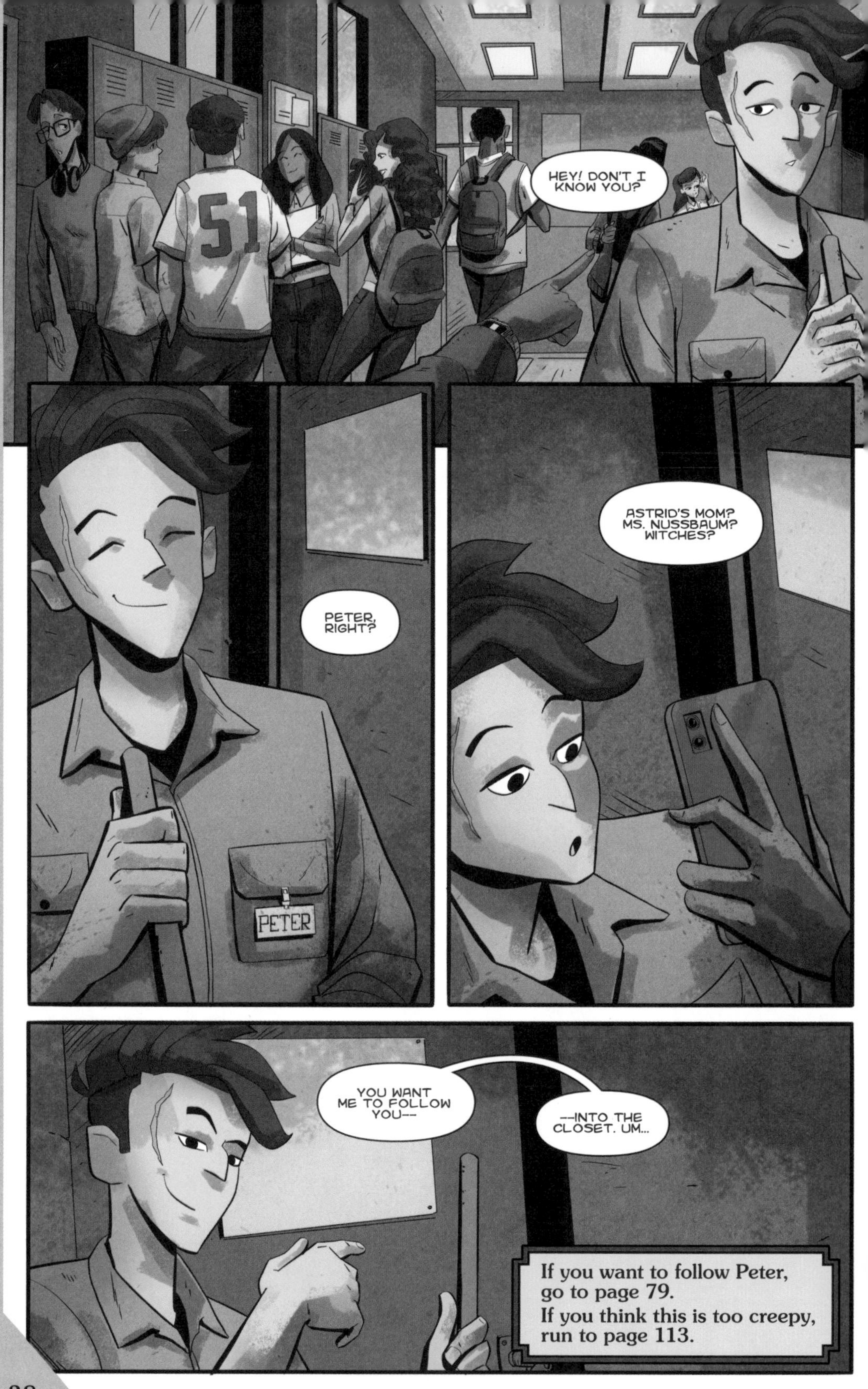
HEY! DON'T I KNOW YOU?
PETER, RIGHT?
PETER
ASTRID'S MOM? MS. NUSSBAUM? WITCHES?
YOU WANT ME TO FOLLOW YOU--
--INTO THE CLOSET. UM...

If you want to follow Peter, go to page 79.
If you think this is too creepy, run to page 113.

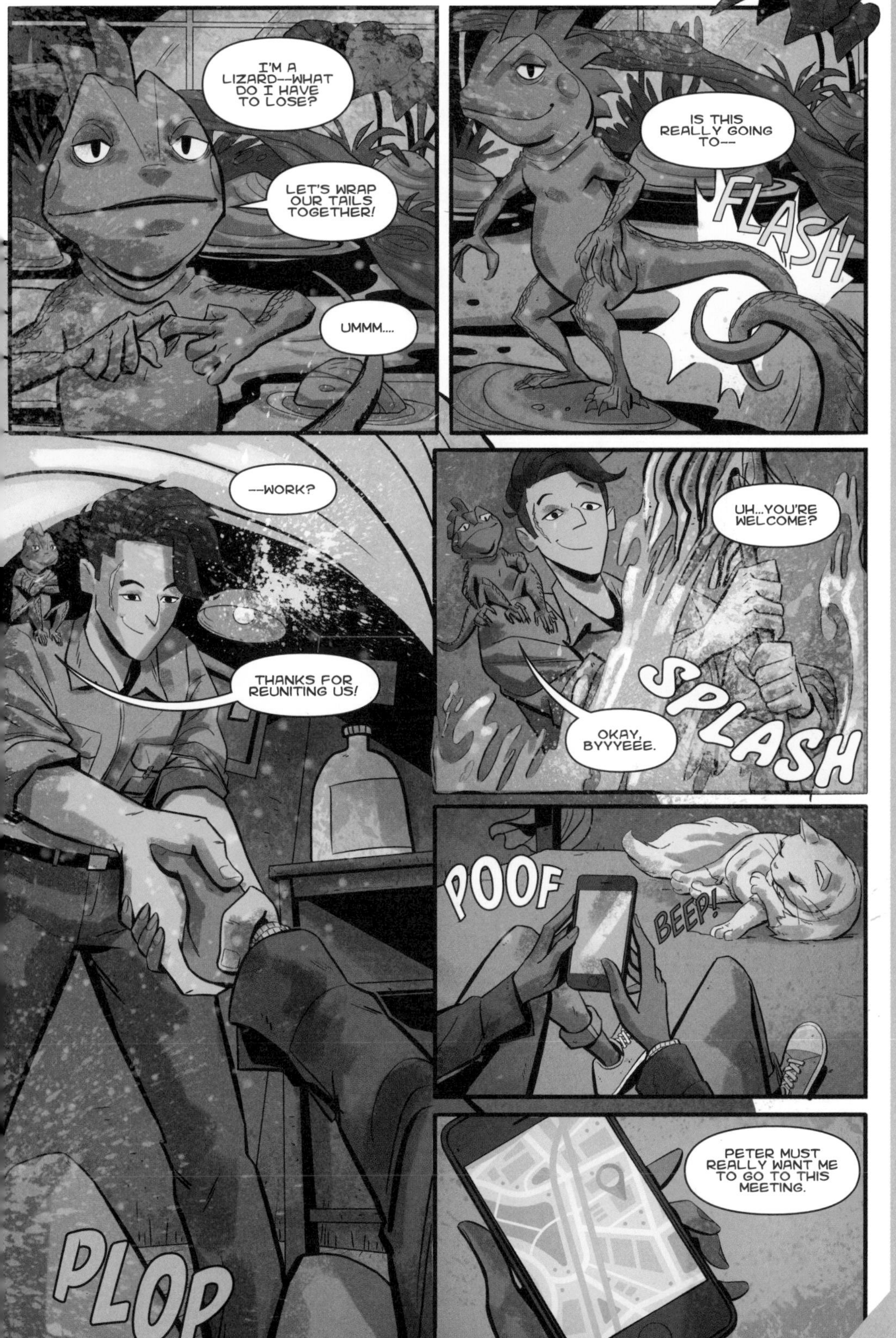
I'M A LIZARD--WHAT DO I HAVE TO LOSE?
LET'S WRAP OUR TAILS TOGETHER!
UMMM....
IS THIS REALLY GOING TO--
FLASH
--WORK?
THANKS FOR REUNITING US!
UH...YOU'RE WELCOME?
OKAY, BYYYEEE.
SPLASH
PLOP
POOF
BEEP!
PETER MUST REALLY WANT ME TO GO TO THIS MEETING.

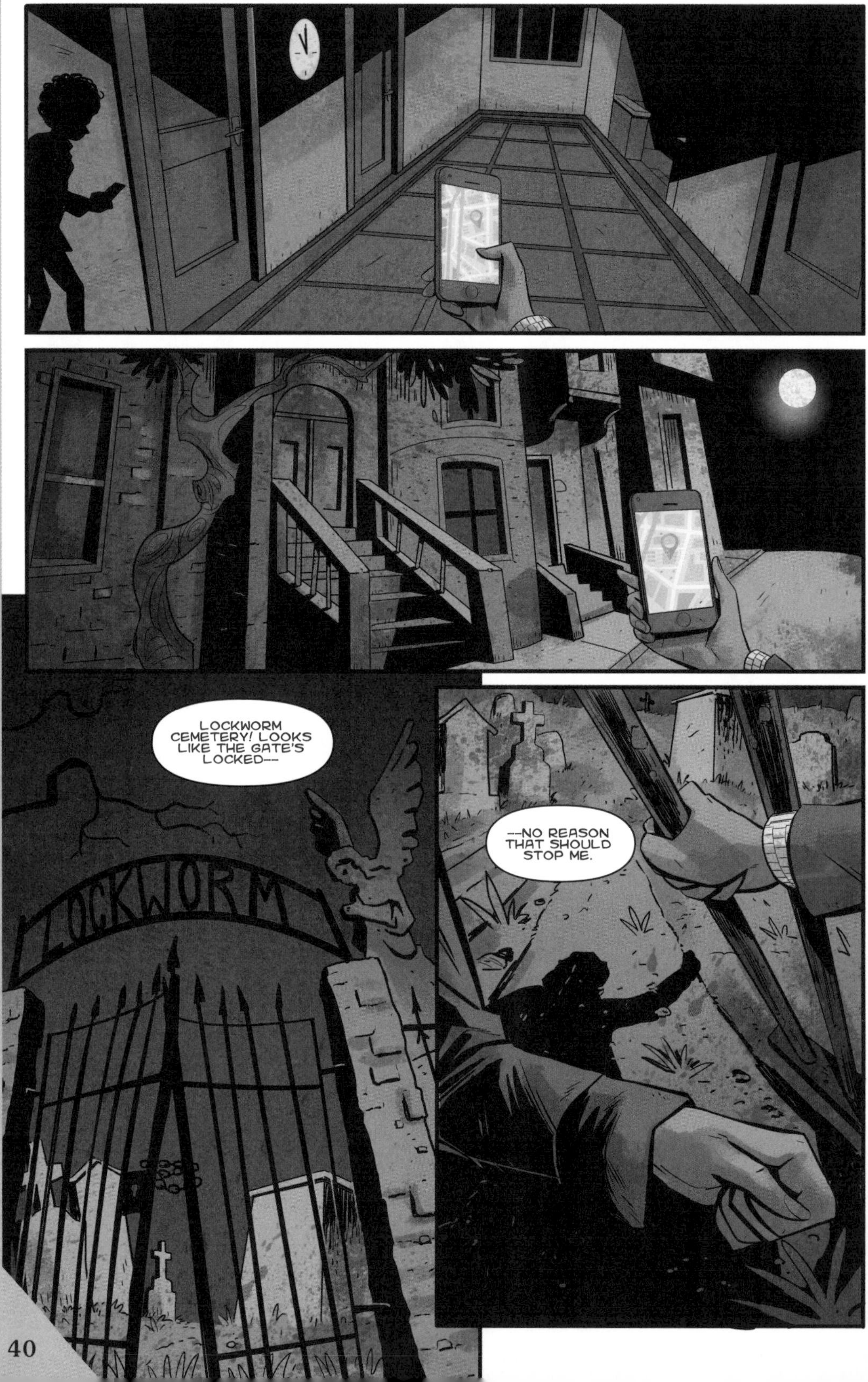
LOCKWORM CEMETERY! LOOKS LIKE THE GATE'S LOCKED--
LOCKWORM
--NO REASON THAT SHOULD STOP ME.

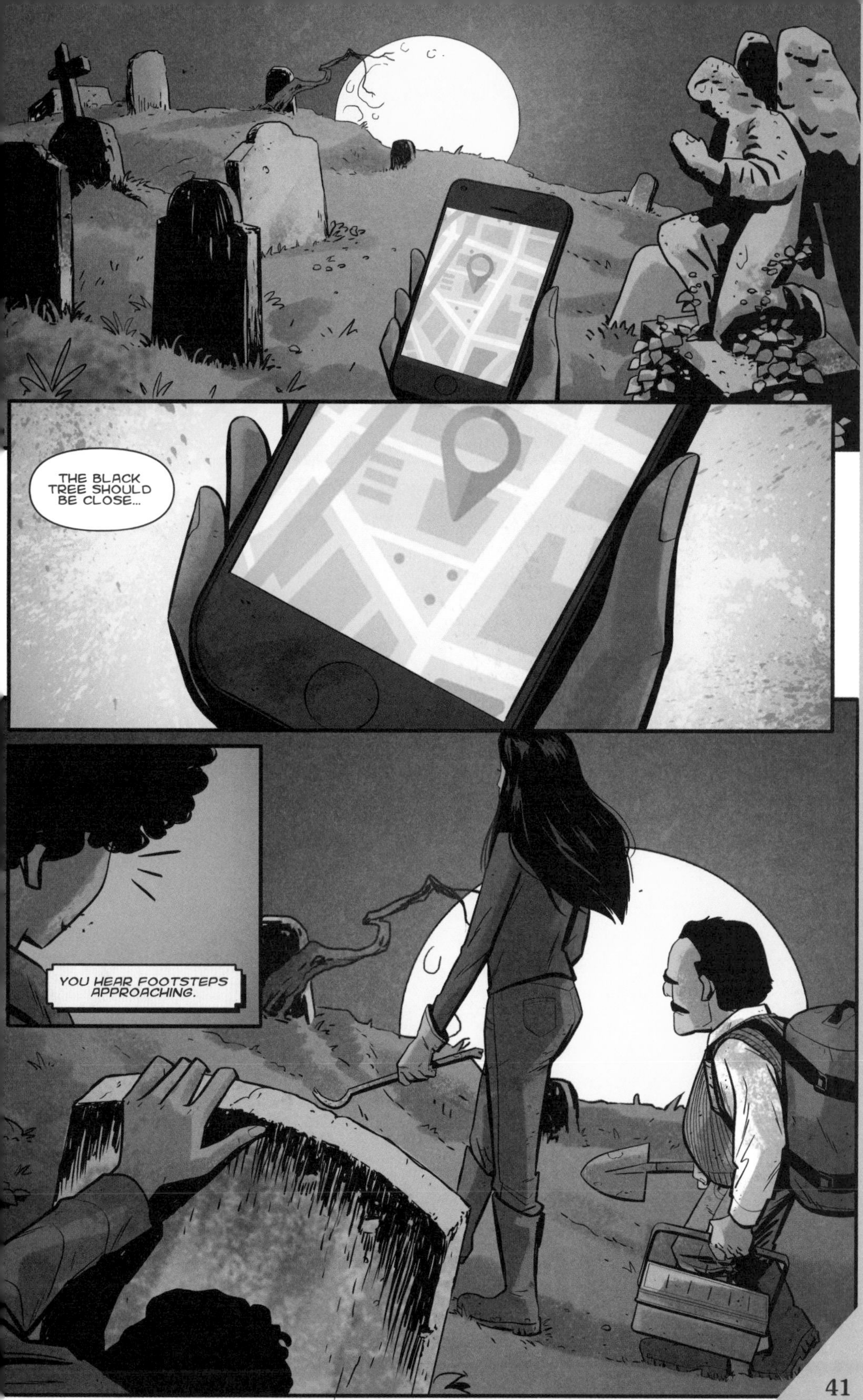
THE BLACK TREE SHOULD BE CLOSE...
YOU HEAR FOOTSTEPS APPROACHING.

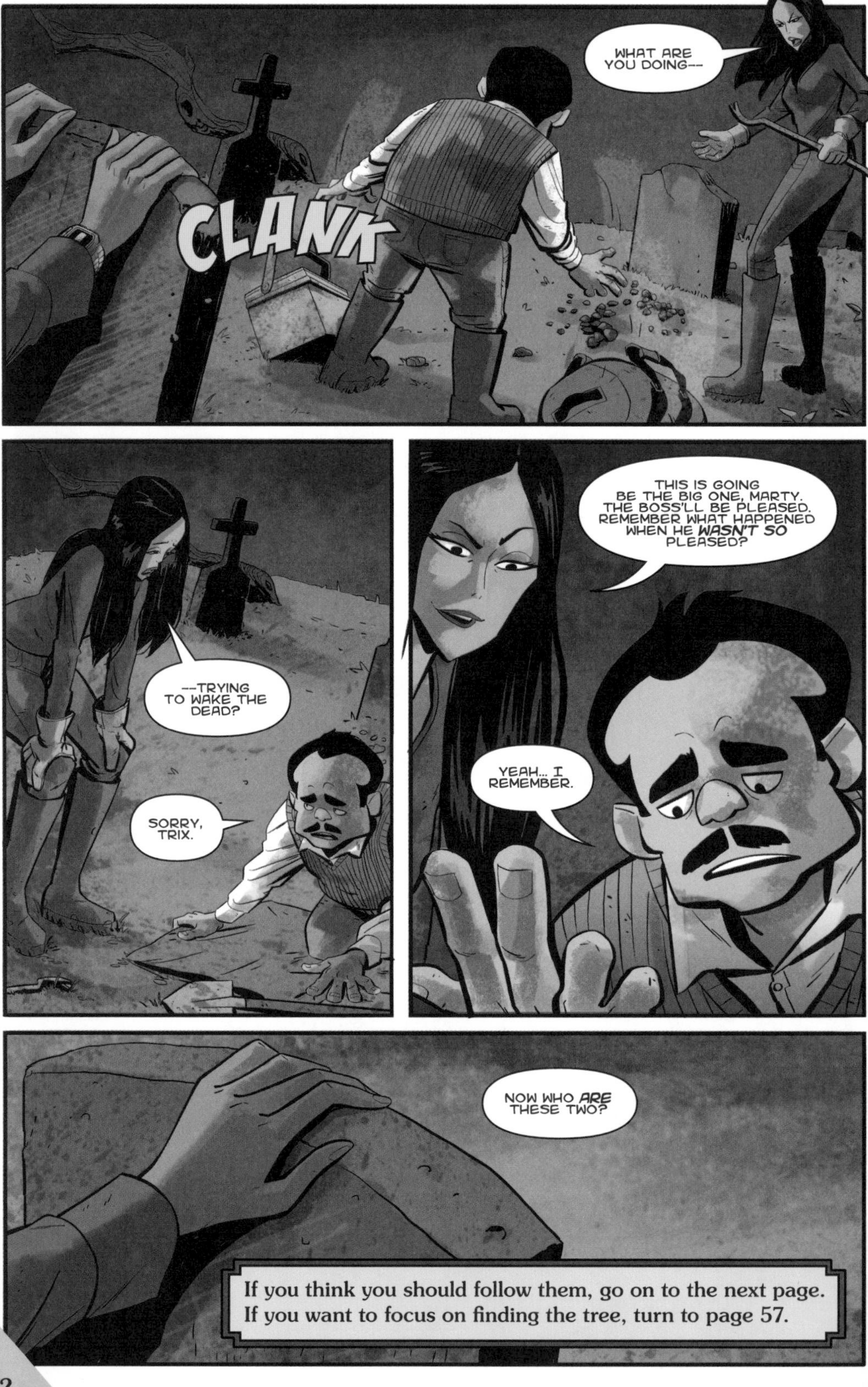
CLANK
WHAT ARE YOU DOING--
--TRYING TO WAKE THE DEAD?
SORRY, TRIX.
THIS IS GOING BE THE BIG ONE, MARTY. THE BOSS'LL BE PLEASED. REMEMBER WHAT HAPPENED WHEN HE WASN'T SO PLEASED?
YEAH... I REMEMBER.
NOW WHO ARE THESE TWO?

If you think you should follow them, go on to the next page.
If you want to focus on finding the tree, turn to page 57.

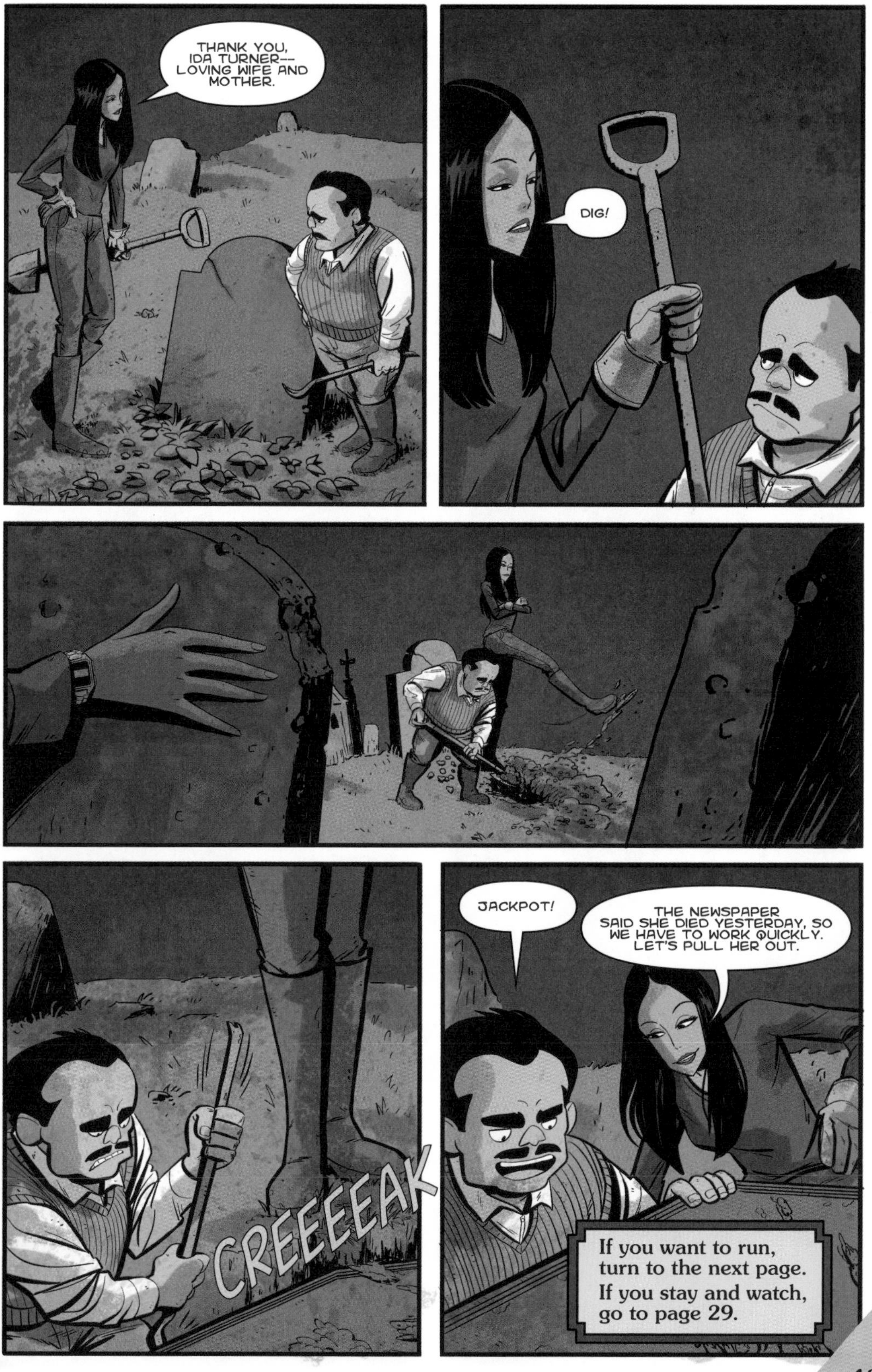

THANK YOU, IDA TURNER-- LOVING WIFE AND MOTHER.
DIG!
CREEEEEAK
JACKPOT!
THE NEWSPAPER SAID SHE DIED YESTERDAY, SO WE HAVE TO WORK QUICKLY. LET'S PULL HER OUT.

If you want to run, turn to the next page.
If you stay and watch, go to page 29.

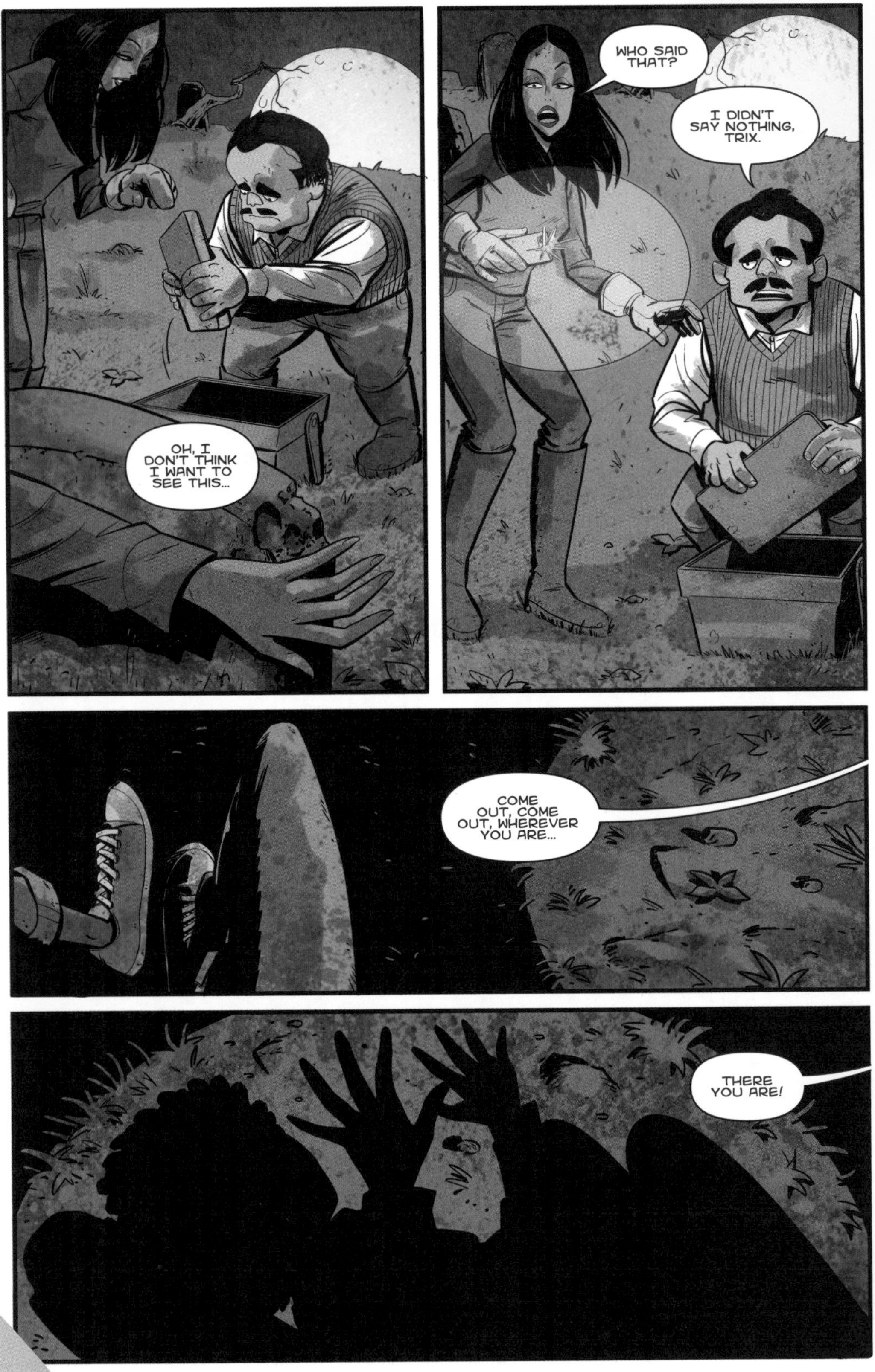
OH, I DON'T THINK I WANT TO SEE THIS...
WHO SAID THAT?
I DIDN'T SAY NOTHING, TRIX.
COME OUT, COME OUT, WHEREVER YOU ARE...
THERE YOU ARE!

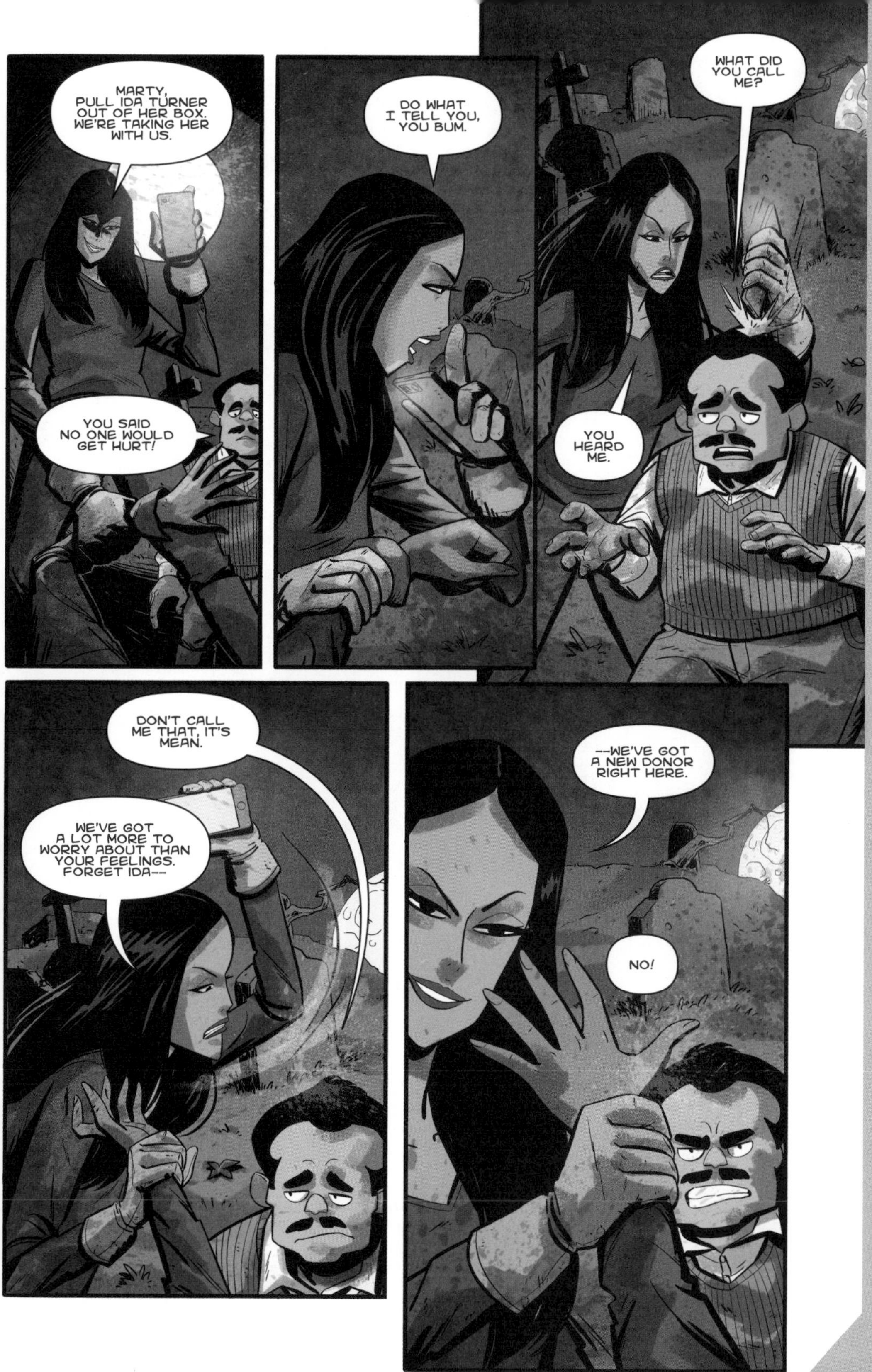
MARTY, PULL IDA TURNER OUT OF HER BOX. WE'RE TAKING HER WITH US.
YOU SAID NO ONE WOULD GET HURT!
DO WHAT I TELL YOU, YOU BUM.
WHAT DID YOU CALL ME?
YOU HEARD ME.
DON'T CALL ME THAT, IT'S MEAN.
WE'VE GOT A LOT MORE TO WORRY ABOUT THAN YOUR FEELINGS. FORGET IDA--
--WE'VE GOT A NEW DONOR RIGHT HERE.
NO!

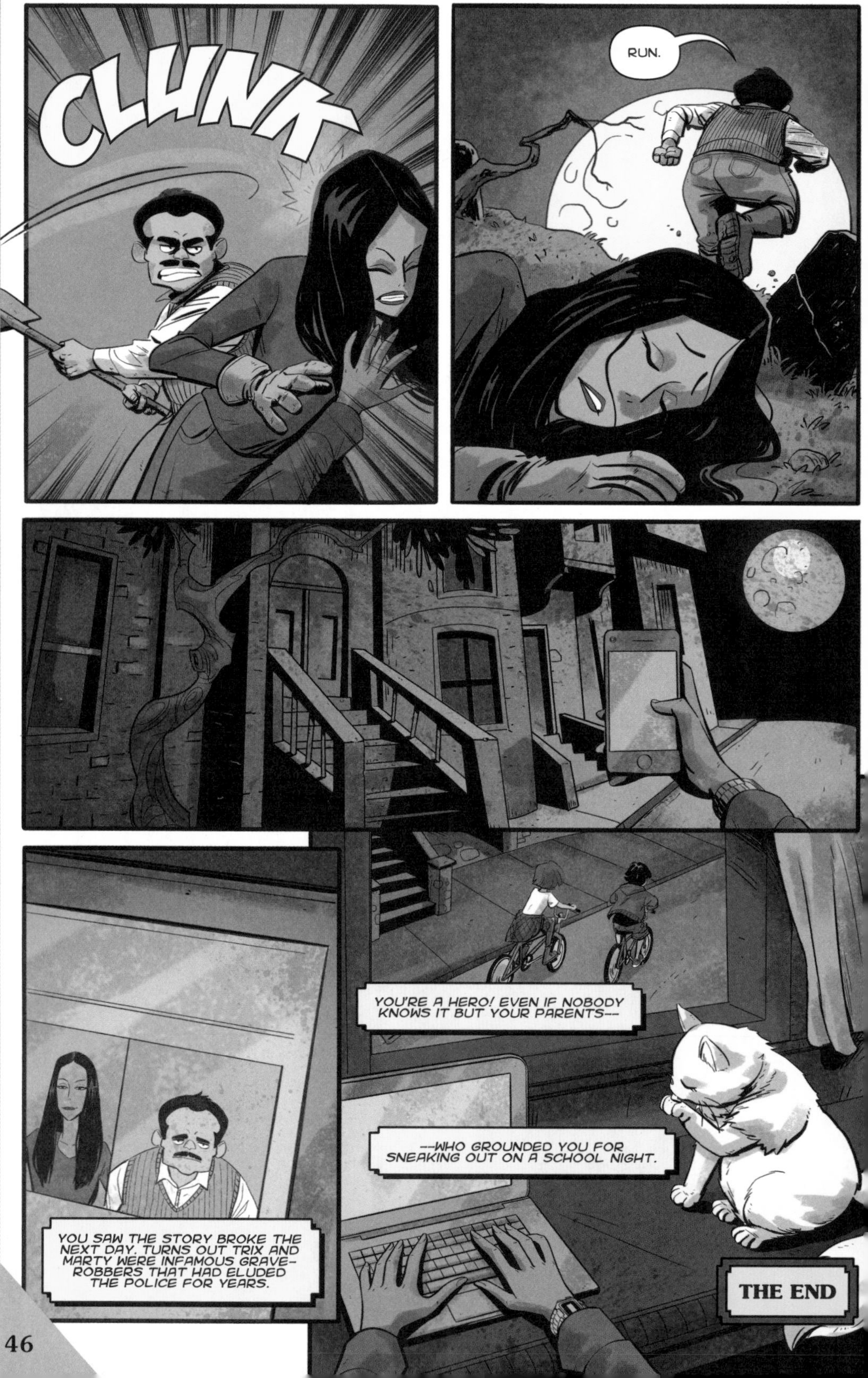
CLUNK
RUN.
YOU'RE A HERO! EVEN IF NOBODY KNOWS IT BUT YOUR PARENTS---
--WHO GROUNDED YOU FOR SNEAKING OUT ON A SCHOOL NIGHT.
YOU SAW THE STORY BROKE THE NEXT DAY. TURNS OUT TRIX AND MARTY WERE INFAMOUS GRAVE-ROBBERS THAT HAD ELUDED THE POLICE FOR YEARS.
THE END

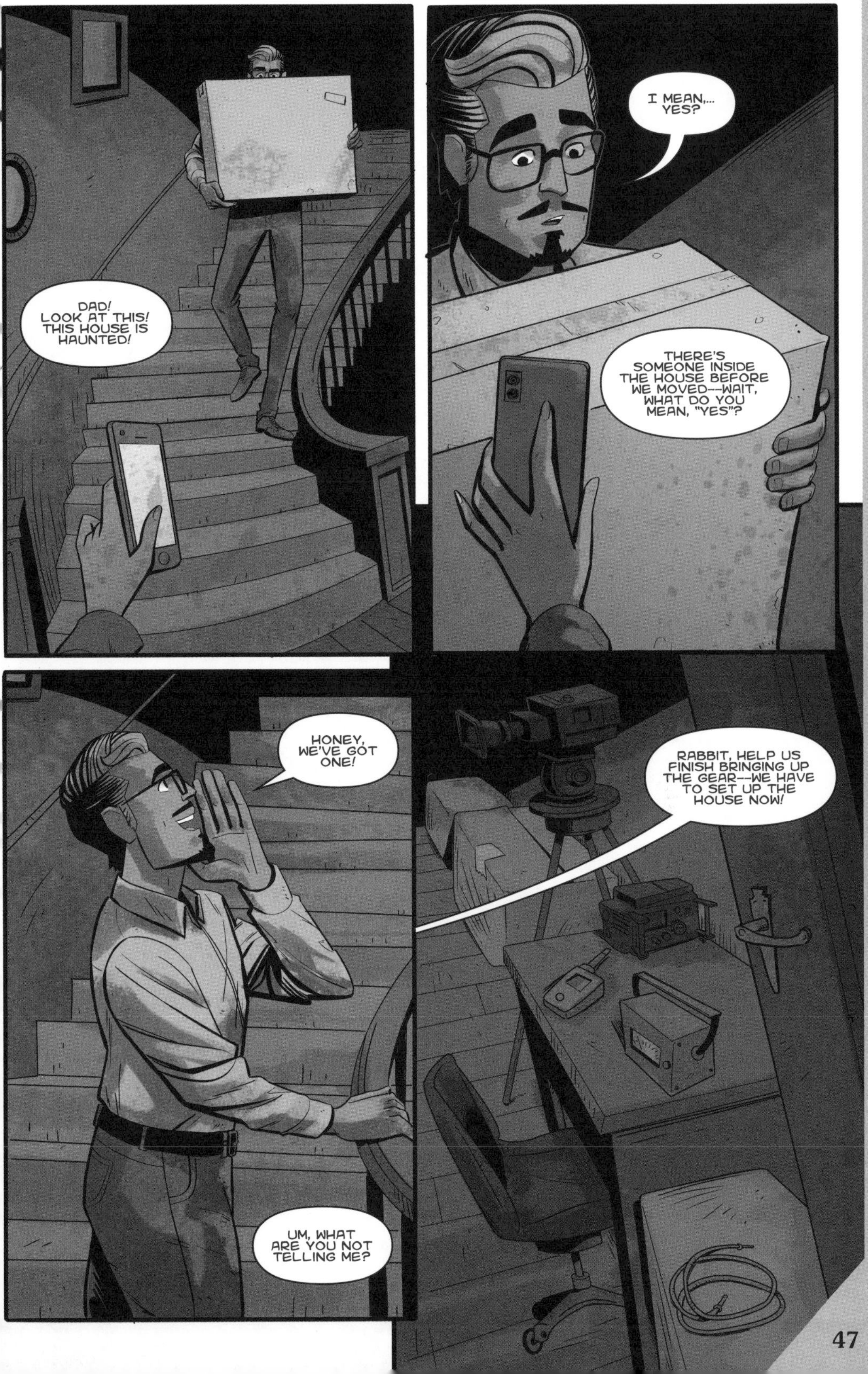
DAD! LOOK AT THIS! THIS HOUSE IS HAUNTED!
I MEAN,... YES?
THERE'S SOMEONE INSIDE THE HOUSE BEFORE WE MOVED--WAIT, WHAT DO YOU MEAN, "YES"?
HONEY, WE'VE GOT ONE!
UM, WHAT ARE YOU NOT TELLING ME?
RABBIT, HELP US FINISH BRINGING UP THE GEAR--WE HAVE TO SET UP THE HOUSE NOW!

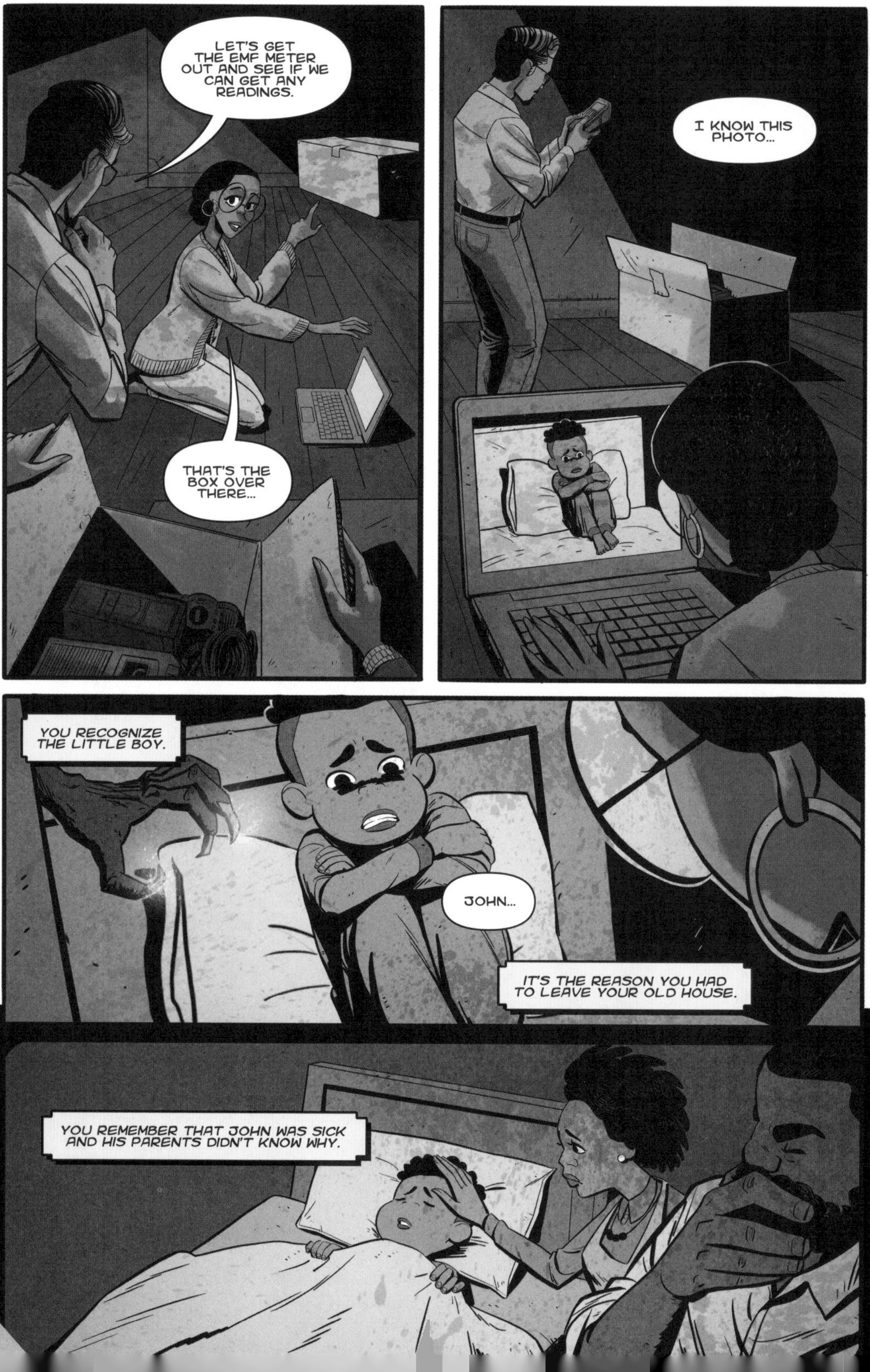
LET'S GET THE EMF METER OUT AND SEE IF WE CAN GET ANY READINGS.
THAT'S THE BOX OVER THERE...
I KNOW THIS PHOTO...
YOU RECOGNIZE THE LITTLE BOY.
JOHN...
IT'S THE REASON YOU HAD TO LEAVE YOUR OLD HOUSE.
YOU REMEMBER THAT JOHN WAS SICK AND HIS PARENTS DIDN'T KNOW WHY.

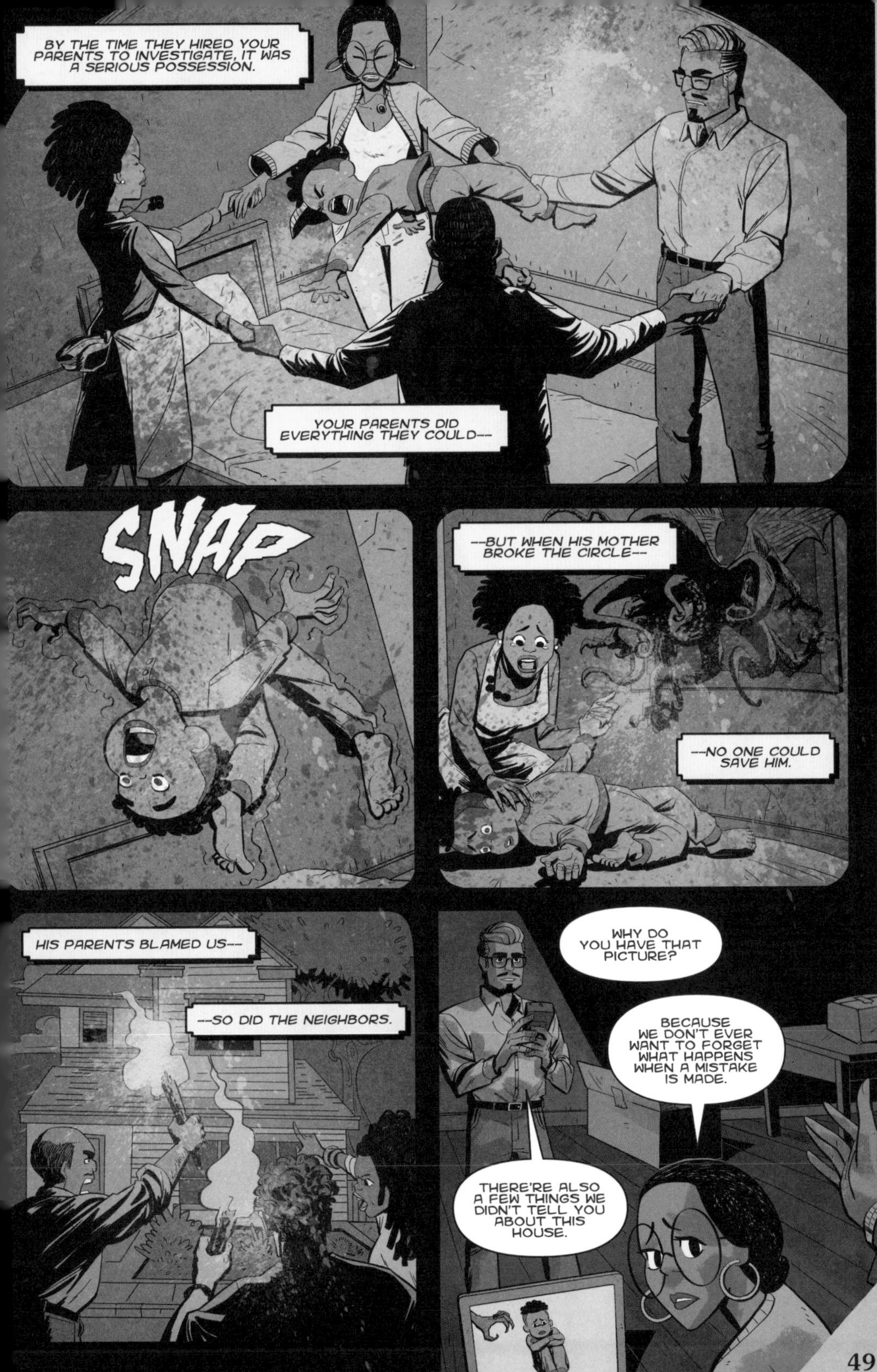
BY THE TIME THEY HIRED YOUR PARENTS TO INVESTIGATE, IT WAS A SERIOUS POSSESSION.
YOUR PARENTS DID EVERYTHING THEY COULD--
SNAP
--BUT WHEN HIS MOTHER BROKE THE CIRCLE--
--NO ONE COULD SAVE HIM.
HIS PARENTS BLAMED US--
--SO DID THE NEIGHBORS.
WHY DO YOU HAVE THAT PICTURE?
BECAUSE WE DON'T EVER WANT TO FORGET WHAT HAPPENS WHEN A MISTAKE IS MADE.
THERE'RE ALSO A FEW THINGS WE DIDN'T TELL YOU ABOUT THIS HOUSE.

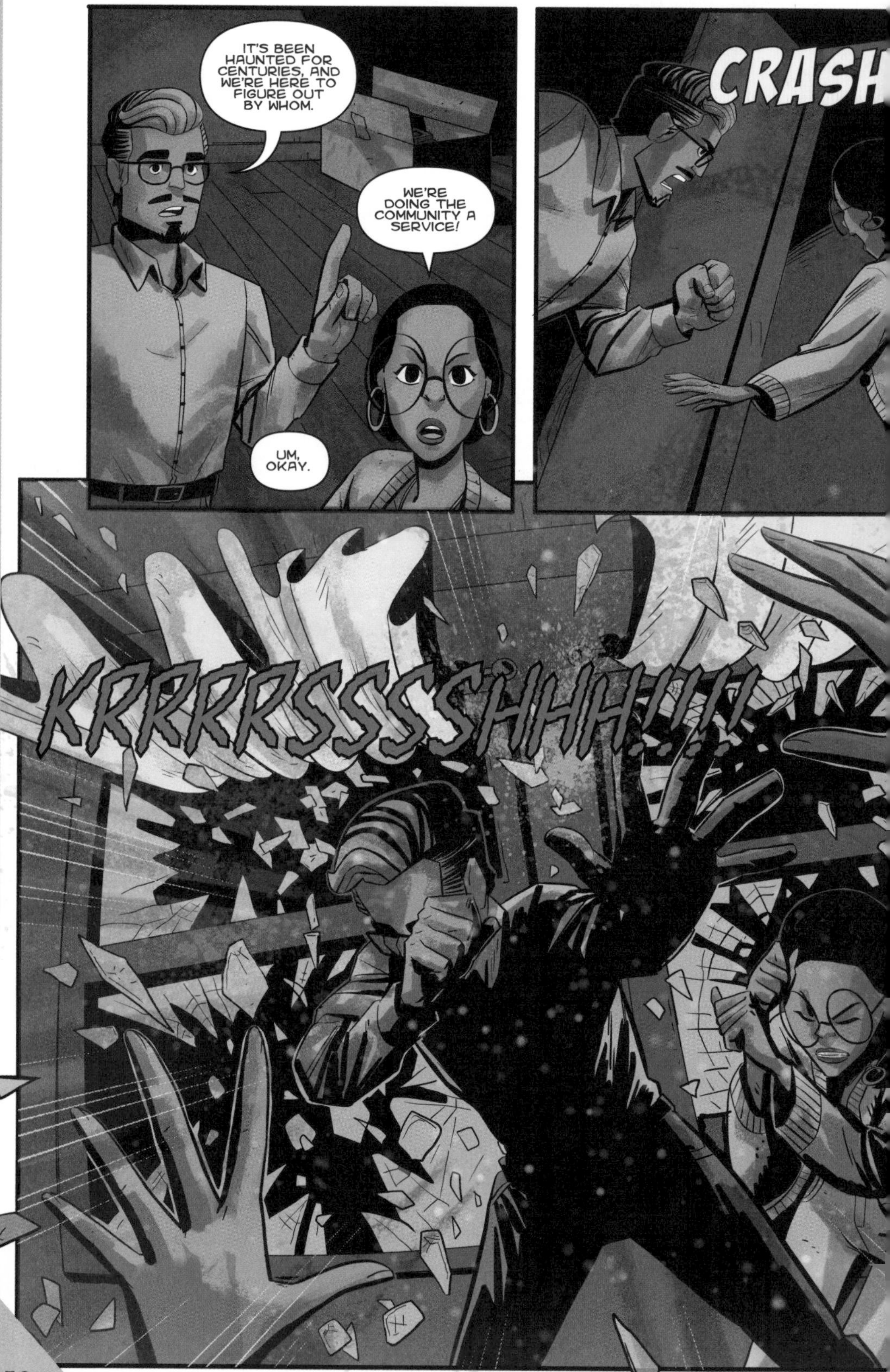
IT'S BEEN HAUNTED FOR CENTURIES, AND WE'RE HERE TO FIGURE OUT BY WHOM.
WE'RE DOING THE COMMUNITY A SERVICE!
UM, OKAY.
CRASH
KRRRRSSSSHHH!!!!!

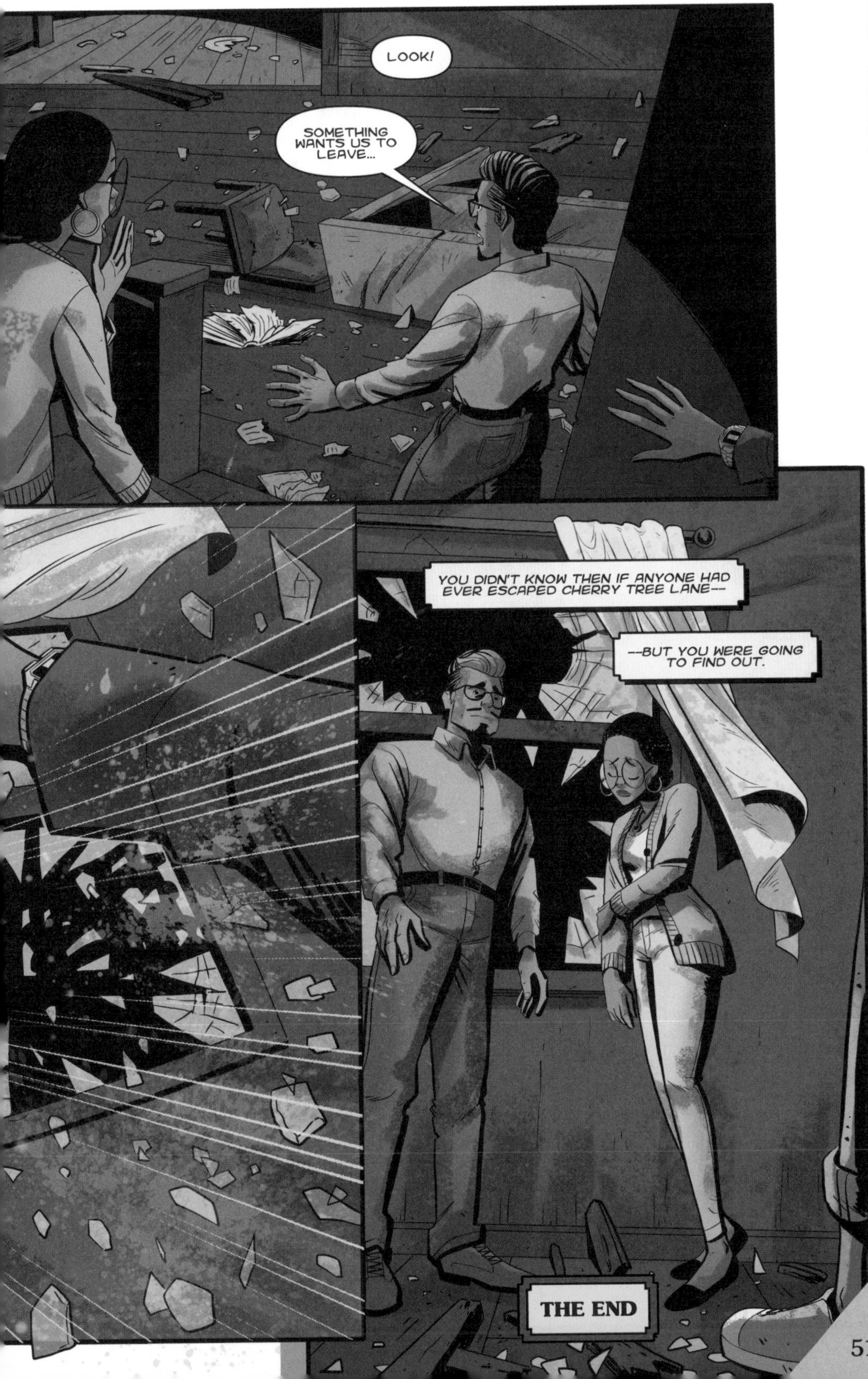
LOOK!
SOMETHING WANTS US TO LEAVE...
YOU DIDN'T KNOW THEN IF ANYONE HAD EVER ESCAPED CHERRY TREE LANE--
--BUT YOU WERE GOING TO FIND OUT.
THE END

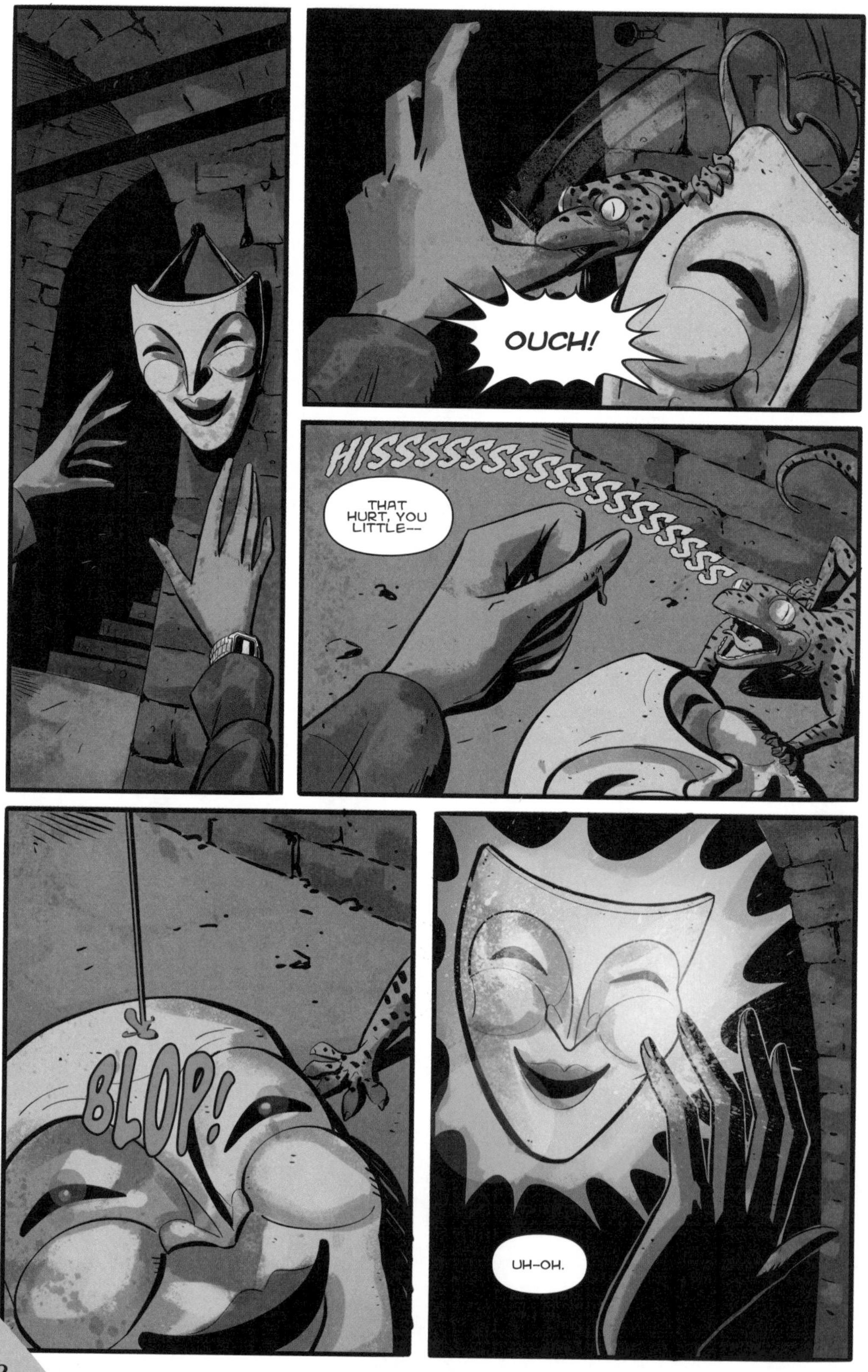
OUCH!
HISSSSSSSSSSSSSSSSSSS
THAT HURT, YOU LITTLE--
BLOP!
UH-OH.

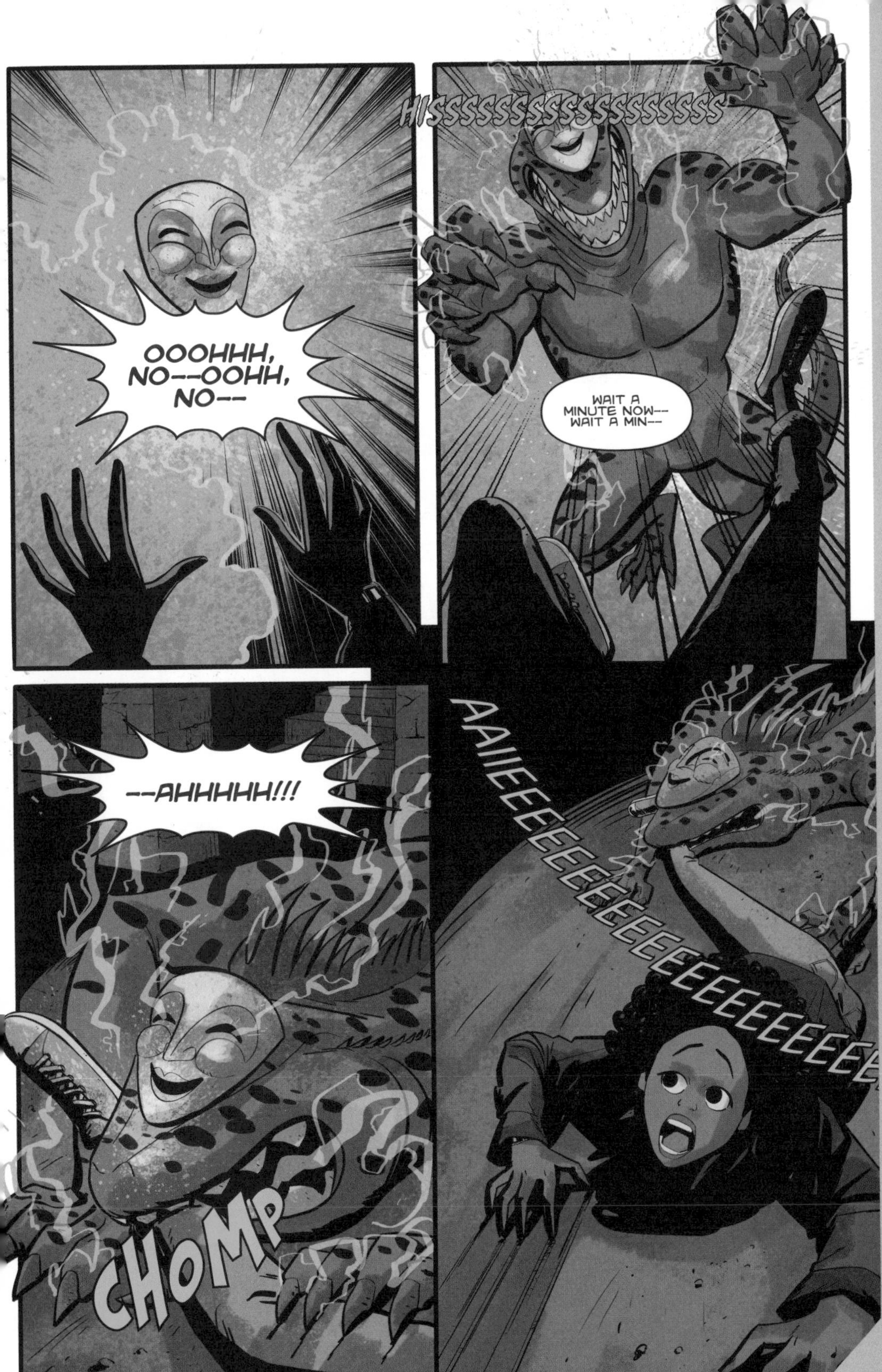
OOOHHH, NO--OOHH, NO--
HISSSSSSSSSSSSSSSSSSS
WAIT A MINUTE NOW-- WAIT A MIN--
--AHHHHH!!!
CHOMP
AAIIEEEEEEEEEEEEEEEEEEEEEEEEEEE

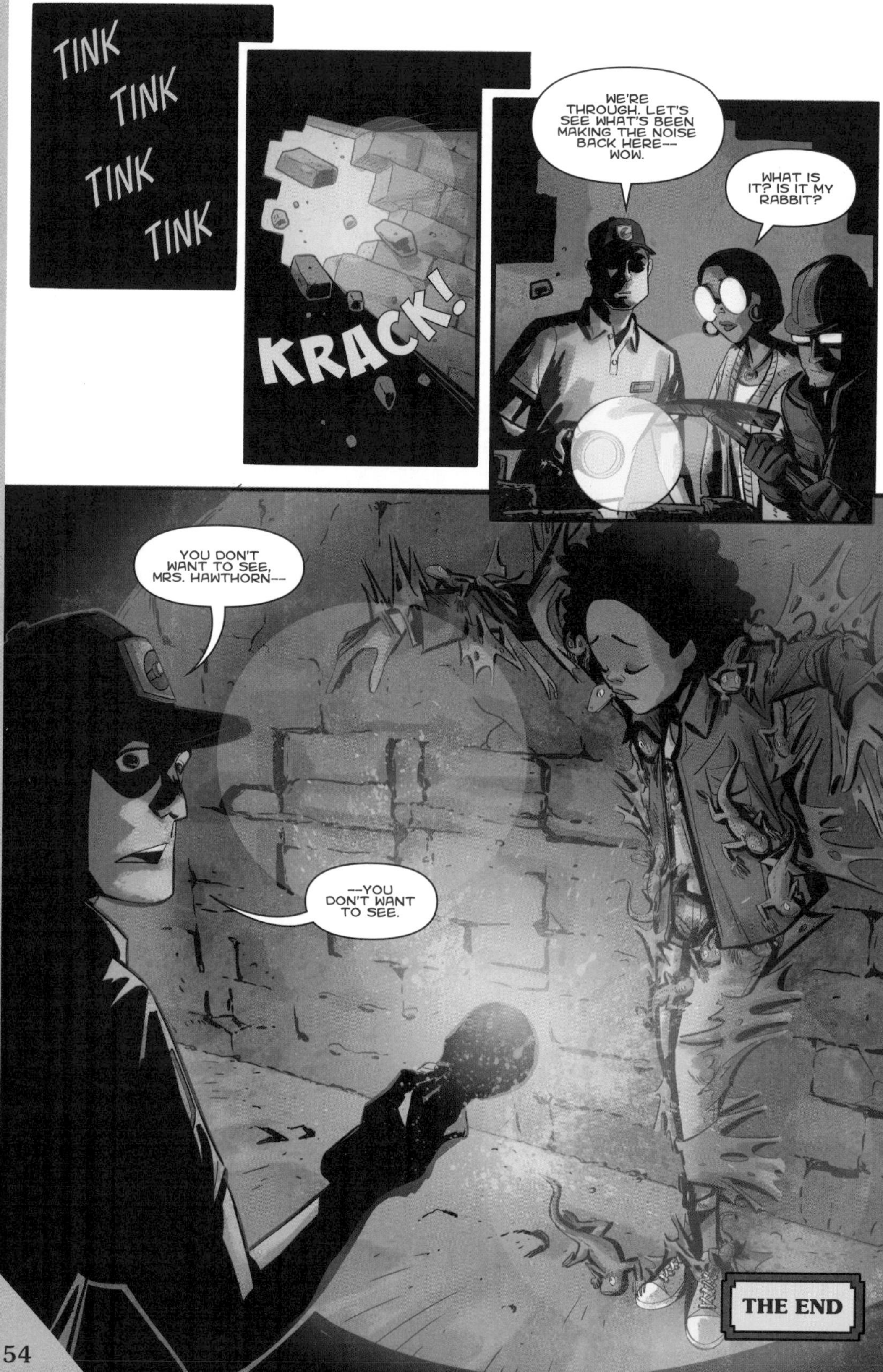
TINK
TINK
TINK
TINK
KRACK!
WE'RE THROUGH. LET'S SEE WHAT'S BEEN MAKING THE NOISE BACK HERE-- WOW.
WHAT IS IT? IS IT MY RABBIT?
YOU DON'T WANT TO SEE, MRS. HAWTHORN--
--YOU DON'T WANT TO SEE.
THE END

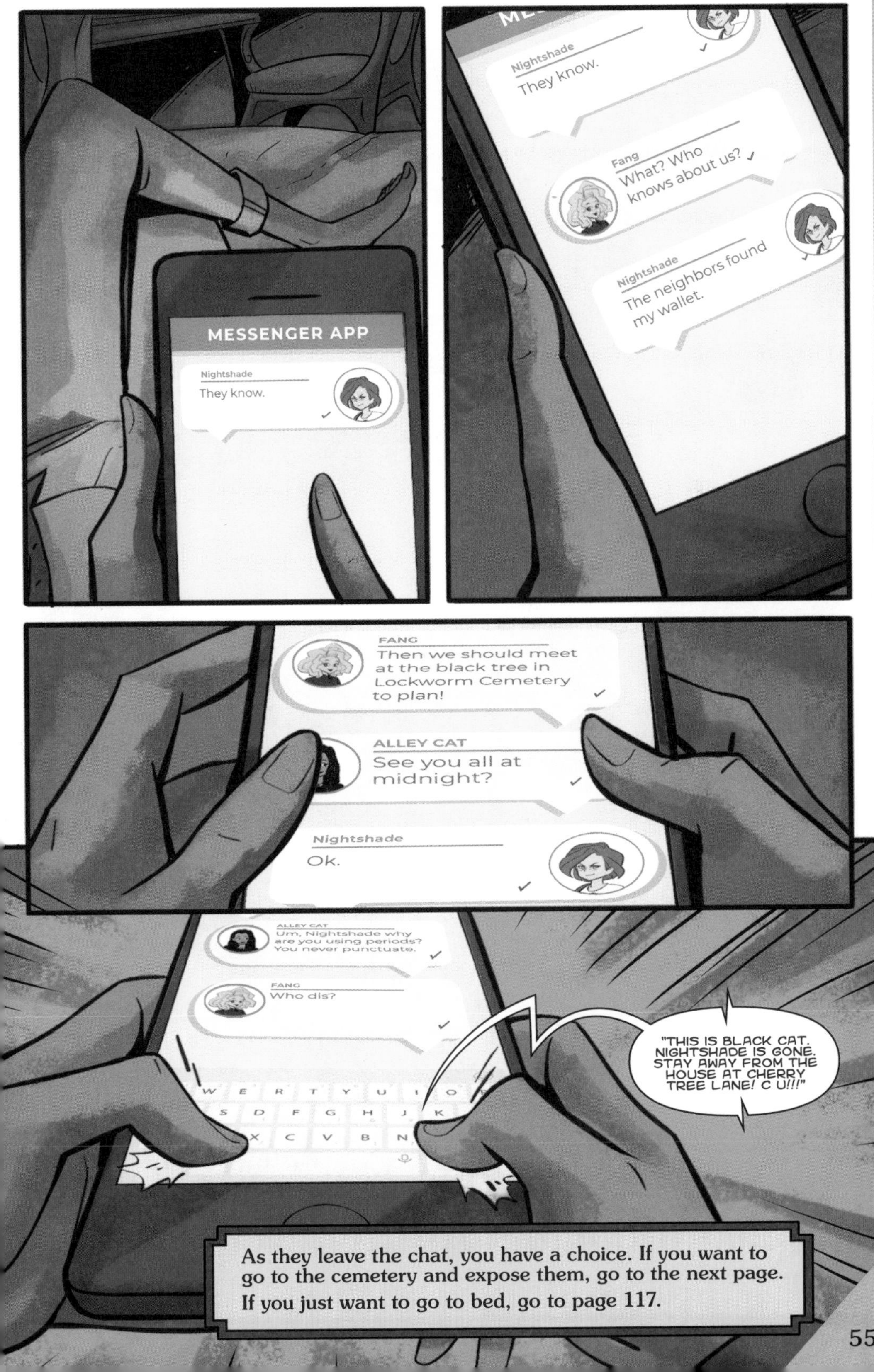
MESSENGER APP
Nightshade
They know.
Nightshade
They know.
Fang
What? Who knows about us?
Nightshade
The neighbors found my wallet.
FANG
Then we should meet at the black tree in Lockworm Cemetery to plan!
ALLEY CAT
See you all at midnight?
Nightshade
Ok.
ALLEY CAT
Um, Nightshade why are you using periods? You never punctuate.
FANG
Who dis?
"THIS IS BLACK CAT. NIGHTSHADE IS GONE. STAY AWAY FROM THE HOUSE AT CHERRY TREE LANE! C U!!!"
As they leave the chat, you have a choice. If you want to go to the cemetery and expose them, go to the next page. If you just want to go to bed, go to page 117.

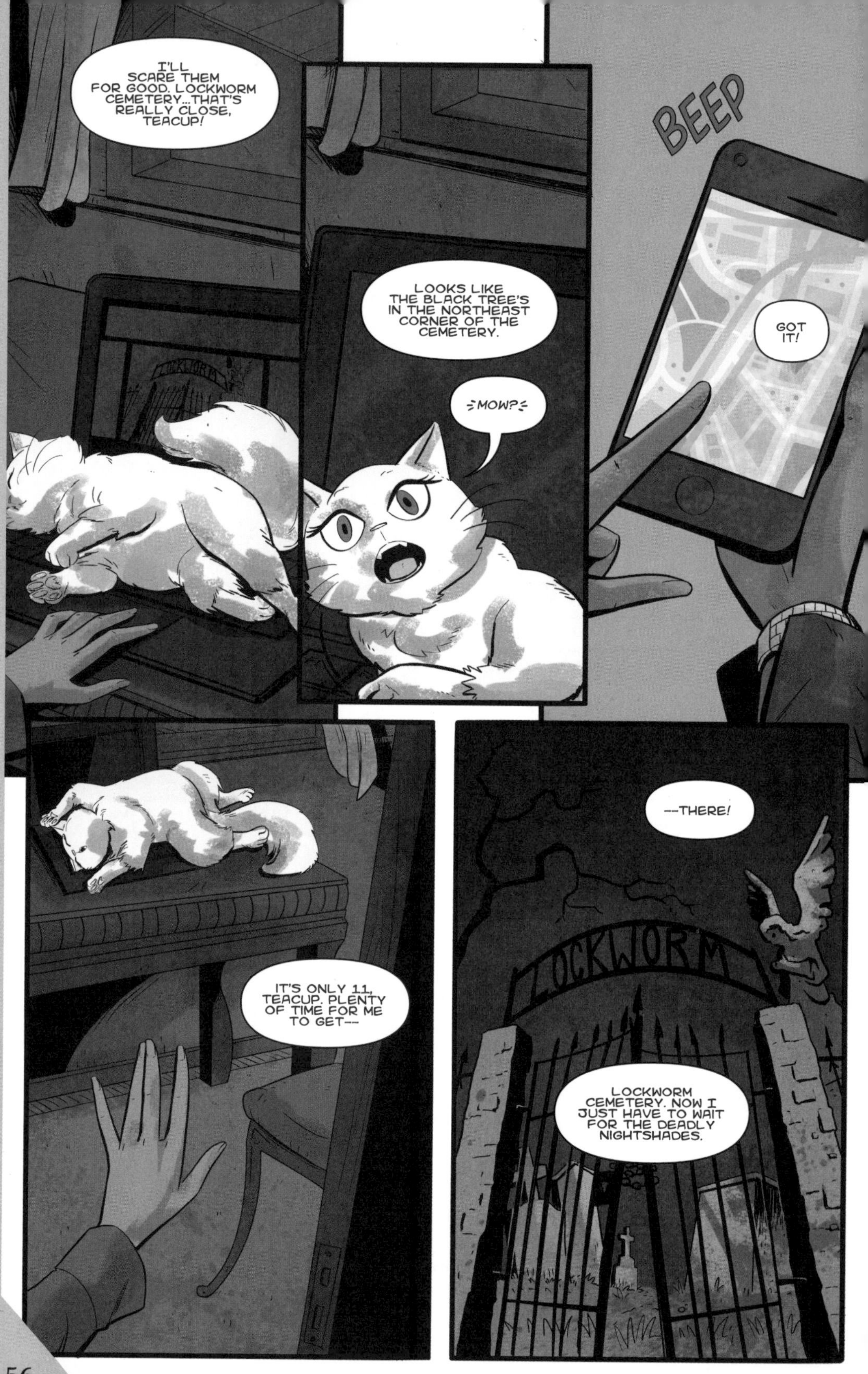
I'LL SCARE THEM FOR GOOD. LOCKWORM CEMETERY...THAT'S REALLY CLOSE, TEACUP!
LOOKS LIKE THE BLACK TREE'S IN THE NORTHEAST CORNER OF THE CEMETERY.
MOW?
BEEP
GOT IT!
IT'S ONLY 11, TEACUP. PLENTY OF TIME FOR ME TO GET--
--THERE!
LOCKWORM
LOCKWORM CEMETERY. NOW I JUST HAVE TO WAIT FOR THE DEADLY NIGHTSHADES.

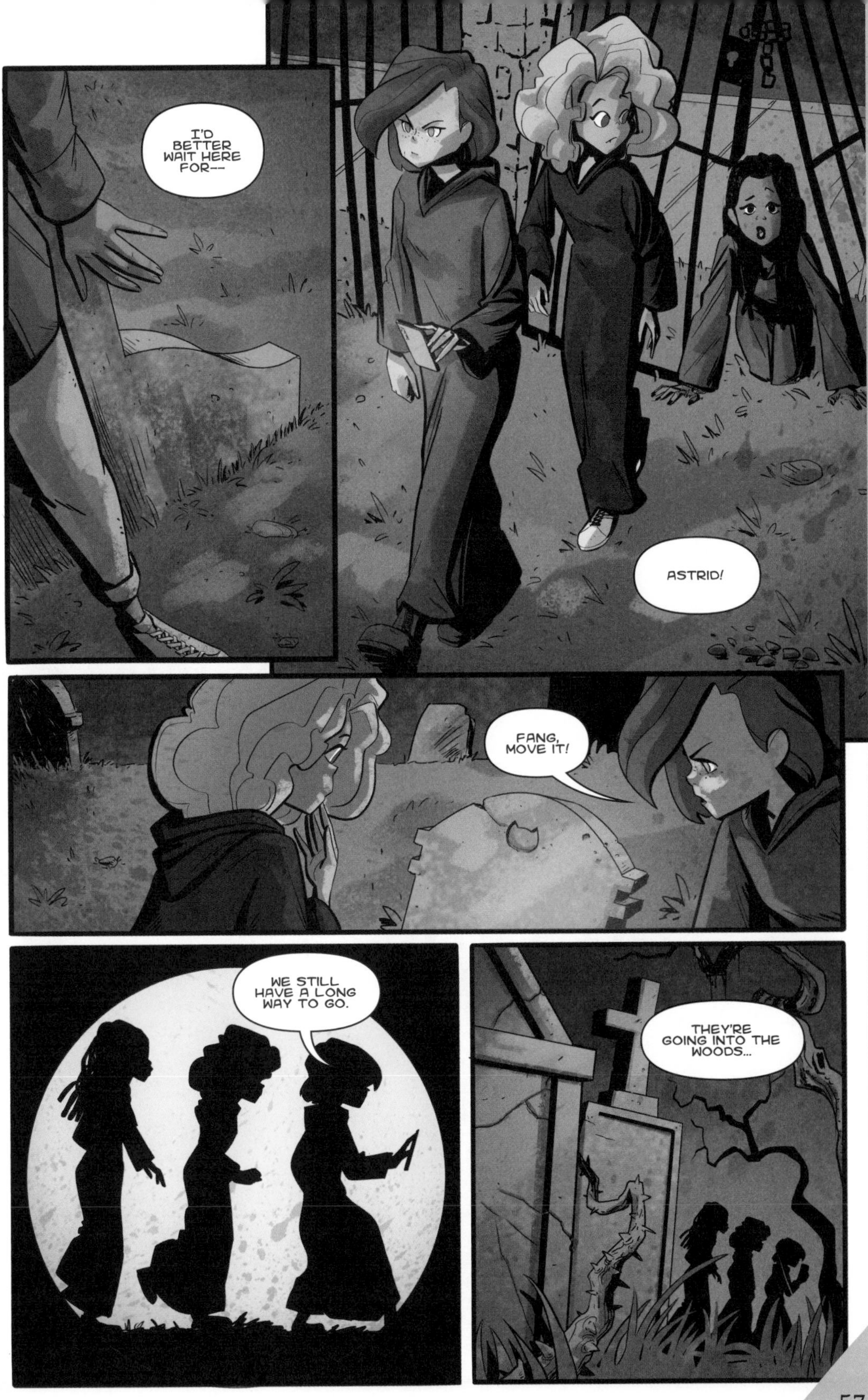
I'D BETTER WAIT HERE FOR--
ASTRID!
FANG, MOVE IT!
WE STILL HAVE A LONG WAY TO GO.
THEY'RE GOING INTO THE WOODS...

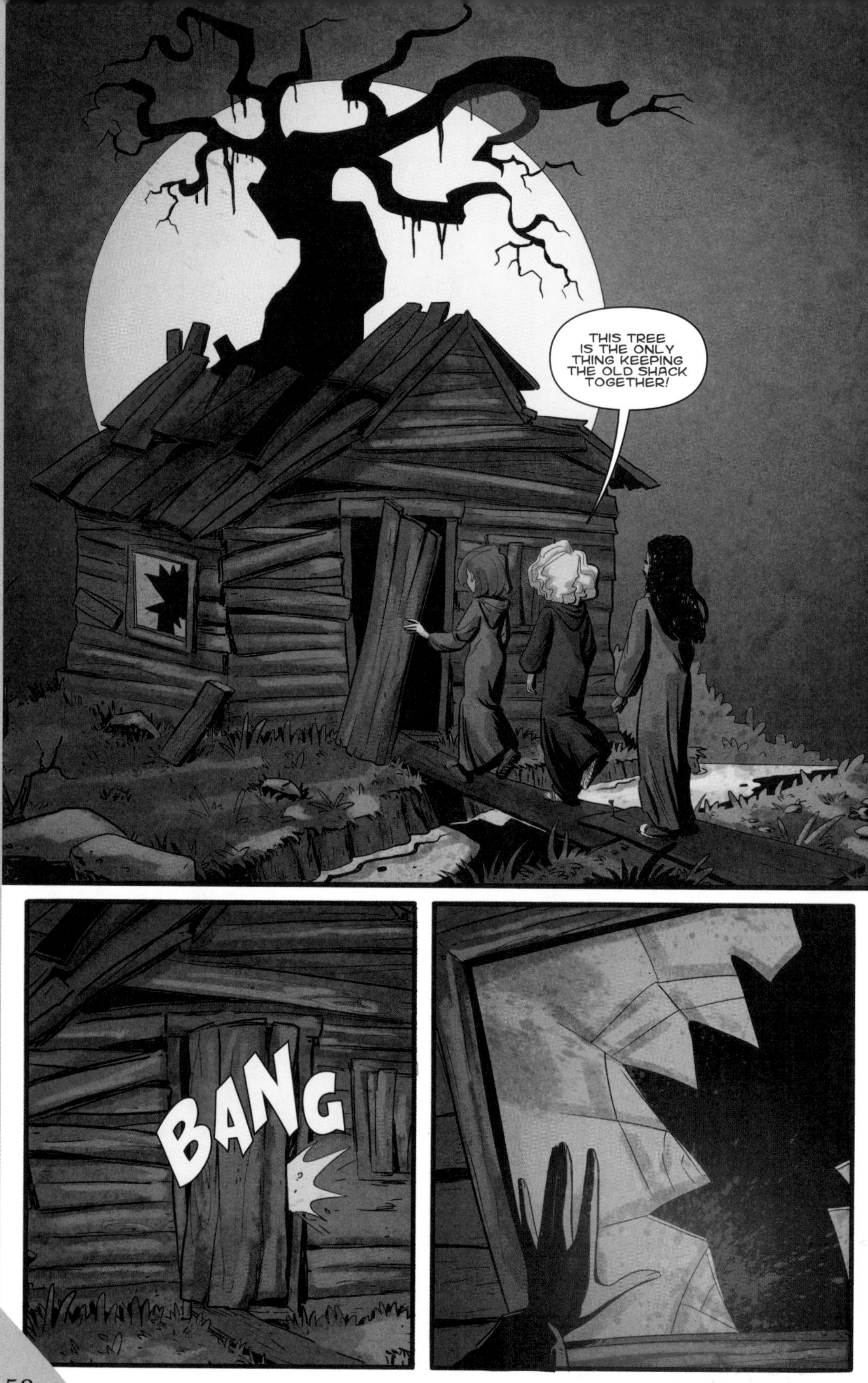
THIS TREE IS THE ONLY THING KEEPING THE OLD SHACK TOGETHER!
BANG

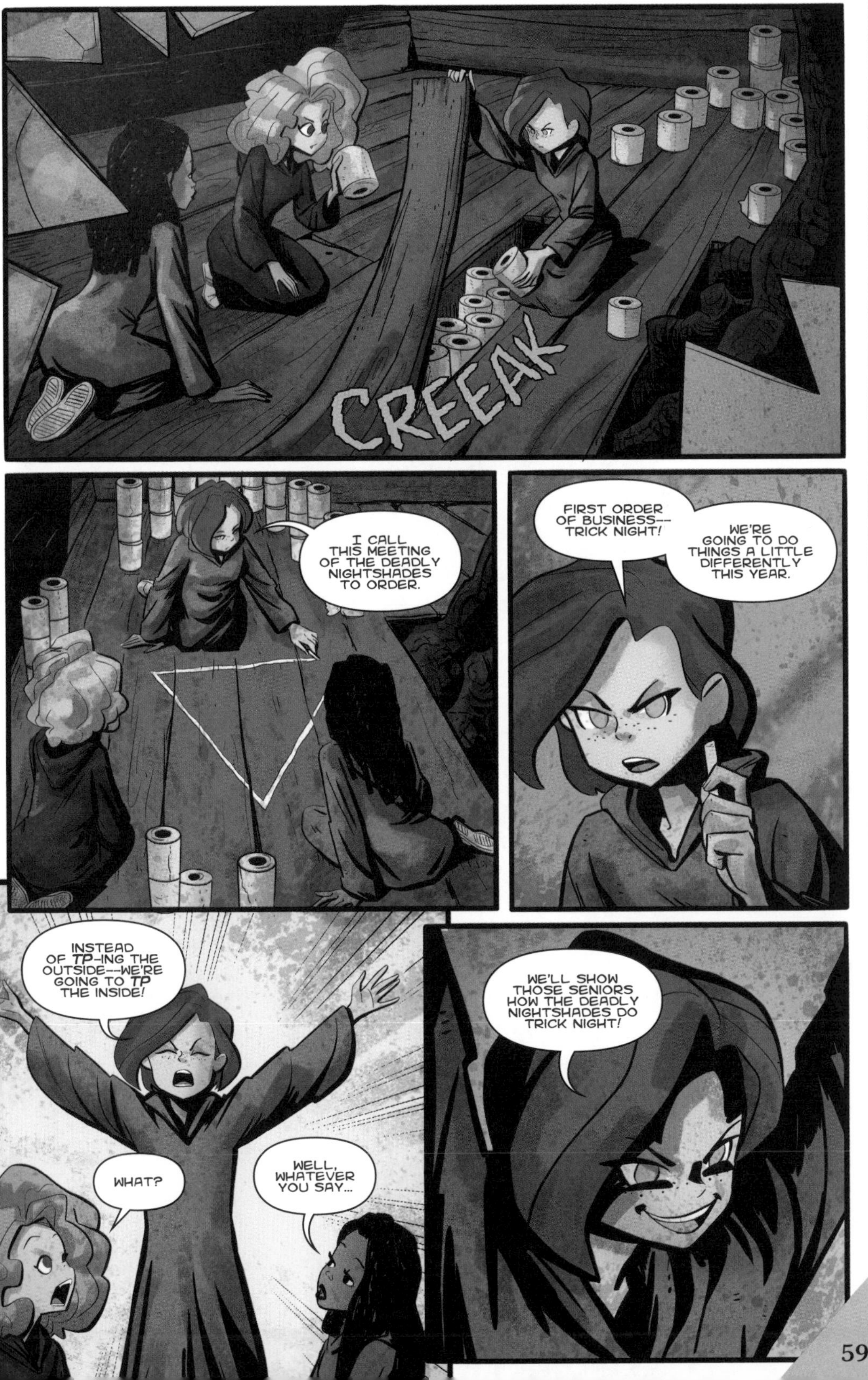

CREEAK
I CALL THIS MEETING OF THE DEADLY NIGHTSHADES TO ORDER.
FIRST ORDER OF BUSINESS-- TRICK NIGHT!
WE'RE GOING TO DO THINGS A LITTLE DIFFERENTLY THIS YEAR.
INSTEAD OF TP-ING THE OUTSIDE--WE'RE GOING TO TP THE INSIDE!
WHAT?
WELL, WHATEVER YOU SAY...
WE'LL SHOW THOSE SENIORS HOW THE DEADLY NIGHTSHADES DO TRICK NIGHT!

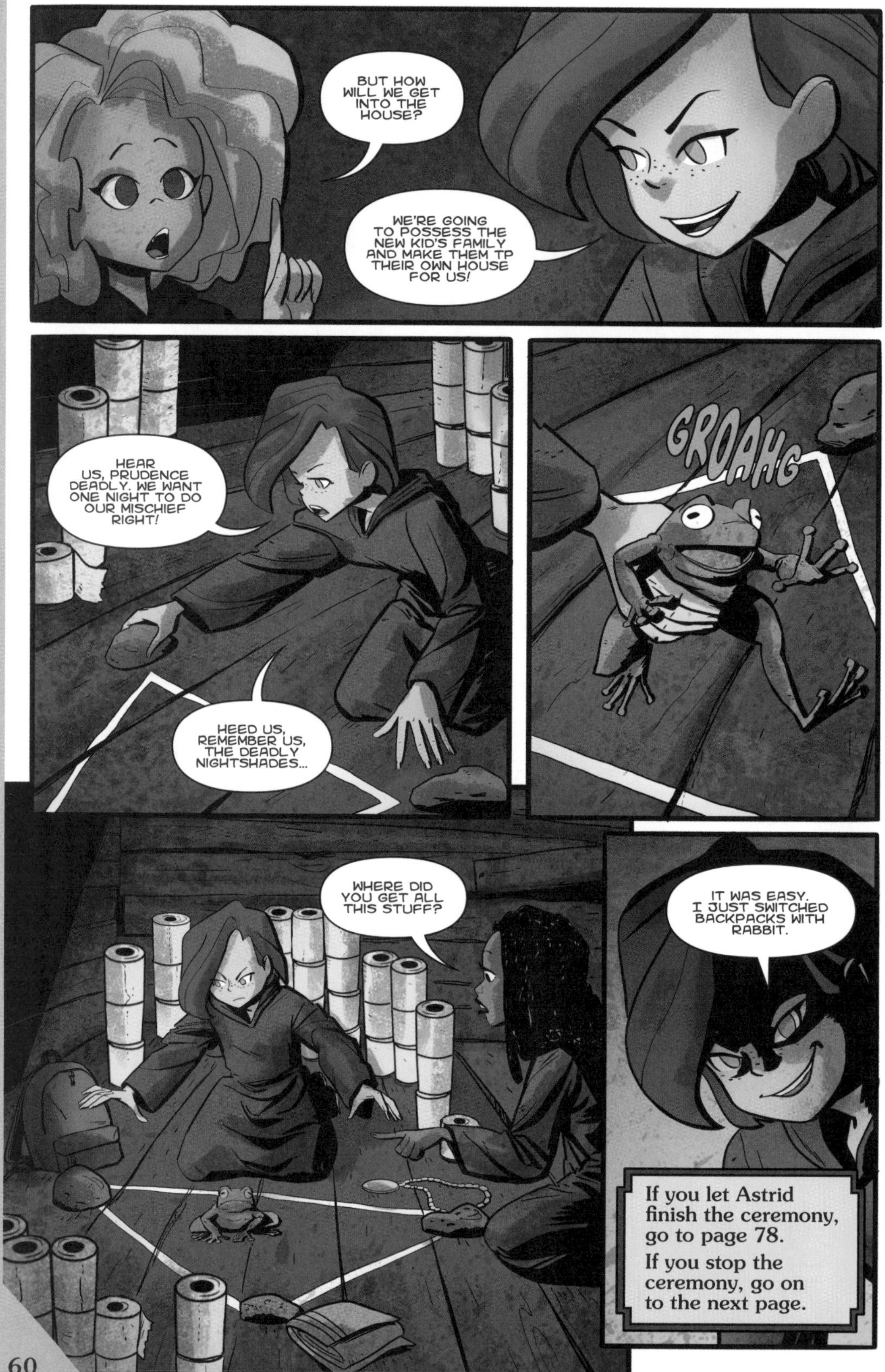
BUT HOW WILL WE GET INTO THE HOUSE?
WE'RE GOING TO POSSESS THE NEW KID'S FAMILY AND MAKE THEM TP THEIR OWN HOUSE FOR US!
HEAR US, PRUDENCE DEADLY. WE WANT ONE NIGHT TO DO OUR MISCHIEF RIGHT!
HEED US, REMEMBER US, THE DEADLY NIGHTSHADES...
GROAHG
WHERE DID YOU GET ALL THIS STUFF?
IT WAS EASY. I JUST SWITCHED BACKPACKS WITH RABBIT.

If you let Astrid finish the ceremony, go to page 78.
If you stop the ceremony, go on to the next page.

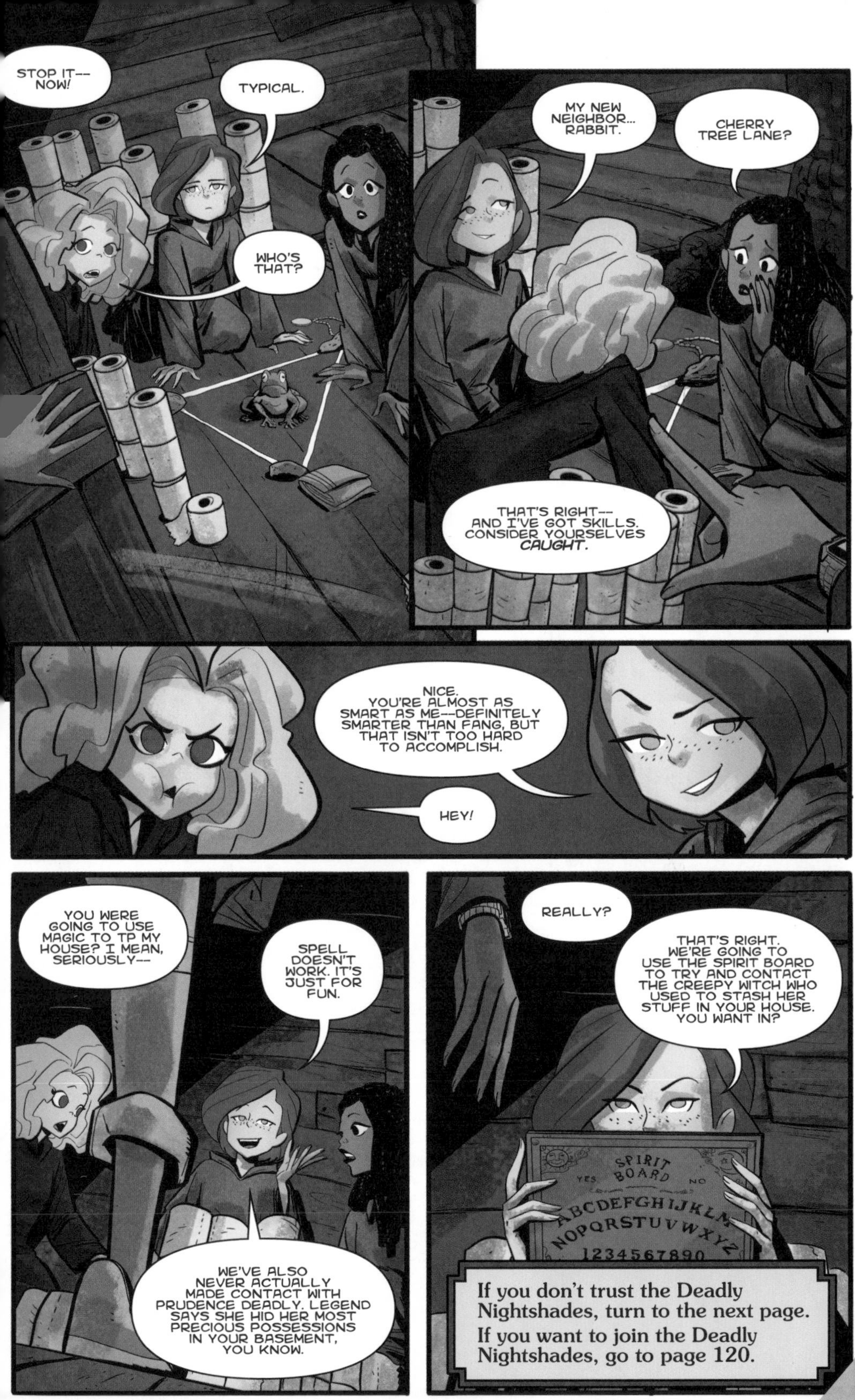

STOP IT-- NOW!
TYPICAL.
WHO'S THAT?
MY NEW NEIGHBOR... RABBIT.
CHERRY TREE LANE?
THAT'S RIGHT-- AND I'VE GOT SKILLS. CONSIDER YOURSELVES CAUGHT.
NICE. YOU'RE ALMOST AS SMART AS ME--DEFINITELY SMARTER THAN FANG, BUT THAT ISN'T TOO HARD TO ACCOMPLISH.
HEY!
YOU WERE GOING TO USE MAGIC TO TP MY HOUSE? I MEAN, SERIOUSLY--
SPELL DOESN'T WORK. IT'S JUST FOR FUN.
WE'VE ALSO NEVER ACTUALLY MADE CONTACT WITH PRUDENCE DEADLY. LEGEND SAYS SHE HID HER MOST PRECIOUS POSSESSIONS IN YOUR BASEMENT, YOU KNOW.
REALLY?
THAT'S RIGHT. WE'RE GOING TO USE THE SPIRIT BOARD TO TRY AND CONTACT THE CREEPY WITCH WHO USED TO STASH HER STUFF IN YOUR HOUSE. YOU WANT IN?
SPIRIT BOARD
YES
NO
ABCDEFGHIJKLM
NOPQRSTUVWXYZ
1234567890

If you don't trust the Deadly Nightshades, turn to the next page.

If you want to join the Deadly Nightshades, go to page 120.

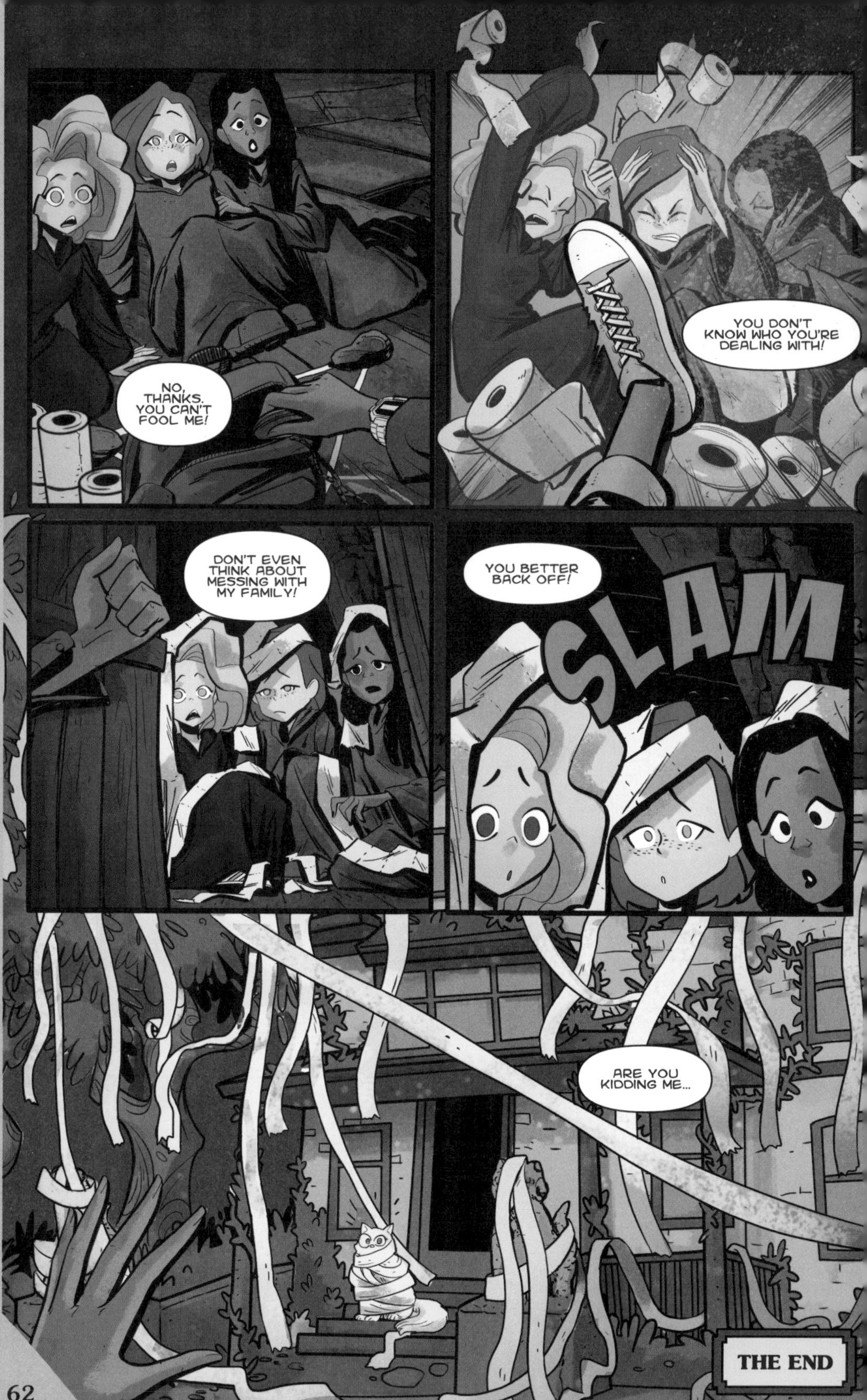
NO, THANKS. YOU CAN'T FOOL ME!
YOU DON'T KNOW WHO YOU'RE DEALING WITH!
DON'T EVEN THINK ABOUT MESSING WITH MY FAMILY!
YOU BETTER BACK OFF!
SLAM
ARE YOU KIDDING ME...
THE END

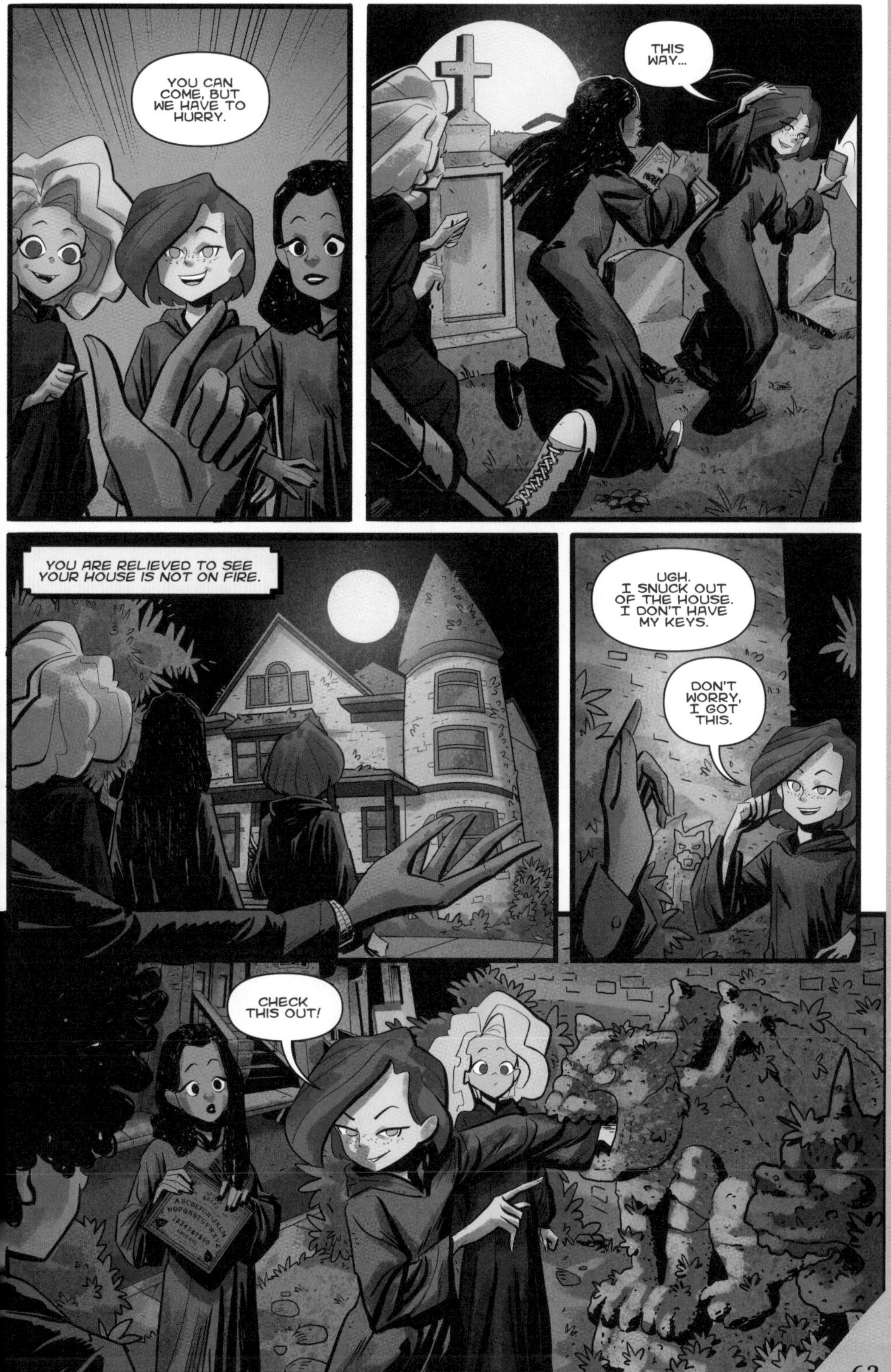

YOU CAN COME, BUT WE HAVE TO HURRY.
THIS WAY...
YOU ARE RELIEVED TO SEE YOUR HOUSE IS NOT ON FIRE.
UGH. I SNUCK OUT OF THE HOUSE. I DON'T HAVE MY KEYS.
DON'T WORRY, I GOT THIS.
CHECK THIS OUT!

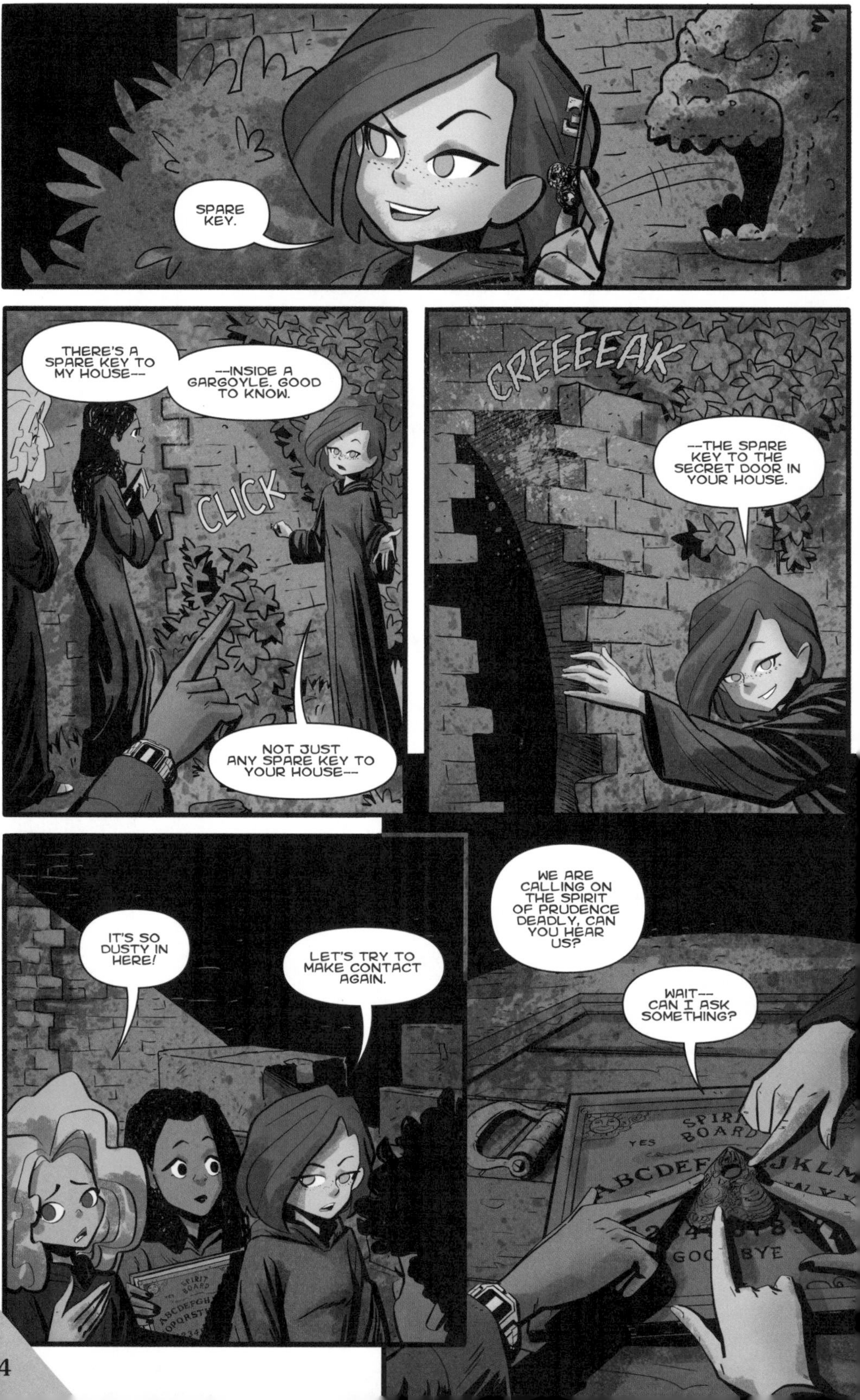
SPARE KEY.
THERE'S A SPARE KEY TO MY HOUSE--
--INSIDE A GARGOYLE. GOOD TO KNOW.
CLICK
NOT JUST ANY SPARE KEY TO YOUR HOUSE--
CREEEEAK
--THE SPARE KEY TO THE SECRET DOOR IN YOUR HOUSE.
IT'S SO DUSTY IN HERE!
LET'S TRY TO MAKE CONTACT AGAIN.
WE ARE CALLING ON THE SPIRIT OF PRUDENCE DEADLY, CAN YOU HEAR US?
WAIT-- CAN I ASK SOMETHING?
SPIRIT BOARD
YES
GOODBYE

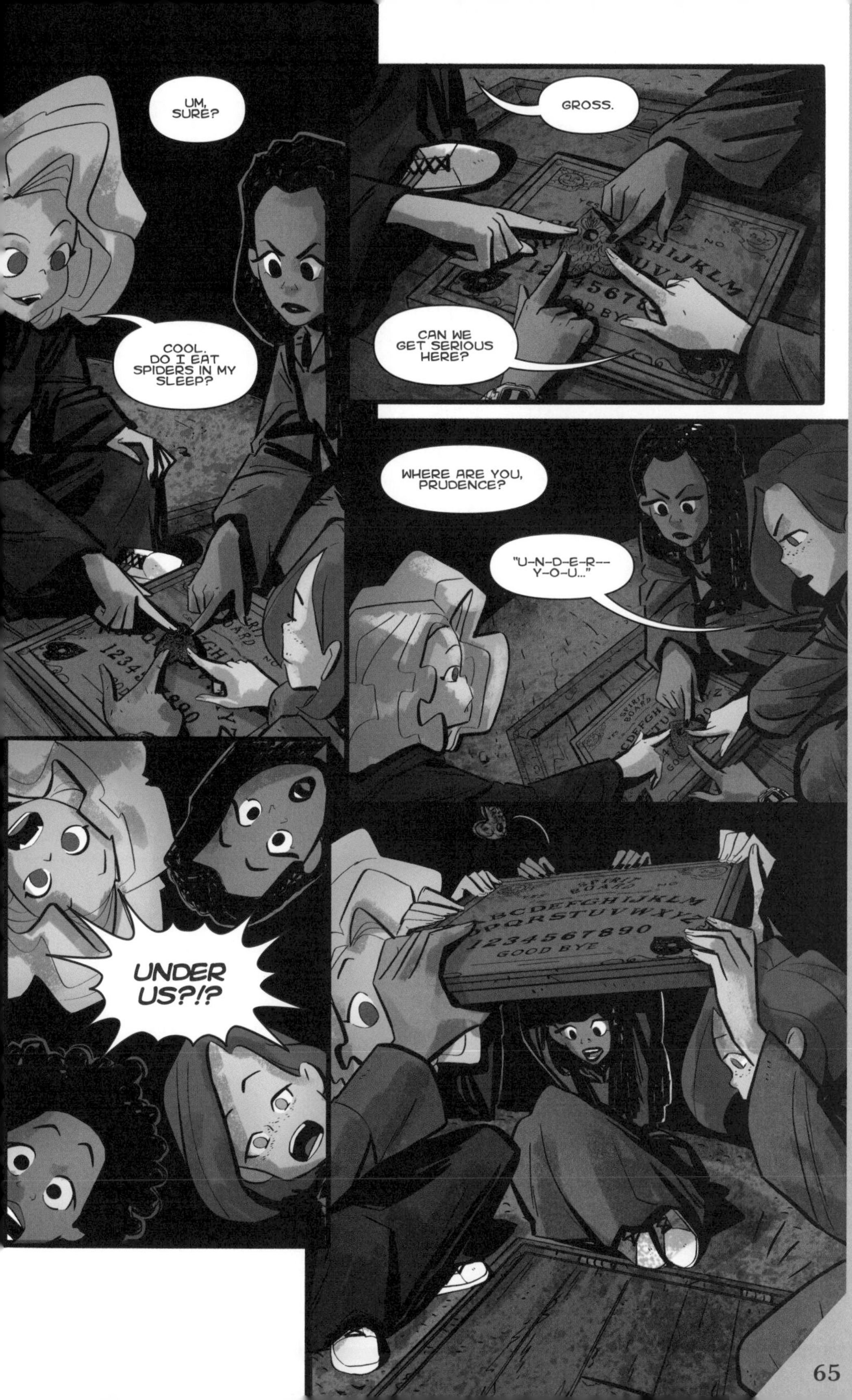

UM, SURE?
GROSS.
COOL. DO I EAT SPIDERS IN MY SLEEP?
CAN WE GET SERIOUS HERE?
WHERE ARE YOU, PRUDENCE?
"U-N-D-E-R-- Y-O-U..."
UNDER US?!?

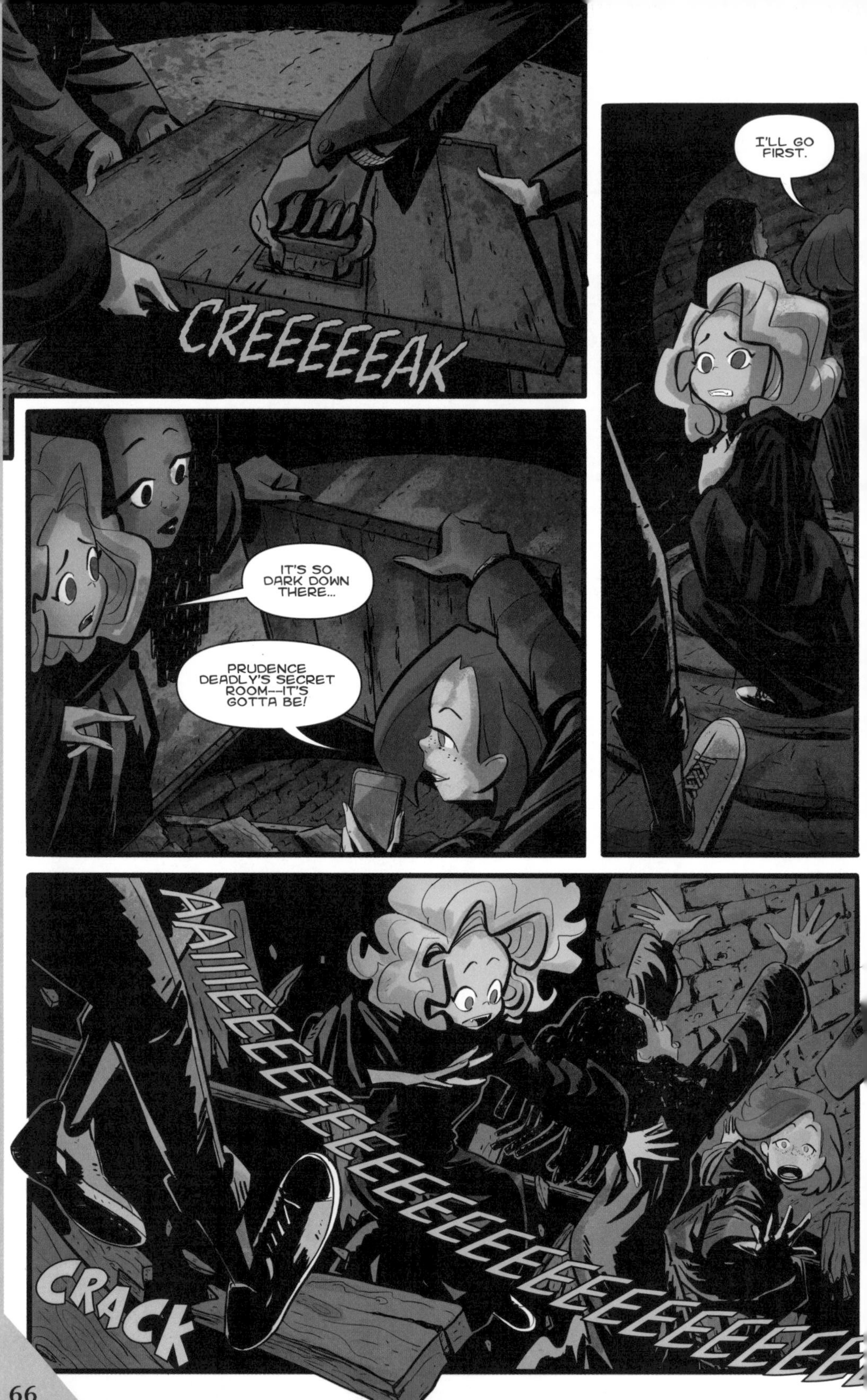

CREEEEEEAK
I'LL GO FIRST.
IT'S SO DARK DOWN THERE...
PRUDENCE DEADLY'S SECRET ROOM--IT'S GOTTA BE!
AAIIIEEEEEEEEEEEEEEEEEEEEEEEEEEEE
CRACK

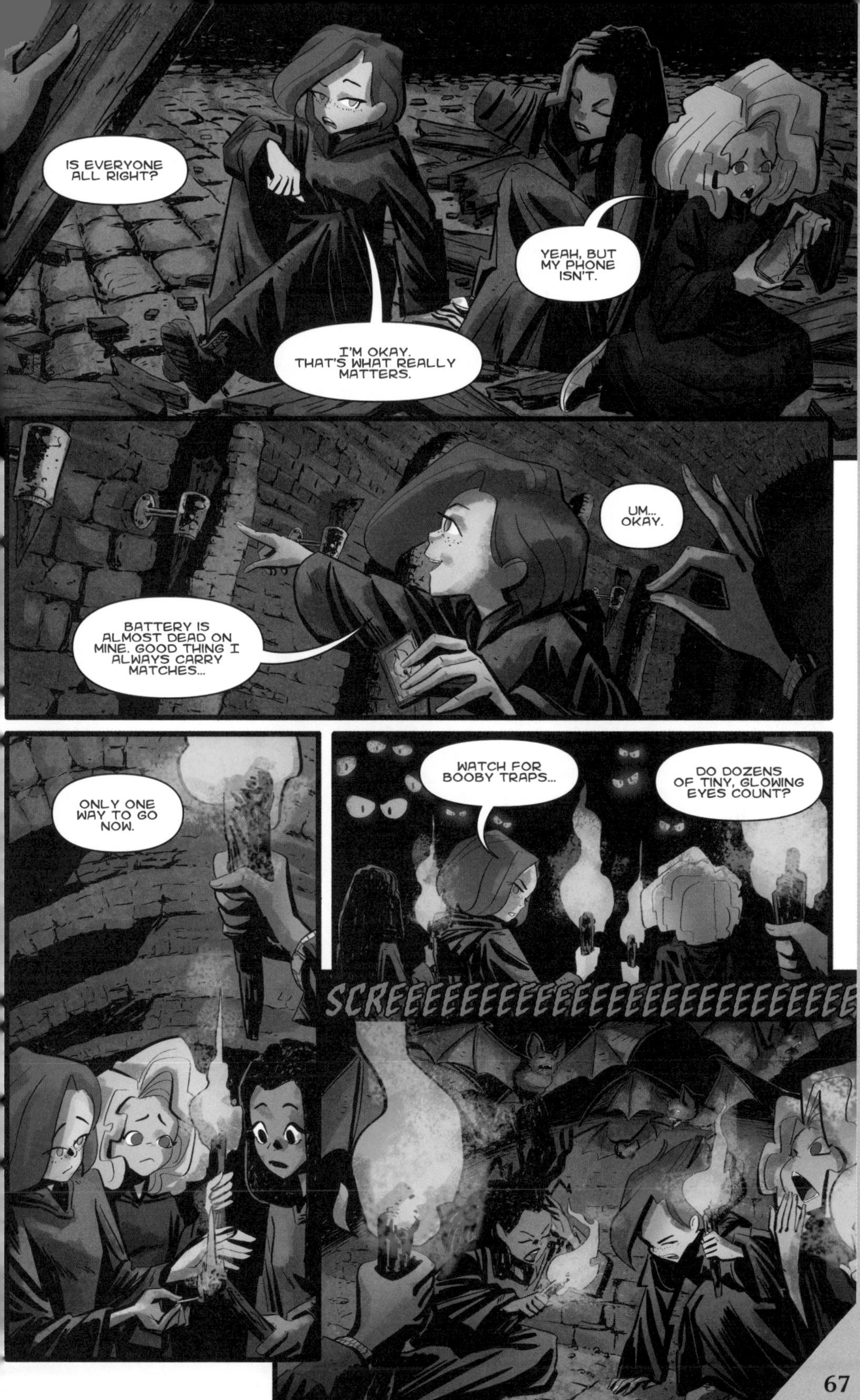
IS EVERYONE ALL RIGHT?
I'M OKAY. THAT'S WHAT REALLY MATTERS.
YEAH, BUT MY PHONE ISN'T.
BATTERY IS ALMOST DEAD ON MINE. GOOD THING I ALWAYS CARRY MATCHES...
UM... OKAY.
ONLY ONE WAY TO GO NOW.
WATCH FOR BOOBY TRAPS...
DO DOZENS OF TINY, GLOWING EYES COUNT?
SCREEEEEEEEEEEEEEEEEEEEEEEEEEE

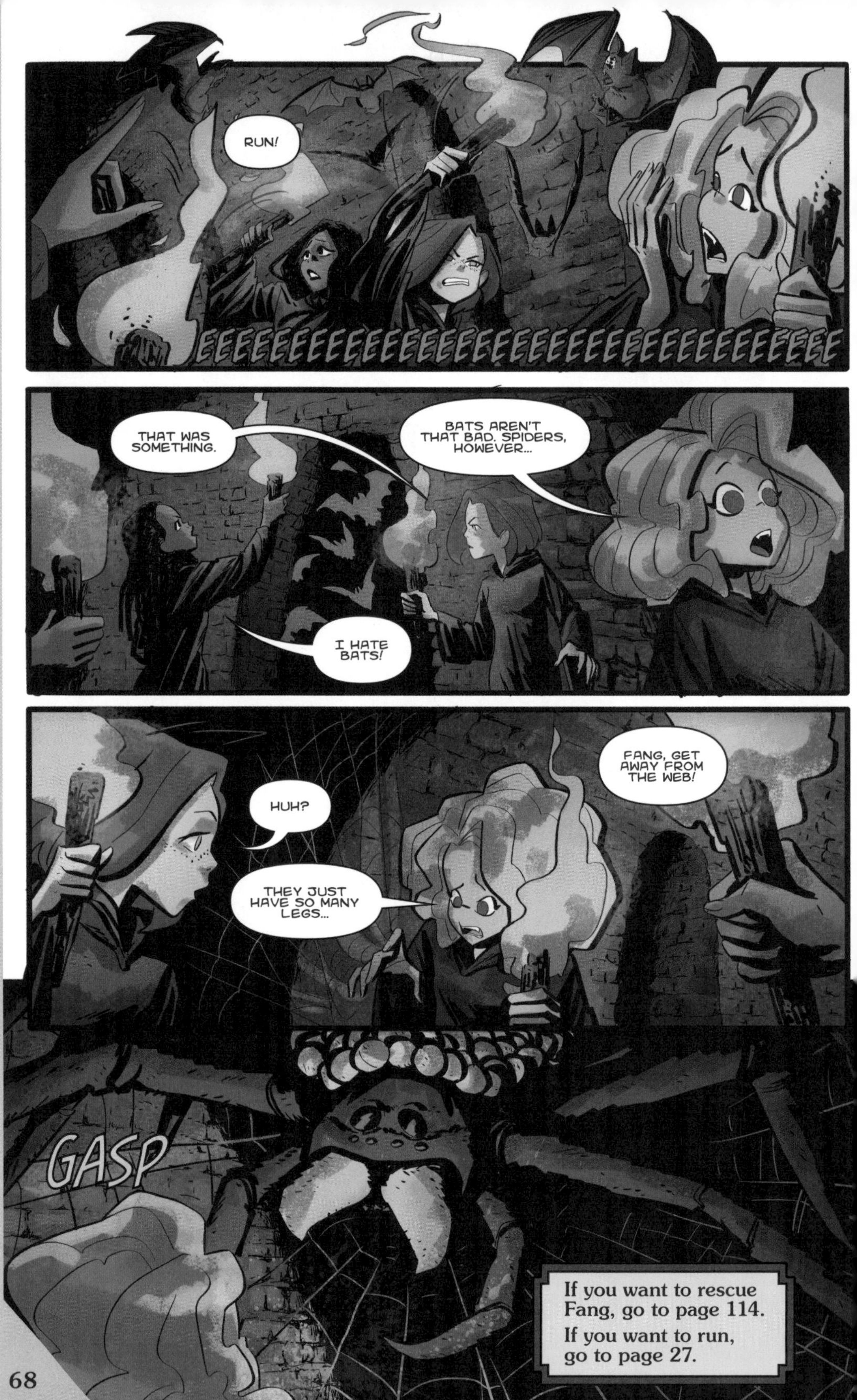
RUN!
EEEEEEEEEEEEEEEEEEEEEEEEEEEEEEE
THAT WAS SOMETHING.
BATS AREN'T THAT BAD. SPIDERS, HOWEVER...
I HATE BATS!
HUH?
FANG, GET AWAY FROM THE WEB!
THEY JUST HAVE SO MANY LEGS...
GASP

If you want to rescue Fang, go to page 114.
If you want to run, go to page 27.

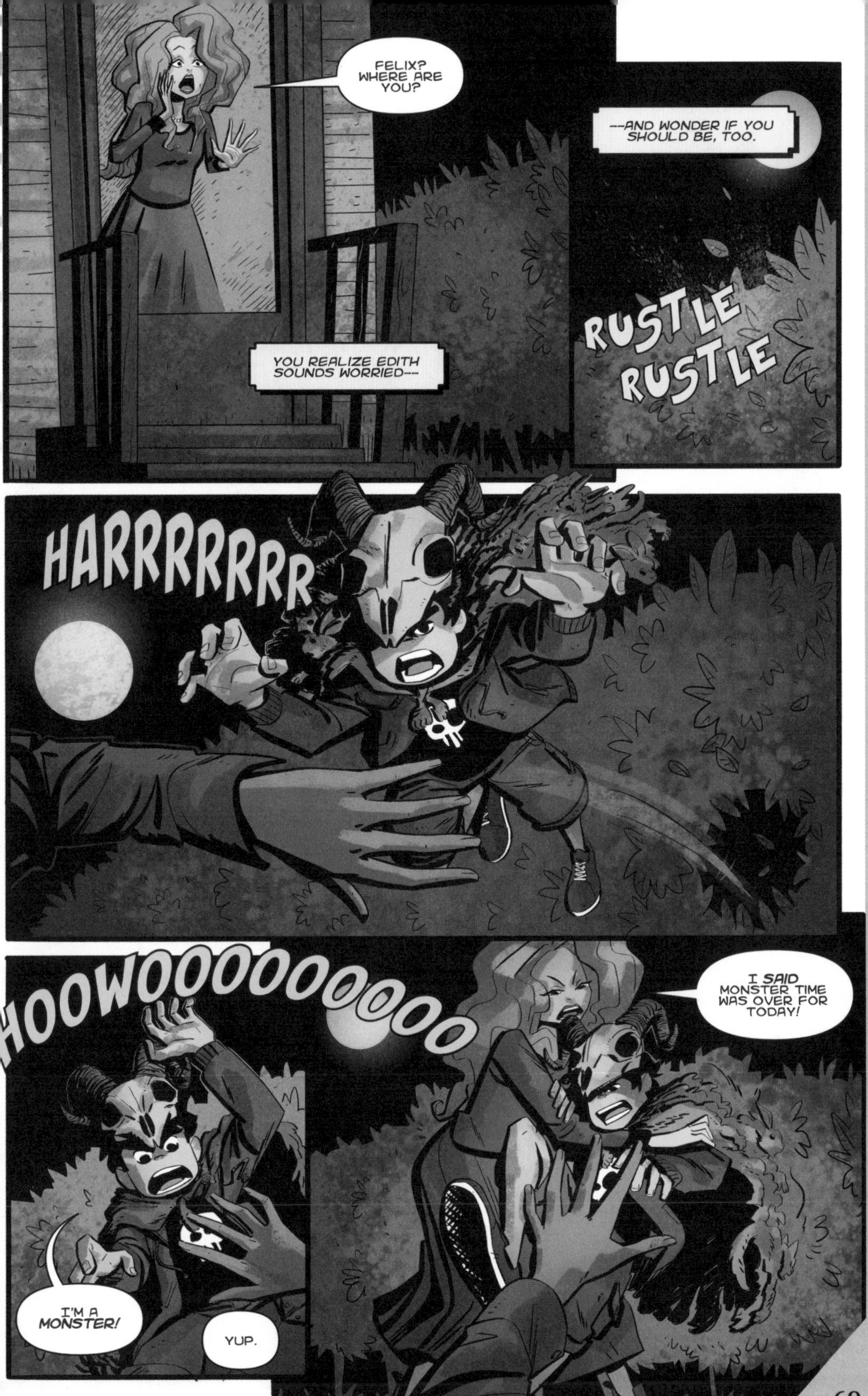
FELIX? WHERE ARE YOU?
YOU REALIZE EDITH SOUNDS WORRIED--
--AND WONDER IF YOU SHOULD BE, TOO.
RUSTLE RUSTLE
HARRRRRRR
HOOWOOOOOOOOO
I'M A MONSTER!
YUP.
I SAID MONSTER TIME WAS OVER FOR TODAY!

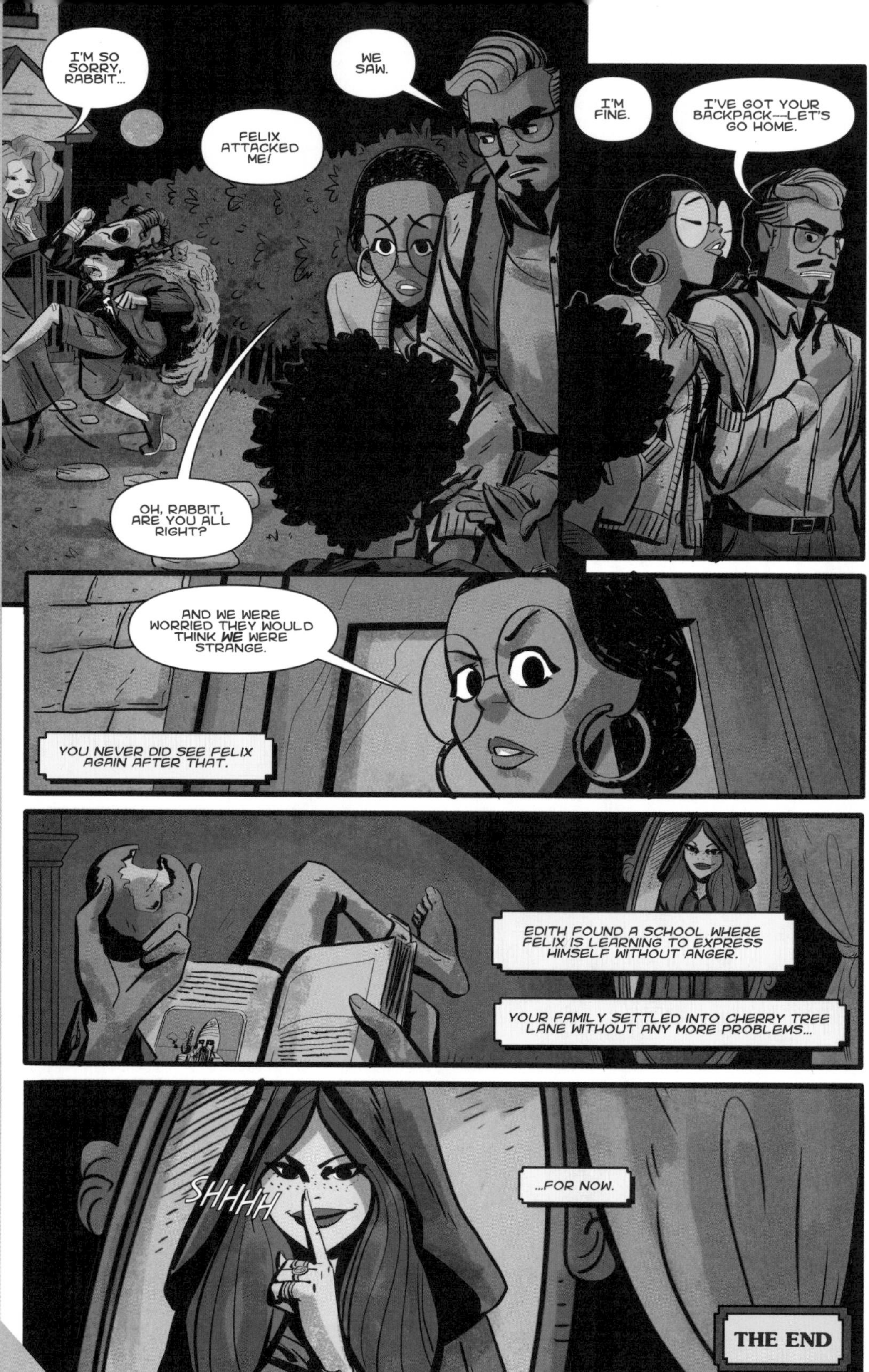
I'M SO SORRY, RABBIT...
FELIX ATTACKED ME!
WE SAW.
OH, RABBIT, ARE YOU ALL RIGHT?
I'M FINE.
I'VE GOT YOUR BACKPACK--LET'S GO HOME.
AND WE WERE WORRIED THEY WOULD THINK WE WERE STRANGE.
YOU NEVER DID SEE FELIX AGAIN AFTER THAT.
EDITH FOUND A SCHOOL WHERE FELIX IS LEARNING TO EXPRESS HIMSELF WITHOUT ANGER.
YOUR FAMILY SETTLED INTO CHERRY TREE LANE WITHOUT ANY MORE PROBLEMS...
SHHHH
...FOR NOW.
THE END

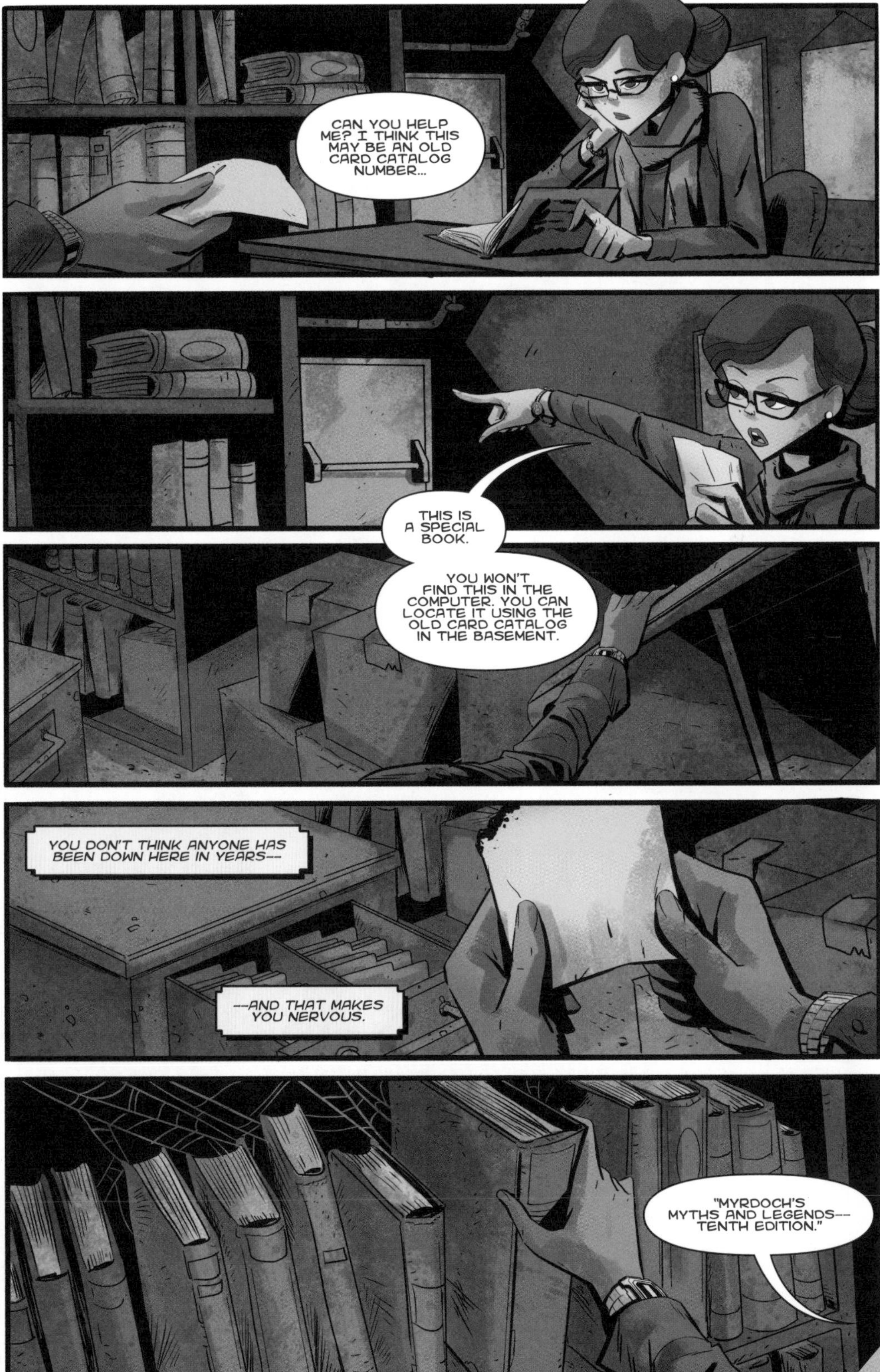
CAN YOU HELP ME? I THINK THIS MAY BE AN OLD CARD CATALOG NUMBER...
THIS IS A SPECIAL BOOK.
YOU WON'T FIND THIS IN THE COMPUTER. YOU CAN LOCATE IT USING THE OLD CARD CATALOG IN THE BASEMENT.
YOU DON'T THINK ANYONE HAS BEEN DOWN HERE IN YEARS--
--AND THAT MAKES YOU NERVOUS.
"MYRDOCH'S MYTHS AND LEGENDS-- TENTH EDITION."

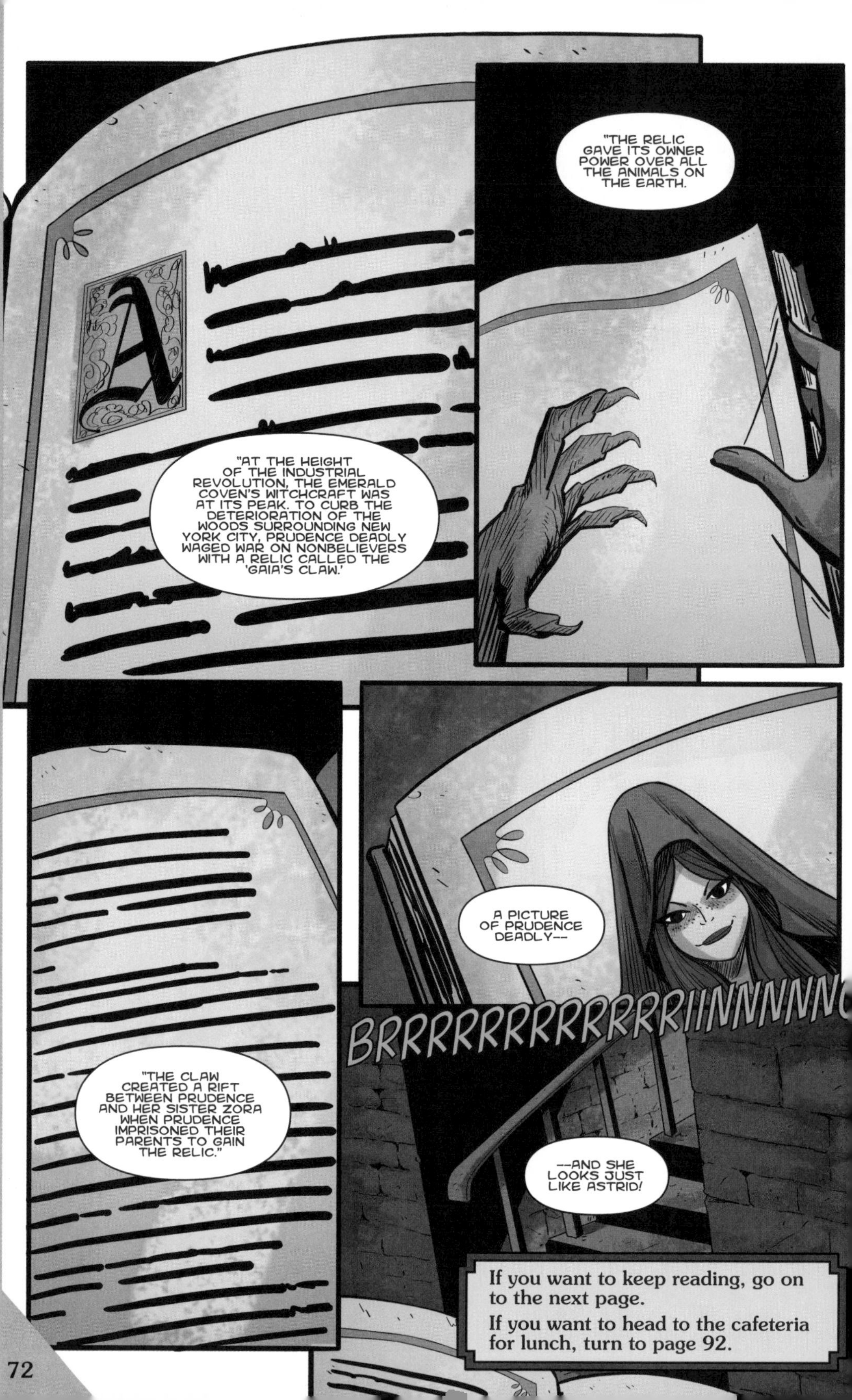
"AT THE HEIGHT OF THE INDUSTRIAL REVOLUTION, THE EMERALD COVEN'S WITCHCRAFT WAS AT ITS PEAK. TO CURB THE DETERIORATION OF THE WOODS SURROUNDING NEW YORK CITY, PRUDENCE DEADLY WAGED WAR ON NONBELIEVERS WITH A RELIC CALLED THE 'GAIA'S CLAW.'
"THE RELIC GAVE ITS OWNER POWER OVER ALL THE ANIMALS ON THE EARTH.
"THE CLAW CREATED A RIFT BETWEEN PRUDENCE AND HER SISTER ZORA WHEN PRUDENCE IMPRISONED THEIR PARENTS TO GAIN THE RELIC."
A PICTURE OF PRUDENCE DEADLY--
BRRRRRRRRRRRRRIINNNNNG
--AND SHE LOOKS JUST LIKE ASTRID!

If you want to keep reading, go on to the next page.
If you want to head to the cafeteria for lunch, turn to page 92.

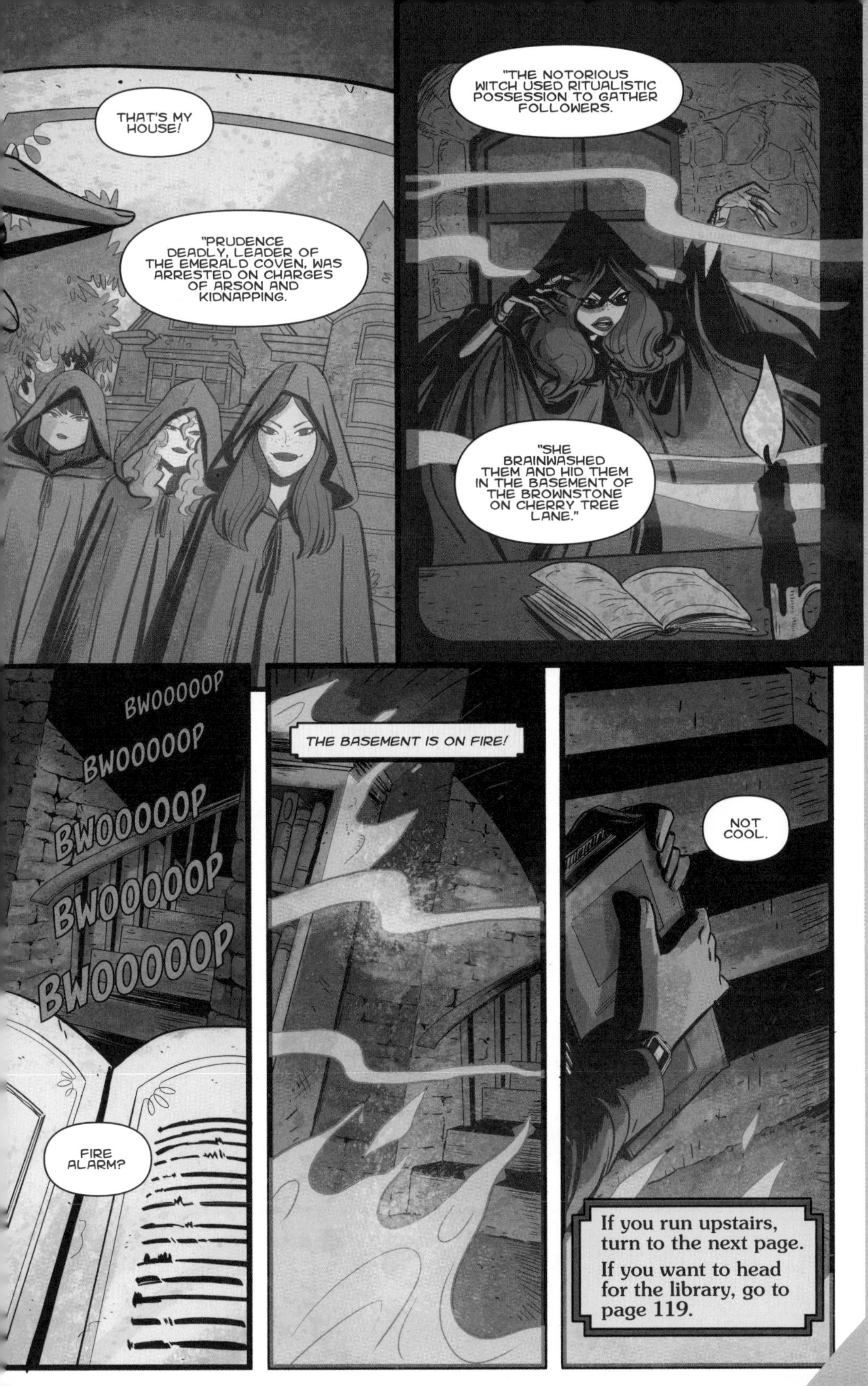
THAT'S MY HOUSE!
"PRUDENCE DEADLY, LEADER OF THE EMERALD COVEN, WAS ARRESTED ON CHARGES OF ARSON AND KIDNAPPING.
"THE NOTORIOUS WITCH USED RITUALISTIC POSSESSION TO GATHER FOLLOWERS.
"SHE BRAINWASHED THEM AND HID THEM IN THE BASEMENT OF THE BROWNSTONE ON CHERRY TREE LANE."
BWOOOOOP
BWOOOOOP
BWOOOOOP
BWOOOOOP
BWOOOOOP
FIRE ALARM?
THE BASEMENT IS ON FIRE!
NOT COOL.

If you run upstairs, turn to the next page.
If you want to head for the library, go to page 119.

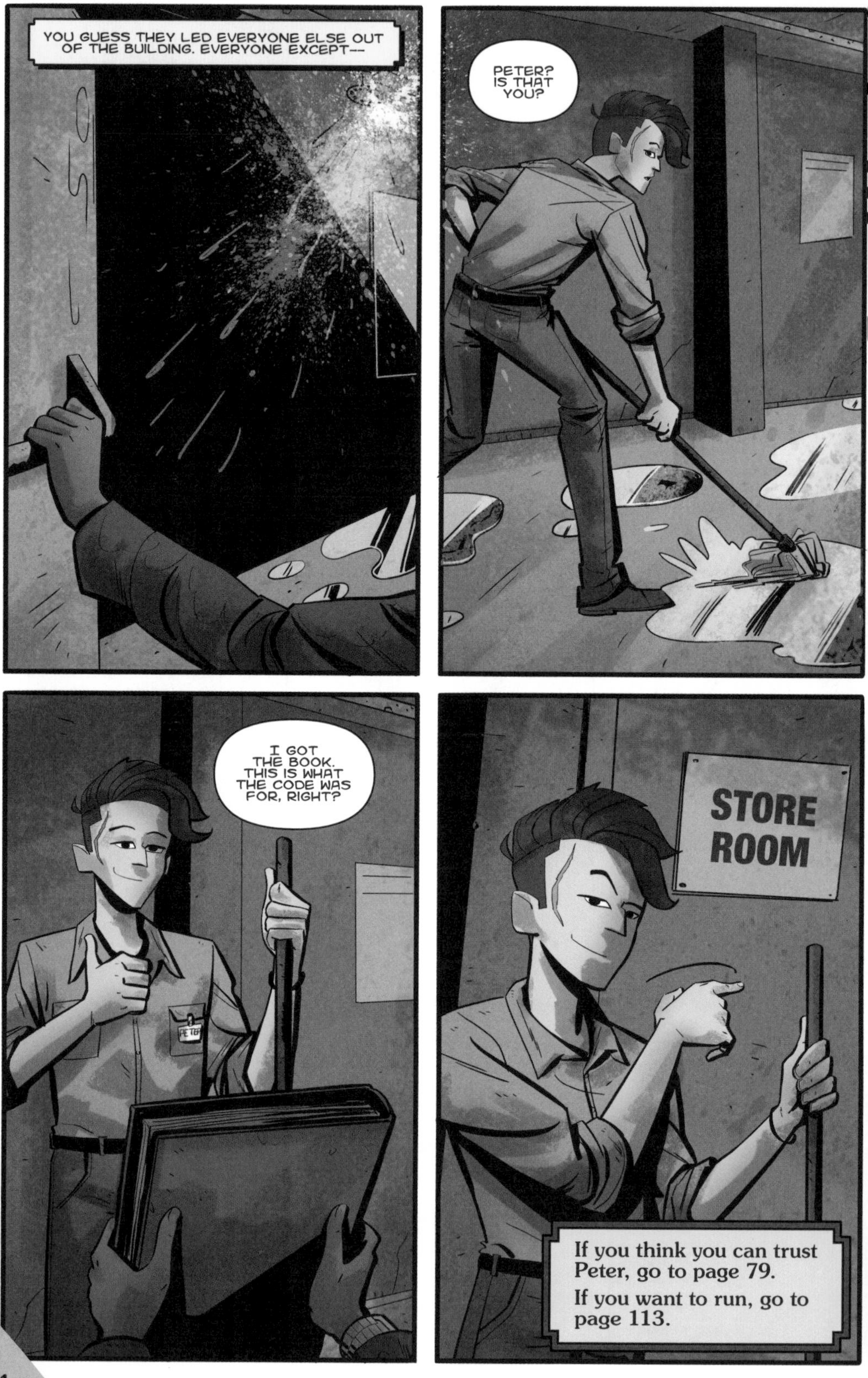
YOU GUESS THEY LED EVERYONE ELSE OUT OF THE BUILDING. EVERYONE EXCEPT--
PETER? IS THAT YOU?
I GOT THE BOOK. THIS IS WHAT THE CODE WAS FOR, RIGHT?
STORE ROOM
If you think you can trust Peter, go to page 79.
If you want to run, go to page 113.

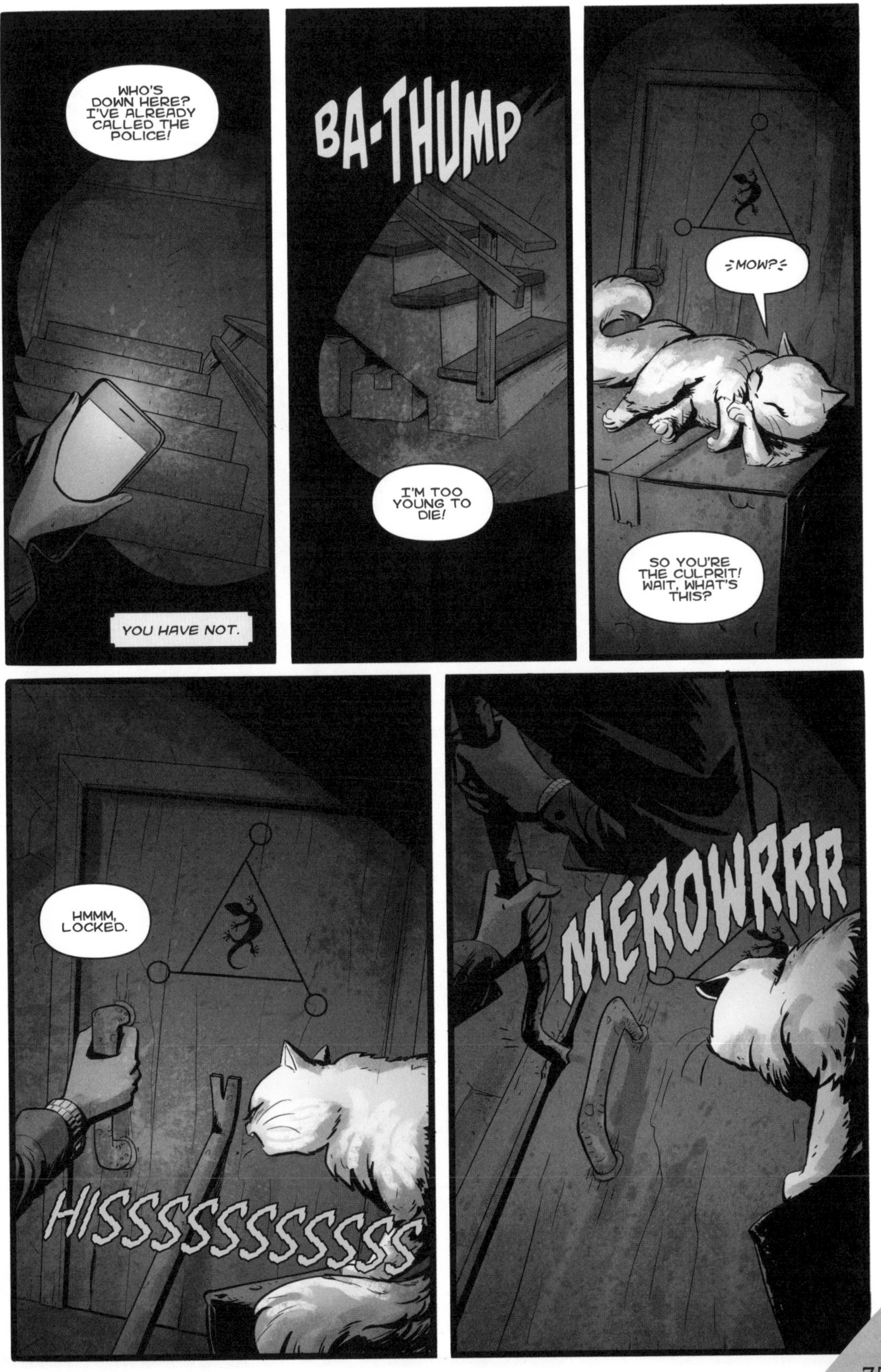
WHO'S DOWN HERE? I'VE ALREADY CALLED THE POLICE!
YOU HAVE NOT.
BA-THUMP
I'M TOO YOUNG TO DIE!
MOW?
SO YOU'RE THE CULPRIT! WAIT, WHAT'S THIS?
HMMM, LOCKED.
HISSSSSSSSSS
MEROWRRR

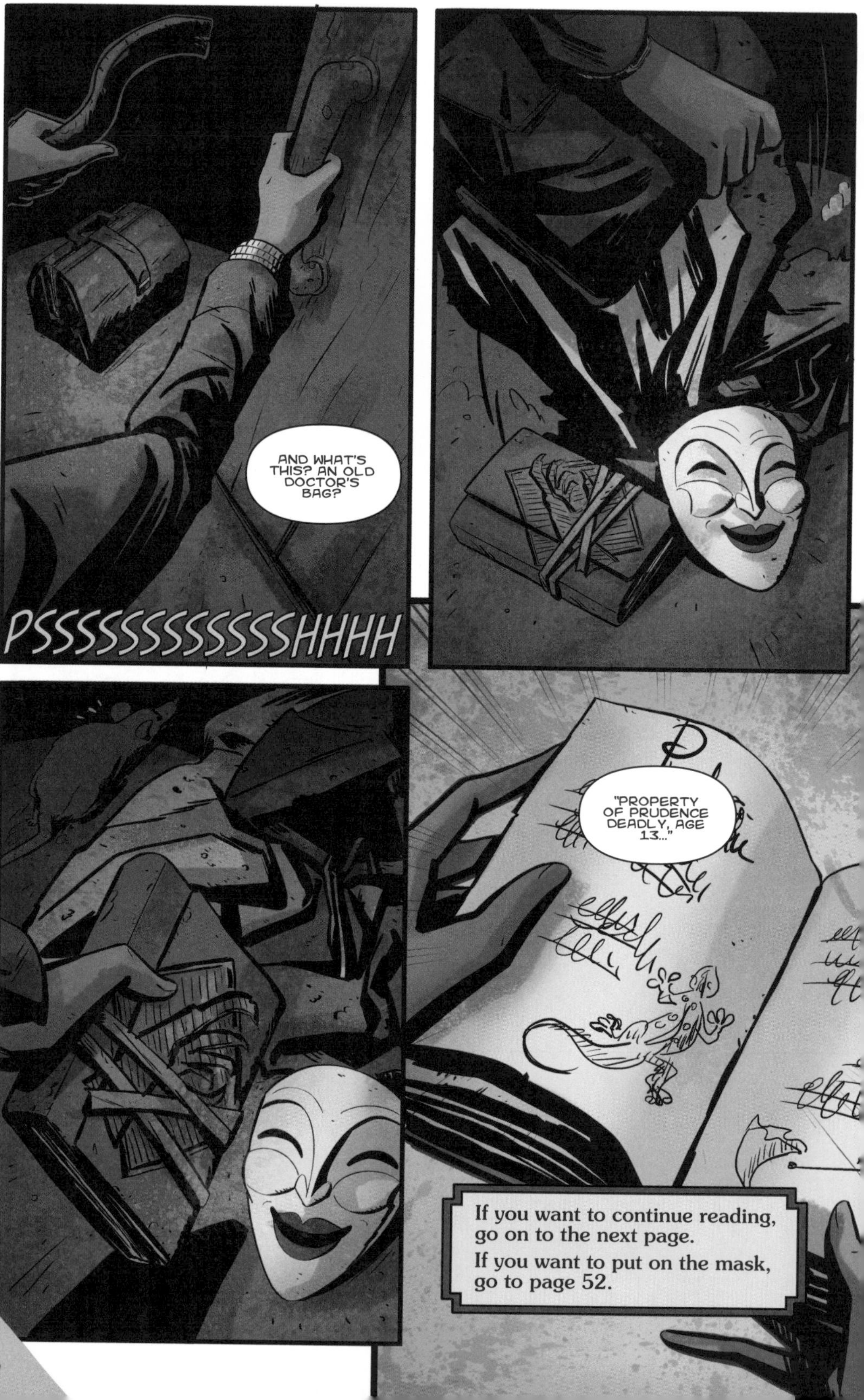
AND WHAT'S THIS? AN OLD DOCTOR'S BAG?
PSSSSSSSSSSSSHHHH
"PROPERTY OF PRUDENCE DEADLY, AGE 13..."

If you want to continue reading, go on to the next page.
If you want to put on the mask, go to page 52.

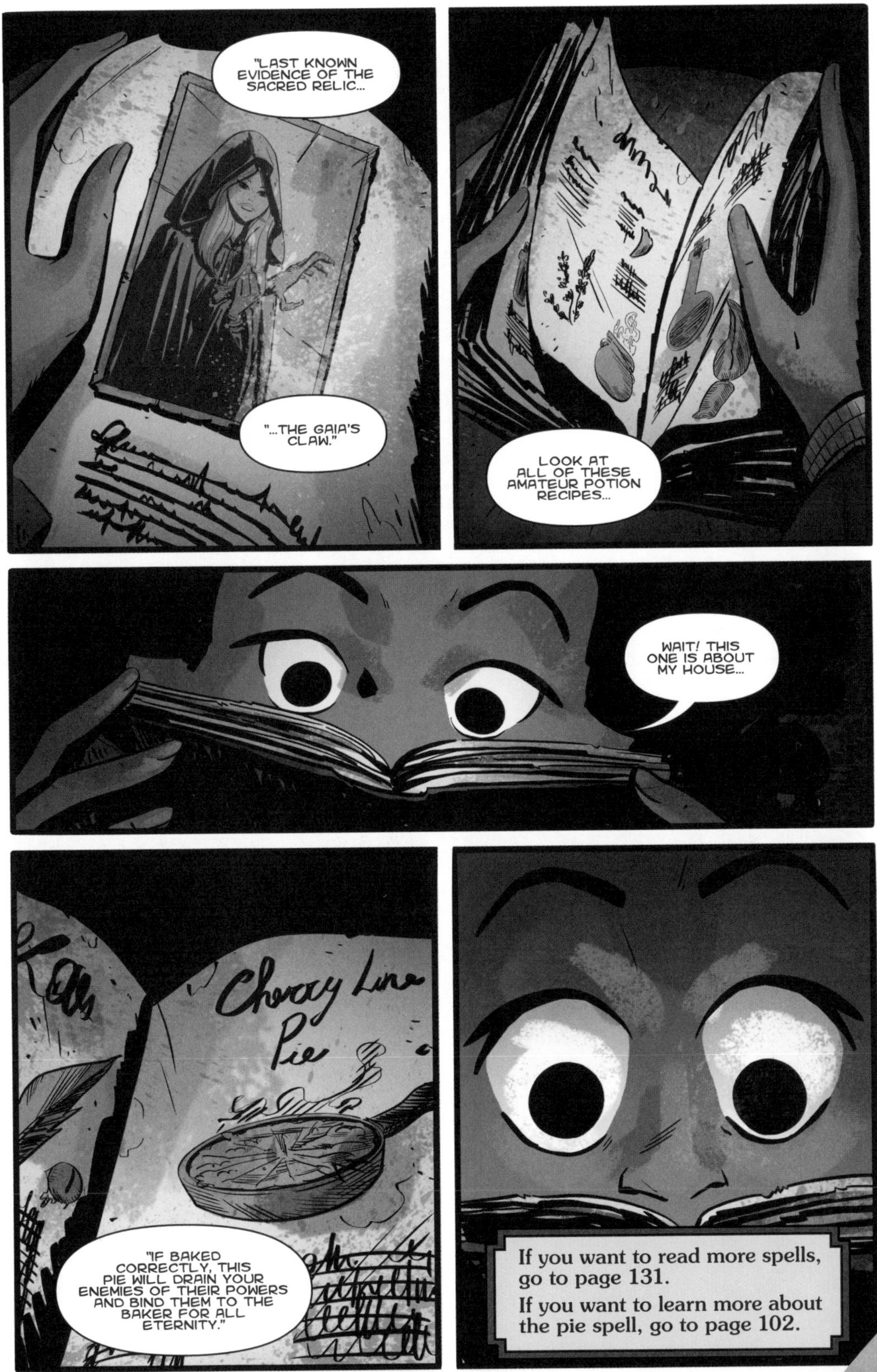
"LAST KNOWN EVIDENCE OF THE SACRED RELIC...
"...THE GAIA'S CLAW."
LOOK AT ALL OF THESE AMATEUR POTION RECIPES...
WAIT! THIS ONE IS ABOUT MY HOUSE...
Cherry Lime Pie
"IF BAKED CORRECTLY, THIS PIE WILL DRAIN YOUR ENEMIES OF THEIR POWERS AND BIND THEM TO THE BAKER FOR ALL ETERNITY."

If you want to read more spells, go to page 131.

If you want to learn more about the pie spell, go to page 102.

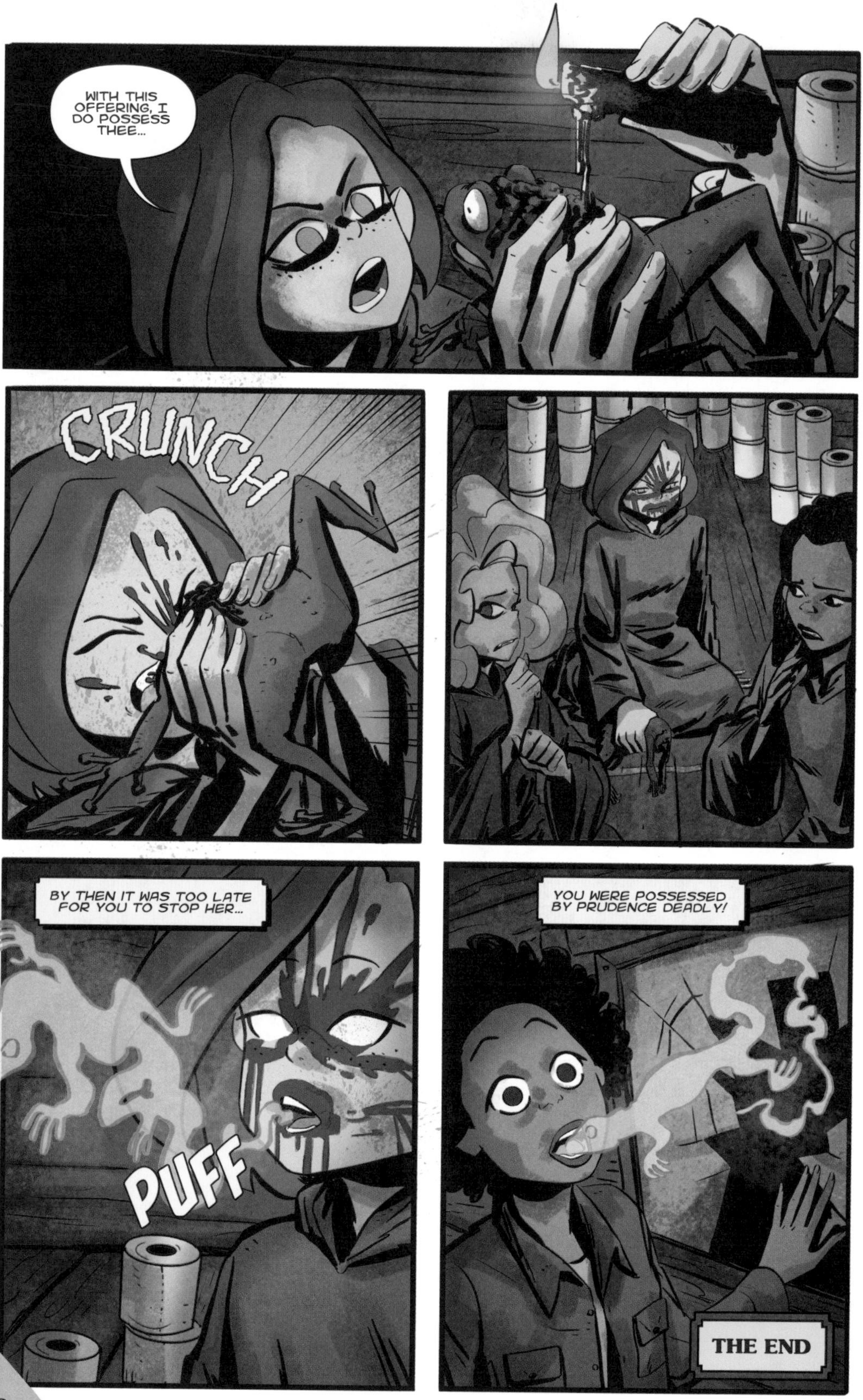
WITH THIS OFFERING, I DO POSSESS THEE...
CRUNCH
BY THEN IT WAS TOO LATE FOR YOU TO STOP HER...
PUFF
YOU WERE POSSESSED BY PRUDENCE DEADLY!
THE END

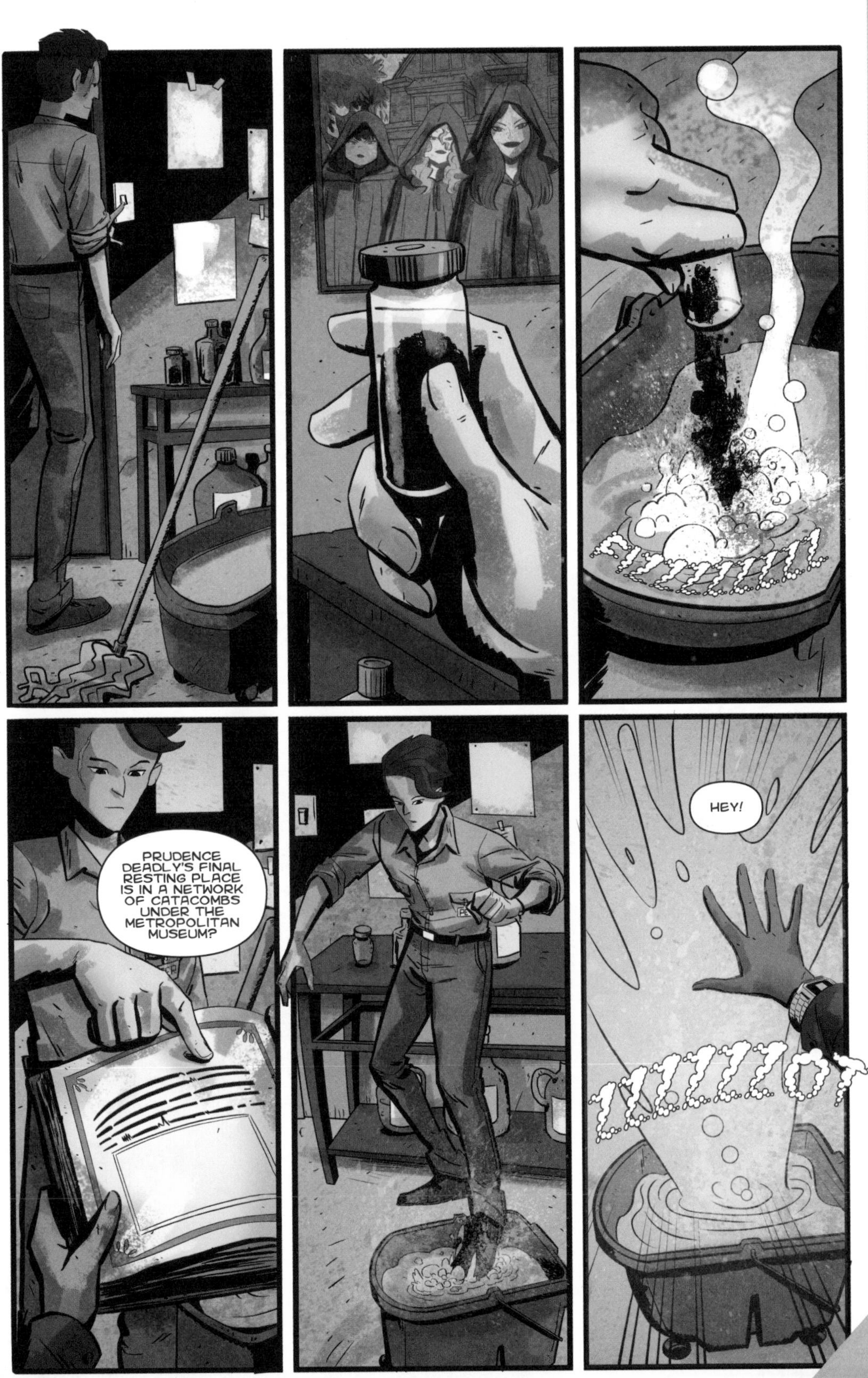
FIZZZZZZZ
PRUDENCE DEADLY'S FINAL RESTING PLACE IS IN A NETWORK OF CATACOMBS UNDER THE METROPOLITAN MUSEUM?
HEY!
ZZZZZZOT

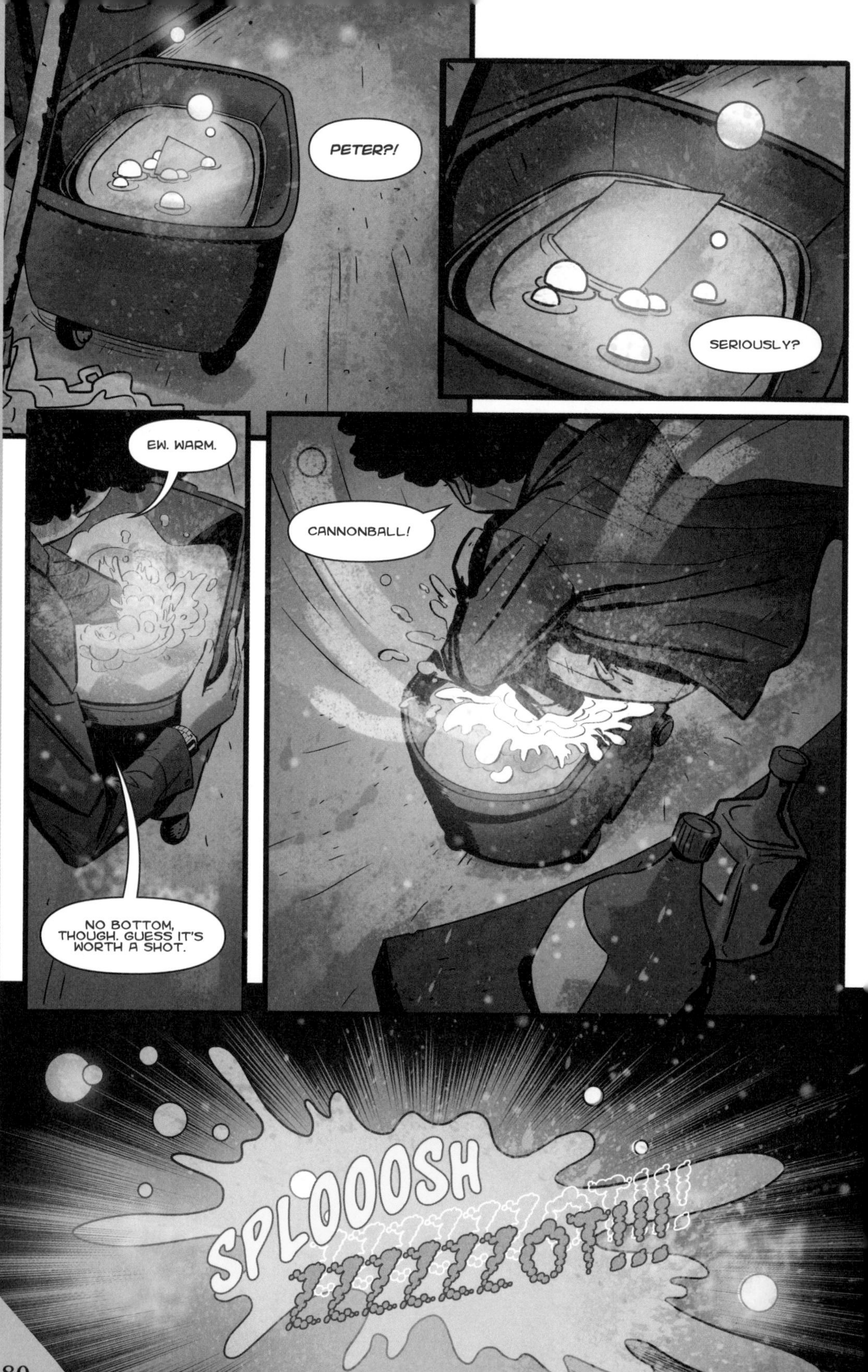
PETER?!
SERIOUSLY?
EW. WARM.
NO BOTTOM, THOUGH. GUESS IT'S WORTH A SHOT.
CANNONBALL!
SPLOOOSH
ZZZZZZOT!!!

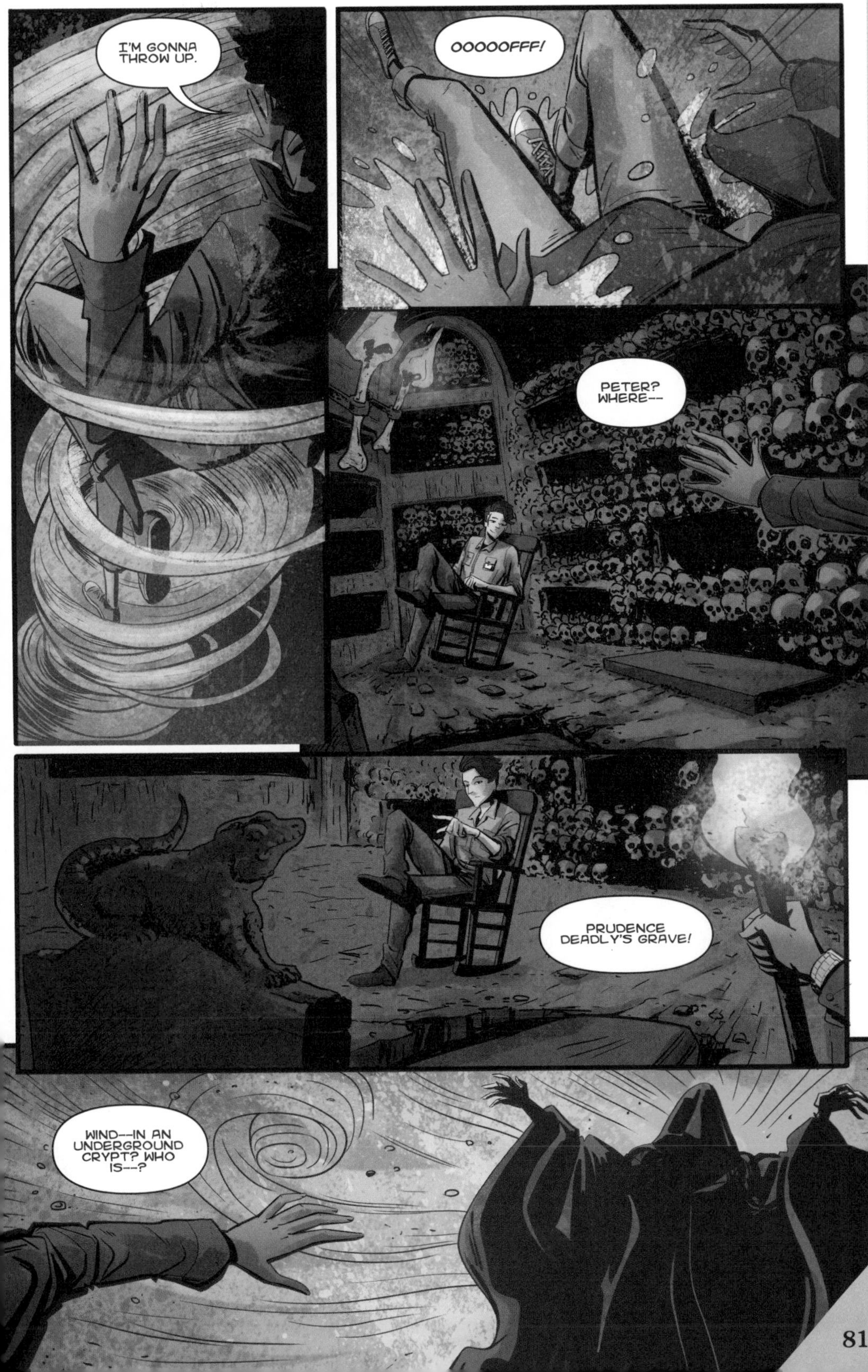
I'M GONNA THROW UP.
OOOOOFFF!
PETER? WHERE--
PRUDENCE DEADLY'S GRAVE!
WIND--IN AN UNDERGROUND CRYPT? WHO IS--?

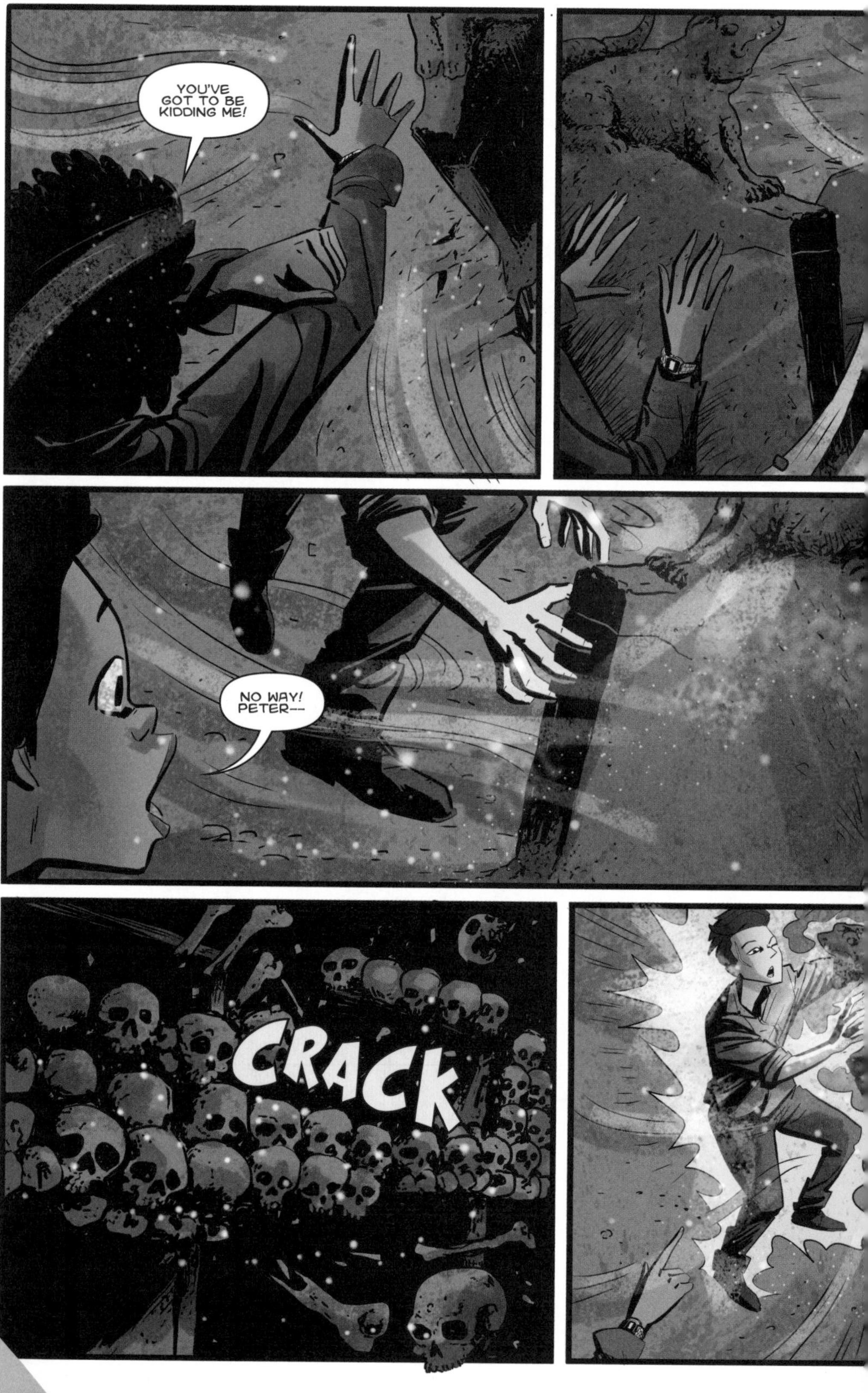
YOU'VE GOT TO BE KIDDING ME!
NO WAY! PETER---
CRACK

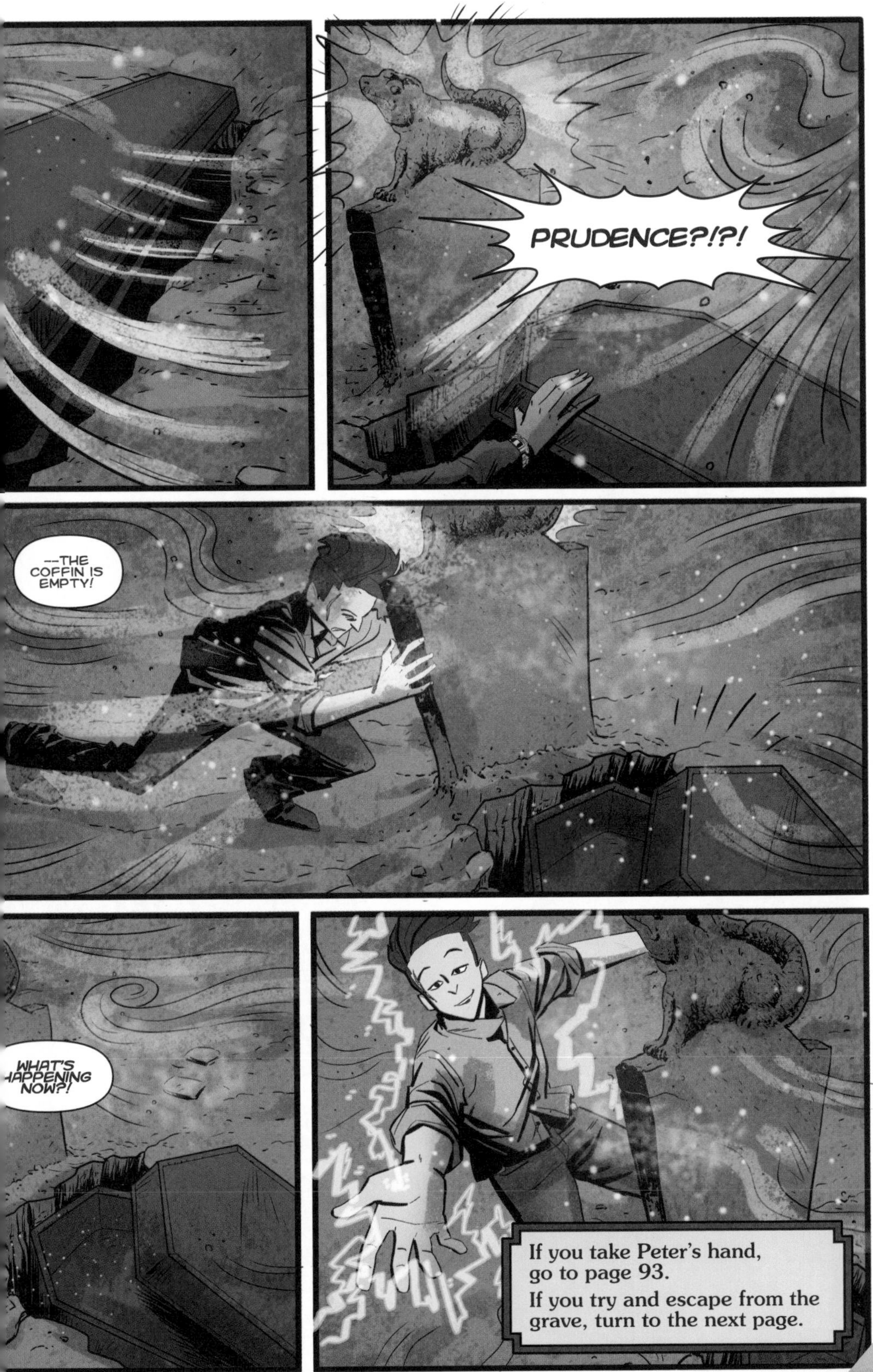
PRUDENCE?!?!
--THE COFFIN IS EMPTY!
WHAT'S HAPPENING NOW?!
If you take Peter's hand, go to page 93.
If you try and escape from the grave, turn to the next page.

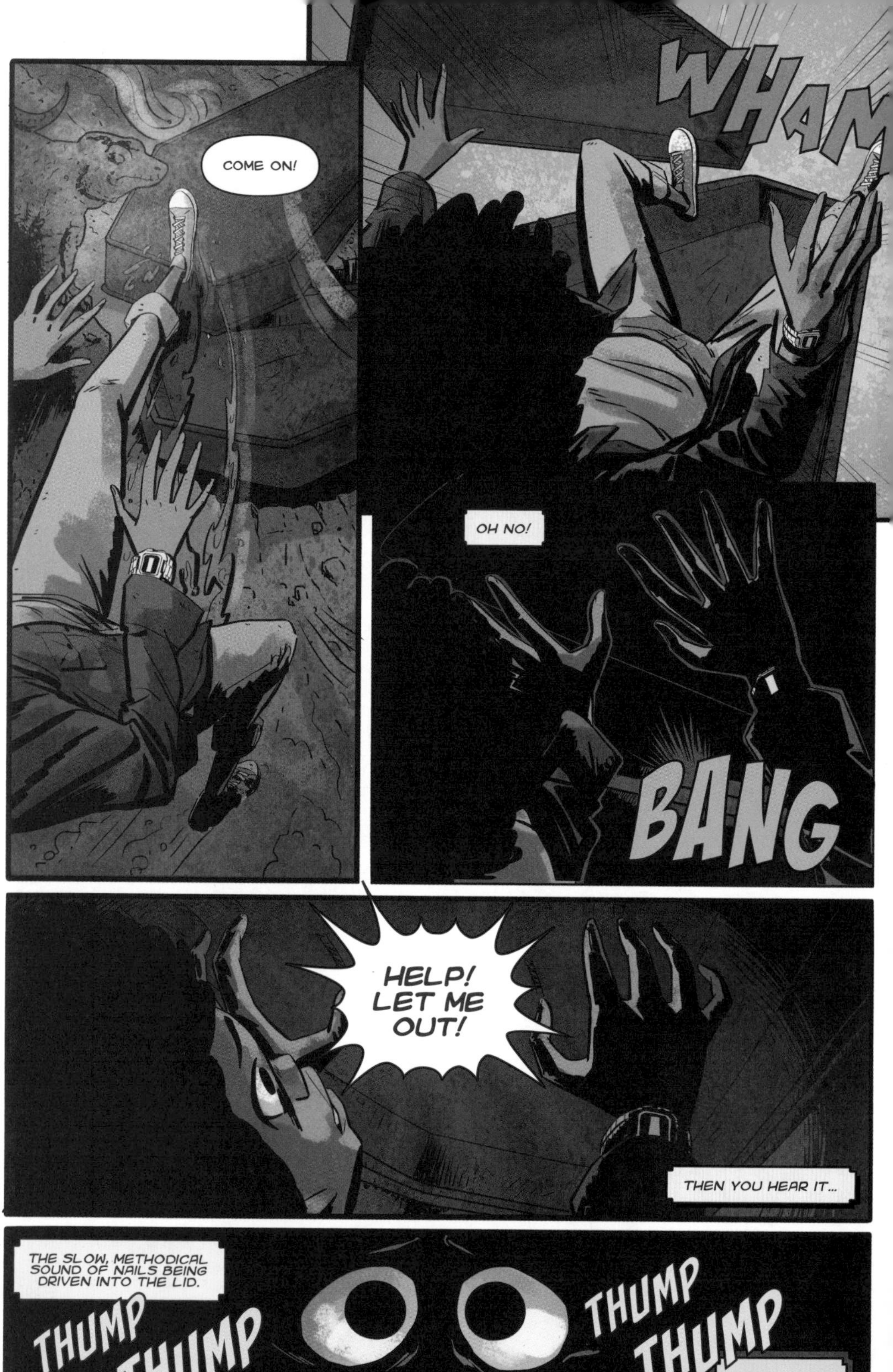
COME ON!
WHAM
OH NO!
BANG
HELP! LET ME OUT!
THEN YOU HEAR IT...
THE SLOW, METHODICAL SOUND OF NAILS BEING DRIVEN INTO THE LID.
THUMP
THUMP
THUMP
THUMP
THE END

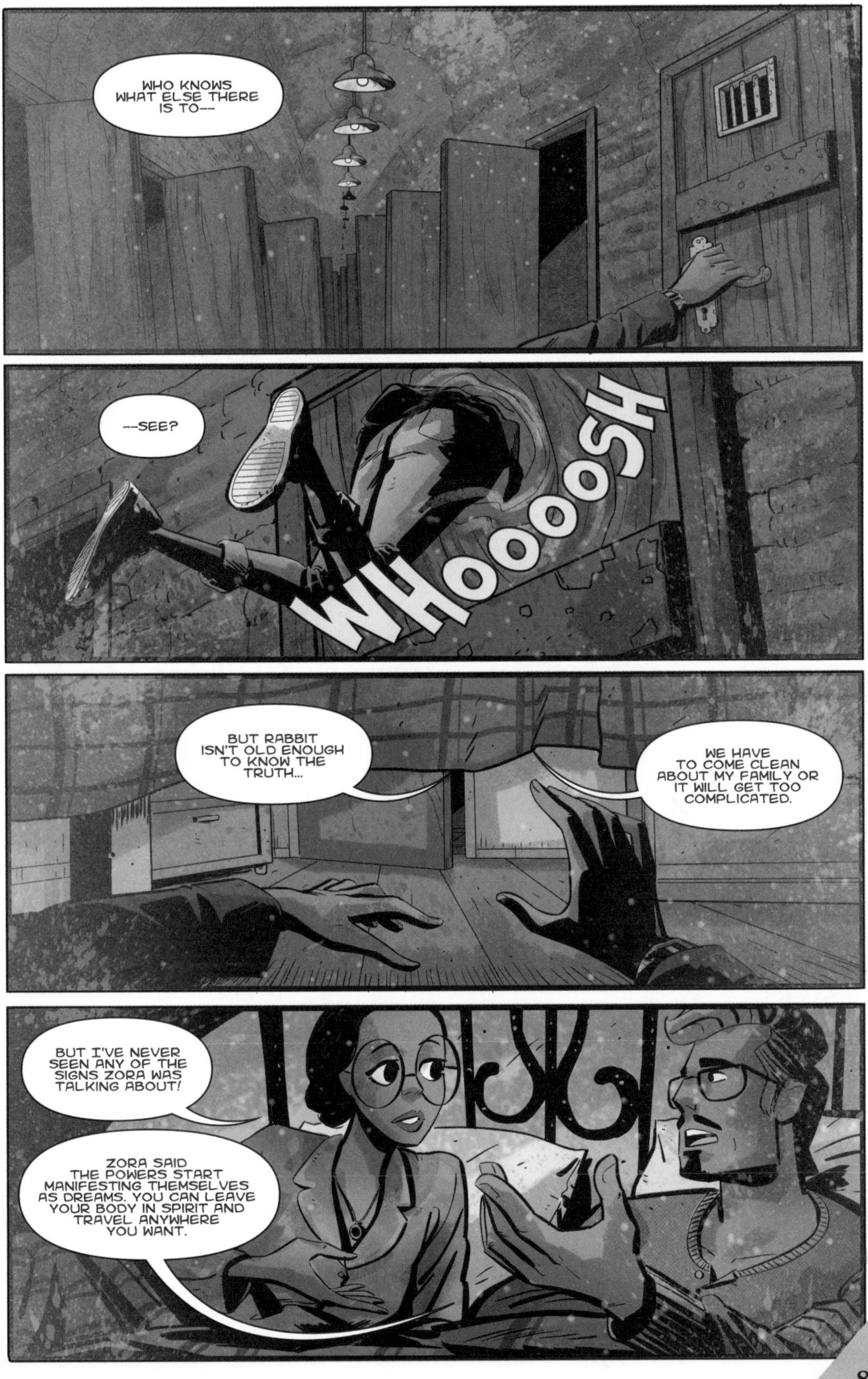
WHO KNOWS WHAT ELSE THERE IS TO--
--SEE?
WHOOOOSH
BUT RABBIT ISN'T OLD ENOUGH TO KNOW THE TRUTH...
WE HAVE TO COME CLEAN ABOUT MY FAMILY OR IT WILL GET TOO COMPLICATED.
BUT I'VE NEVER SEEN ANY OF THE SIGNS ZORA WAS TALKING ABOUT!
ZORA SAID THE POWERS START MANIFESTING THEMSELVES AS DREAMS. YOU CAN LEAVE YOUR BODY IN SPIRIT AND TRAVEL ANYWHERE YOU WANT.

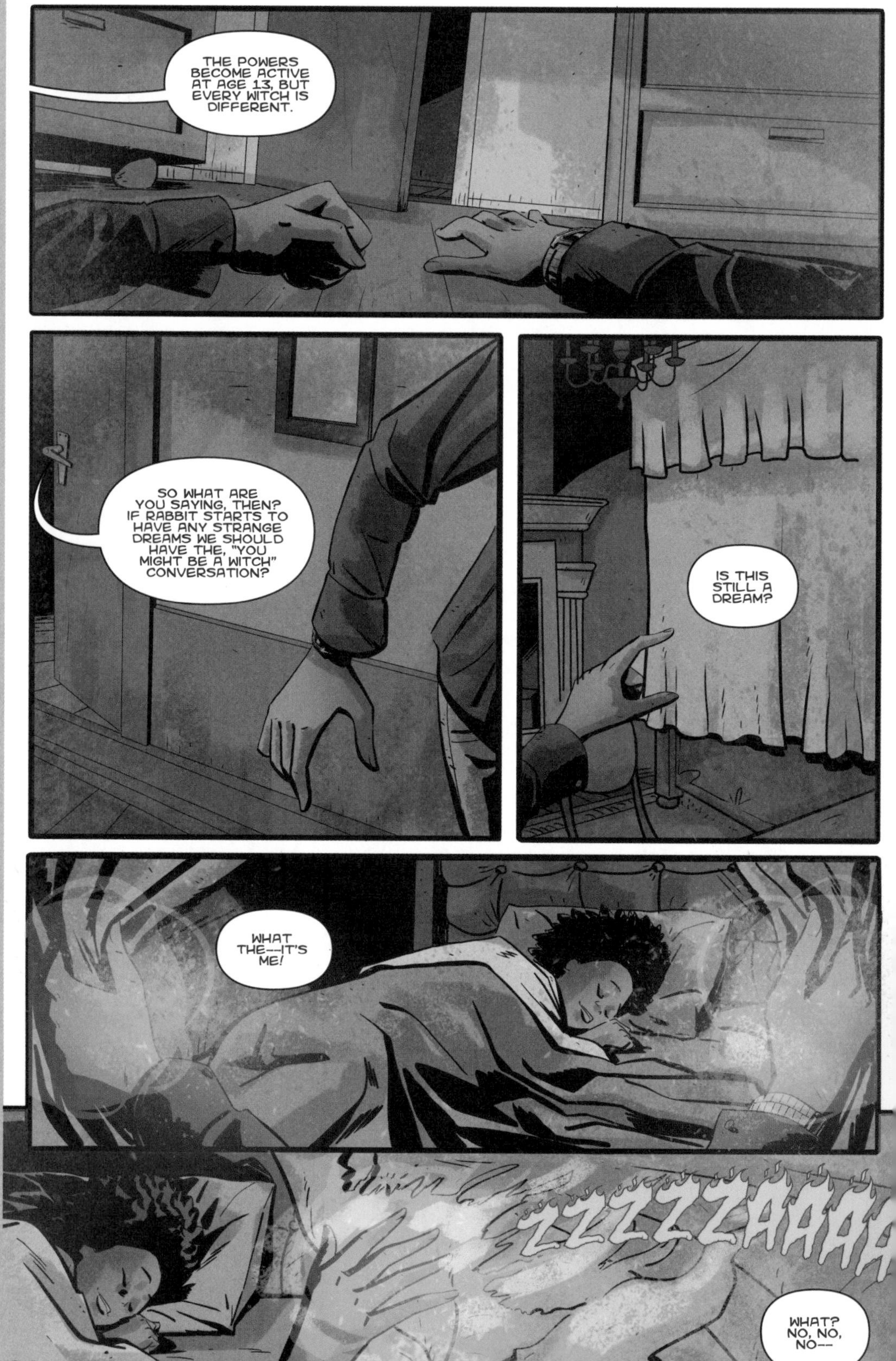
THE POWERS BECOME ACTIVE AT AGE 13, BUT EVERY WITCH IS DIFFERENT.
SO WHAT ARE YOU SAYING, THEN? IF RABBIT STARTS TO HAVE ANY STRANGE DREAMS WE SHOULD HAVE THE, "YOU MIGHT BE A WITCH" CONVERSATION?
IS THIS STILL A DREAM?
WHAT THE--IT'S ME!
ZZZZZAAAA
WHAT? NO, NO, NO--

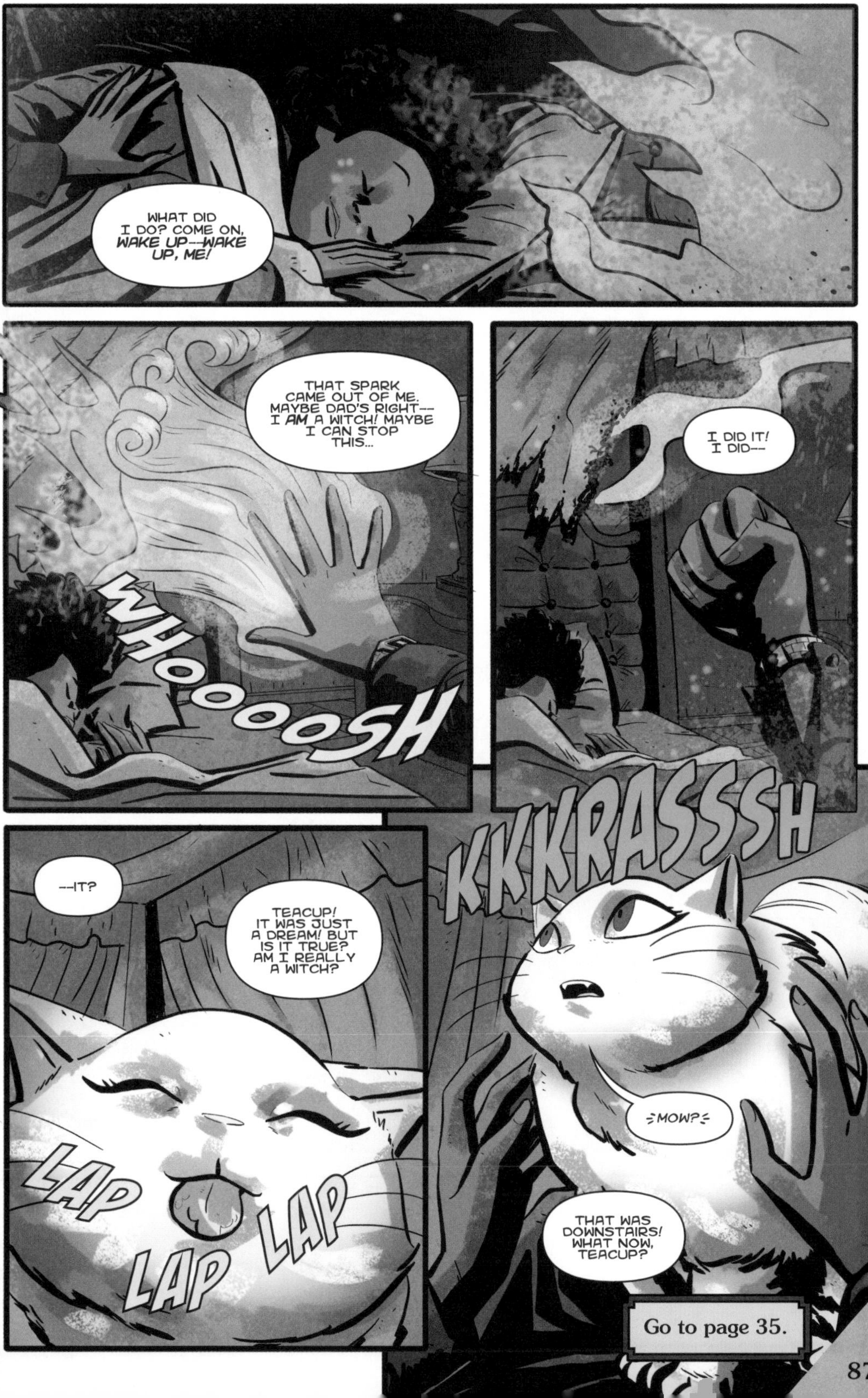
WHAT DID I DO? COME ON, WAKE UP--WAKE UP, ME!
THAT SPARK CAME OUT OF ME. MAYBE DAD'S RIGHT-- I AM A WITCH! MAYBE I CAN STOP THIS...
WHOOOOSH
I DID IT! I DID--
KKKRASSSH
--IT?
TEACUP! IT WAS JUST A DREAM! BUT IS IT TRUE? AM I REALLY A WITCH?
LAP LAP LAP
MOW?
THAT WAS DOWNSTAIRS! WHAT NOW, TEACUP?

Go to page 35.

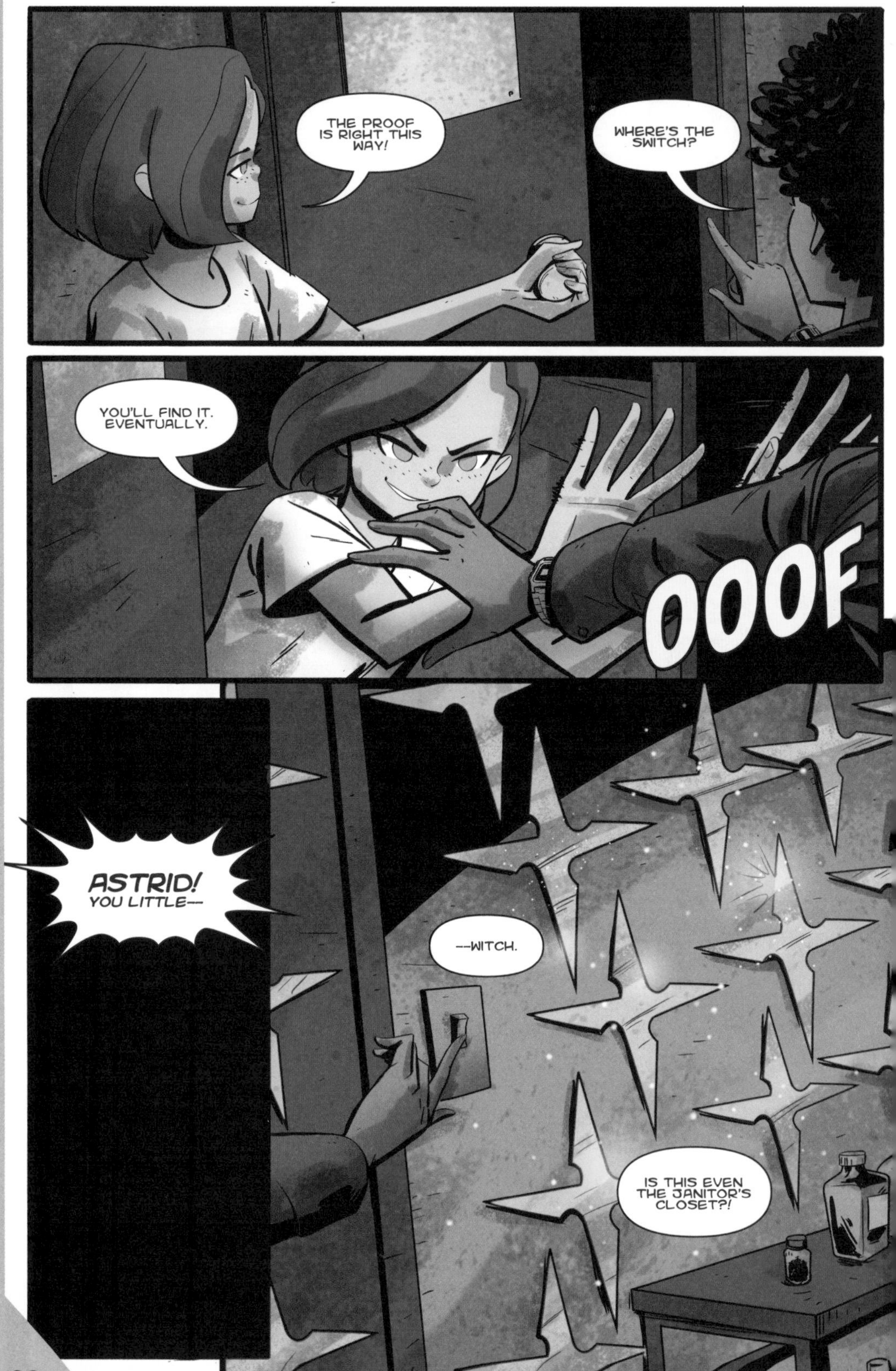
THE PROOF IS RIGHT THIS WAY!
WHERE'S THE SWITCH?
YOU'LL FIND IT. EVENTUALLY.
OOOF
ASTRID! YOU LITTLE--
--WITCH.
IS THIS EVEN THE JANITOR'S CLOSET?!

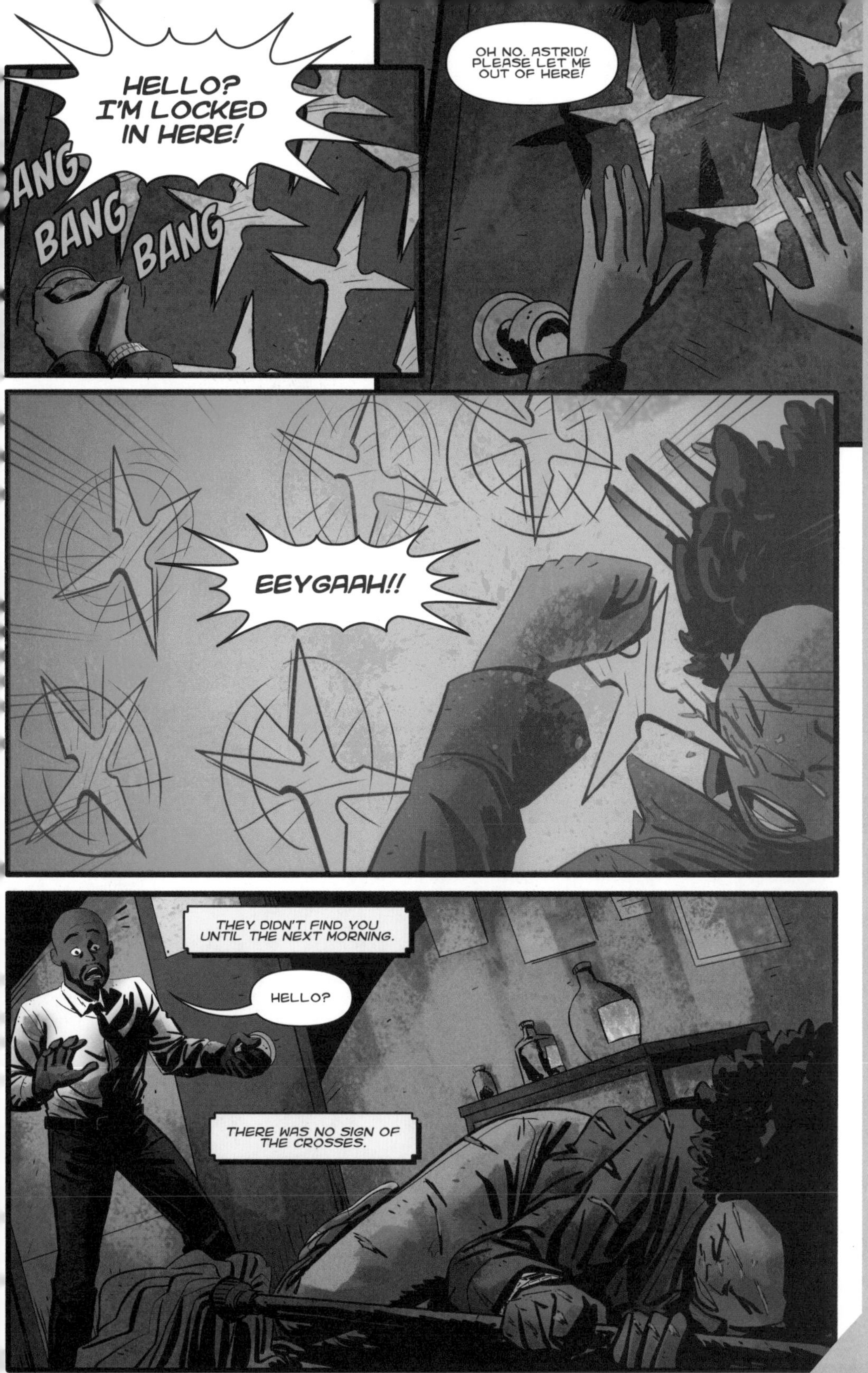
HELLO?
I'M LOCKED
IN HERE!
BANG
BANG
BANG
OH NO. ASTRID!
PLEASE LET ME
OUT OF HERE!
EEYGAAH!!
THEY DIDN'T FIND YOU
UNTIL THE NEXT MORNING.
HELLO?
THERE WAS NO SIGN OF
THE CROSSES.

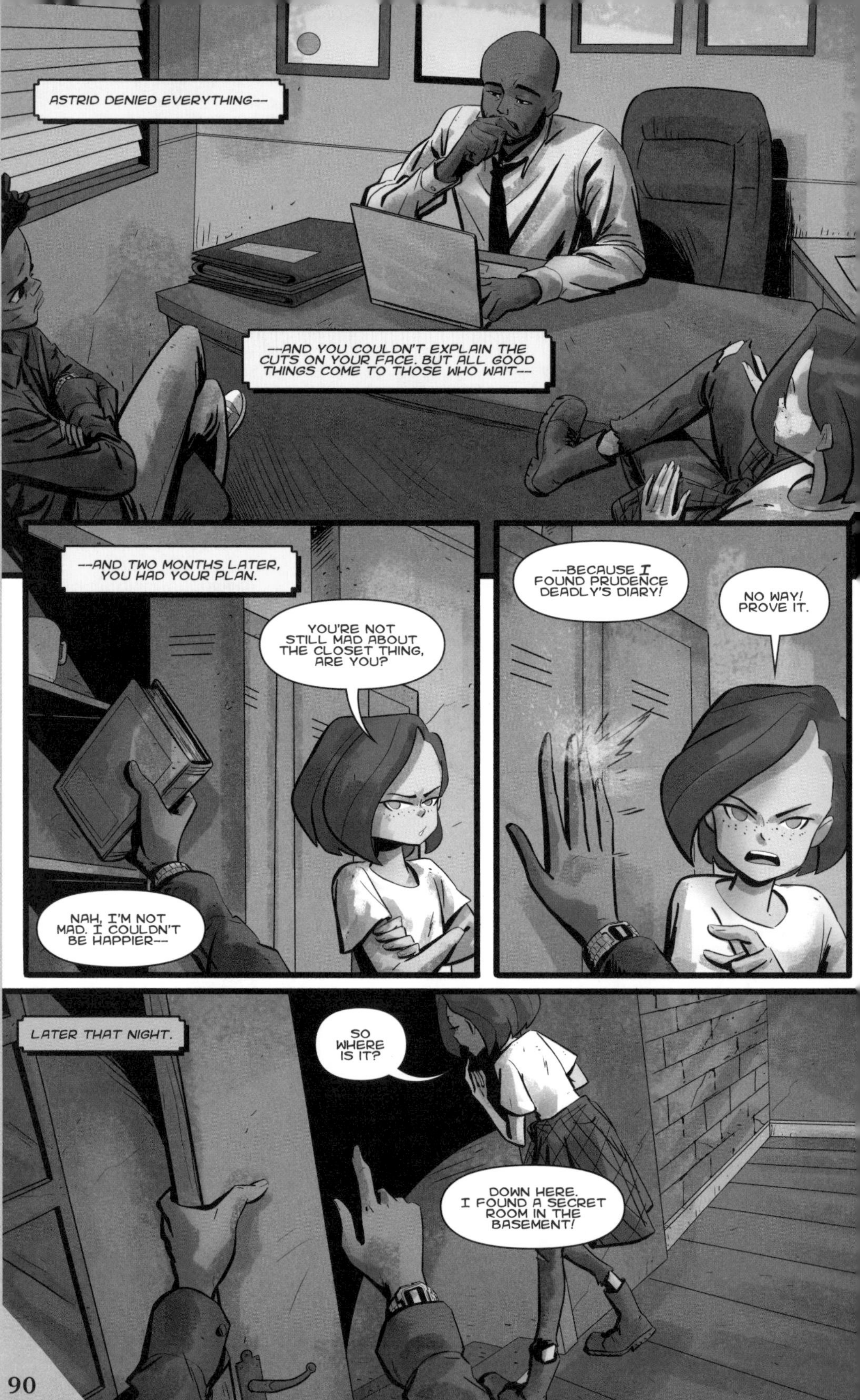
ASTRID DENIED EVERYTHING--
--AND YOU COULDN'T EXPLAIN THE CUTS ON YOUR FACE. BUT ALL GOOD THINGS COME TO THOSE WHO WAIT--
--AND TWO MONTHS LATER, YOU HAD YOUR PLAN.
YOU'RE NOT STILL MAD ABOUT THE CLOSET THING, ARE YOU?
NAH, I'M NOT MAD. I COULDN'T BE HAPPIER--
--BECAUSE I FOUND PRUDENCE DEADLY'S DIARY!
NO WAY! PROVE IT.
LATER THAT NIGHT.
SO WHERE IS IT?
DOWN HERE. I FOUND A SECRET ROOM IN THE BASEMENT!

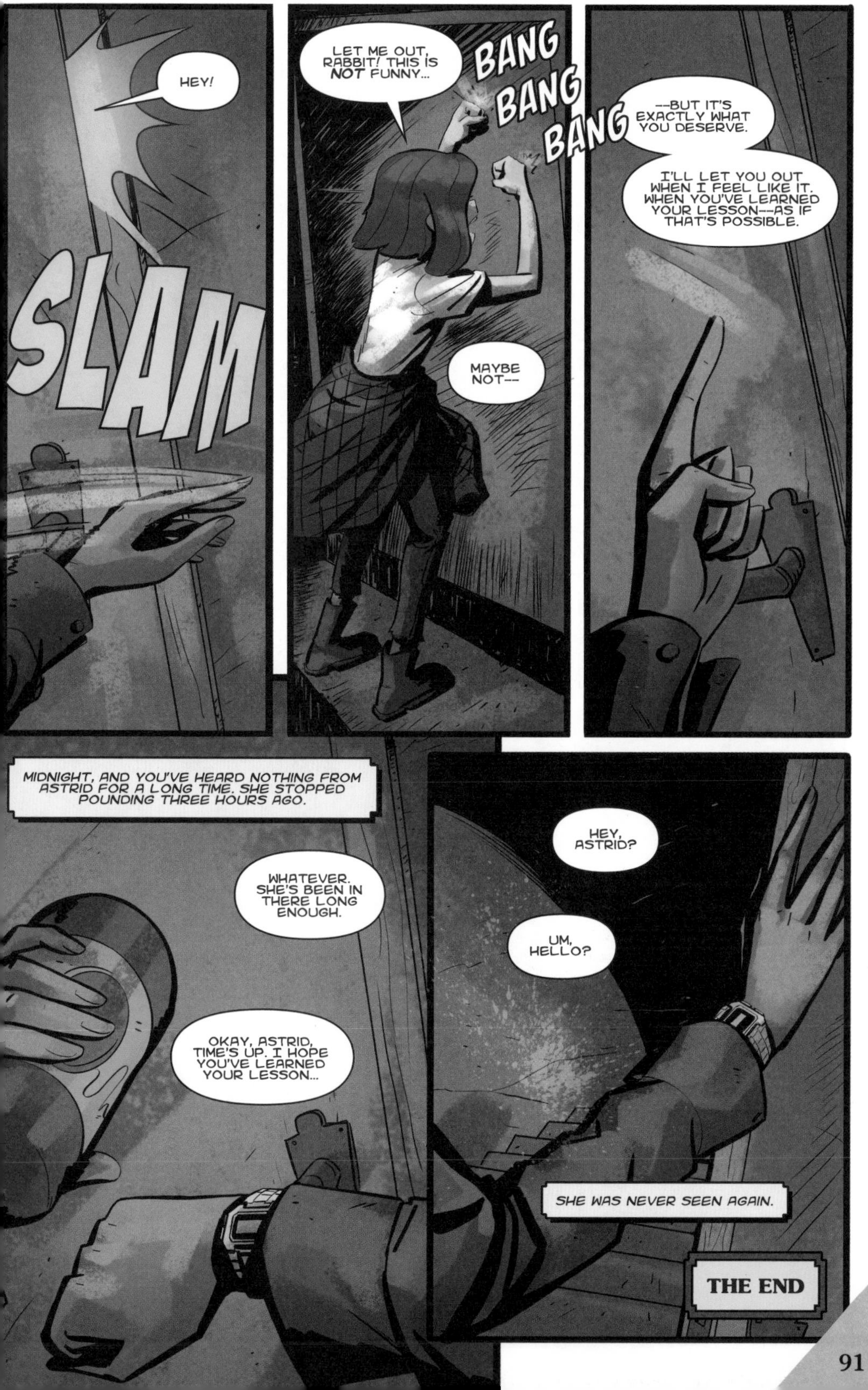
HEY!
SLAM
LET ME OUT, RABBIT! THIS IS NOT FUNNY...
BANG BANG BANG
MAYBE NOT--
--BUT IT'S EXACTLY WHAT YOU DESERVE.
I'LL LET YOU OUT WHEN I FEEL LIKE IT. WHEN YOU'VE LEARNED YOUR LESSON--AS IF THAT'S POSSIBLE.
MIDNIGHT, AND YOU'VE HEARD NOTHING FROM ASTRID FOR A LONG TIME. SHE STOPPED POUNDING THREE HOURS AGO.
WHATEVER. SHE'S BEEN IN THERE LONG ENOUGH.
OKAY, ASTRID, TIME'S UP. I HOPE YOU'VE LEARNED YOUR LESSON...
HEY, ASTRID?
UM, HELLO?
SHE WAS NEVER SEEN AGAIN.
THE END

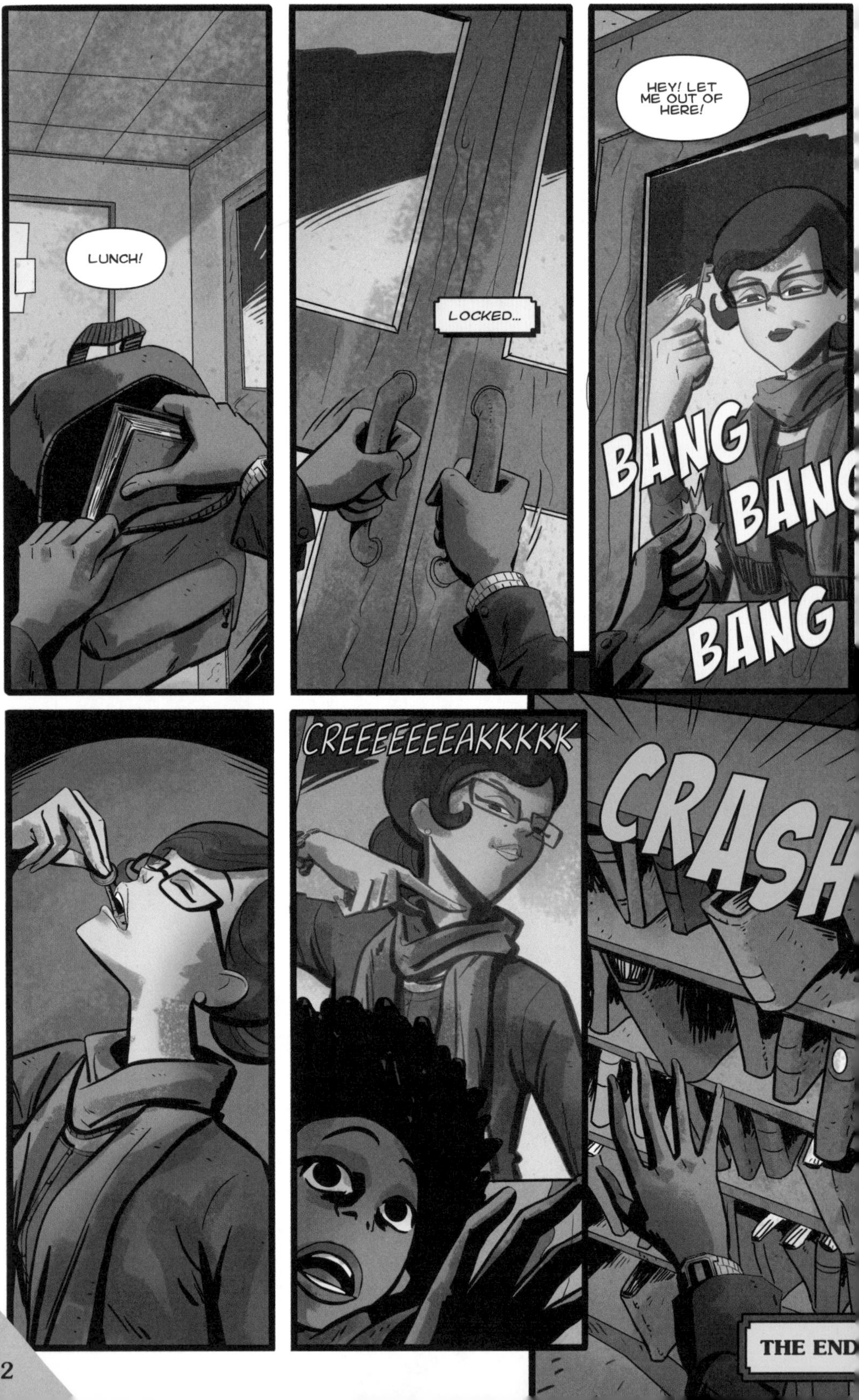
LUNCH!
LOCKED...
HEY! LET ME OUT OF HERE!
BANG
BANG
BANG
CREEEEEEEEAKKKKK
CRASH
THE END

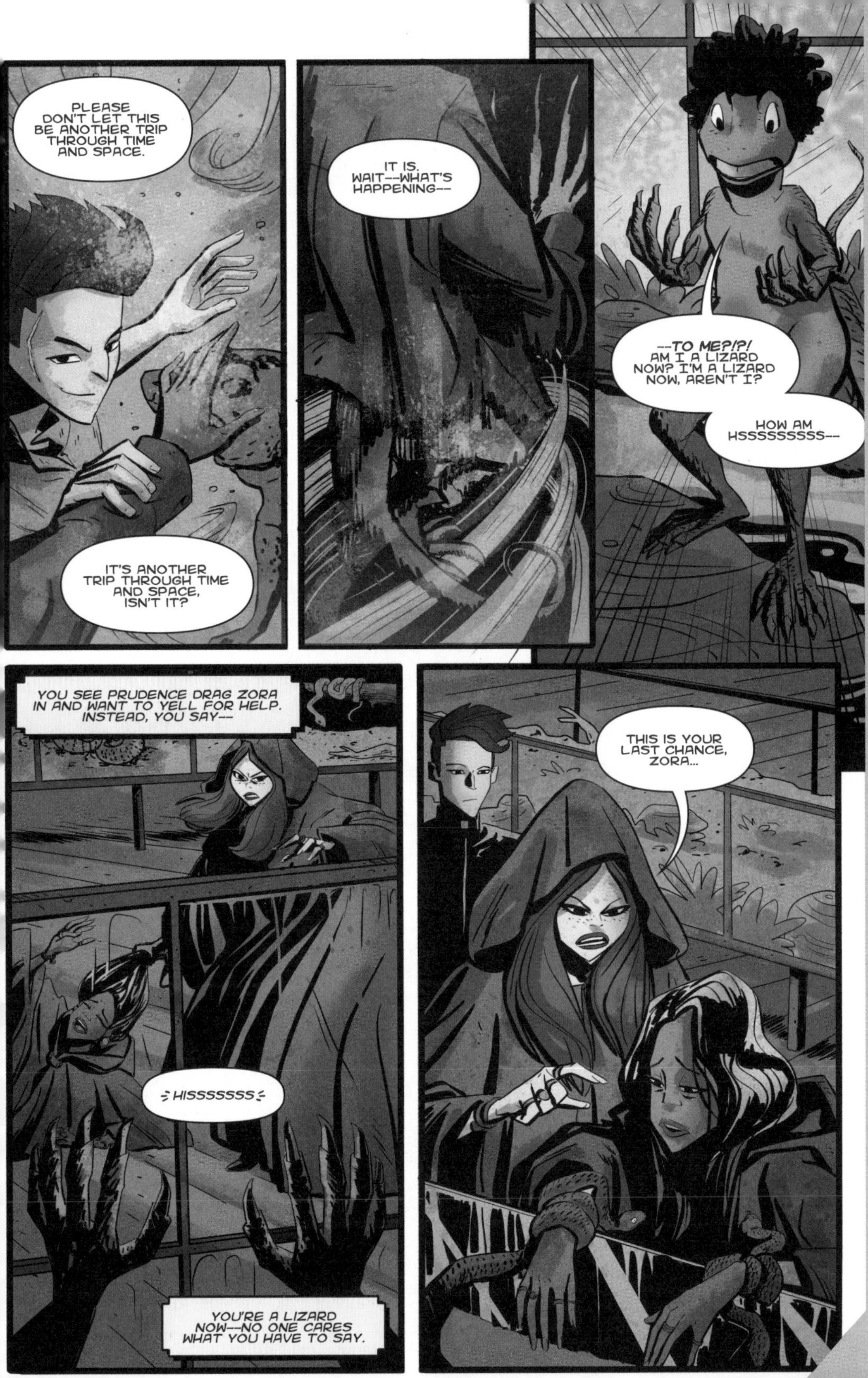
PLEASE DON'T LET THIS BE ANOTHER TRIP THROUGH TIME AND SPACE.
IT'S ANOTHER TRIP THROUGH TIME AND SPACE, ISN'T IT?
IT IS. WAIT--WHAT'S HAPPENING--
--TO ME?!?! AM I A LIZARD NOW? I'M A LIZARD NOW, AREN'T I?
HOW AM HSSSSSSSS--
YOU SEE PRUDENCE DRAG ZORA IN AND WANT TO YELL FOR HELP. INSTEAD, YOU SAY--
HISSSSSSS
YOU'RE A LIZARD NOW--NO ONE CARES WHAT YOU HAVE TO SAY.
THIS IS YOUR LAST CHANCE, ZORA...

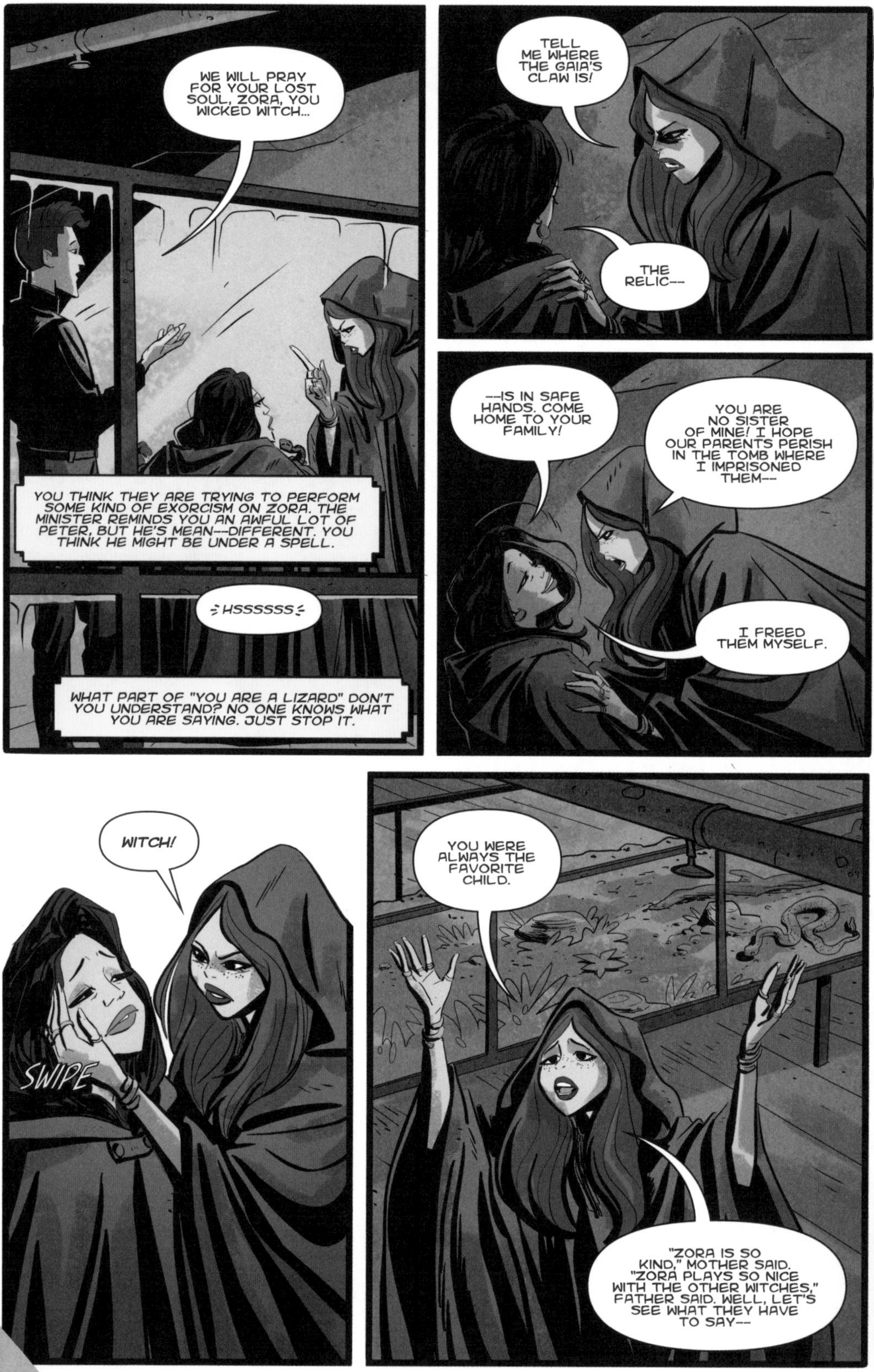
WE WILL PRAY FOR YOUR LOST SOUL, ZORA, YOU WICKED WITCH...
YOU THINK THEY ARE TRYING TO PERFORM SOME KIND OF EXORCISM ON ZORA. THE MINISTER REMINDS YOU AN AWFUL LOT OF PETER, BUT HE'S MEAN--DIFFERENT. YOU THINK HE MIGHT BE UNDER A SPELL.
HSSSSSS
WHAT PART OF "YOU ARE A LIZARD" DON'T YOU UNDERSTAND? NO ONE KNOWS WHAT YOU ARE SAYING. JUST STOP IT.
TELL ME WHERE THE GAIA'S CLAW IS!
THE RELIC--
--IS IN SAFE HANDS. COME HOME TO YOUR FAMILY!
YOU ARE NO SISTER OF MINE! I HOPE OUR PARENTS PERISH IN THE TOMB WHERE I IMPRISONED THEM--
I FREED THEM MYSELF.
WITCH!
SWIPE
YOU WERE ALWAYS THE FAVORITE CHILD.
"ZORA IS SO KIND," MOTHER SAID. "ZORA PLAYS SO NICE WITH THE OTHER WITCHES," FATHER SAID. WELL, LET'S SEE WHAT THEY HAVE TO SAY--

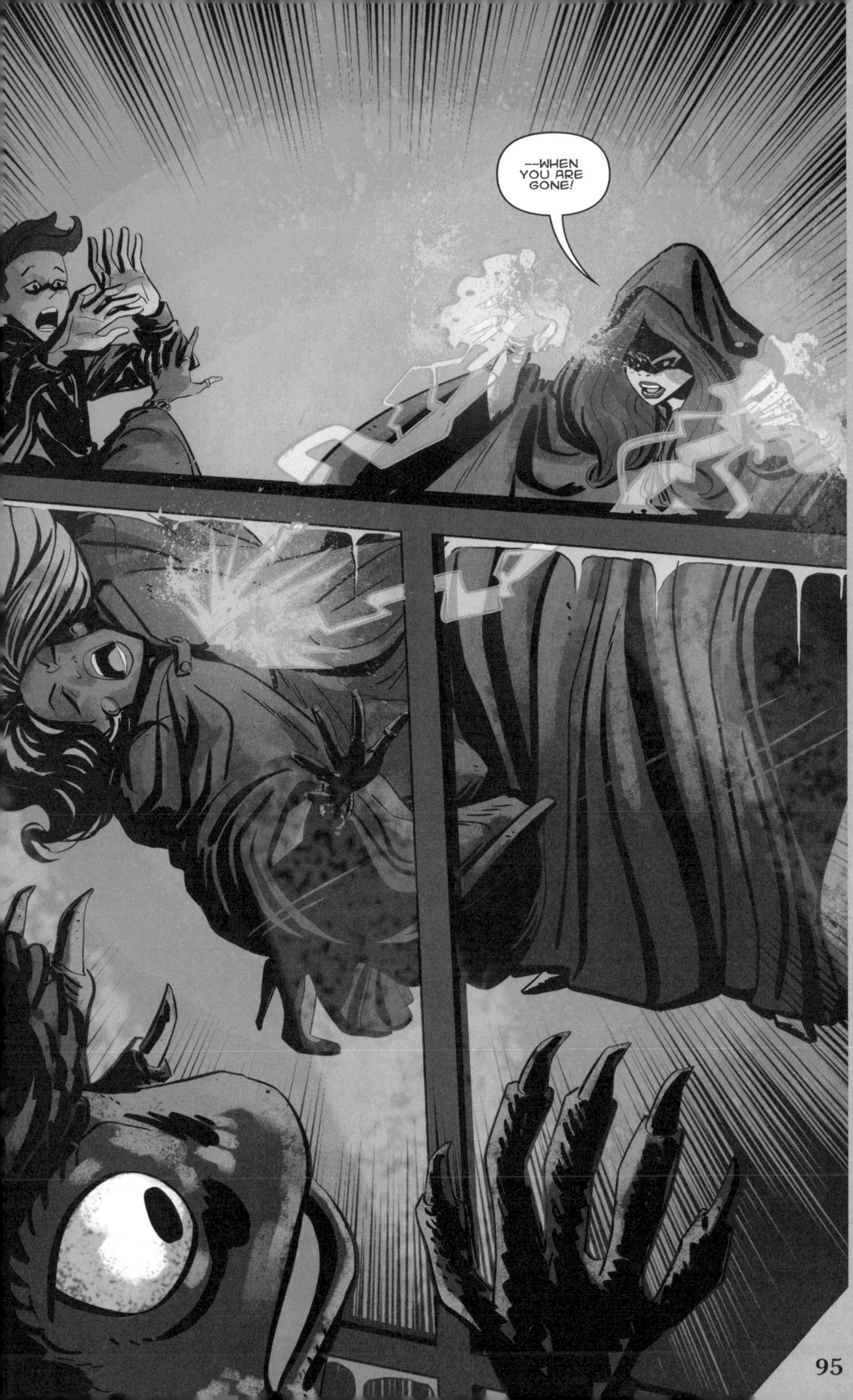
--WHEN YOU ARE GONE!

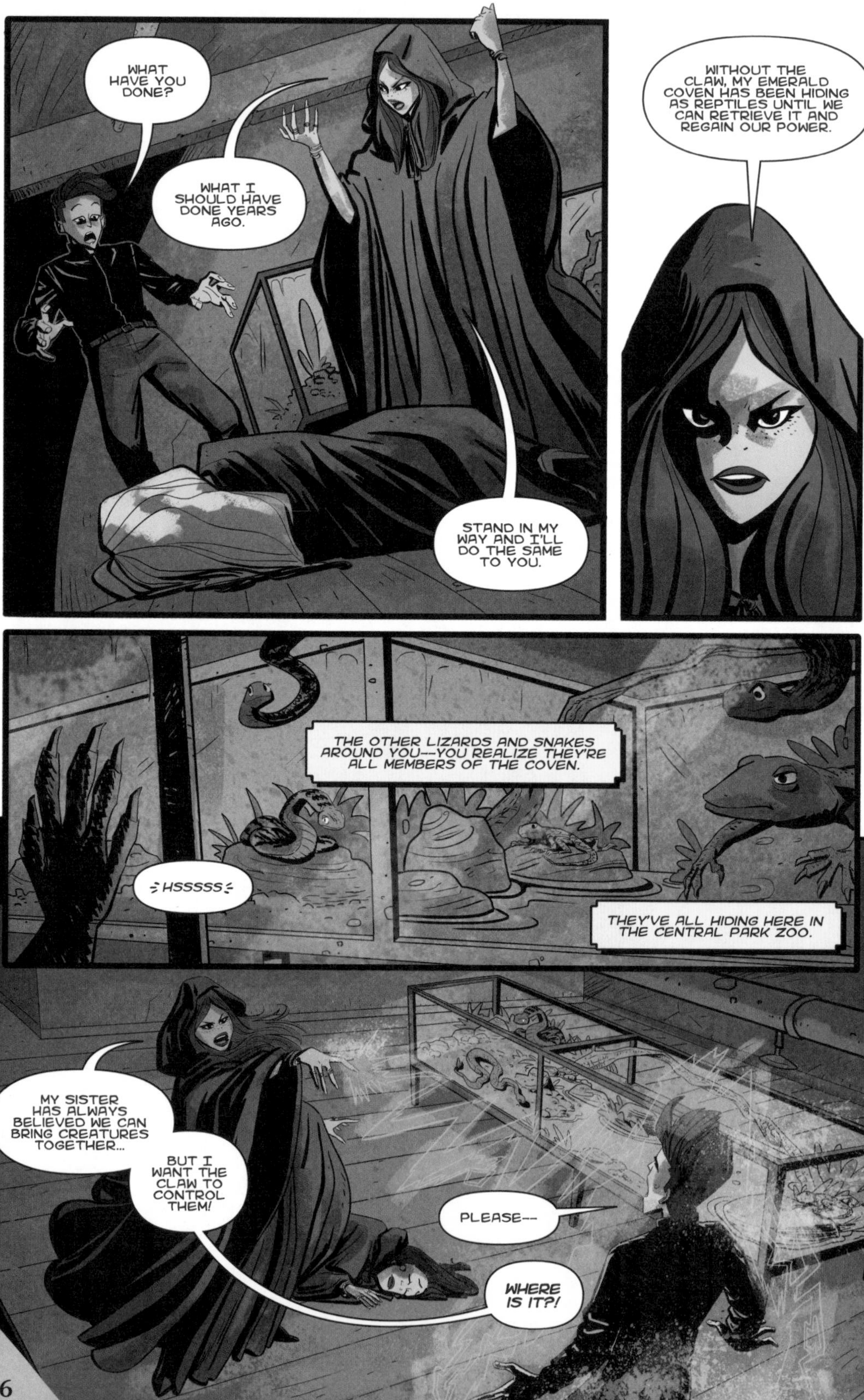
WHAT HAVE YOU DONE?
WHAT I SHOULD HAVE DONE YEARS AGO.
STAND IN MY WAY AND I'LL DO THE SAME TO YOU.
WITHOUT THE CLAW, MY EMERALD COVEN HAS BEEN HIDING AS REPTILES UNTIL WE CAN RETRIEVE IT AND REGAIN OUR POWER.
THE OTHER LIZARDS AND SNAKES AROUND YOU--YOU REALIZE THEY'RE ALL MEMBERS OF THE COVEN.
HSSSSS
THEY'VE ALL HIDING HERE IN THE CENTRAL PARK ZOO.
MY SISTER HAS ALWAYS BELIEVED WE CAN BRING CREATURES TOGETHER...
BUT I WANT THE CLAW TO CONTROL THEM!
PLEASE--
WHERE IS IT?!

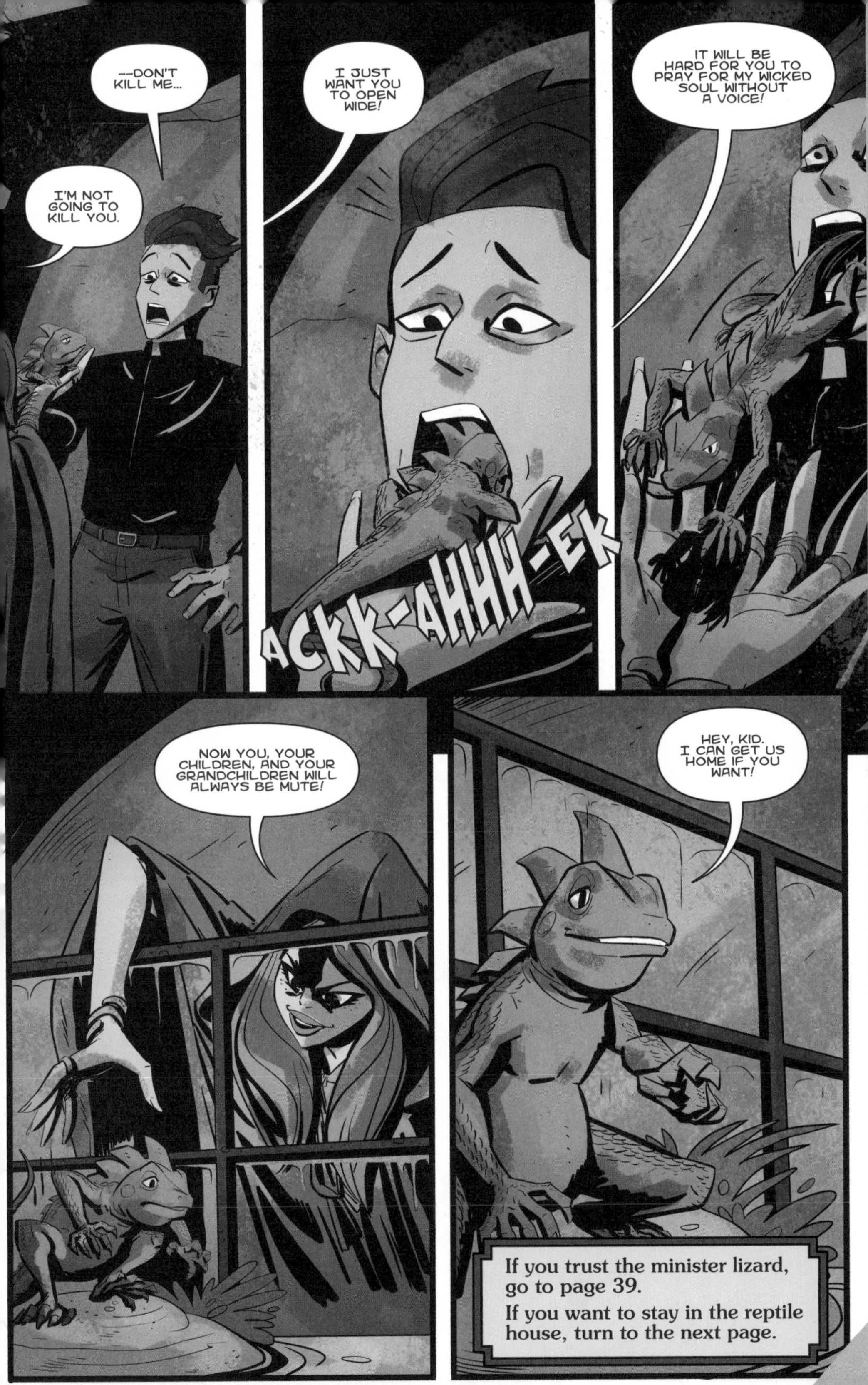
--DON'T KILL ME...
I'M NOT GOING TO KILL YOU.
I JUST WANT YOU TO OPEN WIDE!
ACKK-AHHH-EK
IT WILL BE HARD FOR YOU TO PRAY FOR MY WICKED SOUL WITHOUT A VOICE!
NOW YOU, YOUR CHILDREN, AND YOUR GRANDCHILDREN WILL ALWAYS BE MUTE!
HEY, KID. I CAN GET US HOME IF YOU WANT!

If you trust the minister lizard, go to page 39.
If you want to stay in the reptile house, turn to the next page.

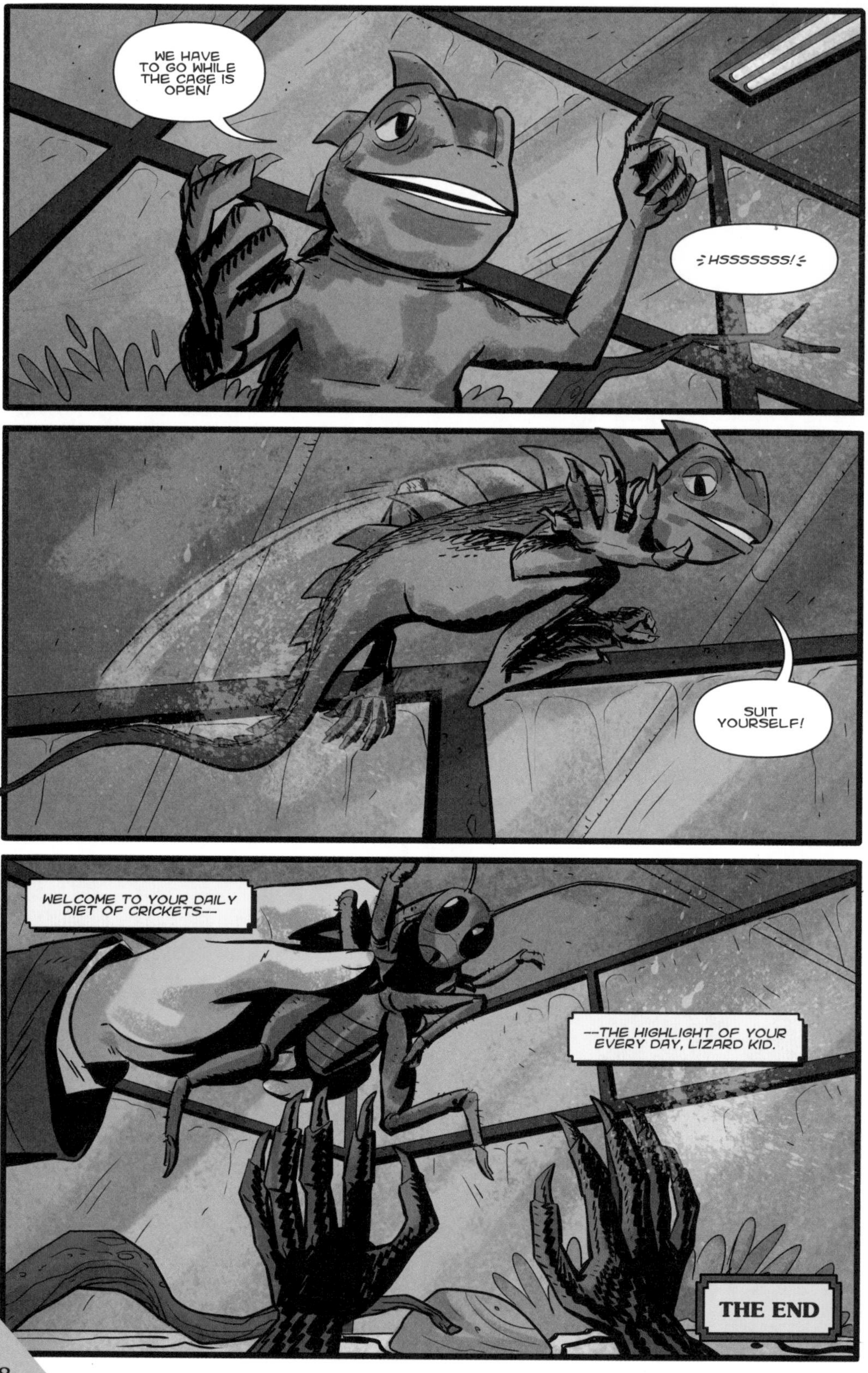
WE HAVE TO GO WHILE THE CAGE IS OPEN!
HSSSSSSS!
SUIT YOURSELF!
WELCOME TO YOUR DAILY DIET OF CRICKETS--
--THE HIGHLIGHT OF YOUR EVERY DAY, LIZARD KID.
THE END

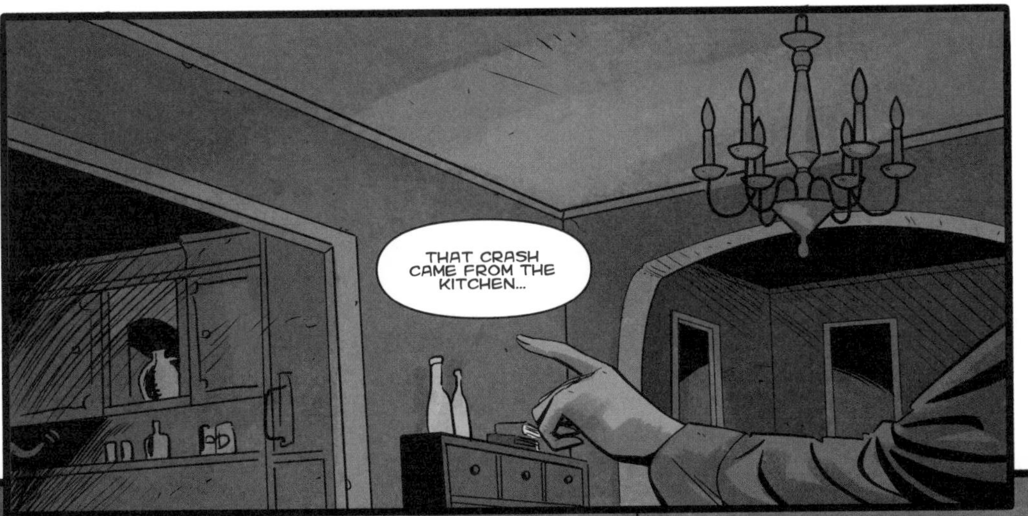
THAT CRASH CAME FROM THE KITCHEN...

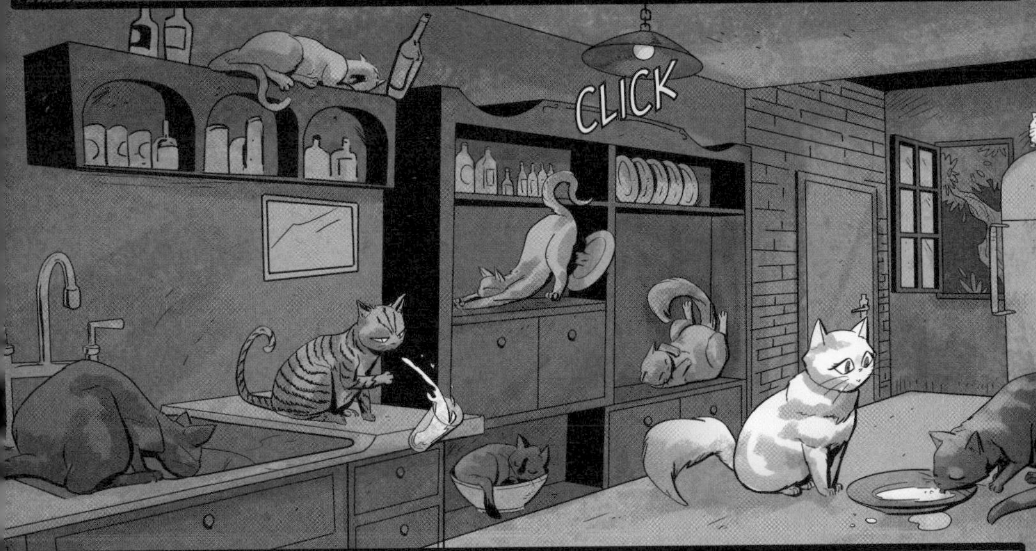
CLICK

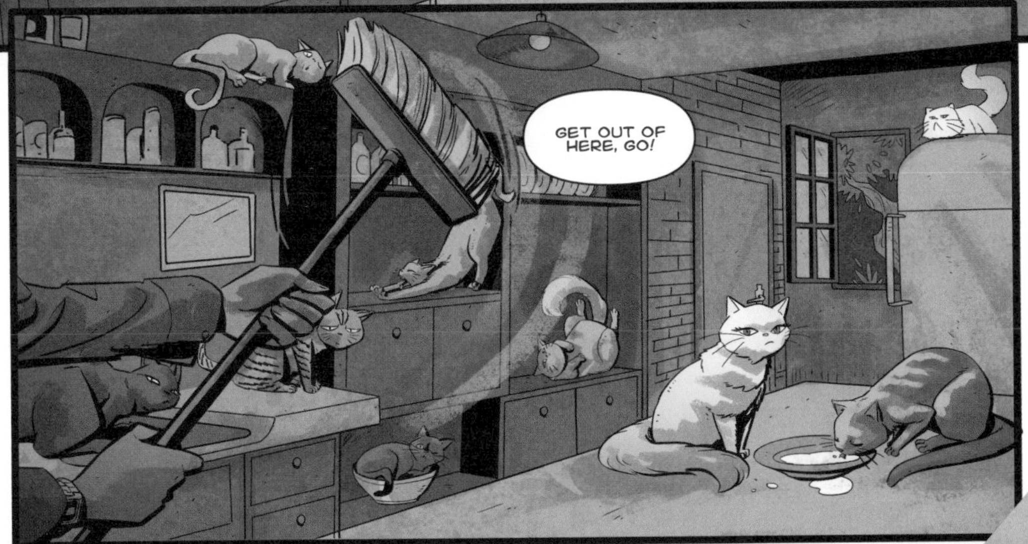
GET OUT OF HERE, GO!

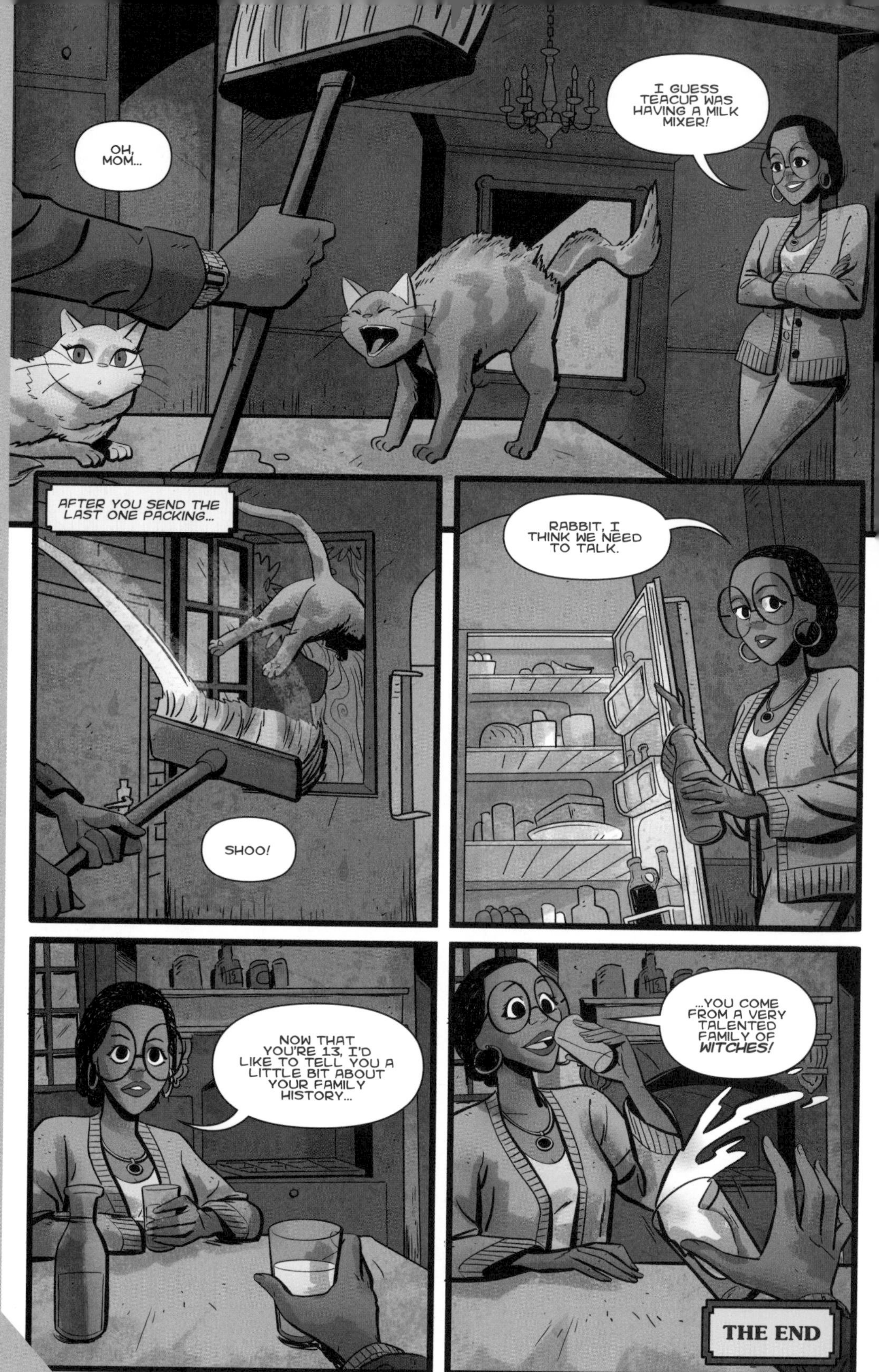
OH, MOM...
I GUESS TEACUP WAS HAVING A MILK MIXER!
AFTER YOU SEND THE LAST ONE PACKING...
SHOO!
RABBIT, I THINK WE NEED TO TALK.
NOW THAT YOU'RE 13, I'D LIKE TO TELL YOU A LITTLE BIT ABOUT YOUR FAMILY HISTORY...
...YOU COME FROM A VERY TALENTED FAMILY OF *WITCHES!*
THE END

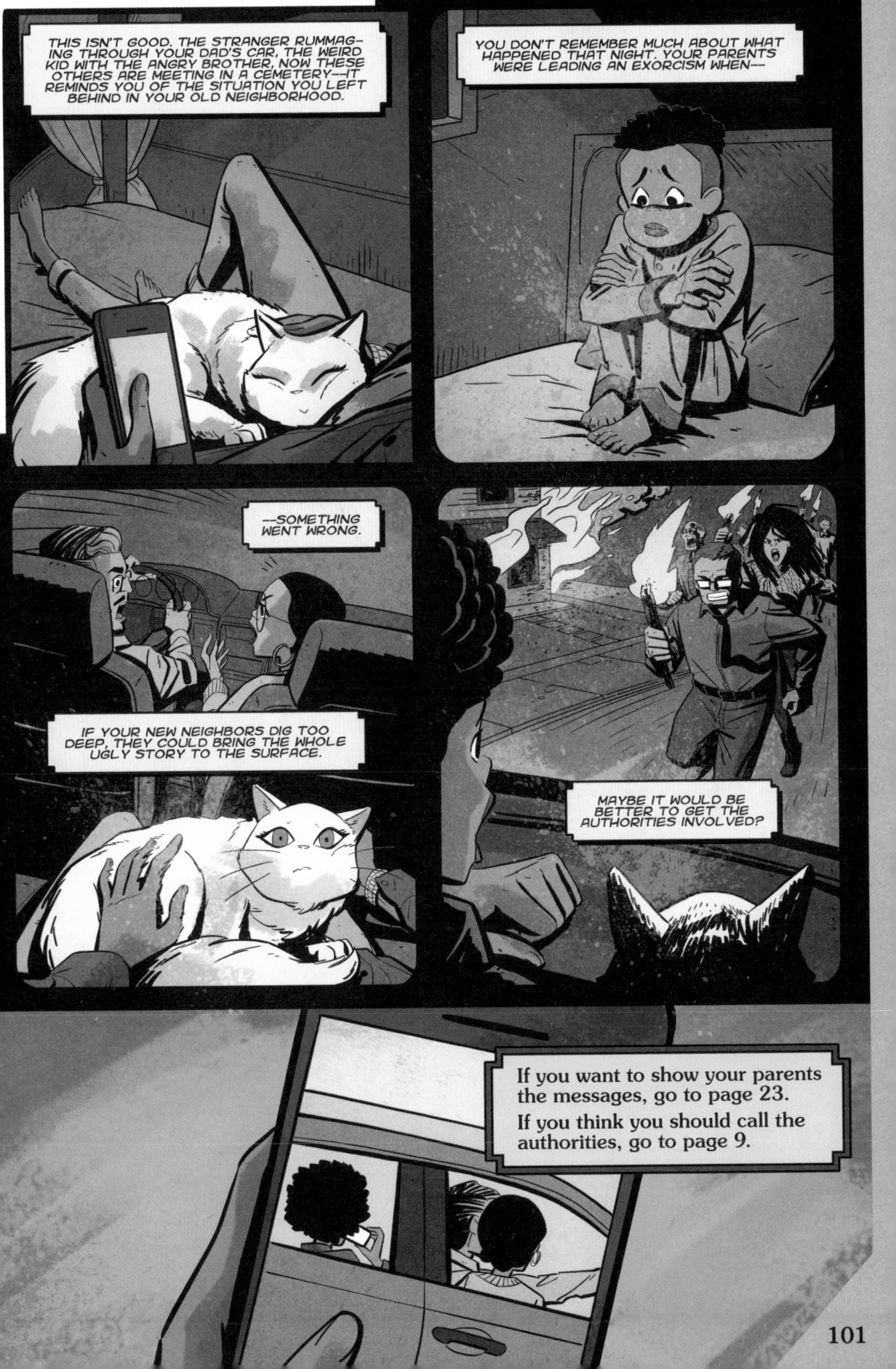
THIS ISN'T GOOD. THE STRANGER RUMMAGING THROUGH YOUR DAD'S CAR, THE WEIRD KID WITH THE ANGRY BROTHER, NOW THESE OTHERS ARE MEETING IN A CEMETERY--IT REMINDS YOU OF THE SITUATION YOU LEFT BEHIND IN YOUR OLD NEIGHBORHOOD.
YOU DON'T REMEMBER MUCH ABOUT WHAT HAPPENED THAT NIGHT. YOUR PARENTS WERE LEADING AN EXORCISM WHEN--
--SOMETHING WENT WRONG.
IF YOUR NEW NEIGHBORS DIG TOO DEEP, THEY COULD BRING THE WHOLE UGLY STORY TO THE SURFACE.
MAYBE IT WOULD BE BETTER TO GET THE AUTHORITIES INVOLVED?
If you want to show your parents the messages, go to page 23.
If you think you should call the authorities, go to page 9.

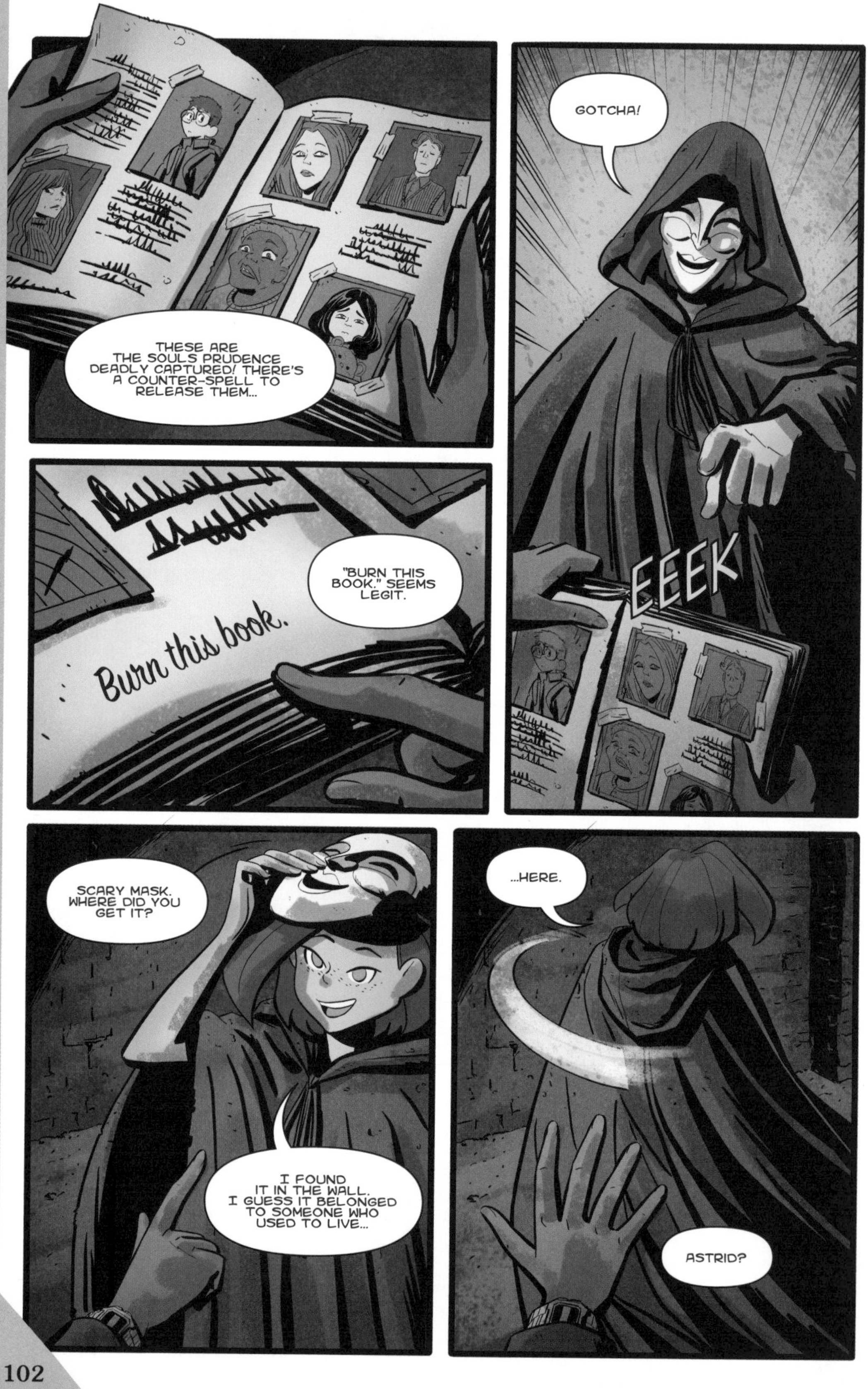
THESE ARE THE SOULS PRUDENCE DEADLY CAPTURED! THERE'S A COUNTER-SPELL TO RELEASE THEM...
GOTCHA!
Burn this book.
"BURN THIS BOOK." SEEMS LEGIT.
EEEK
SCARY MASK. WHERE DID YOU GET IT?
I FOUND IT IN THE WALL. I GUESS IT BELONGED TO SOMEONE WHO USED TO LIVE...
...HERE.
ASTRID?

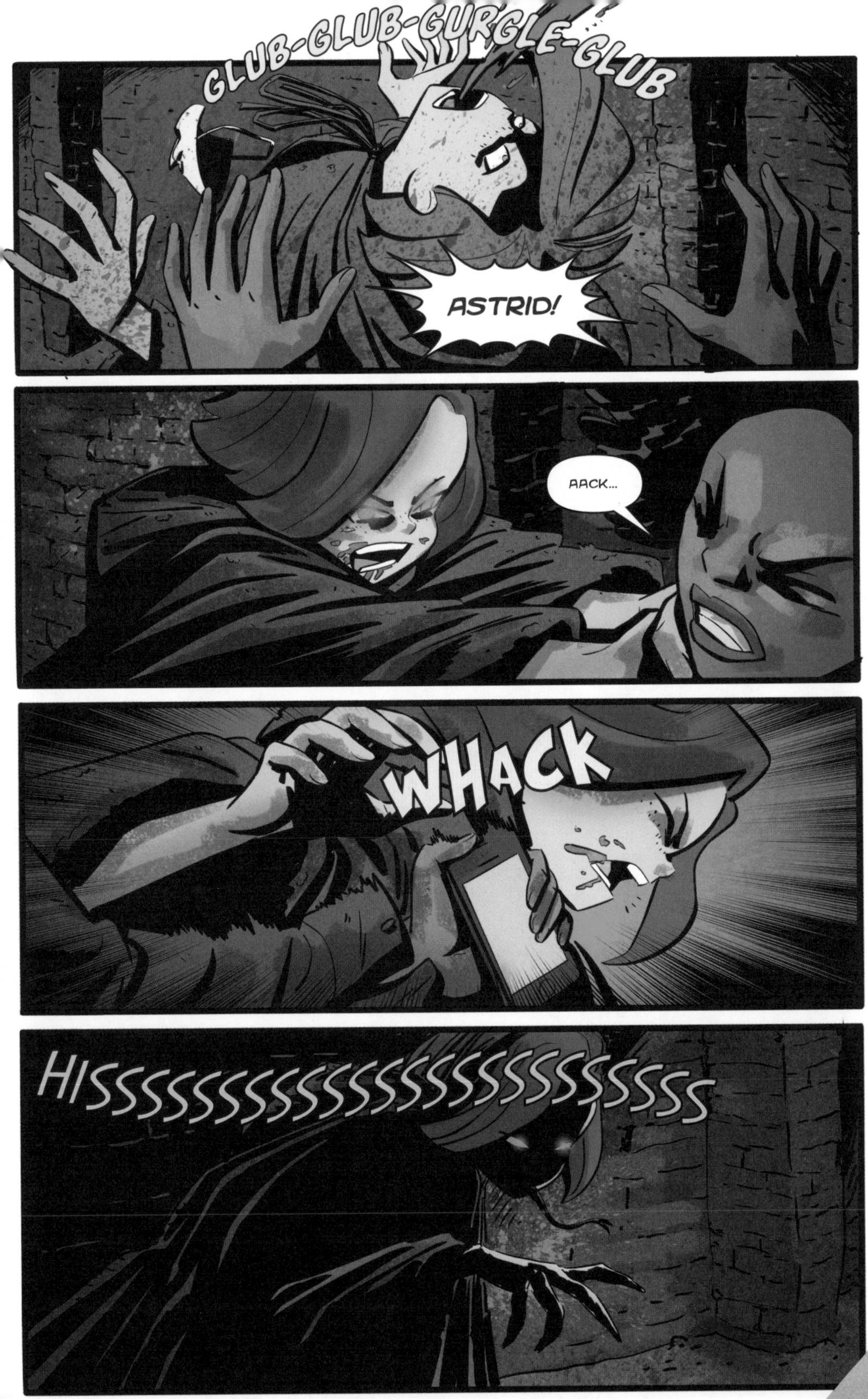
GLUB-GLUB-GURGLE-GLUB
ASTRID!
AACK...
WHACK
HISSSSSSSSSSSSSSSSSSSSSSS

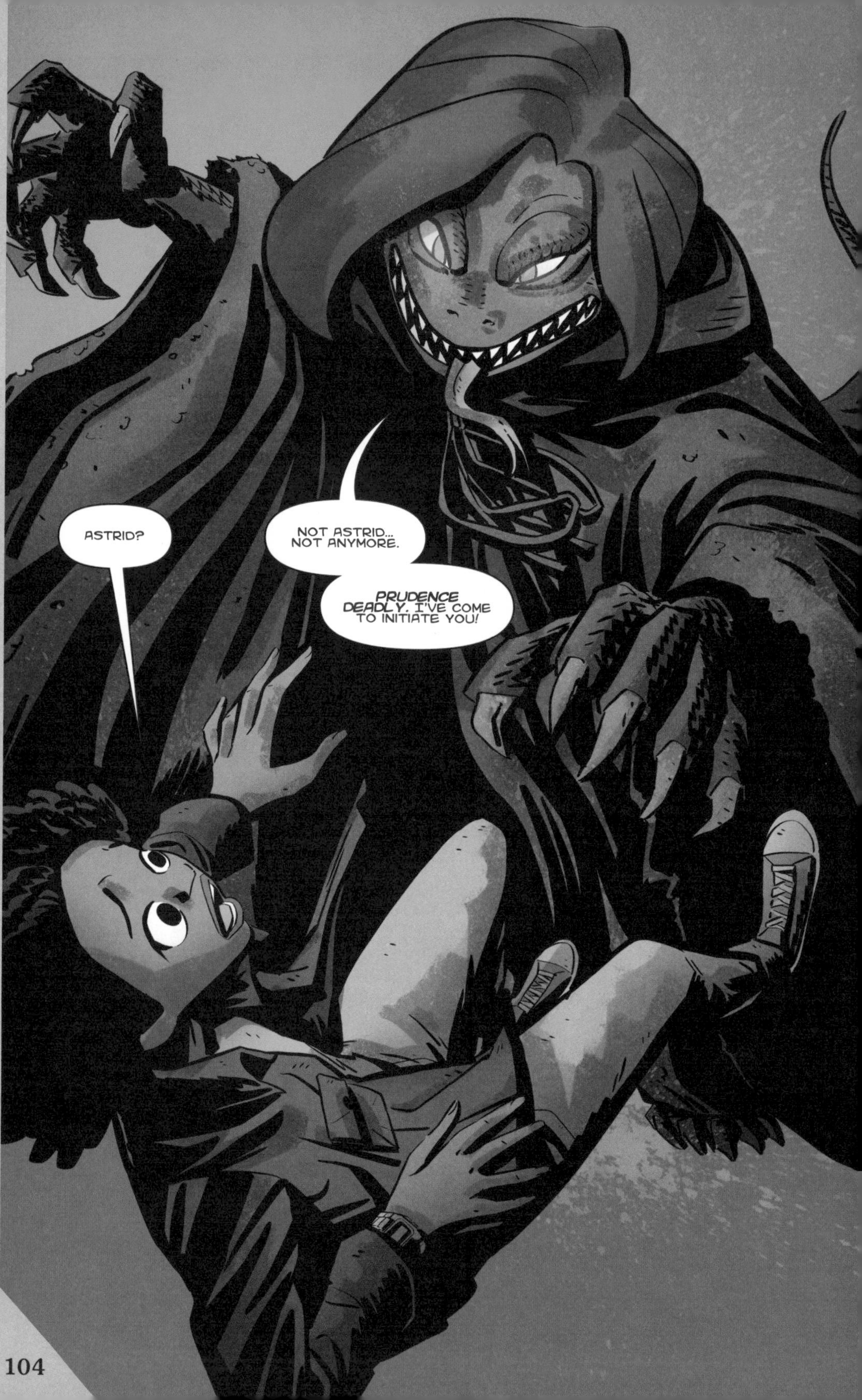
ASTRID?
NOT ASTRID... NOT ANYMORE.
PRUDENCE DEADLY. I'VE COME TO INITIATE YOU!

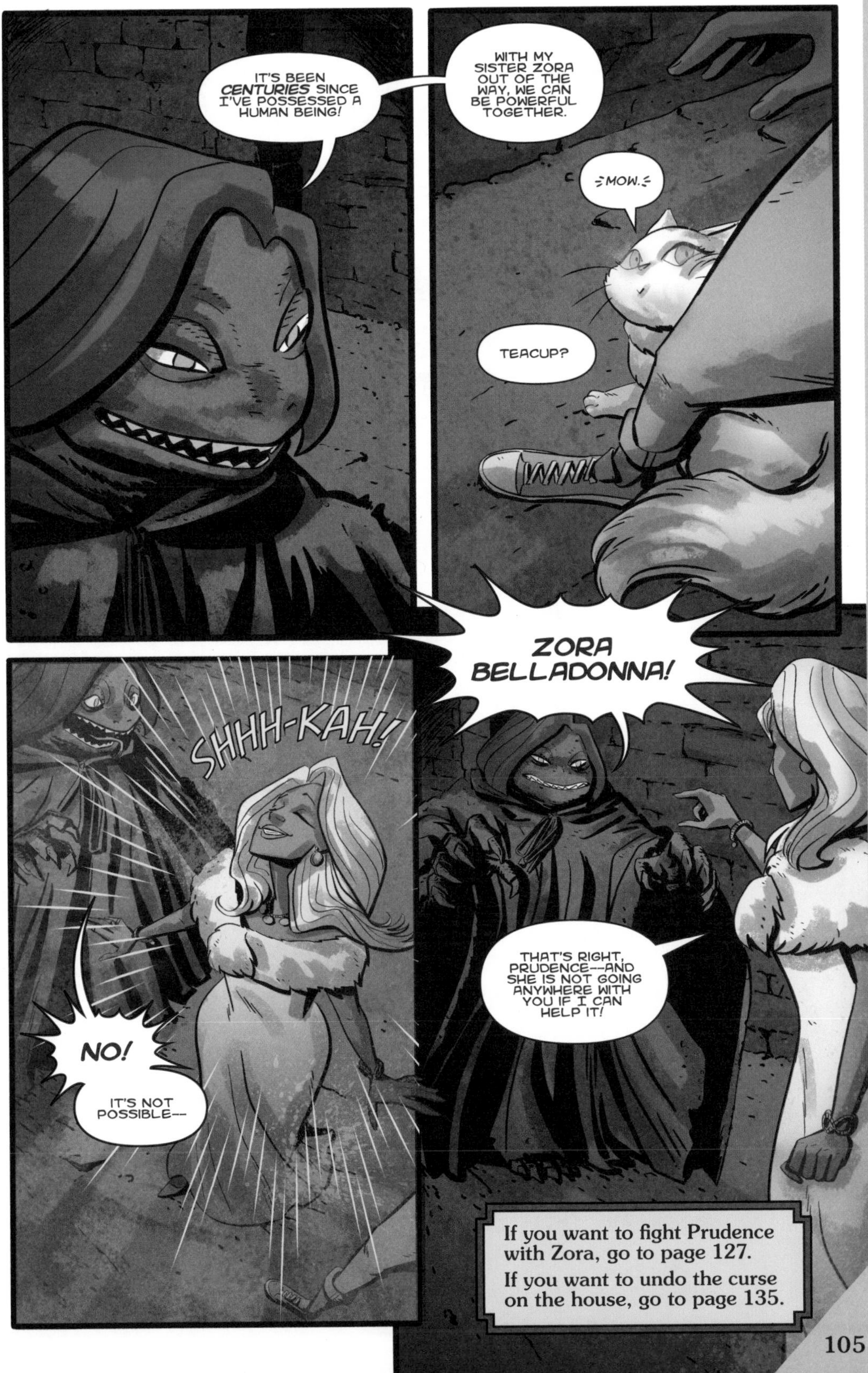
IT'S BEEN CENTURIES SINCE I'VE POSSESSED A HUMAN BEING!
WITH MY SISTER ZORA OUT OF THE WAY, WE CAN BE POWERFUL TOGETHER.
MOW.
TEACUP?
ZORA BELLADONNA!
SHHH-KAH!
NO!
IT'S NOT POSSIBLE--
THAT'S RIGHT, PRUDENCE--AND SHE IS NOT GOING ANYWHERE WITH YOU IF I CAN HELP IT!

If you want to fight Prudence with Zora, go to page 127.

If you want to undo the curse on the house, go to page 135.

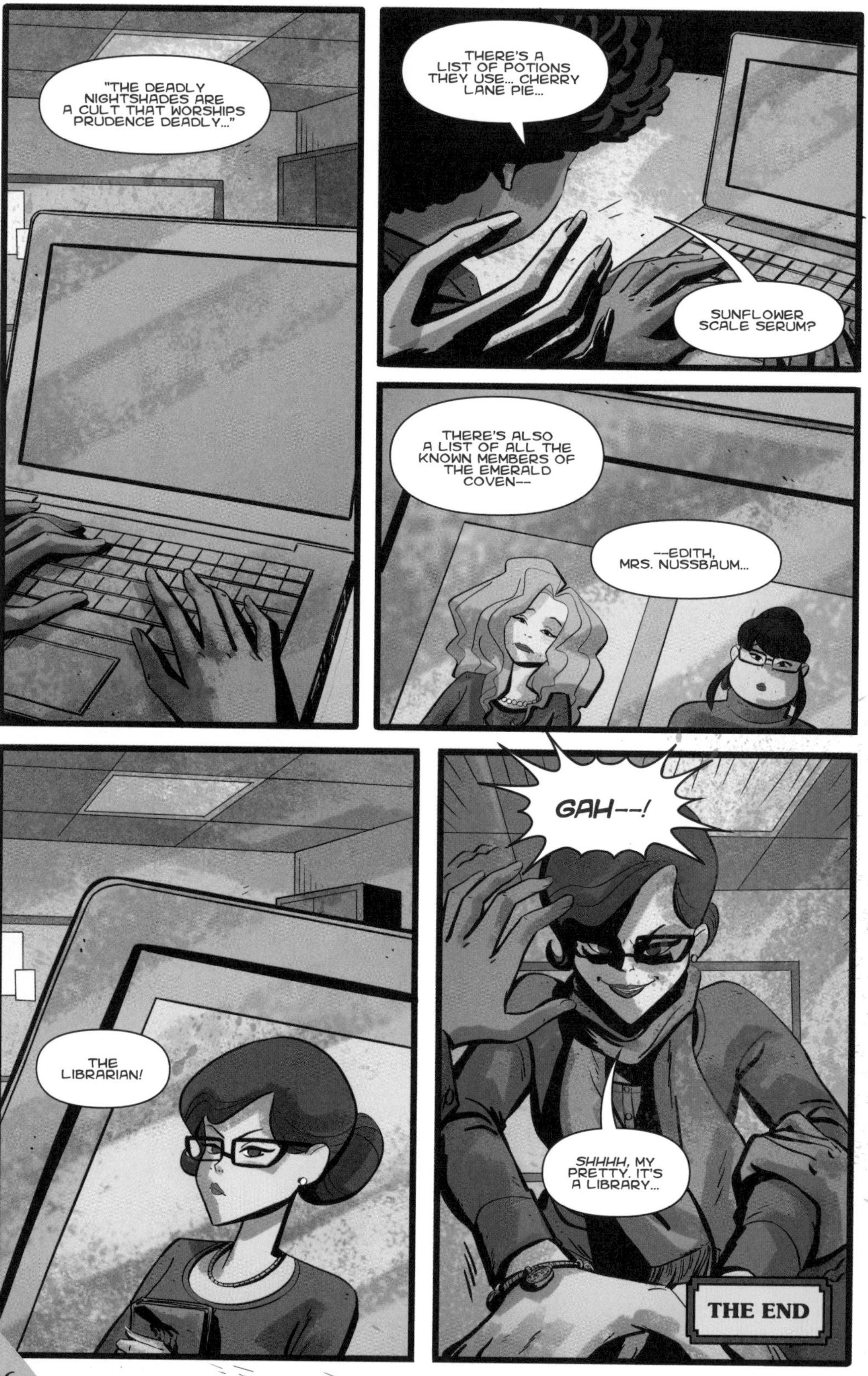
"THE DEADLY NIGHTSHADES ARE A CULT THAT WORSHIPS PRUDENCE DEADLY..."
THERE'S A LIST OF POTIONS THEY USE... CHERRY LANE PIE...
SUNFLOWER SCALE SERUM?
THERE'S ALSO A LIST OF ALL THE KNOWN MEMBERS OF THE EMERALD COVEN--
--EDITH, MRS. NUSSBAUM...
THE LIBRARIAN!
GAH--!
SHHHH, MY PRETTY. IT'S A LIBRARY...
THE END

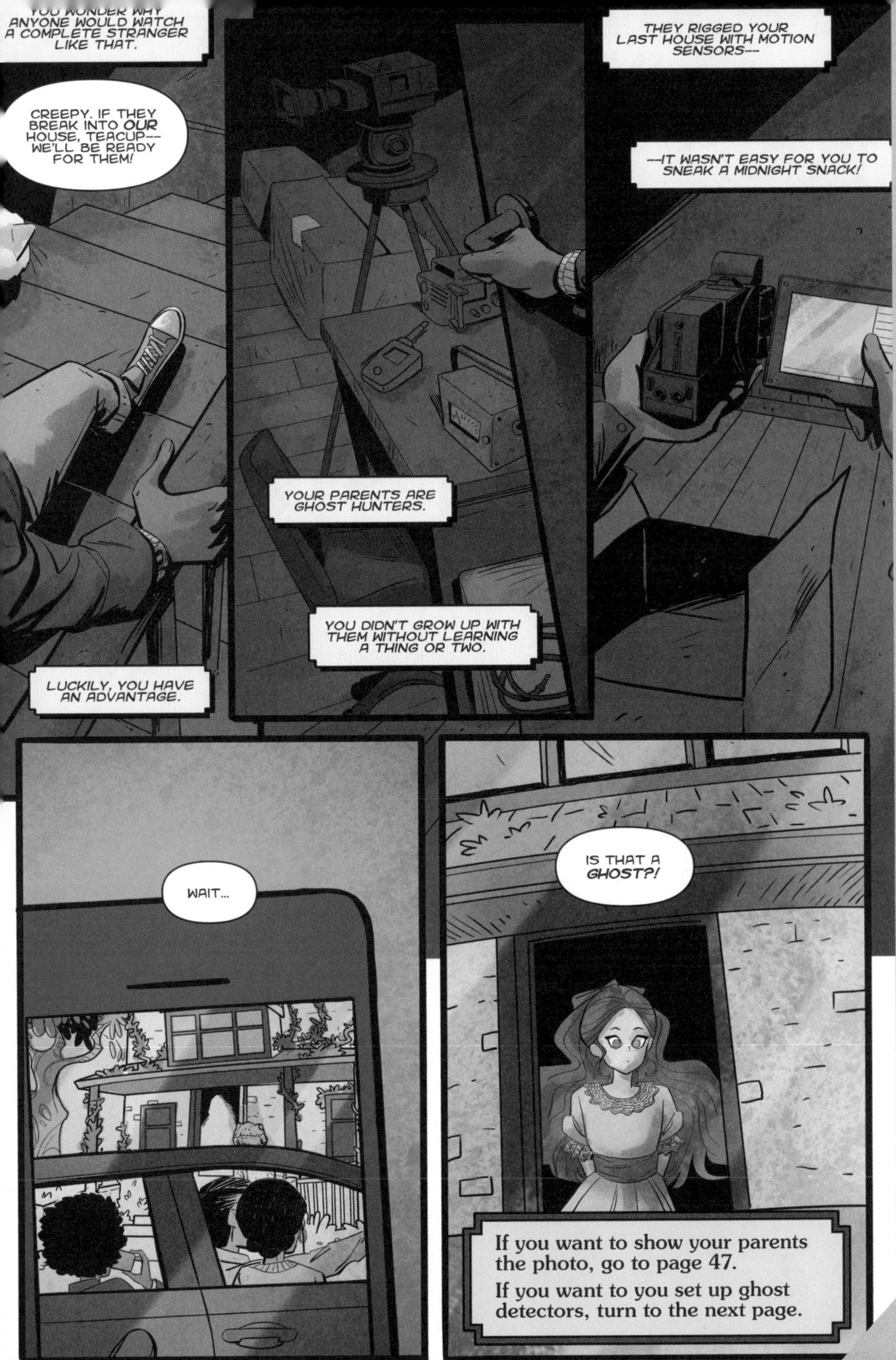
YOU WONDER WHY ANYONE WOULD WATCH A COMPLETE STRANGER LIKE THAT.
CREEPY. IF THEY BREAK INTO OUR HOUSE, TEACUP--WE'LL BE READY FOR THEM!
LUCKILY, YOU HAVE AN ADVANTAGE.
YOUR PARENTS ARE GHOST HUNTERS.
YOU DIDN'T GROW UP WITH THEM WITHOUT LEARNING A THING OR TWO.
THEY RIGGED YOUR LAST HOUSE WITH MOTION SENSORS--
--IT WASN'T EASY FOR YOU TO SNEAK A MIDNIGHT SNACK!
WAIT...
IS THAT A GHOST?!
If you want to show your parents the photo, go to page 47.
If you want to you set up ghost detectors, turn to the next page.

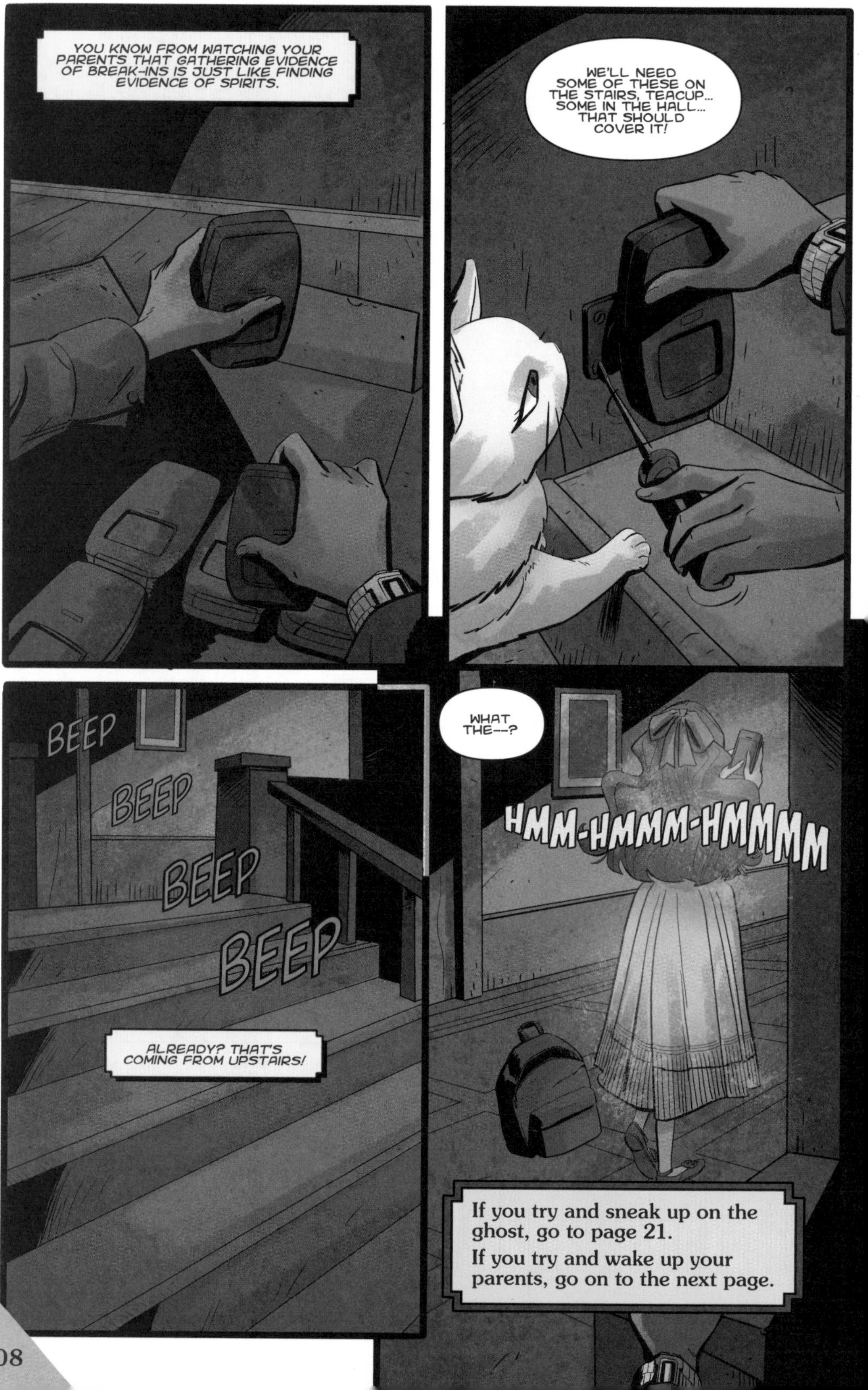
YOU KNOW FROM WATCHING YOUR PARENTS THAT GATHERING EVIDENCE OF BREAK-INS IS JUST LIKE FINDING EVIDENCE OF SPIRITS.
WE'LL NEED SOME OF THESE ON THE STAIRS, TEACUP... SOME IN THE HALL... THAT SHOULD COVER IT!
BEEP
BEEP
BEEP
BEEP
ALREADY? THAT'S COMING FROM UPSTAIRS!
WHAT THE--?
HMM-HMMM-HMMMM

If you try and sneak up on the ghost, go to page 21.
If you try and wake up your parents, go on to the next page.

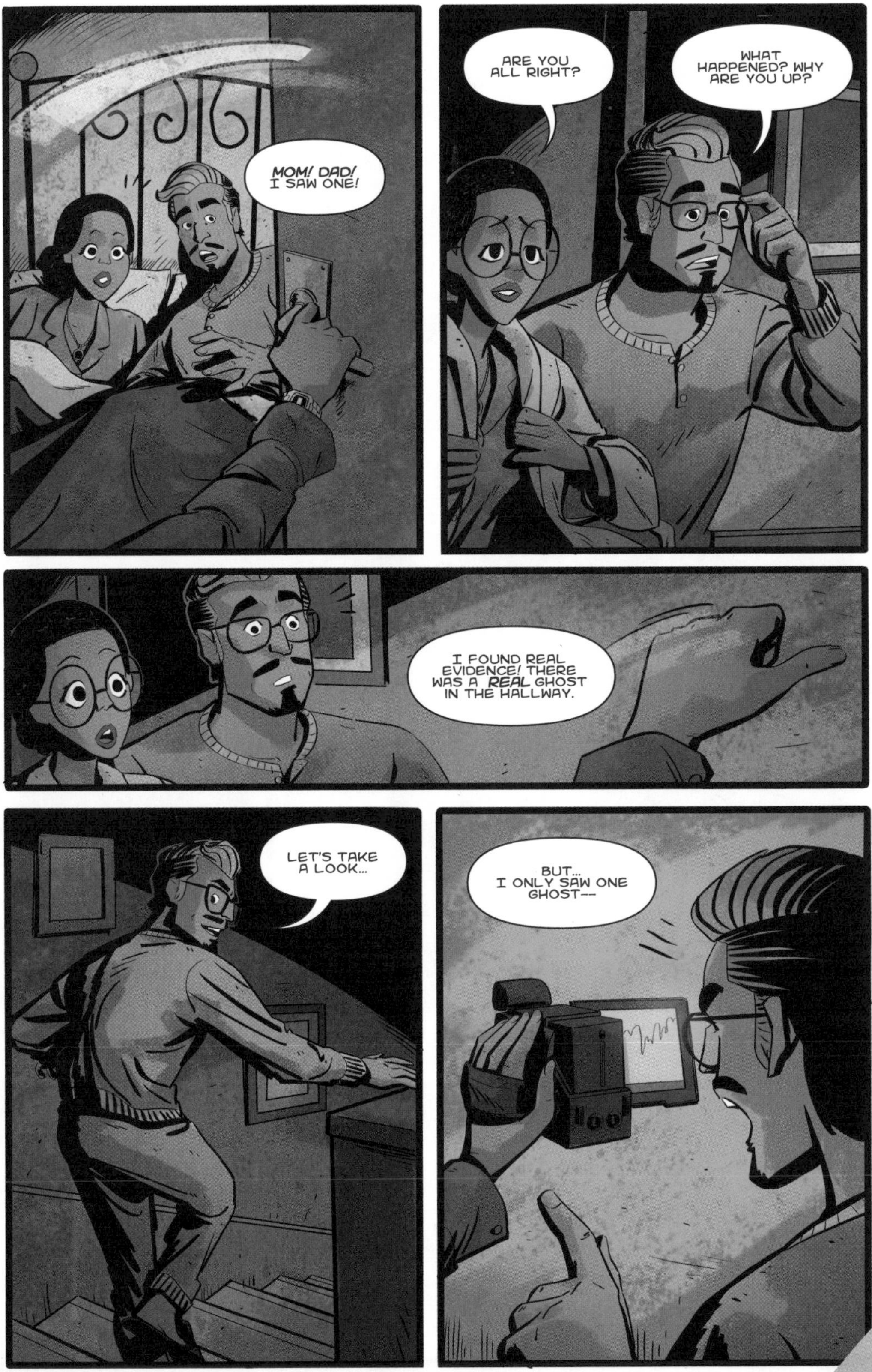
MOM! DAD! I SAW ONE!
ARE YOU ALL RIGHT?
WHAT HAPPENED? WHY ARE YOU UP?
I FOUND REAL EVIDENCE! THERE WAS A REAL GHOST IN THE HALLWAY.
LET'S TAKE A LOOK...
BUT... I ONLY SAW ONE GHOST--

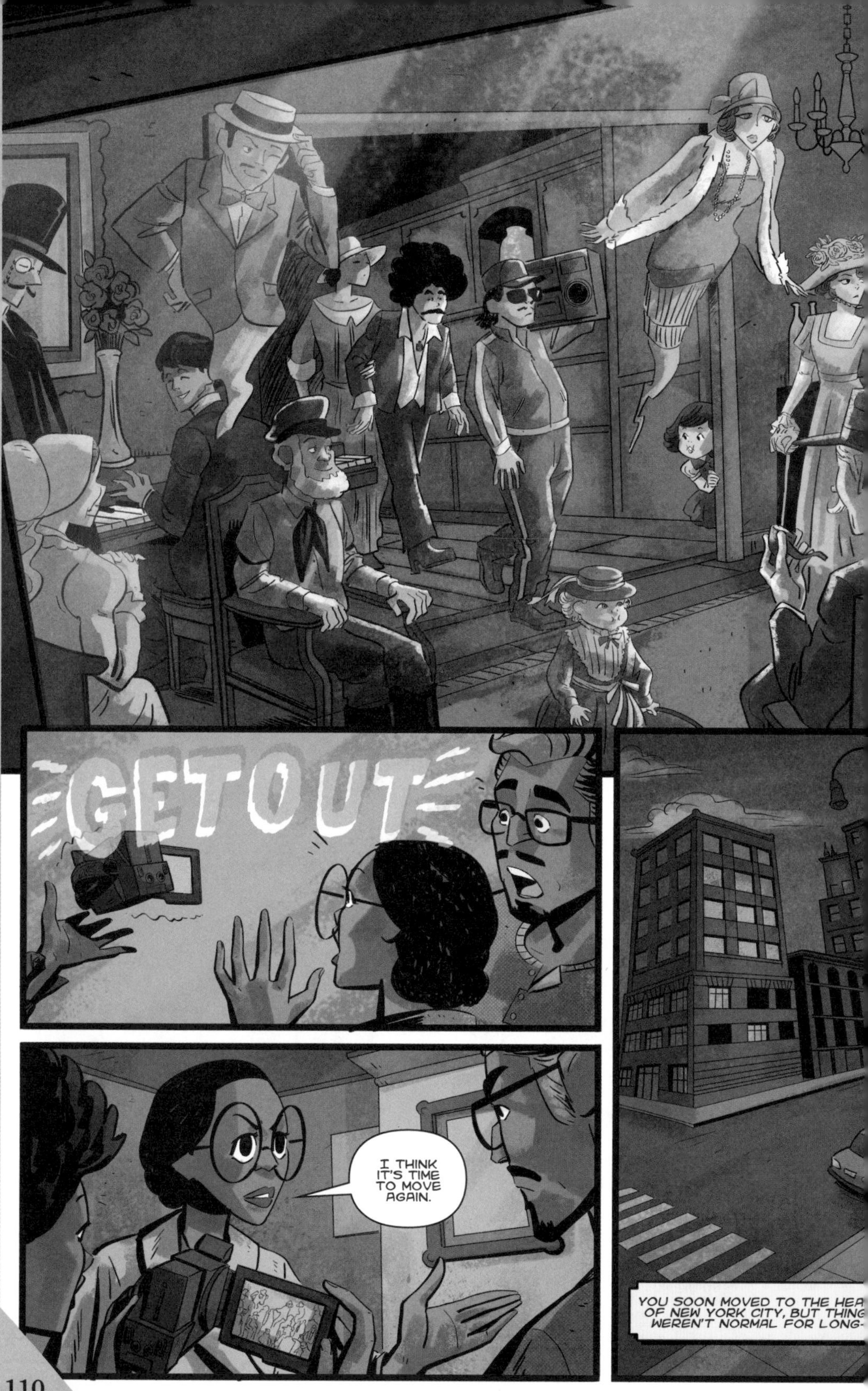
GET OUT
I THINK IT'S TIME TO MOVE AGAIN.
YOU SOON MOVED TO THE HEA
OF NEW YORK CITY, BUT THING
WEREN'T NORMAL FOR LONG-

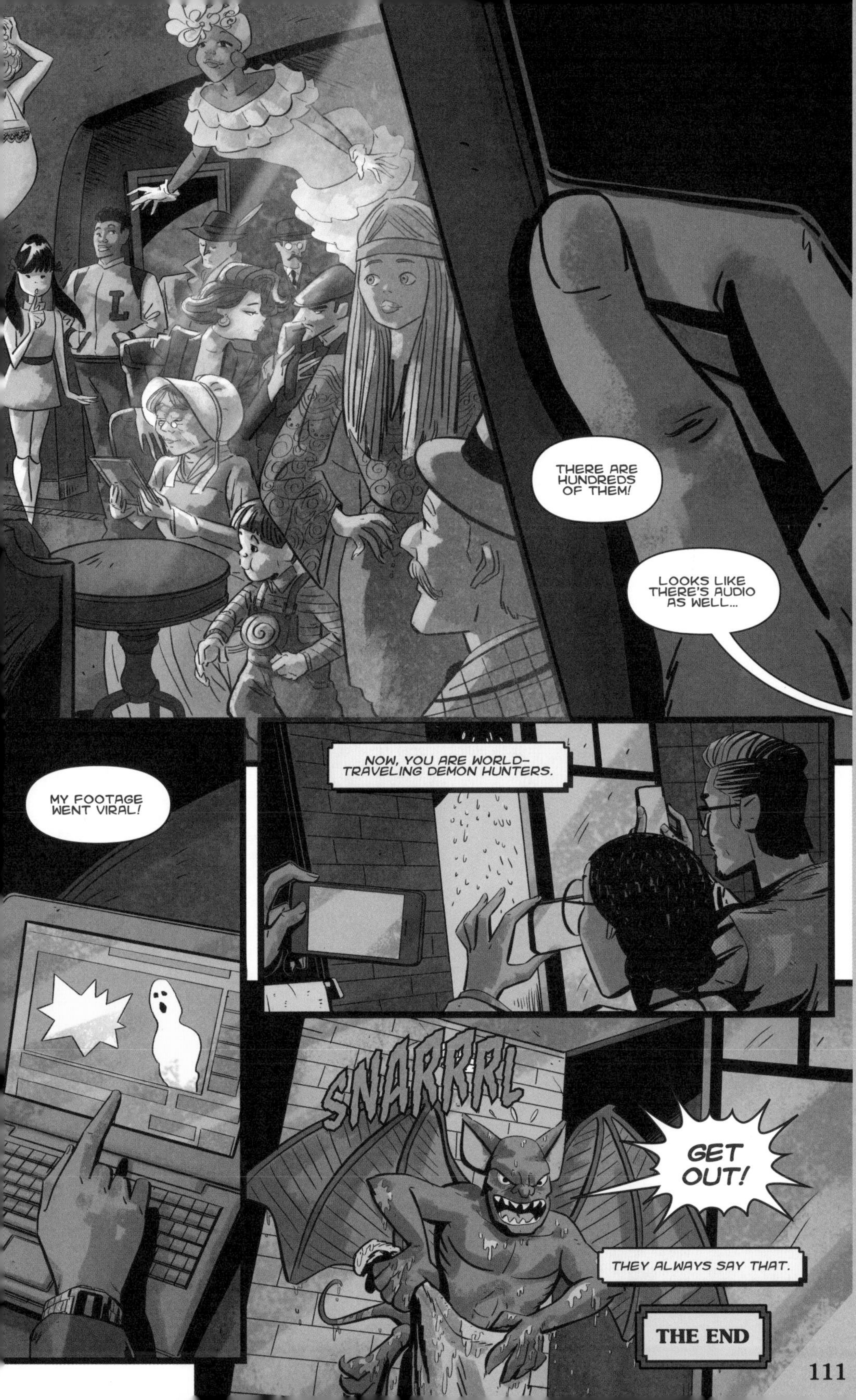
THERE ARE HUNDREDS OF THEM!
LOOKS LIKE THERE'S AUDIO AS WELL...
MY FOOTAGE WENT VIRAL!
NOW, YOU ARE WORLD-TRAVELING DEMON HUNTERS.
SNARRRL
GET OUT!
THEY ALWAYS SAY THAT.
THE END

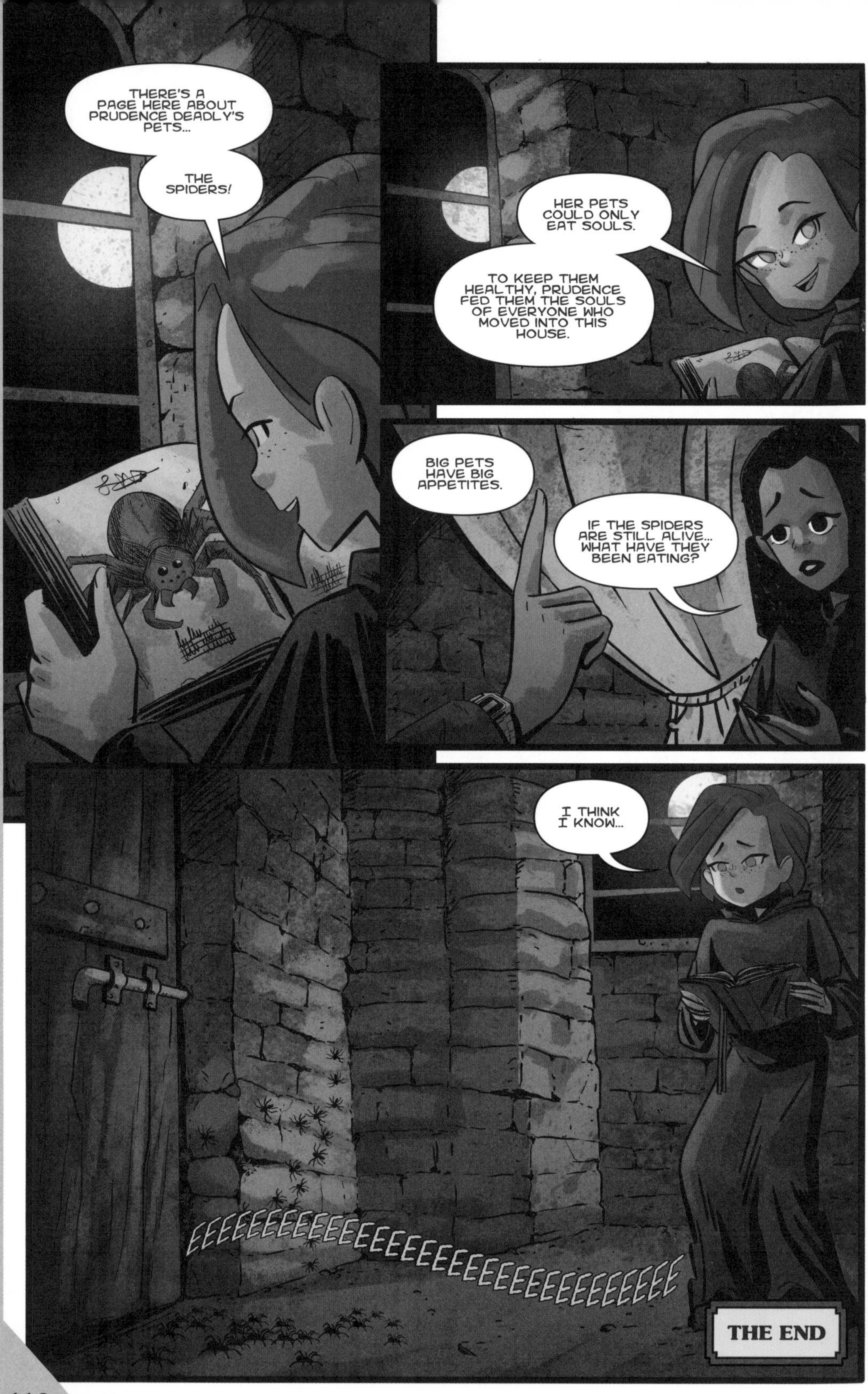
THERE'S A PAGE HERE ABOUT PRUDENCE DEADLY'S PETS...
THE SPIDERS!
HER PETS COULD ONLY EAT SOULS.
TO KEEP THEM HEALTHY, PRUDENCE FED THEM THE SOULS OF EVERYONE WHO MOVED INTO THIS HOUSE.
BIG PETS HAVE BIG APPETITES.
IF THE SPIDERS ARE STILL ALIVE... WHAT HAVE THEY BEEN EATING?
I THINK I KNOW...
EEEEEEEEEEEEEEEEEEEEEEEEEEEEEEEEEEEEEEEE
THE END

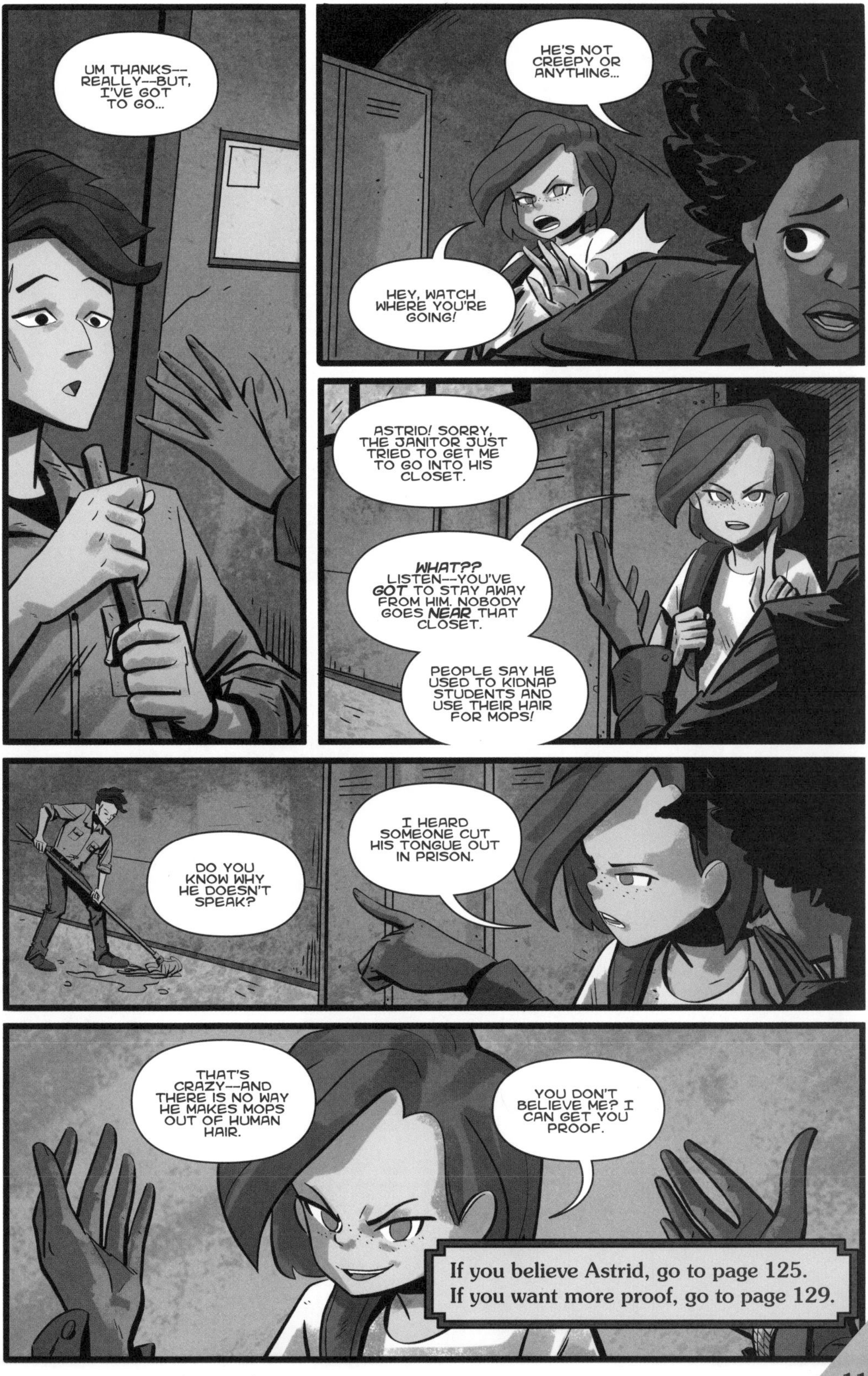
UM THANKS-- REALLY--BUT, I'VE GOT TO GO...
HE'S NOT CREEPY OR ANYTHING...
HEY, WATCH WHERE YOU'RE GOING!
ASTRID! SORRY, THE JANITOR JUST TRIED TO GET ME TO GO INTO HIS CLOSET.
WHAT?? LISTEN--YOU'VE GOT TO STAY AWAY FROM HIM. NOBODY GOES NEAR THAT CLOSET.
PEOPLE SAY HE USED TO KIDNAP STUDENTS AND USE THEIR HAIR FOR MOPS!
DO YOU KNOW WHY HE DOESN'T SPEAK?
I HEARD SOMEONE CUT HIS TONGUE OUT IN PRISON.
THAT'S CRAZY--AND THERE IS NO WAY HE MAKES MOPS OUT OF HUMAN HAIR.
YOU DON'T BELIEVE ME? I CAN GET YOU PROOF.

If you believe Astrid, go to page 125.
If you want more proof, go to page 129.

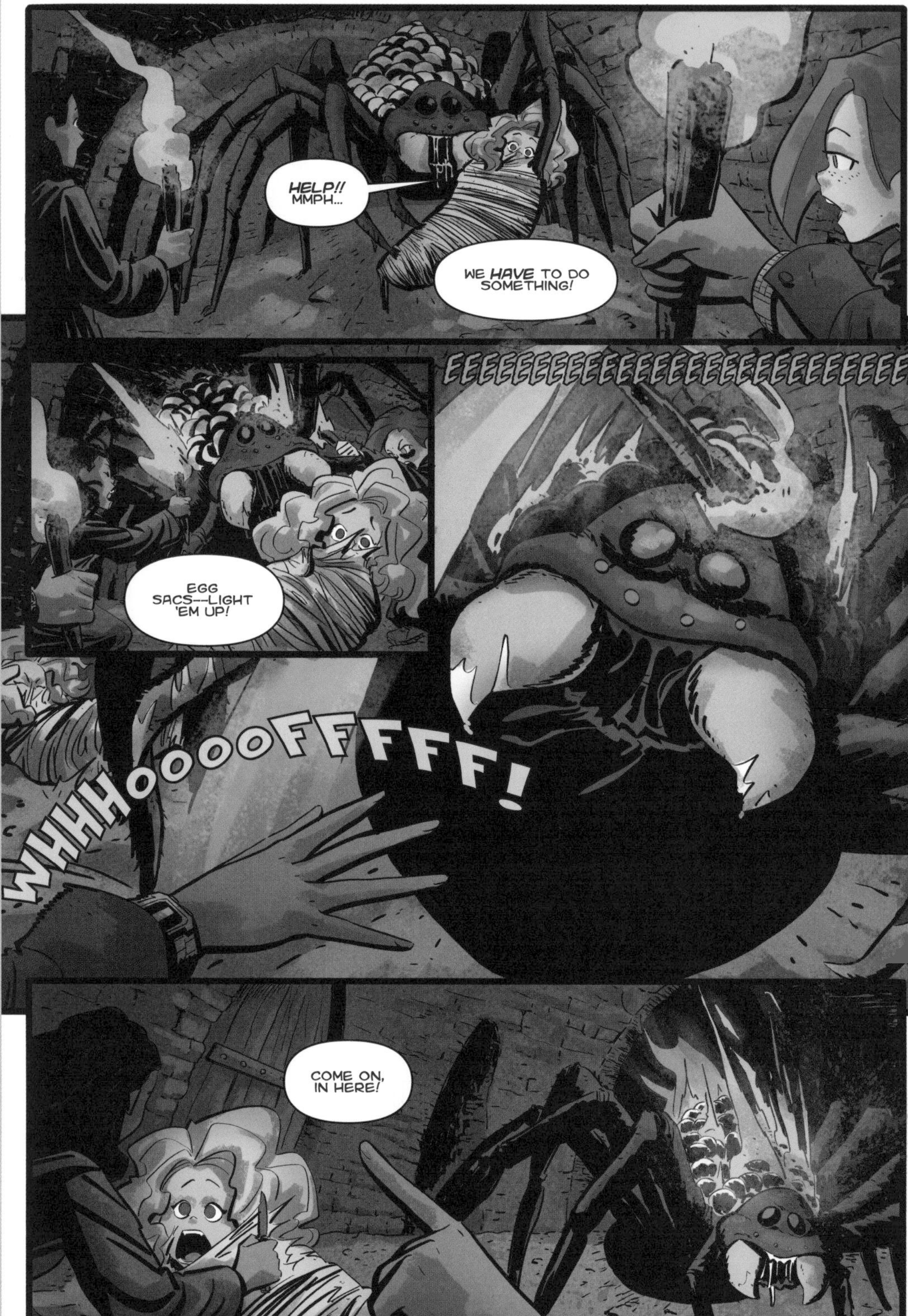
HELP!! MMPH...
WE HAVE TO DO SOMETHING!
EGG SACS--LIGHT 'EM UP!
EEEEEEEEEEEEEEEEEEEEEEEEEEEE
WHHOOOOFFFFFF!
COME ON, IN HERE!

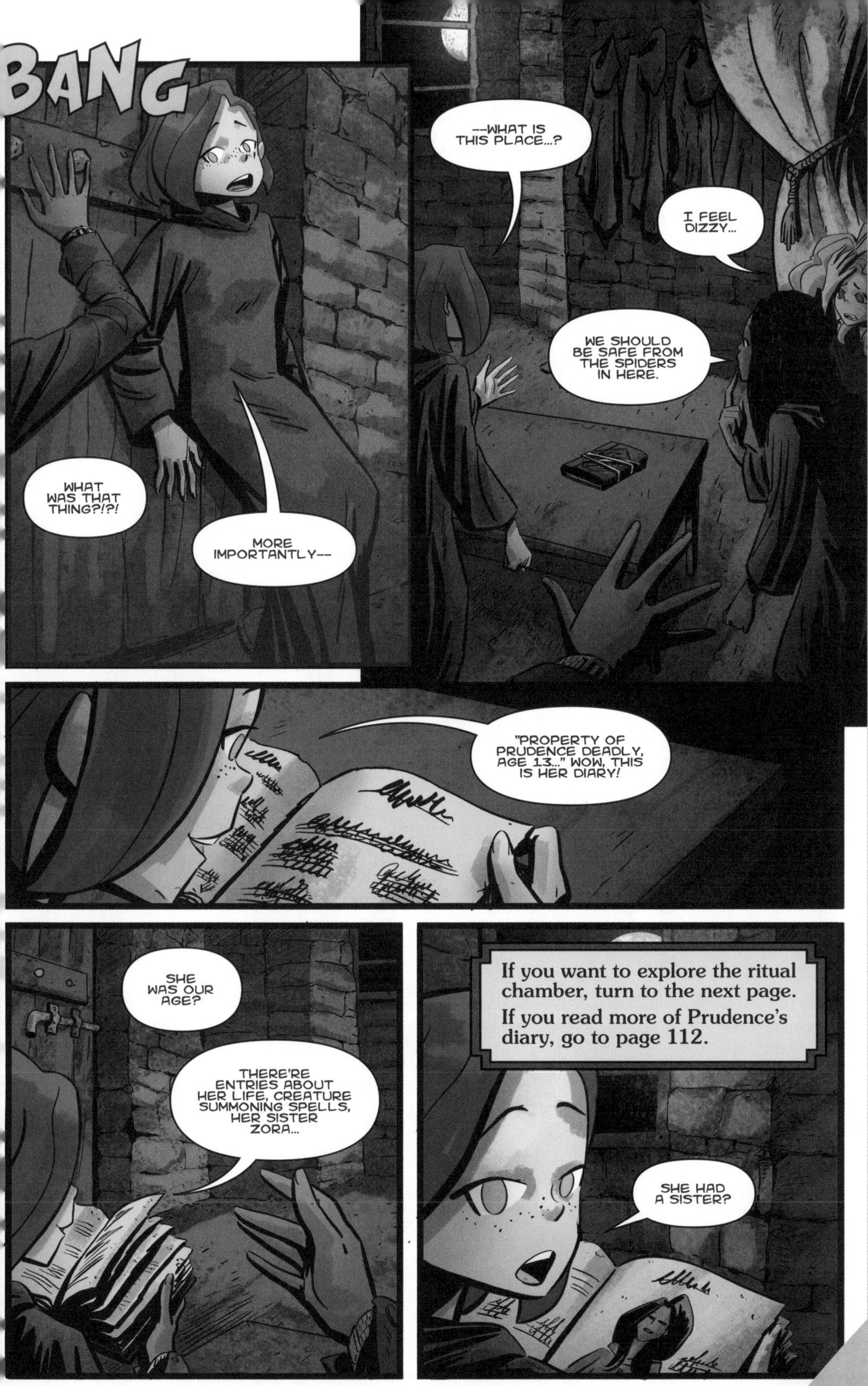
BANG
WHAT WAS THAT THING?!?!
MORE IMPORTANTLY--
--WHAT IS THIS PLACE...?
I FEEL DIZZY...
WE SHOULD BE SAFE FROM THE SPIDERS IN HERE.
"PROPERTY OF PRUDENCE DEADLY, AGE 13..." WOW, THIS IS HER DIARY!
SHE WAS OUR AGE?
THERE'RE ENTRIES ABOUT HER LIFE, CREATURE SUMMONING SPELLS, HER SISTER ZORA...
If you want to explore the ritual chamber, turn to the next page.
If you read more of Prudence's diary, go to page 112.
SHE HAD A SISTER?

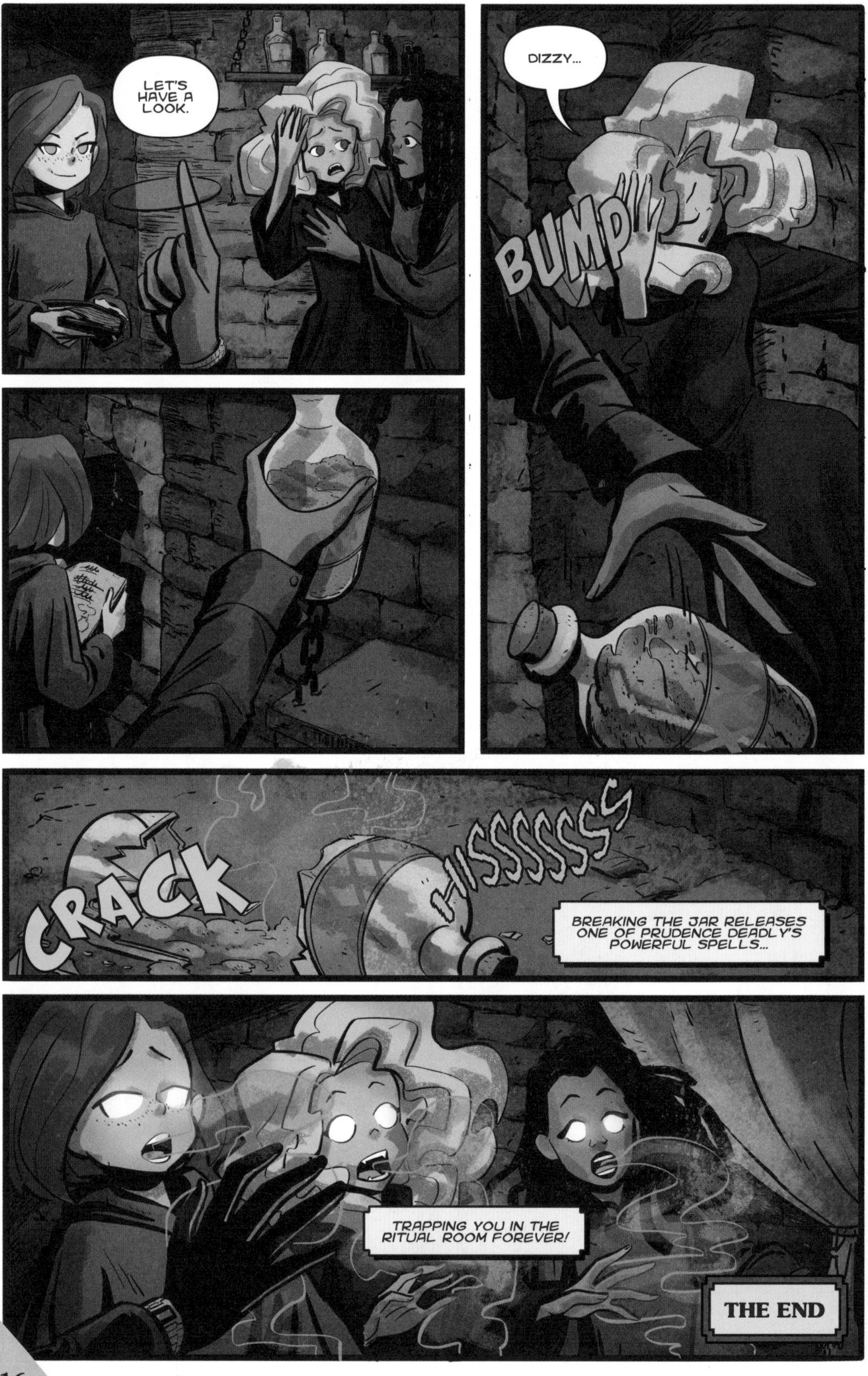
LET'S HAVE A LOOK.
DIZZY...
BUMP
CRACK
HISSSSSSS
BREAKING THE JAR RELEASES ONE OF PRUDENCE DEADLY'S POWERFUL SPELLS...
TRAPPING YOU IN THE RITUAL ROOM FOREVER!
THE END

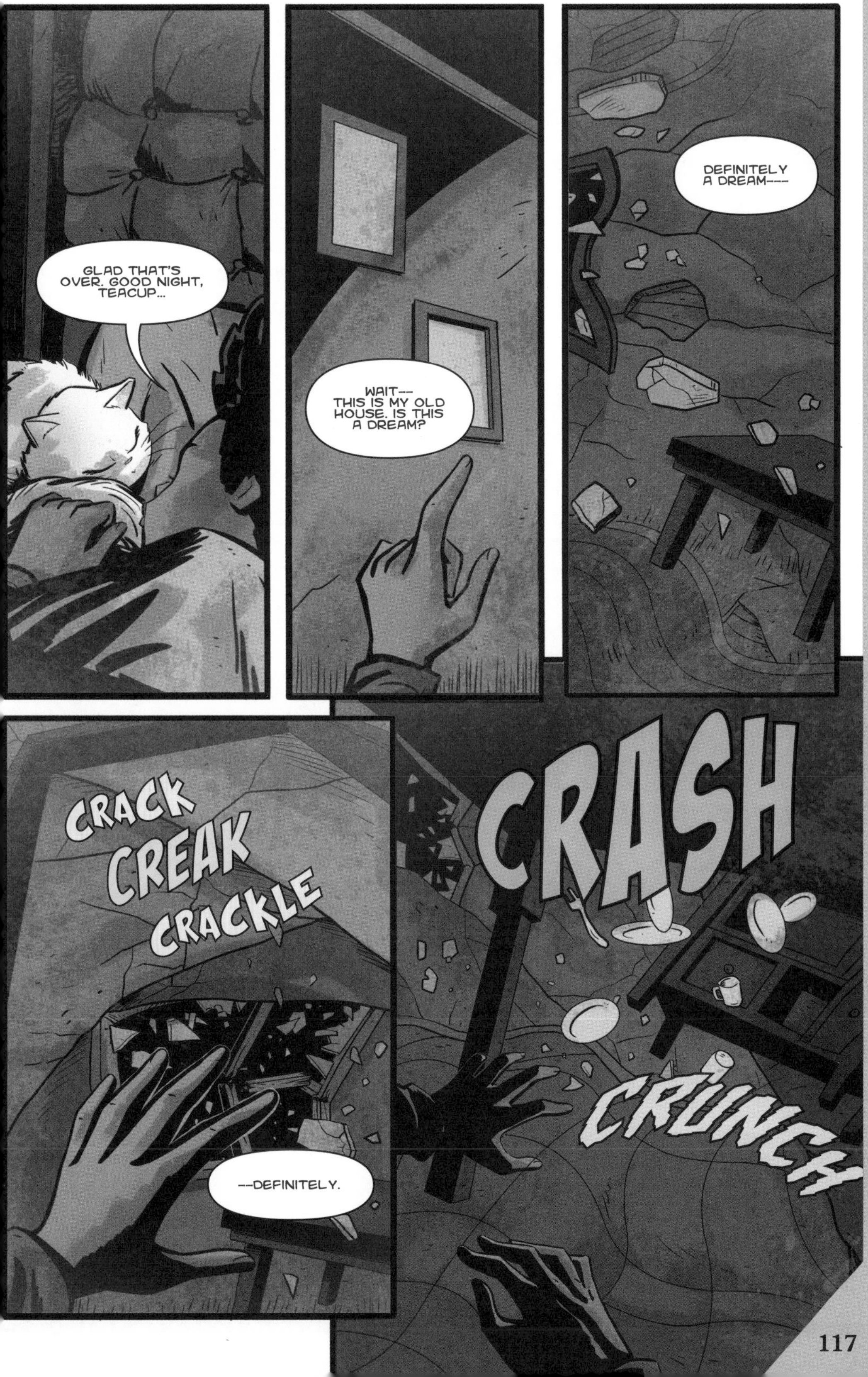
GLAD THAT'S OVER. GOOD NIGHT, TEACUP...
WAIT-- THIS IS MY OLD HOUSE. IS THIS A DREAM?
DEFINITELY A DREAM---
CRACK
CREAK
CRACKLE
--DEFINITELY.
CRASH
CRUNCH

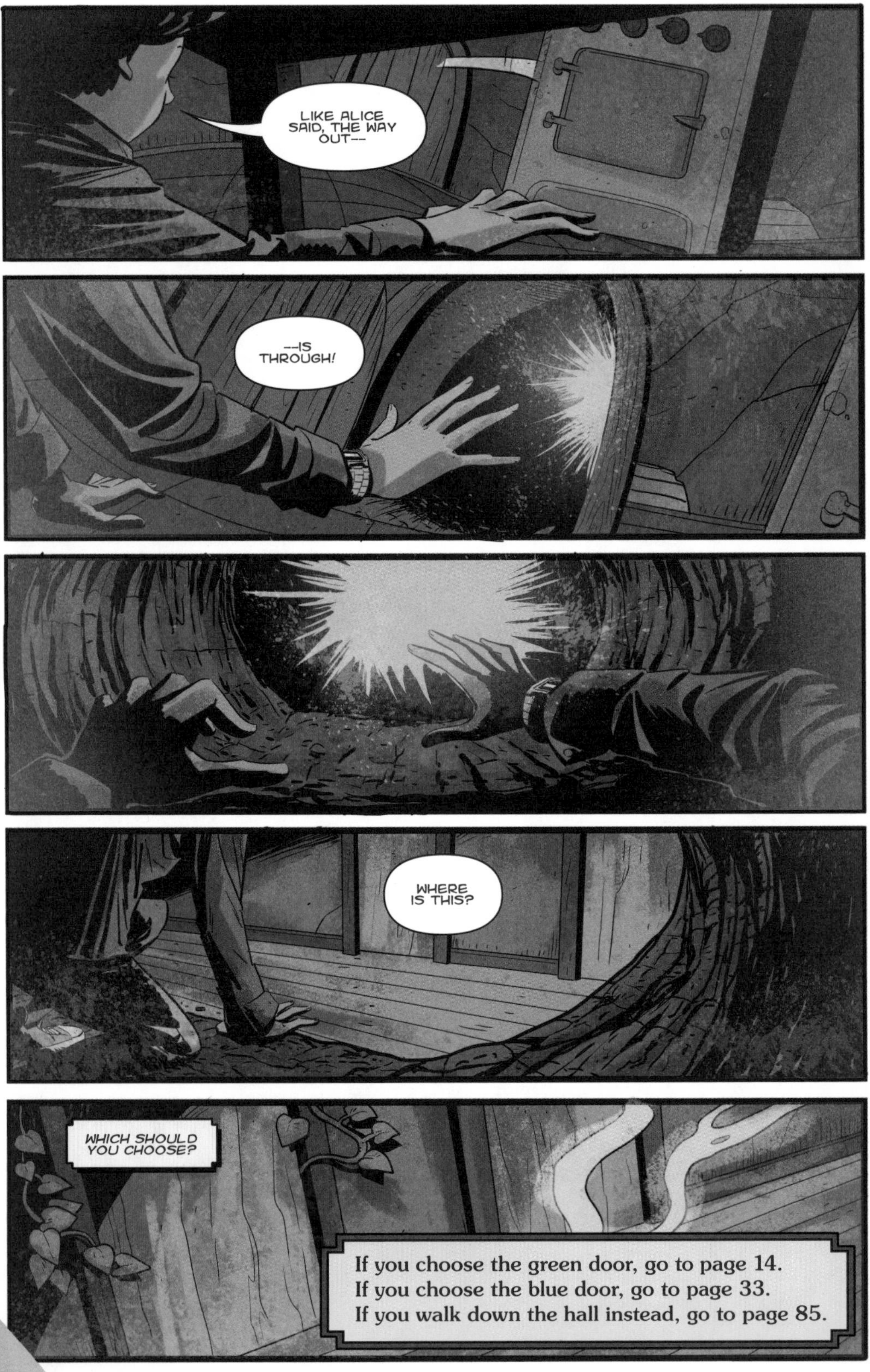
LIKE ALICE SAID, THE WAY OUT--
--IS THROUGH!
WHERE IS THIS?
WHICH SHOULD YOU CHOOSE?
If you choose the green door, go to page 14.
If you choose the blue door, go to page 33.
If you walk down the hall instead, go to page 85.

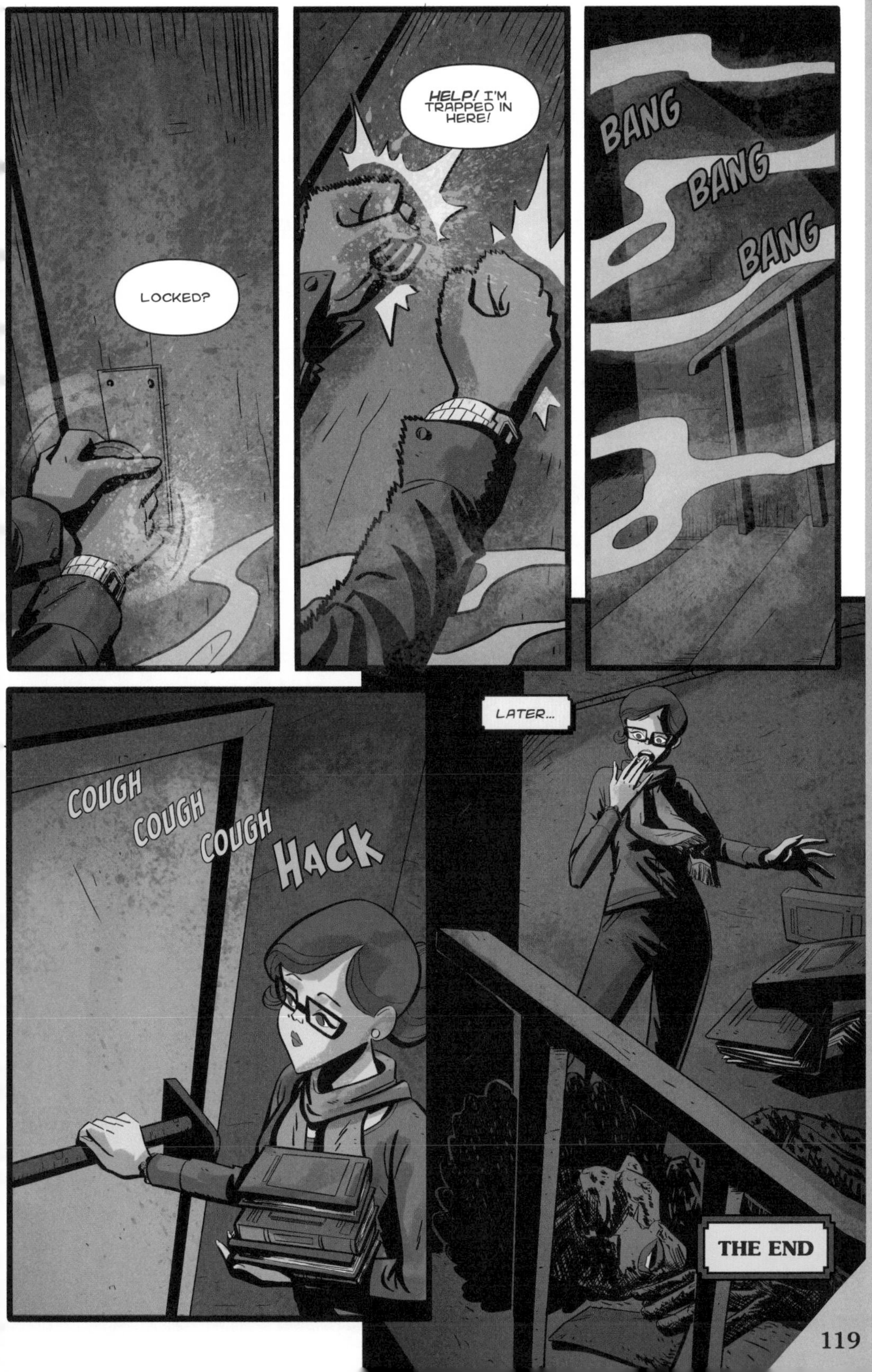
LOCKED?
HELP! I'M TRAPPED IN HERE!
BANG
BANG
BANG
COUGH
COUGH
COUGH
HACK
LATER...
THE END

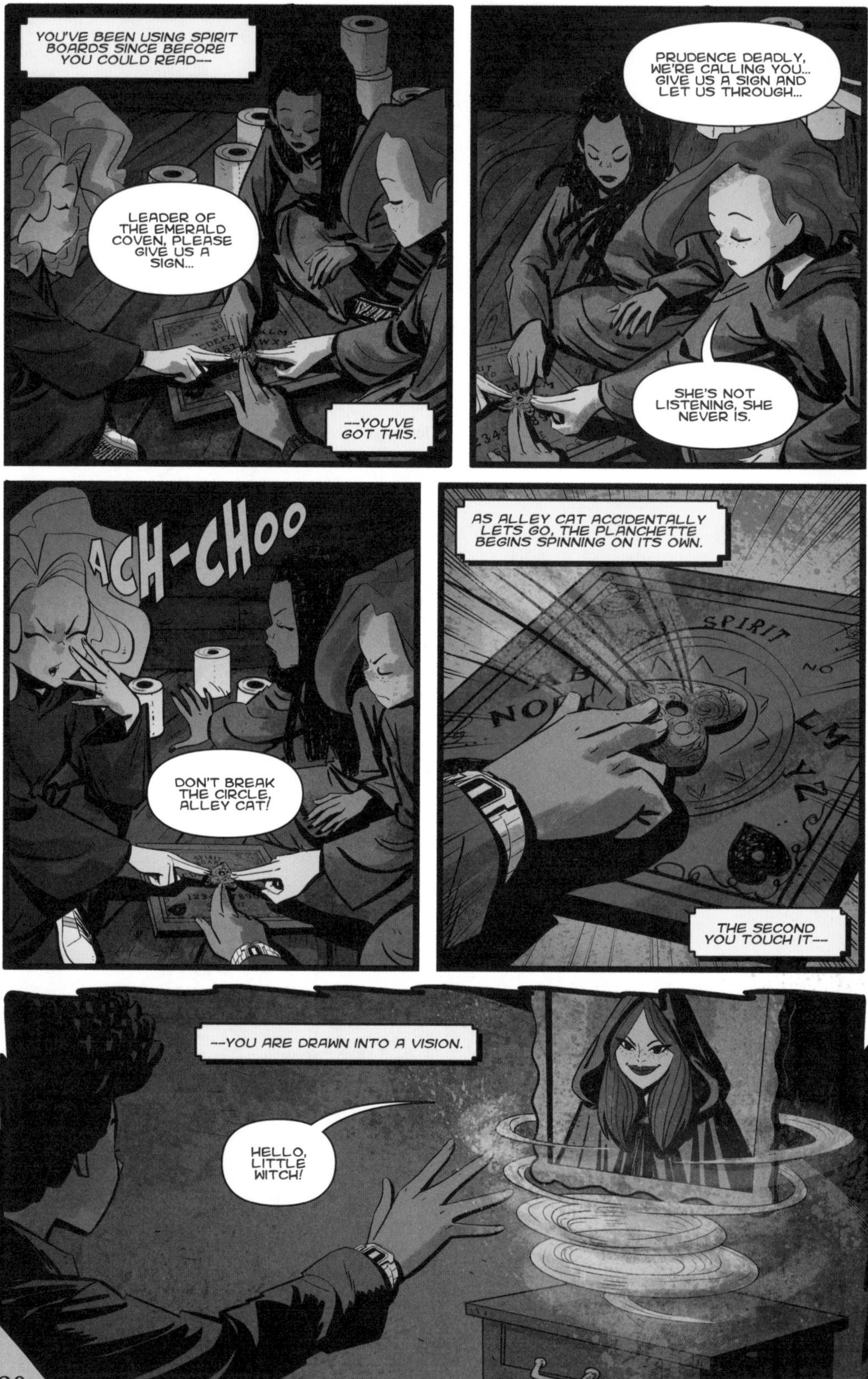
YOU'VE BEEN USING SPIRIT BOARDS SINCE BEFORE YOU COULD READ--
LEADER OF THE EMERALD COVEN, PLEASE GIVE US A SIGN...
--YOU'VE GOT THIS.
PRUDENCE DEADLY, WE'RE CALLING YOU... GIVE US A SIGN AND LET US THROUGH...
SHE'S NOT LISTENING, SHE NEVER IS.
ACH-CHOO
DON'T BREAK THE CIRCLE, ALLEY CAT!
AS ALLEY CAT ACCIDENTALLY LETS GO, THE PLANCHETTE BEGINS SPINNING ON ITS OWN.
SPIRIT
NO
THE SECOND YOU TOUCH IT--
--YOU ARE DRAWN INTO A VISION.
HELLO, LITTLE WITCH!

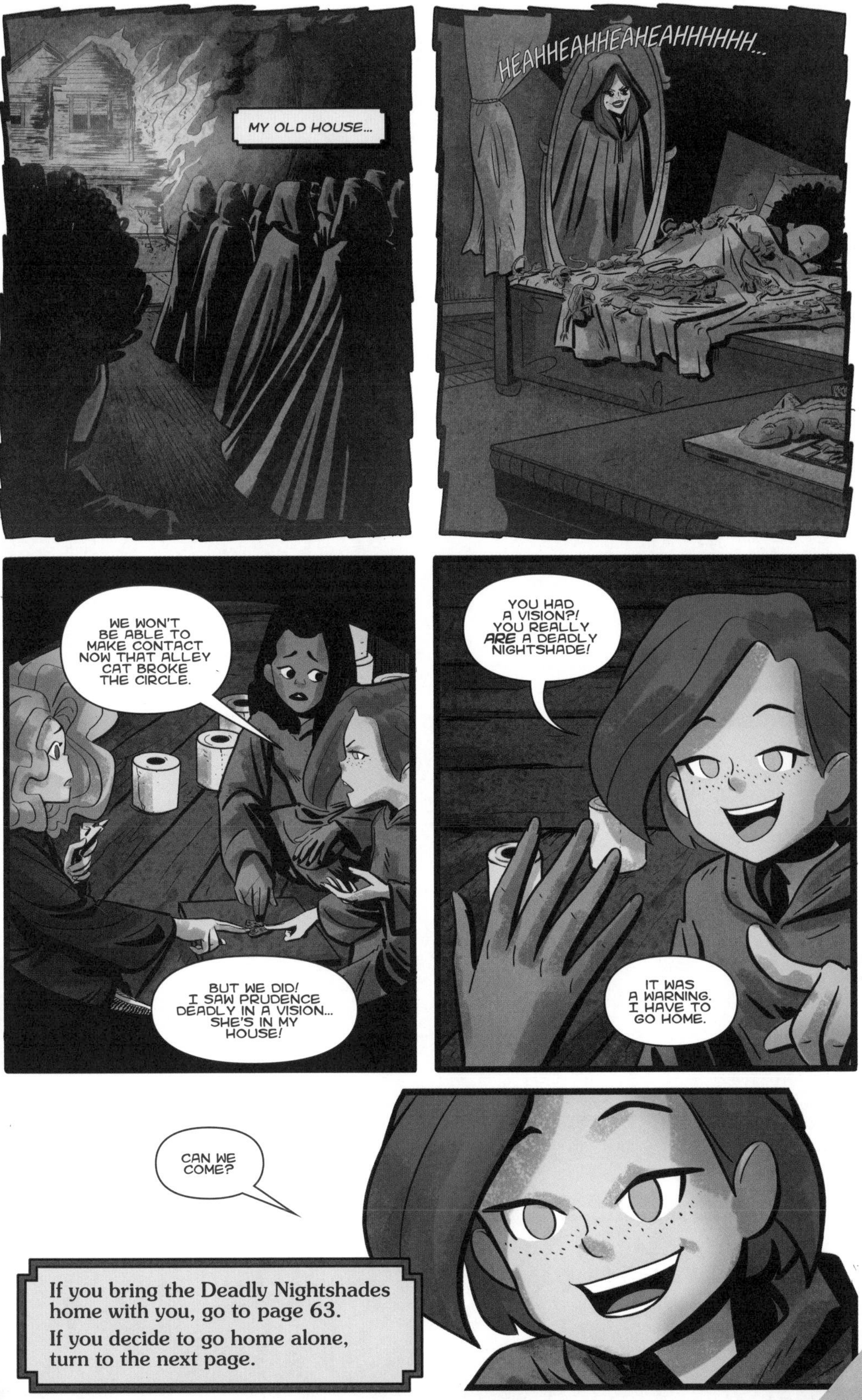
MY OLD HOUSE...
HEAHHEAHHEAHEAHHHHHH...
WE WON'T BE ABLE TO MAKE CONTACT NOW THAT ALLEY CAT BROKE THE CIRCLE.
BUT WE DID! I SAW PRUDENCE DEADLY IN A VISION... SHE'S IN MY HOUSE!
YOU HAD A VISION?! YOU REALLY ARE A DEADLY NIGHTSHADE!
IT WAS A WARNING. I HAVE TO GO HOME.
CAN WE COME?

If you bring the Deadly Nightshades home with you, go to page 63.

If you decide to go home alone, turn to the next page.

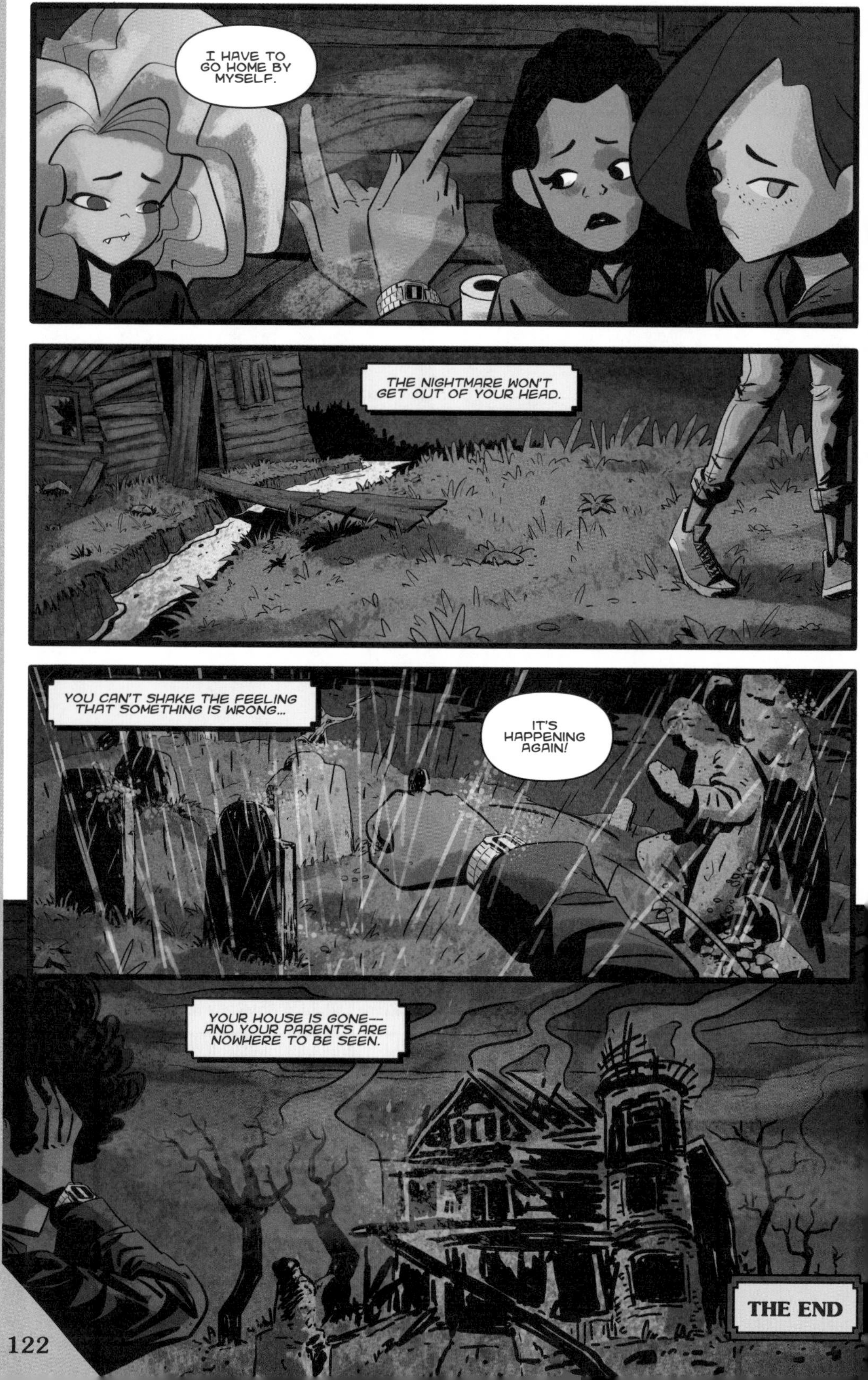

I HAVE TO GO HOME BY MYSELF.
THE NIGHTMARE WON'T GET OUT OF YOUR HEAD.
YOU CAN'T SHAKE THE FEELING THAT SOMETHING IS WRONG...
IT'S HAPPENING AGAIN!
YOUR HOUSE IS GONE-- AND YOUR PARENTS ARE NOWHERE TO BE SEEN.
THE END

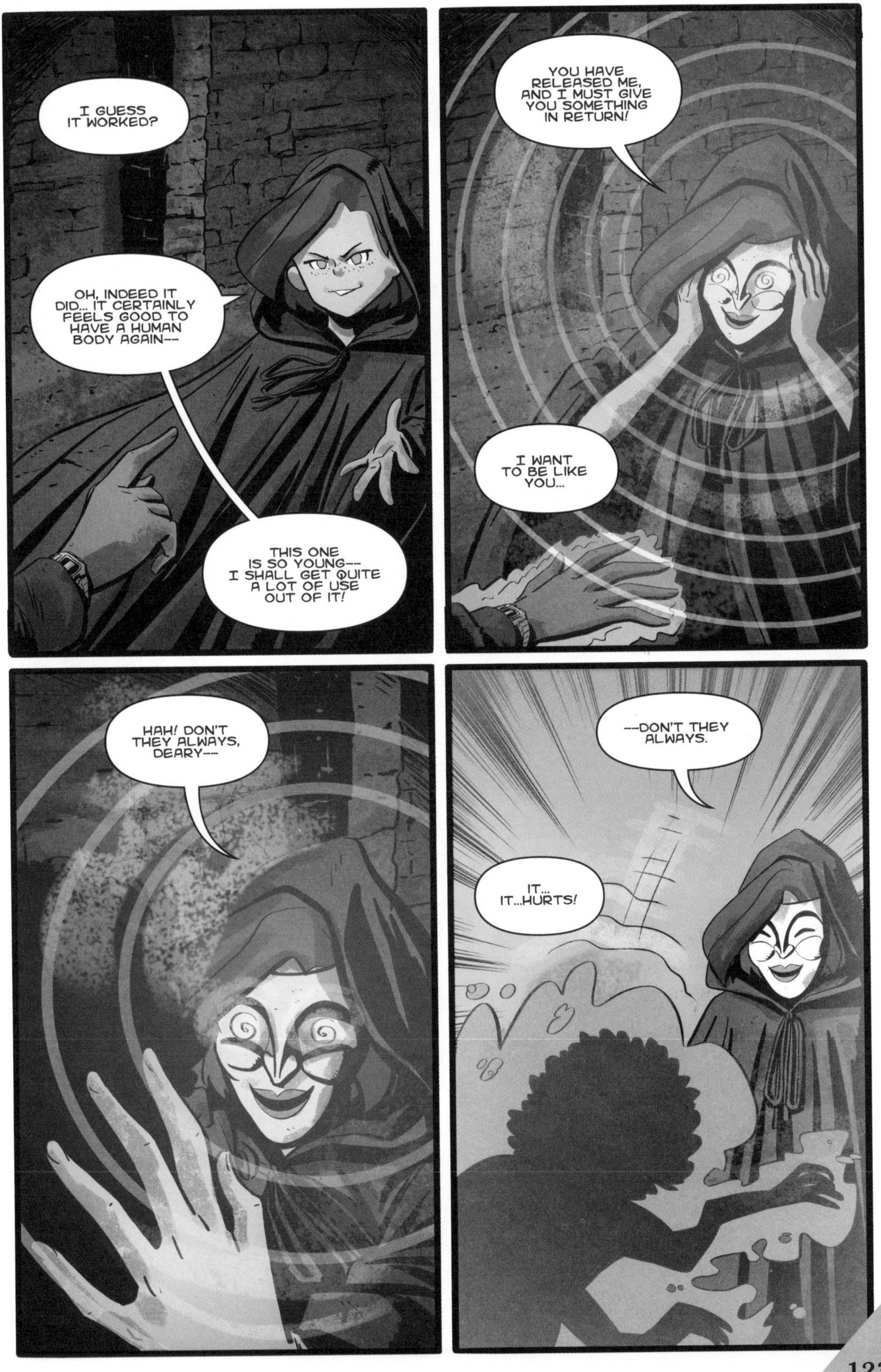
I GUESS IT WORKED?
OH, INDEED IT DID... IT CERTAINLY FEELS GOOD TO HAVE A HUMAN BODY AGAIN--
THIS ONE IS SO YOUNG-- I SHALL GET QUITE A LOT OF USE OUT OF IT!
YOU HAVE RELEASED ME, AND I MUST GIVE YOU SOMETHING IN RETURN!
I WANT TO BE LIKE YOU...
HAH! DON'T THEY ALWAYS, DEARY--
--DON'T THEY ALWAYS.
IT... IT...HURTS!

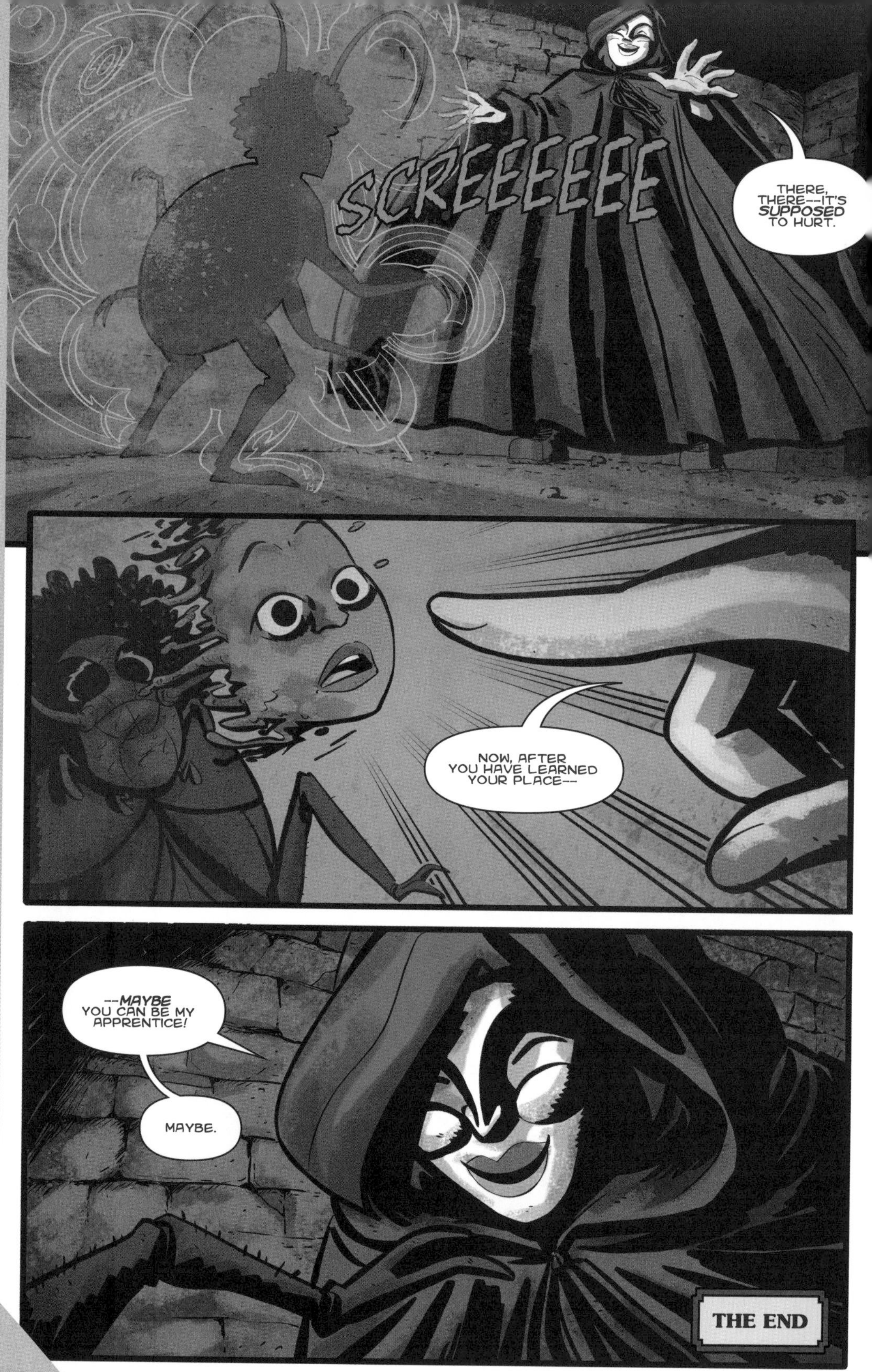
SCREEEEEEE
THERE, THERE--IT'S *SUPPOSED* TO HURT.
NOW, AFTER YOU HAVE LEARNED YOUR PLACE--
--*MAYBE* YOU CAN BE MY APPRENTICE!
MAYBE.
THE END

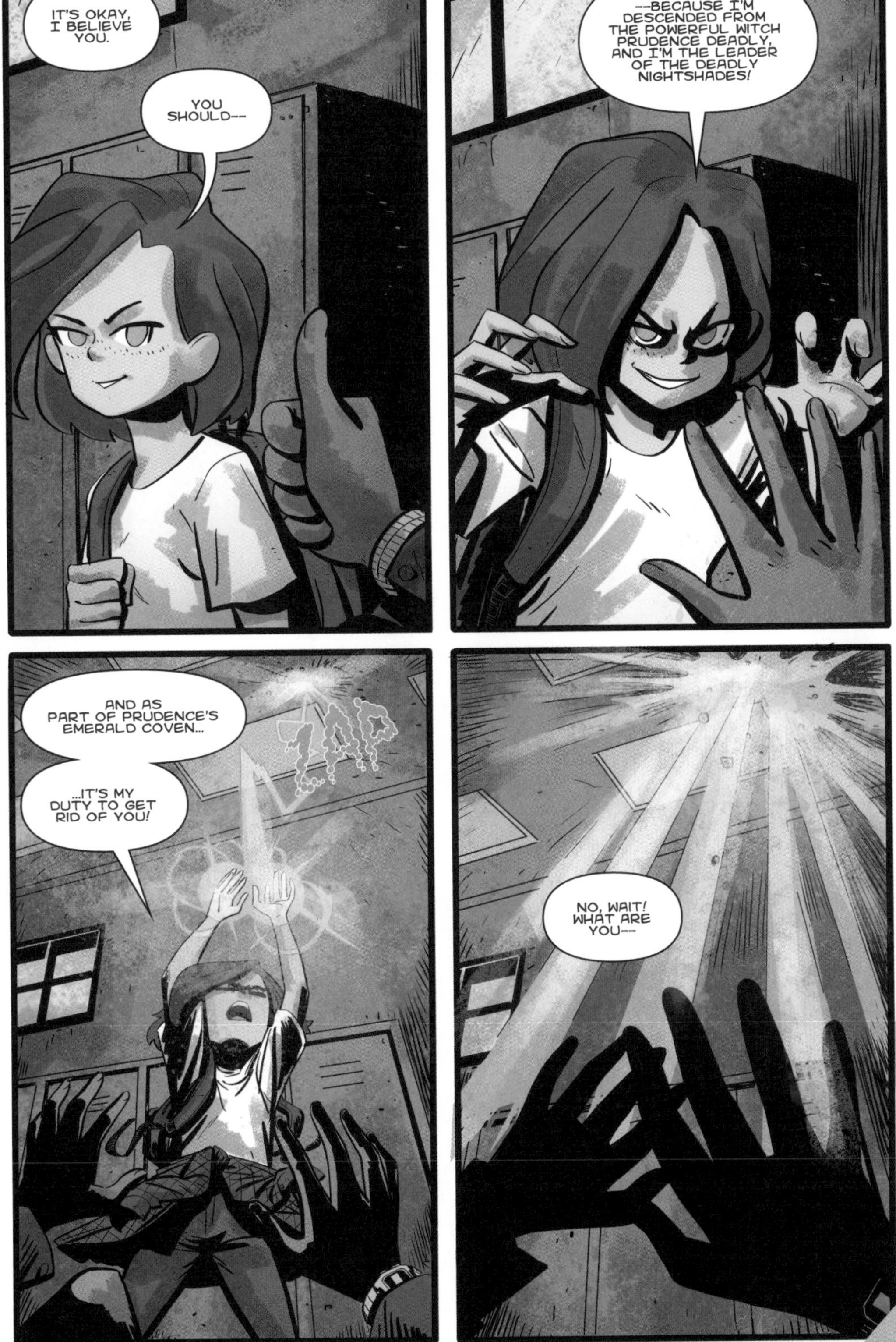
IT'S OKAY, I BELIEVE YOU.
YOU SHOULD--
--BECAUSE I'M DESCENDED FROM THE POWERFUL WITCH PRUDENCE DEADLY, AND I'M THE LEADER OF THE DEADLY NIGHTSHADES!
AND AS PART OF PRUDENCE'S EMERALD COVEN...
...IT'S MY DUTY TO GET RID OF YOU!
ZAP
NO, WAIT! WHAT ARE YOU--

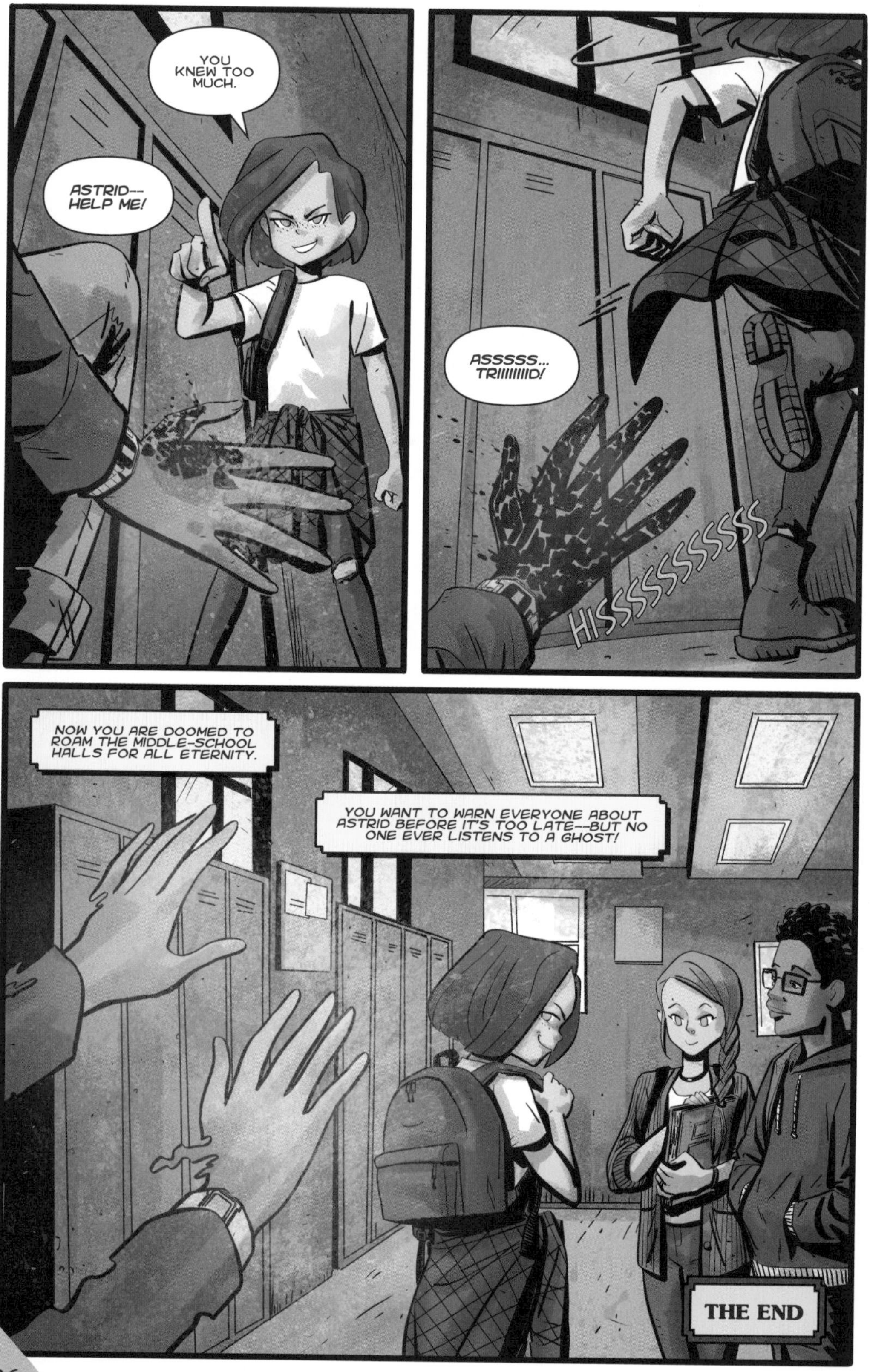
YOU KNEW TOO MUCH.
ASTRID-- HELP ME!
ASSSSS... TRIIIIIIID!
HISSSSSSSSSSSS
NOW YOU ARE DOOMED TO ROAM THE MIDDLE-SCHOOL HALLS FOR ALL ETERNITY.
YOU WANT TO WARN EVERYONE ABOUT ASTRID BEFORE IT'S TOO LATE--BUT NO ONE EVER LISTENS TO A GHOST!
THE END

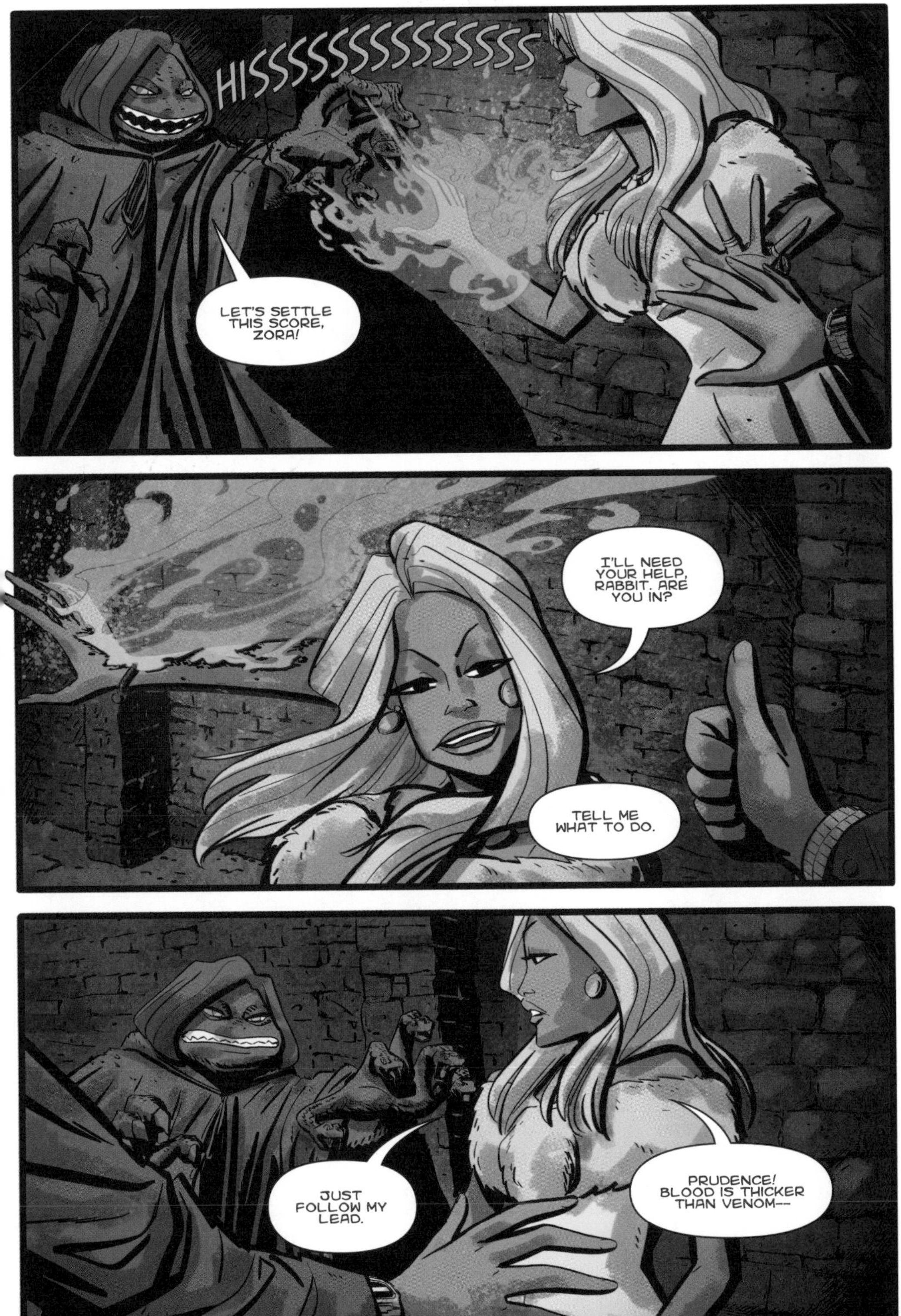
HISSSSSSSSSSSSSS
LET'S SETTLE THIS SCORE, ZORA!
I'LL NEED YOUR HELP, RABBIT. ARE YOU IN?
TELL ME WHAT TO DO.
JUST FOLLOW MY LEAD.
PRUDENCE! BLOOD IS THICKER THAN VENOM--

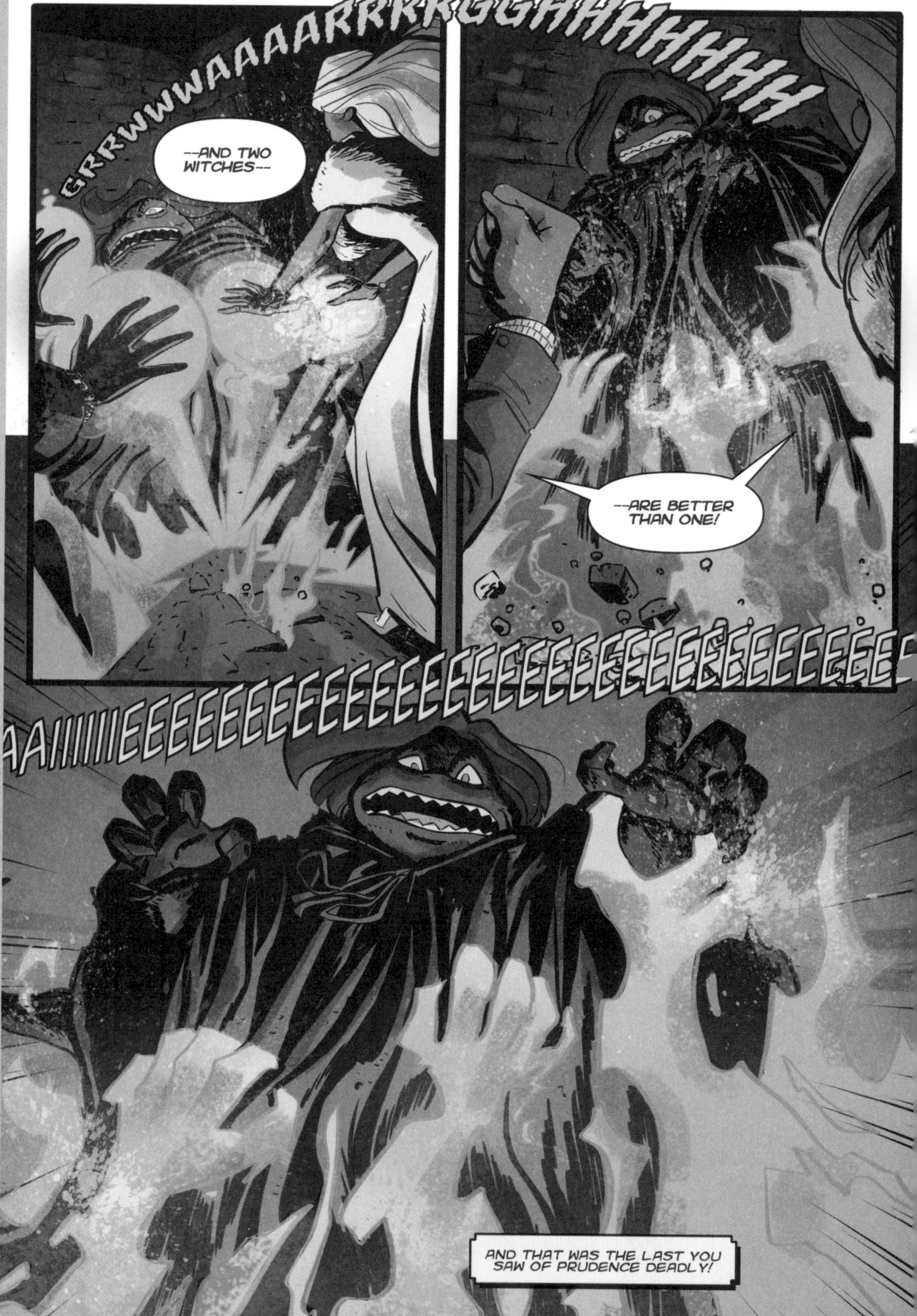
GRRWWWAAAARRRRGGHHHHHHHHH
--AND TWO WITCHES--
--ARE BETTER THAN ONE!
AAIIIIIIEEEEEEEEEEEEEEEEEEEEEEEEEEEEEEEEEEEE
AND THAT WAS THE LAST YOU SAW OF PRUDENCE DEADLY!
THE END

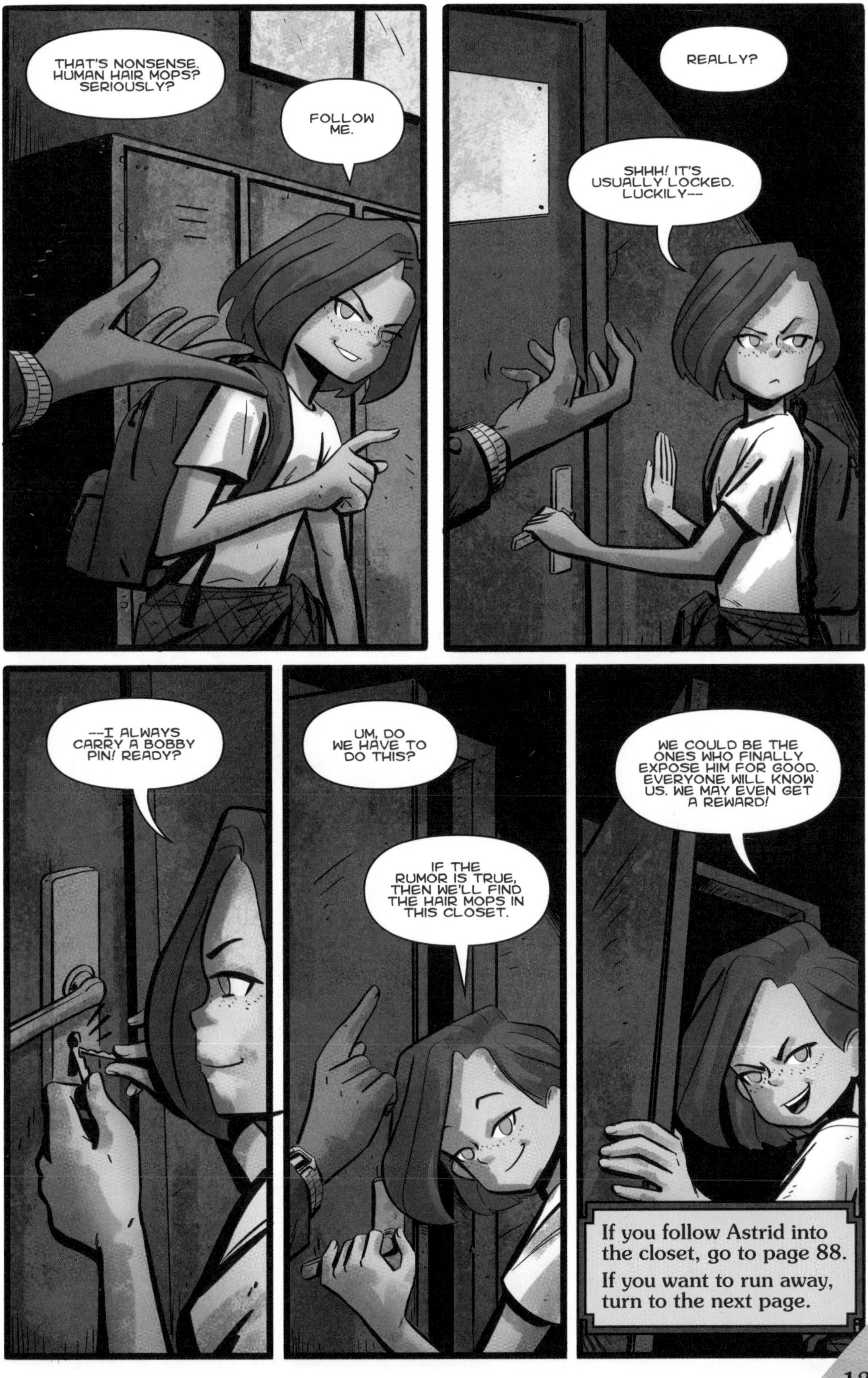
THAT'S NONSENSE. HUMAN HAIR MOPS? SERIOUSLY?
FOLLOW ME.
REALLY?
SHHH! IT'S USUALLY LOCKED. LUCKILY--
--I ALWAYS CARRY A BOBBY PIN! READY?
UM, DO WE HAVE TO DO THIS?
IF THE RUMOR IS TRUE, THEN WE'LL FIND THE HAIR MOPS IN THIS CLOSET.
WE COULD BE THE ONES WHO FINALLY EXPOSE HIM FOR GOOD. EVERYONE WILL KNOW US. WE MAY EVEN GET A REWARD!
If you follow Astrid into the closet, go to page 88.
If you want to run away, turn to the next page.

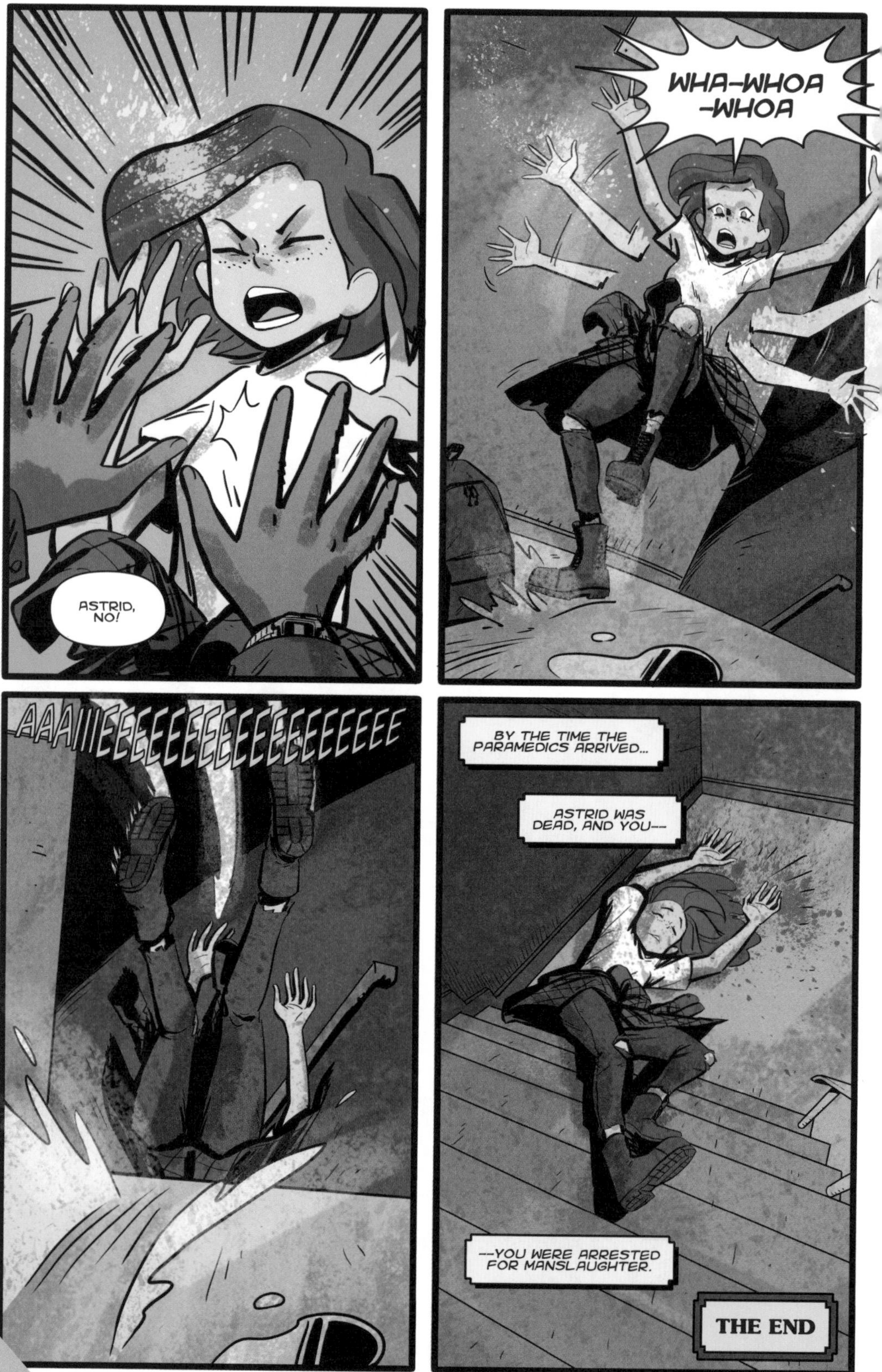
ASTRID, NO!
WHA-WHOA -WHOA
AAAIIIEEEEEEEEEEEEEEEEEEEE
BY THE TIME THE PARAMEDICS ARRIVED...
ASTRID WAS DEAD, AND YOU--
--YOU WERE ARRESTED FOR MANSLAUGHTER.
THE END

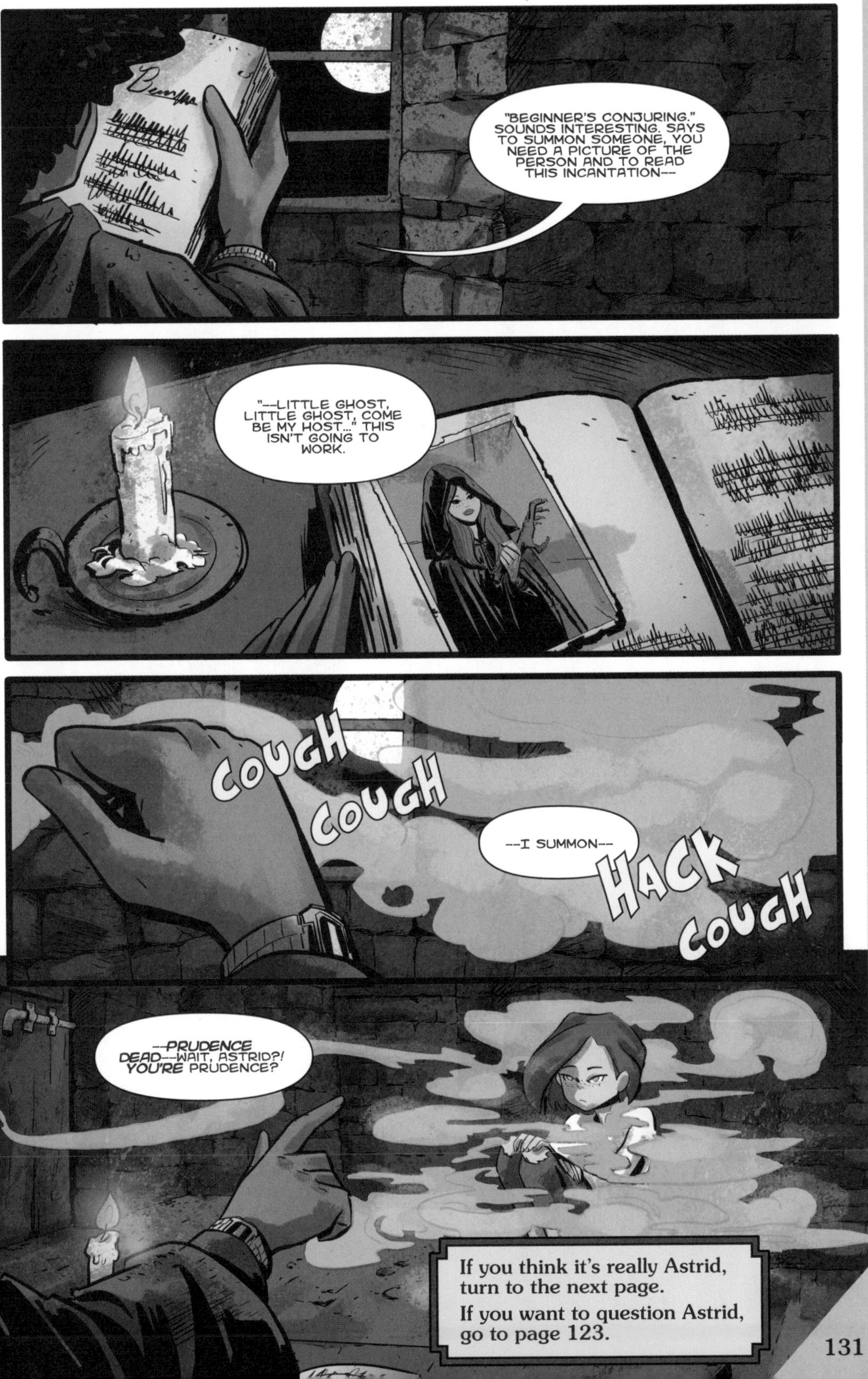
"BEGINNER'S CONJURING." SOUNDS INTERESTING. SAYS TO SUMMON SOMEONE, YOU NEED A PICTURE OF THE PERSON AND TO READ THIS INCANTATION--
"--LITTLE GHOST, LITTLE GHOST, COME BE MY HOST..." THIS ISN'T GOING TO WORK.
COUGH
COUGH
--I SUMMON--
HACK
COUGH
--*PRUDENCE DEAD*--WAIT, ASTRID?! *YOU'RE* PRUDENCE?

If you think it's really Astrid, turn to the next page.
If you want to question Astrid, go to page 123.

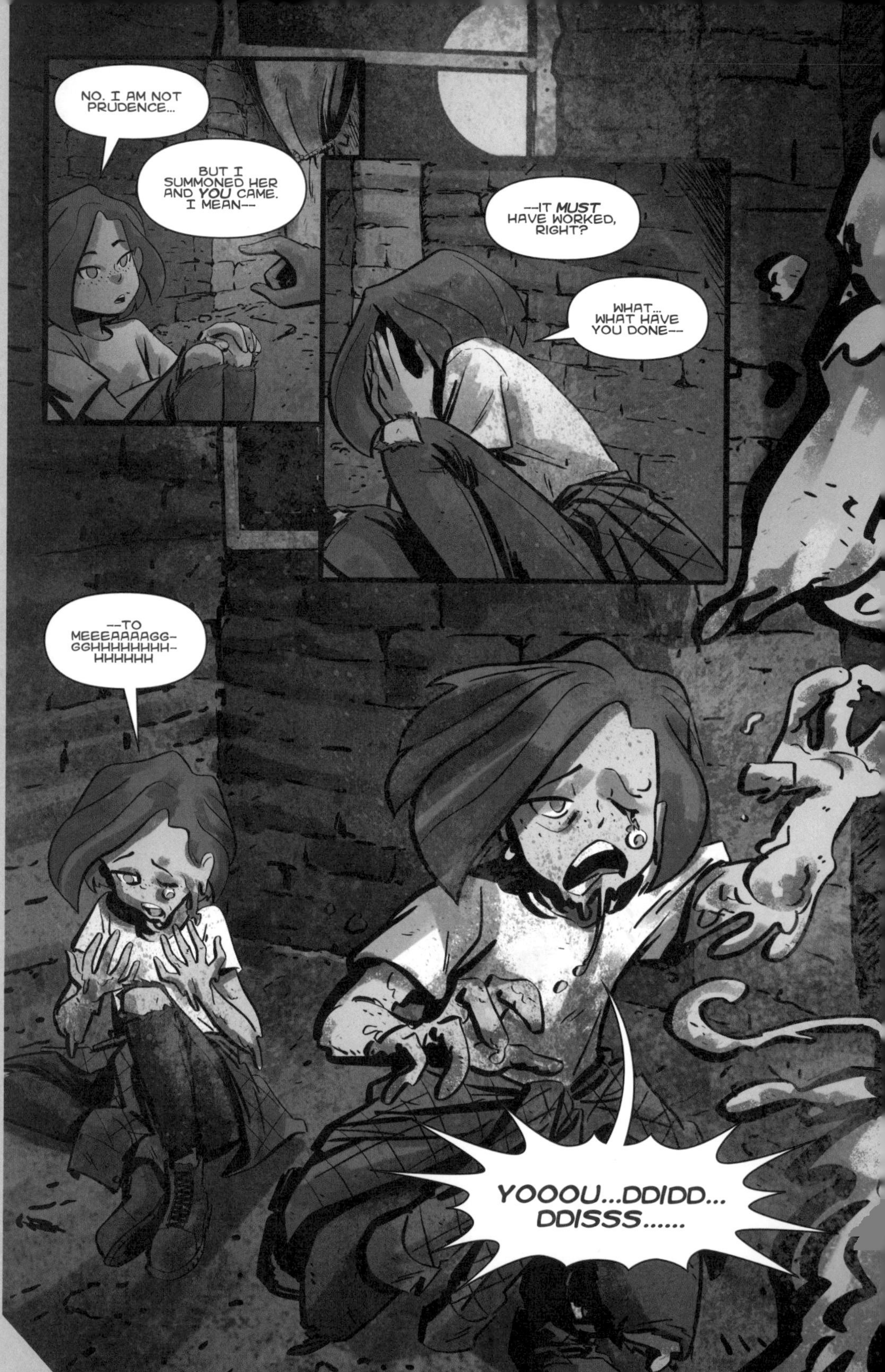
NO. I AM NOT PRUDENCE...
BUT I SUMMONED HER AND YOU CAME. I MEAN--
--IT MUST HAVE WORKED, RIGHT?
WHAT... WHAT HAVE YOU DONE--
--TO MEEEAAAAAGG-GGHHHHHHHHH-HHHHHH
YOOOU...DDIDD... DDISSS......

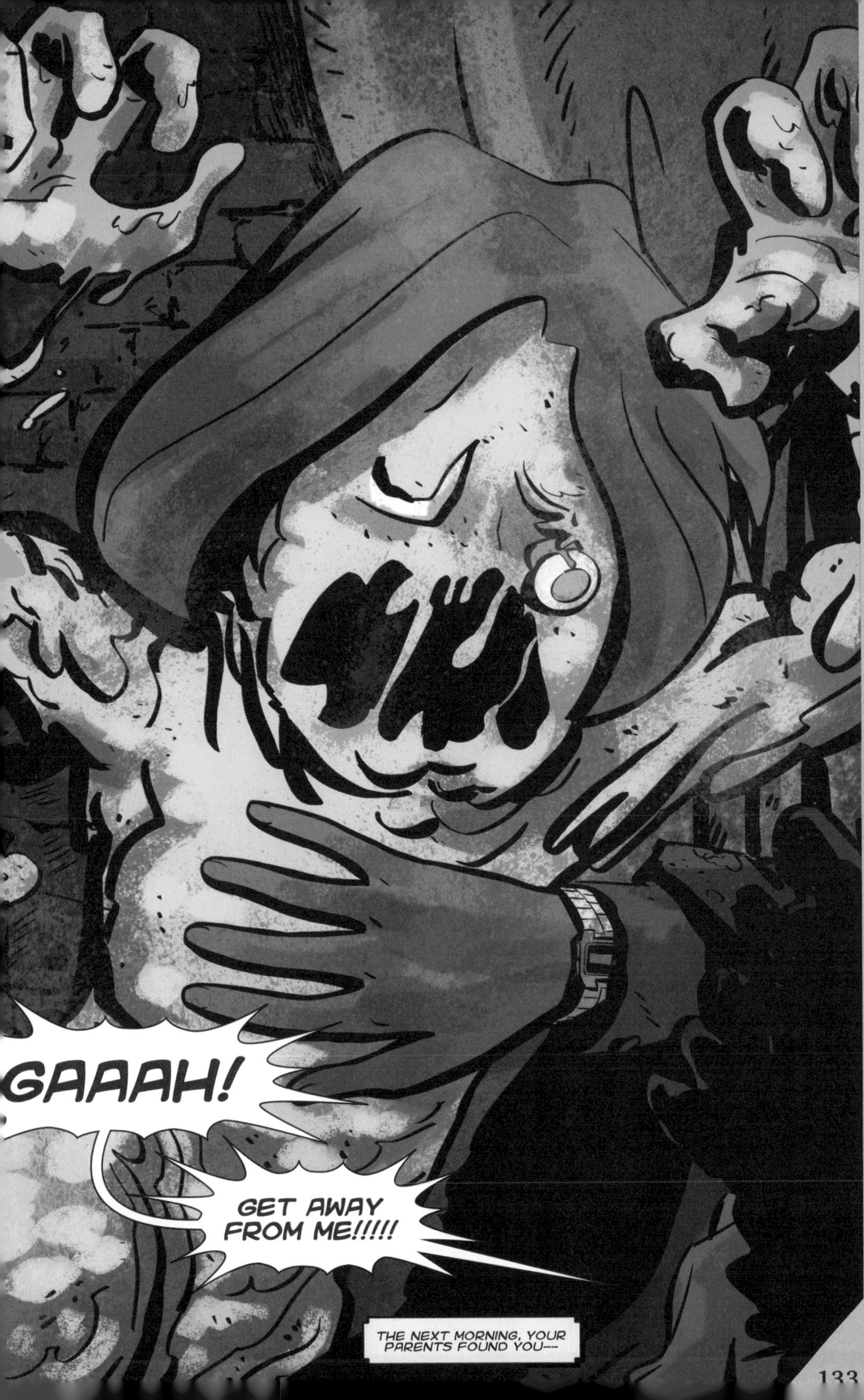
GAAAH!
GET AWAY FROM ME!!!!!
THE NEXT MORNING, YOUR PARENTS FOUND YOU--

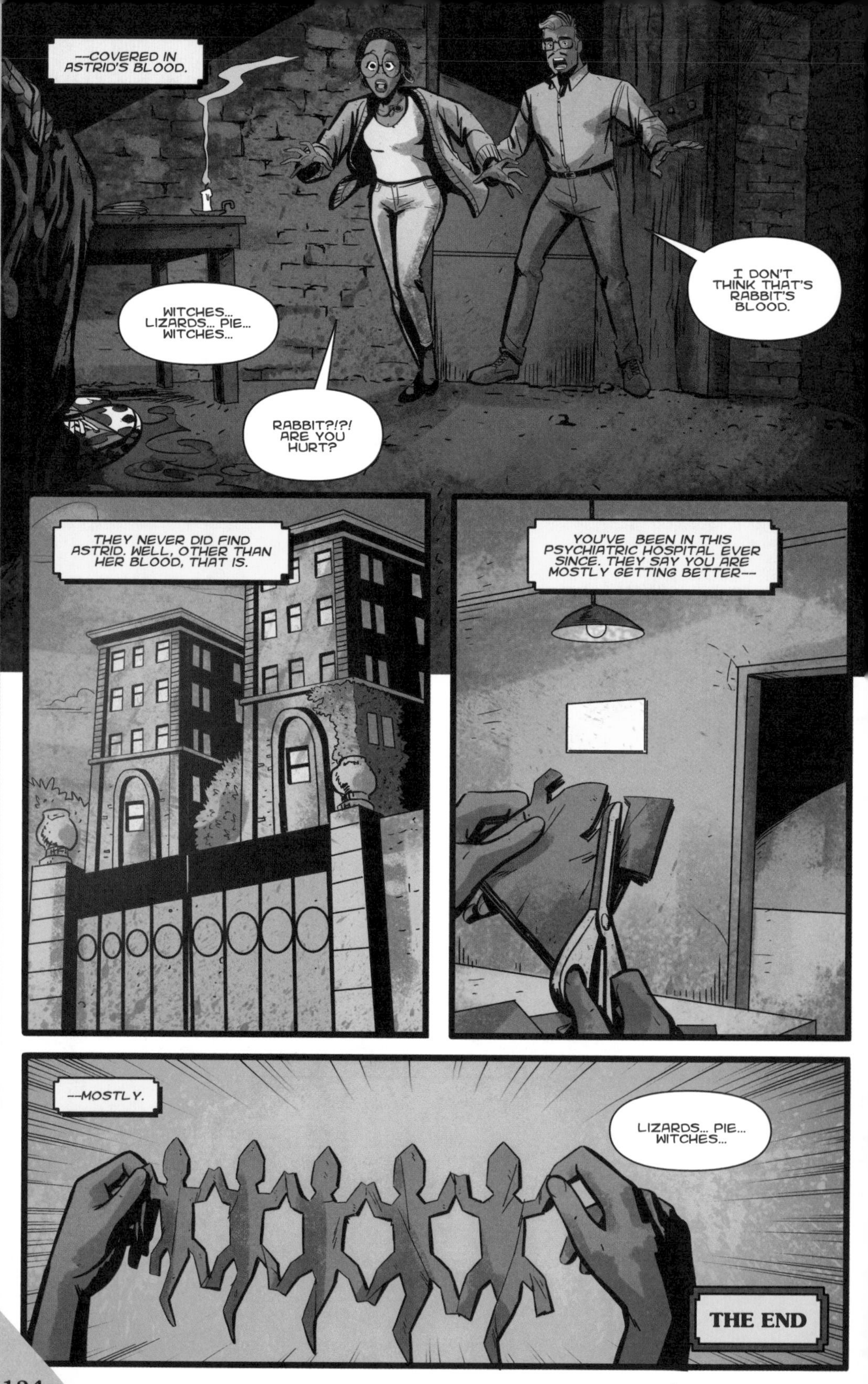
--COVERED IN ASTRID'S BLOOD.
WITCHES... LIZARDS... PIE... WITCHES...
RABBIT?!?! ARE YOU HURT?
I DON'T THINK THAT'S RABBIT'S BLOOD.
THEY NEVER DID FIND ASTRID. WELL, OTHER THAN HER BLOOD, THAT IS.
YOU'VE BEEN IN THIS PSYCHIATRIC HOSPITAL EVER SINCE. THEY SAY YOU ARE MOSTLY GETTING BETTER--
--MOSTLY.
LIZARDS... PIE... WITCHES...
THE END

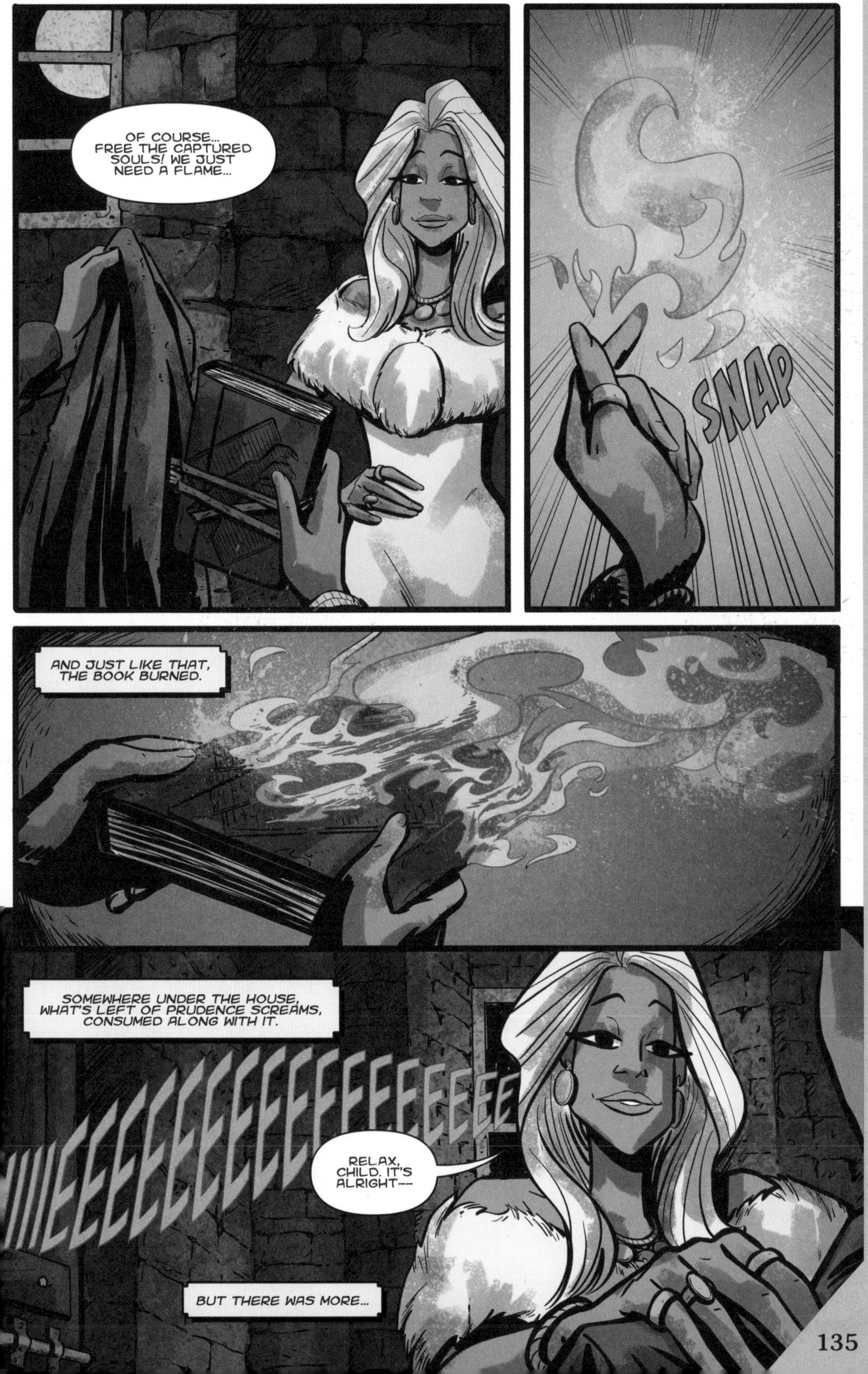
OF COURSE... FREE THE CAPTURED SOULS! WE JUST NEED A FLAME...
SNAP
AND JUST LIKE THAT, THE BOOK BURNED.
SOMEWHERE UNDER THE HOUSE, WHAT'S LEFT OF PRUDENCE SCREAMS, CONSUMED ALONG WITH IT.
IIIIEEEEEEEEEEEEEEEEEE
RELAX, CHILD. IT'S ALRIGHT--
BUT THERE WAS MORE...

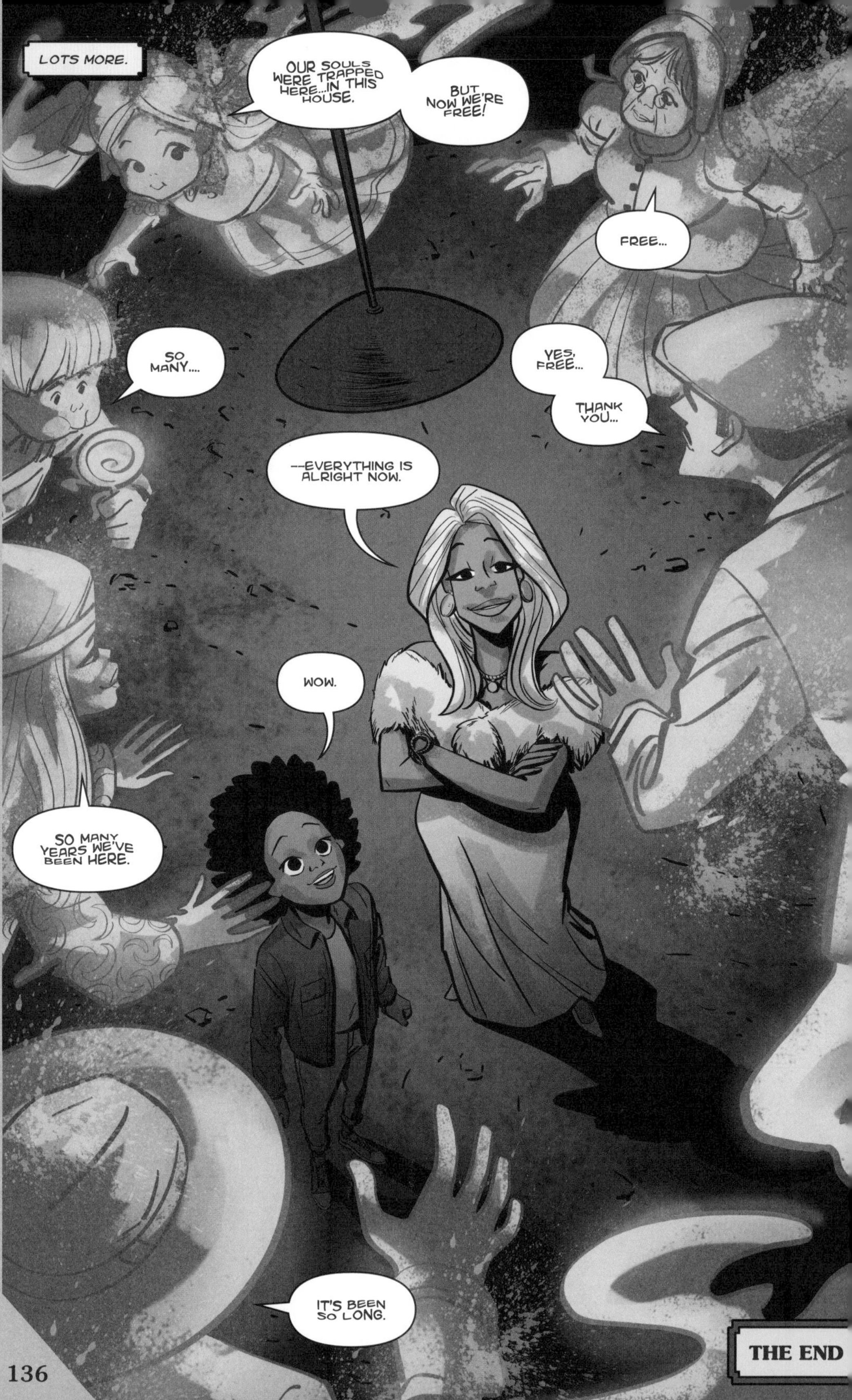
LOTS MORE.
OUR SOULS WERE TRAPPED HERE...IN THIS HOUSE.
BUT NOW WE'RE FREE!
FREE...
SO MANY....
YES, FREE...
THANK YOU...
--EVERYTHING IS ALRIGHT NOW.
WOW.
SO MANY YEARS WE'VE BEEN HERE.
IT'S BEEN SO LONG.
THE END

LOOK FOR MORE ADVENTURES IN *JOURNEY UNDER THE SEA*!

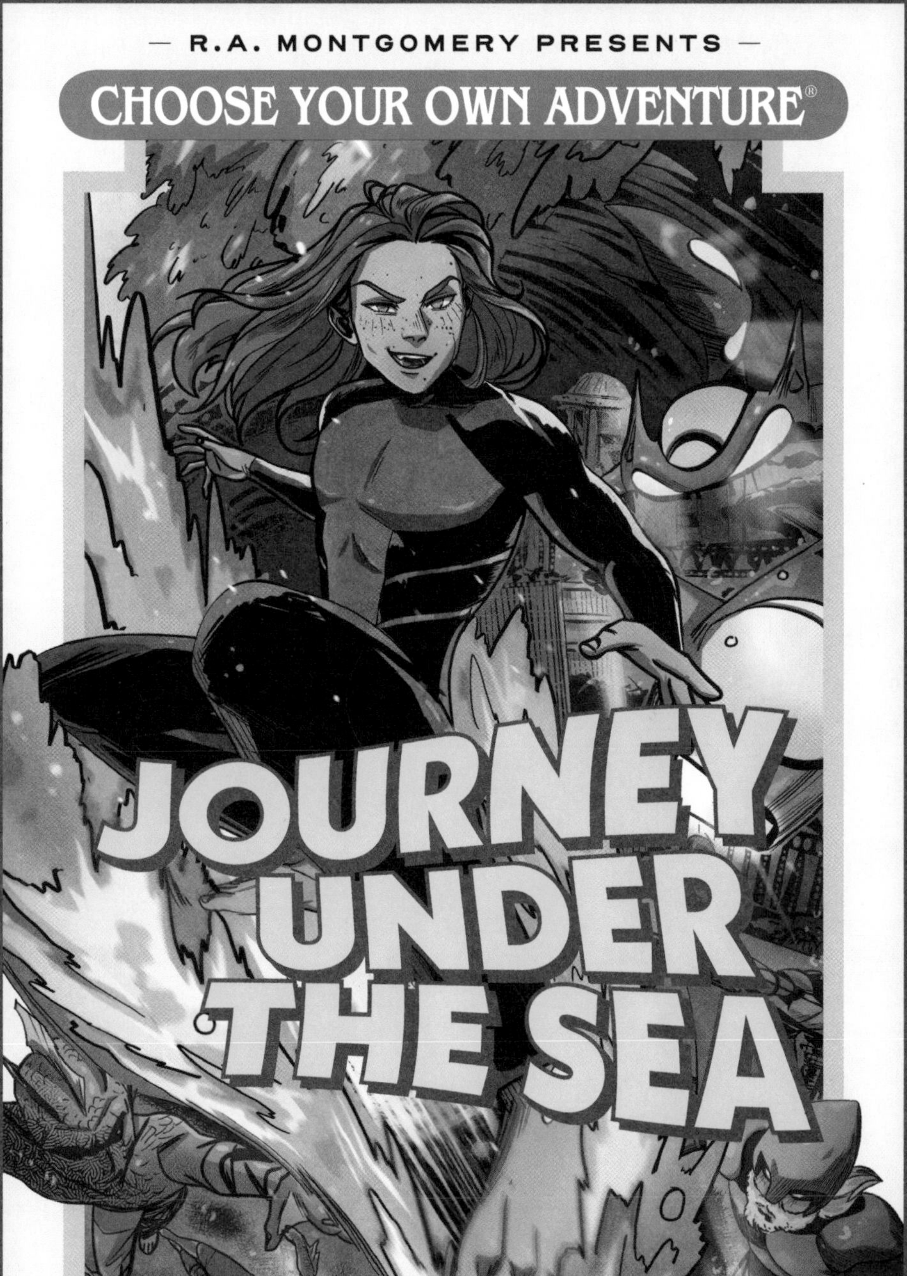
— R.A. MONTGOMERY PRESENTS —
CHOOSE YOUR OWN ADVENTURE®
JOURNEY UNDER THE SEA

C.E. SIMPSON

Char Simpson (they/them) is a nonbinary artist, interactive writer, creative producer, and teacher. They specialize in the crafting and mapping of compelling, immersive stories. Their work has been featured by the Tribeca Film Festival, Cannes XR, DEFCON, and others. They work in the space between comedy and horror; even when it gets really scary, there is still a flicker of fun. Find out more at charsimp.com.

ANDREW E. C. GASKA

An Ennie Award–winning game writer, creative director, and sci-fi author with twenty years of industry experience, Drew is also the Senior Development Editor and Head Writer for Lion Forge Animation. In addition to developing STEAM education projects, Drew has adapted three classic *Choose Your Own Adventure* books to graphic novel form. He is a freelance consultant to 20th Century Fox, maintaining continuity and canon bibles for *Predator* and *Planet of the Apes*. The lead writer of the ALIEN Roleplaying Game, he lives beneath a pile of action figures with his glutenous feline, Adrien.

E.L. THOMAS

E.L. Thomas is a writer and game designer who has worked on numerous treatments, story bibles, and scripts for animation. His most recent credits include adapting *Choose Your Own Adventure* titles into graphic novels and co-writing the pilot for the *Orglanauts* animated series. He is the co-creator of the gaming periodical *Rolled & Told*. His additional game credits include working on supplements for the *Aliens* RPG. He lives in the Midwestern United States with his comely wife and three spoiled dogs.

VALERIO CHIOLA

Valerio Chiola is an Italian comic book artist living in Rome. He is co-creator and illustrator of *Bulloni*, a children's books series published by Round Robin Editrice in Italy and Carambuco Ediciones in Spain (with the title *El Tuerca*). He has also collaborated with Italian Edizioni Erickson and ABCmouse.com.

THIAGO RIBEIRO

Is a Brazilian artist who lives and works in São Bernardo do Campo in São Paulo, Brazil. Thiago is an international comic colorist working with U.S. and European publishers such as Titan Comics, IDW, and others. He divides his time between illustration work, digital coloring, and painting on canvases. He has exhibited his paintings at numerous shows, including Campus Party 2018, Studio Bazzini in Milan, Italy, 3rd place in the VIII International Exhibition of Visual Arts Plastic, sat in the National Union of Plastic Artists /AIA- International Association of Fine Arts, Art at the Collective Exhibitions of Art, and Collective Brazil Forum in Torres Vedras in Portugal.

JOAMETTE GIL

Joamette Gil is an award-winning editor, cartoonist, and letterer extraordinaire. Her letters grace the pages of such Oni-Lion Forge titles as *Archival Quality*, *Girl Haven*, and, of course, *Mooncakes*! She's best known for her groundbreaking imprint P&M Press, home to *POWER & MAGIC: The Queer Witch Comics Anthology* and *HEARTWOOD: Non-binary Tales of Sylvan Fantasy*.

CHOOSE YOUR OWN ADVENTURE®

EIGHTH GRADE WITCH

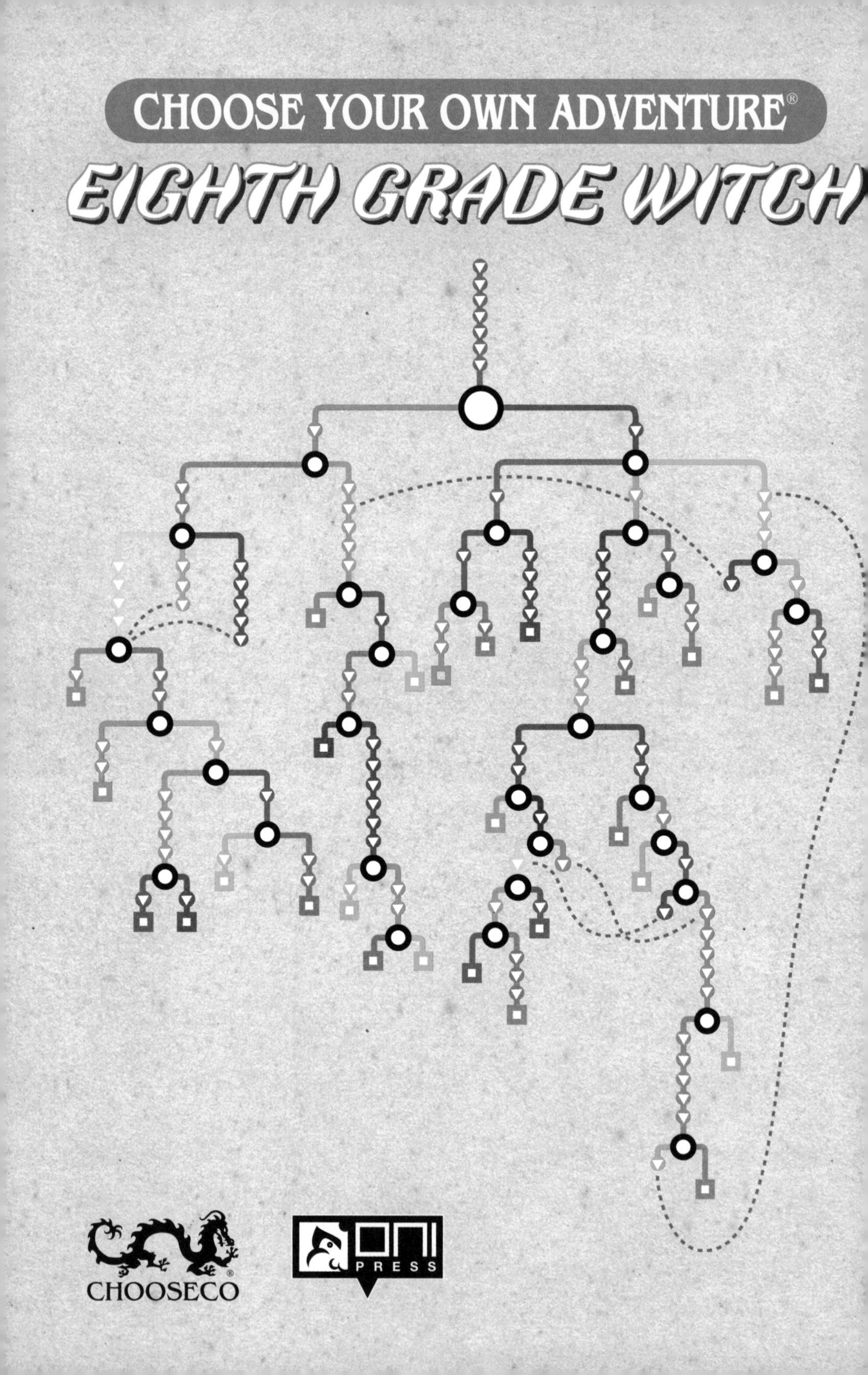

CHOOSECO

ONI PRESS